STRANGE TALES OF
HORROR

AN ANTHOLOGY

EDITED BY
MATT NORD

We dedicate this book to all of the people in our lives who have confidence in us. Thank you Karen, Bonny, Drew and Matt D.

Strange Tales of Horror is an anthology put together by a group of dedicated short story writers and screenplay enthusiast. For many years we have all enjoyed crafting stories of the macabre and the strange. We at NorGus Press have been lucky to have a wide range of stories submitted from around the world. Some of the stories will have the author's regional spellings for certain words. This adds flavor to the story and the way they write it. We feel that they fit exactly what we had been looking for. The stories within are not for the timid. This anthology is not "G" rated, so do not be surprised to encounter adult content or colorful language. *Do* expect chills and thrills from all the talented Authors with in. Please feel free to review and email us with your opinions and views on the stories and we would love to hear which story was your favorite. With out further review we present you with NorGus Press flagship release, *Strange Tales of Horror*.

- Jeffrey Angus

NorGus Press began as an idea between two friends. We were both getting back into the writing game, submitting short stories to various small presses with various degrees of success. We decided to start our own small publishing company in order to put out books full of stories that we felt people would want to read written by authors who may not get a chance somewhere else.

This anthology itself, *Strange Tales of Horror*, was the product of receiving a ton of great stories that didn't quite fit into the themes of any of the anthologies we were accepting for already. I couldn't take them, because they didn't fit, but I hated the fact that I would just have to let such great writing go.

So, we decided to go ahead and open up a brand new anthology to submissions, and the response was fast and hard. You are holding the result. It wasn't even originally planned for NorGus Press, and it ended up being the first to come to fruition.

But sometimes surprises are pleasant. Of course, that all depends on your definition of pleasant. Is it puppies and kittens, or is it zombies, demons and other evil things? If so, this book is sure to please. Enjoy...

- Matt Nord

TABLE OF CONTENTS

MATT NORD

HUNGER

You can't even understand
the hunger I feel.
The need to feed
is too great to deny.
The flesh is soft,
the blood flows over my lips.
Satisfaction
for another night.

HAIR

Hair falls over my eyes.
Blood and sweat form drops at the tips
Before finally falling to the concrete.
Blonde hair stained red.
The hammer falls again.

THE LEAF PEOPLE
BY C.H. POTTER

Duke had known about the leaf people for twelve days before they decided to attack his home.

He remembered because his birthday had been twelve days previous, and what a depressing birthday it had been. Not a single person had noted the milestone that was the beginning of Duke's sixtieth year on this earth. It was true that he no longer had many close associates whom he could reasonably expect to know the special date, but there was a son, Alex, off trotting the globe with some adventure company, too busy to spare the old man a phone call or so much as a postcard marking the occasion.

Duke never would have guessed how disheartening it was not to have anyone to utter those two words when the day came. It was a task that Shannon had performed beautifully for thirty-five years. She always insisted on singing "Happy Birthday" to him, no matter if she had thrown a big surprise party or if it was just the two of them, lounging in bed with a bottle of wine. It was one of the quirks of their marriage that Duke missed so damned much. Like a thousand other parts of his life in the past few years, he simply didn't know *what* to do, how he was supposed to act without his other half by his side.

It was in this mood that Duke found himself stumbling towards his house from Parker's Bar & Grill, where he had sampled both the bar and the grill, but the former with much more enthusiasm. He didn't know what time it was, only that the cute blonde bartender had said something about how she "can't serve you anymore drinks, sir. We're closing soon and you need to sober up for the drive home."

Duke had said emphatically that it was *his birthday*, and he would drink as much as he wanted on *his birthday, dammit*. The girl only shook her head and went about cleaning up for the night.

That had been nearly half an hour ago, and the truth was Duke hadn't sobered up much at all. He made it into his driveway without running over any STOP signs or seeing any flashing lights in the mirror, however, and he was perfectly content to walk inside, turn the television to *The Tonight Show* (or whatever program happened to be on, as Jay Leno had likely gone off the air hours before), and pass out in the recliner. He'd wake up with a sore back and a brutal hangover, yes, but at least the pain would give him something to think about other than the worse birthday he could remember.

Duke was halfway to the backdoor when his foot seemed to catch on something, as if he was walking along an uneven sidewalk and jammed his toes into an upraised slab of concrete. In his inebriated state, the impact was more than enough to send him sprawling onto the ground, head first into the grass.

Maybe it was the force of the collision, maybe it was the booze (probably it was a combination of the two, with the booze figuring more heavily in the equation), but either way, Duke was knocked unconscious. How long, he had no idea. All he knew was that when he came to, there was a set of tiny feet directly in his line of vision. He looked up, wondering what the hell a little kid was doing in his lawn at this ungodly hour. Standing before him wasn't a kid, but a man, a *miniature* man, no more than two feet tall, clothed in what appeared to be matching miniature blue jeans and sweatshirt. To complete Duke's amazement, the little man reached out and pinched his nose.

"Where's Tommy?" he asked in a voice that immediately took Duke back to his son's childhood, when *Alvin and the Chipmunks* reigned supreme. "He was over here just a few minutes ago. Where is he?"

Duke didn't answer, *couldn't* answer. Answering would have been admittance that what was standing over him was more than just the delusions of a heavily intoxicated mind.

"I need to quit drinking," he mumbled. He put his head back on the soft turf of the lawn and closed his eyes, perfectly content with spending the remainder of the night under the stars. In the morning there would be birds chirping and the sun would be shining, and all thought of tiny men would be nothing more than a drunken dream.

WHAP!

Something smacked into Duke's temple hard enough to throw his equilibrium into a tailspin, ending his hopes of a peaceful night's rest in the back lawn. He opened his eyes again. The miniature man was still there, much to Duke's chagrin.

"Wake up, asshole!" the man piped. "What did you do with my brother?"

"Children shouldn't swear."

"I'm not a child, you *jackass*! My name is Timmy, and I'm an adult."

He stroked his reddish handlebar mustache to drive the point home.

"You're two feet tall."

"And you're a *jackass*!" he exclaimed, jabbing Duke in the eye for good measure.

"Ow!" Duke shifted away from the little terror. The movement made him realize that something was poking him in the gut, probably a fallen stick from one of the nearby oaks. Duke judged that "Timmy," as the miniature man called himself, was now standing just beyond the reach of his arms. Moving with all the speed his inebriated body could muster, Duke grabbed the stick and swung it at the interloper. Timmy, presumably with the advantage of perfectly sober reflexes, easily avoided the blow. Duke cursed and threw the stick at the miniature man. It connected, knocking his slight frame to the ground.

"Take that, you little booger!"

Duke got to his feet in triumph. He imagined that Timmy would proceed to shout more profanities at the giant and then flee the scene, a would-be David soundly defeated by Goliath. He blinked several times, taking a moment to process the picture before him.

Timmy was still there, back on his feet, but it seemed to Duke as though another teeny man had suddenly materialized out of the October air. He was lying in the grass, not half a foot from where Timmy now stood.

"What the…?" Duke uttered, before what must have happened occurred to him in a camera flash of understanding. Drunk or no, Duke was an intelligent man, one with a knack for deduction. He quickly pictured this second teenybopper rummaging about in the lawn, perhaps searching for acorns (*yeah acorns Alvin and the Chipmunks bet yer ass*), oblivious, then along comes Duke, drunken Duke, tripping over the little bastard, falling on him, smothering him with his sizable midsection (*sure have packed on the pounds the past couple years yes, yes, that's what happened*). Duke had mistaken the lifeless body (*Tommy*) for a stick, and thrown it at Timmy, his brother. Quite the picture.

Timmy was looking down at the recently departed, shaking. He shouted something in an alien tongue, never glancing away from the dead body of his sibling. More tiny people began to appear, two-six-eight of them, miniature men and women dressed plainly. Most were coming from around the house. None of them spoke, and none of them looked Duke's way. They seemed entirely fixated on their fallen comrade, as if the sight of the corpse and the nature of Timmy's howl had cast a spell on the whole lot. Six of them propped the body up on their shoulders, three on each side. They began marching back towards the front of the house. Timmy lingered for a moment, still staring morosely at the ground, before finally turning and joining the procession.

Duke remained rooted to the earth, agape, until the last little person had disappeared around the corner of his home. Finally, with some effort, he managed to close his mouth. He took a step. The first few chuckles began then, and with each footfall the laughter grew in frequency and volume, starting with a few trickles of water from a leaky faucet and ending in the roar of Niagara Falls. By the time he got to the front of the house his gut was aching from the exertion, as Duke laughed as he hadn't laughed in years.

He had to blink back tears to clear his vision. Only Timmy remained. The rest of his fellows had apparently vanished with the same suddenness with which they had arrived. Timmy was standing on the sidewalk that bordered Duke's lawn and the street, next to a great pile of leaves.

"What are you?" Duke asked.

"I'm Timmy, and now I'm your nightmare," the teeny man proclaimed, shaking his fist. He turned his back on Duke, and dove into the leaf pile as if it was a pool of water, vanishing.

Duke paused for a moment, trying to comprehend the outrageous events that had occurred over the past few minutes. He tried, but he only succeeded in bursting into the biggest laughing fit yet. It was all too absurd for any attempt at rationalization.

He finally went inside, shaking his head and giggling the entire way. He proceeded to go up and down the house, gathering every ounce of alcohol on the premises. He put it all – really just a few beers from the fridge and several old bottles of wine and liquor from the basement – on the kitchen table. He spent the next few minutes dumping every drop into the sink. When the last bottle was emptied, the laughing had stopped, and he suddenly realized that he was quite drunk, and quite tired. Duke went upstairs, passing out on the bed before he could so much as untie his shoes.

It would be his last peaceful night's sleep for some time.

When the sun rose the next day, Duke managed to put all thought of the leaf people, as he would eventually come to call them, out of his mind. He spent the majority of his time watching football, not thinking much about anything other than the ineptitude of his beloved Buffalo Bills.

His dreams that night were stalked by tiny, two-foot tall terrors with razor sharp incisors and the blood red eyes of demons. The dreams varied through the night, the details slightly changing, but the end result was always the same. They would flow into the house by the dozens, overtaking him on the living room sofa or the stairs or cowering in the shower, slice his Achilles heel with a steak knife, drag him to his room and tie him down to the bed, and slowly hack off his limbs, one by agonizing one. They would go parading about the room with his arms and legs carried on their shoulders like bloody spoils of war. Finally, when Duke's body was nothing more than an amorphous hunk of flesh, Timmy would loom over him, the tomahawk in his hands dripping warm blood onto Duke's chest. "I *told* you I was your worst nightmare," he said in that high-pitched voice that no longer bore any hilarity. He would swing the tomahawk high, screaming, and Duke would wake up just as the tip of the blade was about to cleave his head from his body, the scream transferred to his own lips.

Duke wasn't all that surprised to find the tires of his Jeep Wrangler had been slashed sometime during the night. He went through the motions of filing a police report, but the vivid dreams had convinced him that his encounter with the leaf people had been more than an unlikely case of delirium tremens. The officer asked if he had any enemies, and Duke had had an insane urge to jokingly say "None that stand above my knees!," but then the memory of Timmy standing on his chest, eyes seeping hate and murder, sent goose bumps down his arms, and the trace of a smile on his face faltered.

No, the police wouldn't be of any help in this matter.

The leaf people continued to pull smaller pranks for the next week and a half – feces spread all over his doors, the garbage can overturned and strewn across the lawn, various other acts of childish vandalism. Duke had taken to locking the Jeep in the garage, and he was content to wait the leaf people out. He didn't see how he had any other choice. Picking up after them was becoming a part of his morning routine, as regular as brushing his teeth.

The status quo changed the morning Duke almost stepped on the mutilated body of a cat placed just outside his front door. The head had been crudely cut off. A small pool of blood had caked to the concrete where it had once lain. Sickened, Duke got a shovel and buried the poor creature in the back lawn before anyone could see it.

He found the head about an hour later when he opened up his mailbox. The mailman hadn't swung by yet, but the leaf people had been kind enough to leave a special delivery. The cat's head stared back at him when he looked inside, its teeth bared and its eyes wide open, forever frozen in a grimace of shock and fear.

Duke didn't find any nasty presents waiting for him as he went about inspecting his property the next morning. He stood out by the mailbox in pajamas and a bathrobe, staring blankly at the newspaper.

City, union negotiations remain deadlocked, said the main headline.

Maybe the leaf people had tired of toying with him, Duke thought, and the sacrifice of the cat had been a last act of retribution for the death of little Tommy. Maybe, but Duke didn't buy it. The dreams wouldn't let him.

The wind blew, shooting icy air around the exposed flesh of his ankles. It had been unseasonably warm for the past few weeks, but the weather service had promised that a storm front was brewing, bringing with it cold weather. Leaves were sent flying about the street like a colorful snow shower.

Damn leaves, Duke thought. *Damned leaf people. Damned town officials. Damn strike.*

An entire season's worth of leaves was piled up and down the street, often covering sidewalks and overflowing into the edge of the road itself. Mountains of brown, orange, and red, just sitting there. One of the jobs of the town's highway department was to pick up the leaves in the fall, but the majority of the town's employees had been on strike for the past month, demanding higher wages and better benefits. Duke hadn't paid much attention to the whole fiasco. He had raked his leaves into a pile in the front lawn, just as he always did this time of year, playing into the hands of both sides in the controversy, as both claimed the littered streets to be a symbolic victory and a sure sign of their righteousness. Duke figured they would come to terms before winter really hit, regardless of the rhetoric being tossed about. Then the leaves would be gone. In the meantime, however, it appeared as though Timmy & Co. had somehow taken refuge in the mounds during the day.

Duke seized on the idea, amazed that he hadn't done so before now. He spent the rest of the morning bagging up every single leaf in the pile. By ten o'clock he had worked up a heavy sweat despite the chill air, and seven bulging garbage bags now sat where Timmy had disappeared into the pile on that first fateful night. No, Duke's rake didn't scoop up any cursing miniature people, but he did find something that interested him a great deal. His toil had uncovered a storm drain in between the white line on the road and the curb of the sidewalk.

Little shits must be using the leaves as a camouflage to mask their movements, he thought.

He bent over and tried to pry the cover off the drain. It wouldn't budge, no matter how much he wrenched on it. Perplexed, he stood back up, back cracking in protest. He spat down into the drain, hoping it would land right on Timmy's little red head. The comical image helped him put the whole matter out of mind for the rest of the day.

Apparently unimpressed by Duke's efforts, that was the first night the leaf people tried to get inside the house. He awoke with a start around two a.m., his ears immediately keying on the *patter-patter-patter* of their little footsteps running around on the roof. He hadn't the slightest clue how they had managed to get up there, but he took care to creep downstairs and pass the rest of the night on couch, listening intently for any signs of entrance. He didn't want them to know where he slept.

It was the next night, the twelfth night since he had stumbled home from Parker's Bar & Grill on his birthday, which had forced his hand. The leaf people's reconnaissance had taught them that the bay window in the living room was their easiest point of access to the house. Exhausted from the lack of sleep the past several days, Duke had passed out in front of the television early, around ten o'clock.

He didn't hear the first few rocks hit the window. When the sharp *pink* sound of stone ricocheting off glass brought Duke out of his slumber, a crack had already formed up the center of the window. By the time he got up and realized what was happening, the crack had spread, forming a spider web of fissures.

"Doesn't this just *figure*," Duke said.

A final rock slammed through the window, shattering the glass. Duke looked for lights to come on in a neighboring house, but they remained as dark as they always were at this late hour. Help wasn't coming.

Duke walked as close to the window as he dared. There, barely visible in the faint glow of the streetlamps, were the leaf people. *A shit-load of leaf people*, Duke thought. They were massed no more than fifteen feet from the house, staring in at him like an angry mob sizing up a corrupt ruler. One of them stepped forward, and Duke wasn't the least bit surprised to see that it was Terrible Timmy, he of the red handlebar mustache.

"I'm sorry about your brother," Duke said. "I didn't even know he was there."

"You have been marked," was all Timmy said in reply.

With a slight of hand that would have made a Las Vegas card shark envious, one of the leaf people slipped a rock into Timmy's open palm. He flung it at Duke nearly all in one motion. Duke somehow managed to jump out of the way before it could impact his skull. The rock went crashing into the wall behind him, knocking a framed photograph of him and Shannon to the floor.

"You have one more day." Timmy raised his fist and extended one finger, just in case Duke didn't already get the picture, one hundred percent. Then, seemingly as one, the whole crowd began to move. Duke rushed over to the other window, the one with a view of the street. The leaf people walked right over the drain cover, paying it no heed, quickly moving their little legs across the road. He watched in utter amazement as they jumped into the massive pile in the Jenson's lawn, simply vanishing into the leaves without displacing a single, solitary one.

That was how Duke found himself here, hiding in his garage from two-foot tall terrors bent on doing God only knows what to him, although he was reasonably certain they didn't have a massage or a neighborly chat on the agenda.

He reckoned that the garage afforded his best chance at making it through the night. It didn't have any windows, and the only entry point he was mildly worried about was the side door, which was locked. Let them bust another window and break into the house. They would find it empty and assume that Duke had skipped town, bested after all. That was the plan, at least. And if they did somehow get inside the garage, well, he might just have a surprise or two in store for the little bastards.

Duke curled up in the back seat of the Jeep, attempting sleep. He had never been in the military, but he imagined that soldiers for time immemorial felt the way he did then, sitting on the brink of battle, of near certain bloodshed. Duke couldn't help but chuckle at the comparison. Here he was, a sixty-year-old man, preparing himself for mortal combat with *leaf people*, to whom a Chihuahua would likely appear as large and ferocious as a Rottweiler. Ridiculous.

Don't underestimate your opponents, Shannon's voice popped into his head, as it often did. She had frequently spoken those exact words to their son, an All-County quarterback, before football games. Now she was giving Duke the same advice.

He got out of the Jeep. He looked around the darkened garage, trying to figure out what he might have overlooked. He was wary of turning the lights on, lest the leaf people notice the radiance through the cracks along the outline of the side door. He reached into his jeans for his cell phone. It wasn't there. Duke gave his pockets the obligatory pat down, but he knew he had left the phone sitting on the kitchen table, had known it since the first search produced nothing but lint.

Duke cursed at himself. Not only was he without the flashlight effect of the cell phone, but he now had no way of telling what time it was. It was going to be a long night.

He set to pacing about the garage, walking laps around the Jeep. Duke hadn't enjoyed a cigarette in nearly fifteen years, but he suddenly craved a smoke more than at any other time since the first few days after Shannon's death. He was popping in a piece of gum as a substitute when he thought he heard a scratching sound at the side door. Duke froze, the peppermint gum inches from his mouth. He strained to pick up the slightest break in the total silence of the garage. Nothing.

Must have been a mouse, Duke thought. *Or maybe I'm just a little too wound up, imagining things that aren't there. Shit, maybe the leaf people themselves are figments of my crazed imagination. Maybe I've sat home by myself one too many nights. Maybe this is the final embarkation of the Duke Crazy Train, soundtrack courtesy of Ozzy Osbourne. Maybe –*

Scccratttch.

There it was again, this time accompanied by a rattle on the door handle. Duke walked over as quietly as he could manage. The handle was shaken again. He saw it move this time, even through the darkness. There was an audible bump, and then a *knock-knock-knock* came from the bottom half of the door. Duke would have laughed if he wasn't so terrified. The little leaf people were here to murder him, to cut off his limbs before his head went the way of Marie Antoinette, if his dreams were in fact a premonition, but they still had the courtesy to knock on the door. How polite of them.

Let us in, good sir. We're here for the decapitation, the knock seemed to say. *We have to catch the leaf pile back to Hades in an hour, so can we hurry this along, please?*

Duke didn't answer. He went back to the Jeep and grabbed the .22 gauge revolver he had stashed in the seat. It was a long forgotten Christmas present of his son's, designed to mimic the appearance of the guns of the old west. The knock was repeated on his way back to the door, and then the garage was once again as silent as an abandoned graveyard. Quieter, perhaps.

Duke allowed himself to hope that his ruse had fooled the leaf people, that they were currently going back to wherever it was they came from, having a good laugh over that chicken shit Duke. He had himself half convinced when something began to slam into the door, sending fragments of wood splintering into the garage.

At first he didn't quite realize what was happening. Did they have a battering ram? Were they pounding on the door with their hands, hands that probably couldn't even palm a donut? Did they have telekinetic powers? Were they miniature X-Men?

Then the tomahawk peeked through the wood, the tomahawk of Duke's dreams. He already knew that it would look like the axe of a lumberjack when wielded by one of the leaf people.

It had only taken them three blows to crack a hole in the door, alarmingly fast work. Duke could only look on with growing dismay as the small crack became wider with each smack of the blade. One of the cretins eventually stuck his head through before the job was complete, and Duke took more than a little satisfaction in punting his face back onto the other side. He heard the Curious George slam into several of his compatriots, sending the bunch of them into a ruckus.

"There's more where that came from!" Duke hollered. There was no longer any point in playing coy; they meant to get inside, and after that the game was up, one way or another.

The tomahawk slammed back into the door, answering Duke's challenge. It cleaved through the hole easily, the door offering less and less resistance as its integrity was comprised. After a few more strokes it was large enough for the leaf people to jump through, which they immediately began to do.

Duke, however, had anticipated this move. He stood to the side, allowing them to enter unmolested. He then greeted the first wave with the business end of his three-iron. He was sickened by the flat *thud* he felt through the metal when it connected with skull, but that couldn't be helped. This was war, a war between the man of the street and the man of the leaf, Duke was vaguely aware of telling himself.

He kept swinging away, but the invaders of the garage kept coming. His aim didn't miss a single one of them. Men and women alike were sent skittering across the floor, many of them not stirring after they came to a stop.

Duke was kept busy teeing off on the leaf people, busy enough that he didn't notice that those on the outside had continued the assault on the door. He didn't realize it until they began crashing inside two at a time, screaming through bared teeth. He kept the three-iron in the constant motion of a speeding windmill, but eventually one of them was able to break through. It latched onto his leg and, to Duke's mutual terror and amazement, it began to *scurry* up his body, as if it wasn't a miniature man but instead enjoyed a closer relationship to some type of animal that he didn't wish to consider.

He was forced to let go of the golf club. The attacker was now up to his chest, almost sitting on the jut of his belly. With both hands, he grabbed hold of the little demon, wrenching him from his body with all the strength his fatigued arms could summon. He tossed him away, knocking down five more leaf people who had crept within three feet. They dropped like bowling pins. The respite gave him a moment to pull the revolver from the small of his back. A throng of perhaps twenty leaf people were now inside the garage. Duke shot into the crowd five times, aiming indiscriminately. Leaf people keeled over here and there. He cocked the hammer back again, preparing for the sixth and final shot, when his peripheral vision caught one of the bastards on the roof of the Jeep. Duke tried to swing around, but it had already leapt into the air. It landed on his back, its arms grasped firmly around his neck.

"Remember me?" a voice snarled into his ear, and Duke didn't need a game of Guess Who to know that it was Timmy that had maneuvered his way to the neck that he was so desperate to slash.

Duke tried to raise the gun behind his back, meaning to shoot blindly at Timmy, even if it meant accidentally hitting himself. He tried, but he could barely lift the .22 above his waist. He looked down. Two leaf people were wrapped around his arm, acting as lead weights. He watched as three more began to climb up his leg. The rest of the crowd was gathered at his feet, jeering, waiting their turn to scale the walls of Castle Duke.

Duke winced as one of the leaf people bit into his hand. His fingers began to open up compulsively, threatening to drop the revolver into the eager arms of the mob. He managed to fling the gun towards the abandoned door before it fell out of his grasp.

Desperate, Duke saw only one option before his body was covered from head to toe with clawing, biting, kicking leaf people. Bracing himself as best he could, he launched himself into the pile, intending to crush as many of them as possible, granting them the same fate as their beloved Tommy.

Duke took no small measure of satisfaction in the suddenly shocked and terrified faces of the crowd below as he rapidly crashed towards the ground. The impact with the concrete floor immediately knocked him breathless. He turned over onto his back, coughing. The pain consumed his midsection, he was reasonably certain he'd dislocated his right shoulder, his always-balky back screamed in protest, but what he *didn't* feel made it all worth it – there was no longer any writhing masses on his body. The belly flop had worked.

I always knew this gut would come in handy sometime, he thought wryly.

The garage had gone quiet again, as if nothing had happened and the whole battle had been played out solely in Duke's mind. That image almost frightened him more than the leaf people, and Duke opened his eyes.

Timmy was standing above him, grinning, actually *grinning*, although the smile beamed murderous intent rather than any trace of mirth.

"Nightmare isn't over yet, you *jackass*," he said.

Duke glanced around. The faint figures of the remaining leaf people loomed, their faces masked in shadow, but he imagined they were all wearing that same grin, evil little shits that they were.

He looked back up at Timmy. The tomahawk was in his hands, the scimitar of death. He raised it high, pausing at the apex, likely relishing the look on Duke's face before the hammer blow struck, turning off his light in this world. Duke closed his eyes, waiting for the end to arrive.

The back of his eyelids were suddenly awash in light, light that seemed to take on a reddish tint (*oh my God is that my blood I thought this would be over swiftly*). There was a crack of thunder, a thud as something fell to the ground, and a loud clang seemingly right next to his eardrum.

Duke winced, and the pain convinced him that he wasn't dead quite yet. He opened his eyes slowly. Timmy was gone, no longer looming over him. All he could see was the illuminated ceiling of the garage. Duke propped himself up on his elbows. He briefly considered that maybe he was destined for the loony bin after all, because standing in front of him was an impossible sight.

It was his son, Alex, clutching the old western .22 he had received for Christmas twenty years ago.

"Hi, Dad," he said.

"What…how…where is…," Duke stuttered, thoroughly shaken.

Alex came over and knelt beside his father. "Take it easy," he said.

"What happened?" Duke asked. "Where's Timmy?"

"Well if you mean the two foot tall man with the tomahawk, he's right behind you."

Duke swung around, still ready for the strike of the blade against his neck. The tomahawk, however, was sitting next to him, and Timmy was laying a few feet away, a lifeless lump of flesh. Duke looked back to his son, shaking his head in disbelief.

"Alex, what are you doing here?"

"I came back for your birthday. Sixty is quite the milestone, don't you think?"

Duke grunted.

"My company has been conducting some business in northeast India, so I had a little trouble making it on time. It was quite the ordeal getting here, but I guess you're going to have me topped in the story department, judging by the looks of this place."

"Yeah, you could say that. Help your old man up."

Duke took stock of the garage when both men were on their feet. Dead bodies littered the floor. The bottom quarter of the door was completely demolished.

"The majority of them ran out the door after I shot the guy with the tomahawk, ran right past me like their asses were on fire and there was a river outside. What are you going to do about the mess?" Alex asked.

Duke had a sudden flash of inspiration. "Let's put them all in there," he said, pointing to a wheelbarrow propped against the far wall.

They counted eighteen dead bodies in all. Duke hung back when it came time to take care of Timmy's corpse. He didn't want his imagination to have any more material than it already possessed.

They rolled the wheelbarrow out of the garage, across the deserted street, into the Jenson's yard. Duke tipped it up, spilling the bodies into the leaf pile. They all vanished into seeming nothingness. Alex gasped a bit, but didn't say anything. Duke wondered at that.

They went back inside and sat at the kitchen table. Now Alex spoke.

"They just disappeared, didn't they?"

"They're the leaf people," Duke said, as if that explained everything. "You didn't seem completely surprised."

"During the course of my work the past few years I've…uh, seen some things."

"Sounds like we both have stories to tell," Duke said, "but let me ask you something first."

Alex raised his eyebrows.

"Would you mind if I moved out west, where the leaves don't fall quite so hard?"

"Not at all, Dad."

"Thanks. I've had it with leaves."

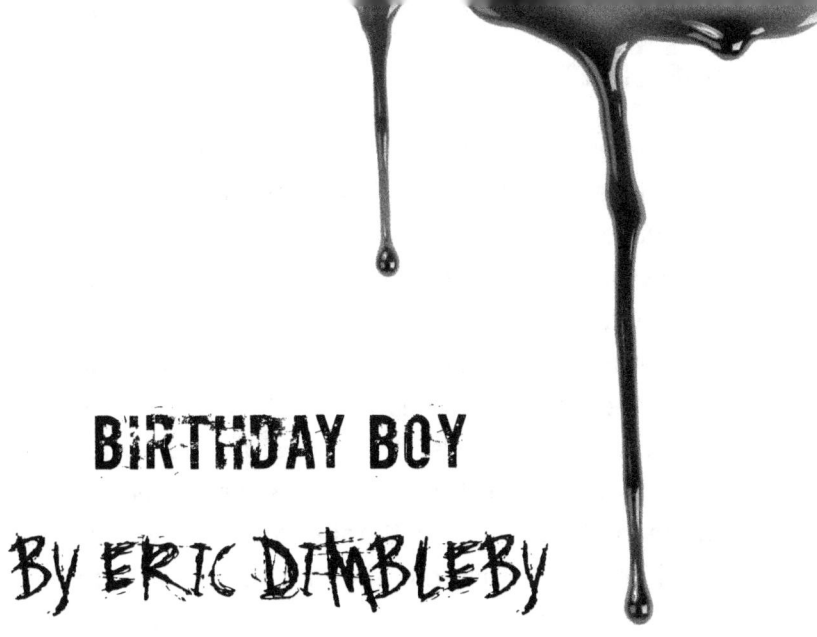

BIRTHDAY BOY

BY ERIC DIMBLEBY

Billy eased himself behind the unwelcoming dumpster, gripping his hand around the rear of the wide and grimy metallic container, holding tightly on to a bar that was used to slide the rear hatch open for easy access to its raunchy innards. Perhaps, if he could keep his movements to a nearly inaudible level, he could crawl inside that hatch, to bury himself in the refuse and rats that were surely scampering about inside. Both the miscellaneous trash and the unkempt vermin would be preferable to his lurking Birthday Monster. A rat would bite him and cause limited pain, but his Birthday Monster would effectively undo him from the land of the living if it had its way.

A low breathing was accompanied by slow padded footsteps, his Birthday Monster's clawed feet clacking on the dirty pavement of the alleyway as it trudged forward with animalistic purpose. It had found him, yet again, for the twenty-third consecutive year. Each year the thing had become more aggressive in its pursuits. Billy had reasoned that this tactical growth stemmed from his own physical prowess, increasing exponentially through his teenage years and into early adulthood. Billy felt that his newly acquired adult body was now in better condition than it had ever been in previous chases. And in likewise measures, the Birthday Monster took after him with fleeting hasty paces, growling and sniffling all the way, its mucus-laden snout and moistened eyeballs scanning every nook and cranny that the Boy of his vicious desires may hide in.

Billy held his breath in a meditative measure, careful not to alert his Monster that there was anything afoot in the murky depths of the treacherous hidden alcoves of the city and its alleyways. It had only just rained a few hours earlier, and there was a looming steam that seemed to blanket everything in sight. Lucky for Billy, this aided in masking him from the diabolical eyes of his fervent and obsessive pursuer. Billy gave silent thanks to the thick soupy camouflage that would not have existed earlier in the day. With nightfall upon them, the midnight hour grew ever closer. For this, as well, Billy was also grateful.

Since moving to the city six months earlier, away from his family for the first time in his life, Billy had quickly familiarized himself with the gulley-works and interconnected networks of the back alleys and shadowy grooves in which the underbelly of society lived and breathed. Where he now hid, somewhere between America Avenue and Prospect Street, served as a China Star's (fantastic Egg Foo Young) delivery area and dumpster. The wait service at China Star was abysmal, but the food was of another world. The scent of disposed greasy egg rolls and cold Lo mein infested Billy's sensitive nostrils. Though he desired these comforting foods while seated at China Star's dirty tables, especially after a long day of running from his yearly predator, they now only served to sicken him to the very pits of his trembling hollow stomach. It seemed to Billy that he may expose himself, were he to climb inside of the bright red dumpster, from the unavoidable sounds of wrenching up yellow bile at the villainous odors that would surround him. Added to that, it would paint him into a corner. Once trapped with no way out, your only hope existed in winning a physical scuffle, of which Billy would assuredly lose.

He eased around the edge of the dumpster, looking into a cloud of steamy moisture that had meandered down the alley. Through the mist stepped his Birthday Monster, slowing to a plodding crawl, its dark brown fur swinging like pendulums, a sort of beastly Cousin It that sought to wreak havoc upon his rapidly beating heart. Biting at his lip, Billy readied himself, clenching his muscles in a precursor to darting away if the thing caught sight of him. He would not allow it his mortal body. He would not allow it his infinite soul. One more hour. One more year. One day, he would be rid of the Birthday Monster, forevermore.

Often, Billy would lay awake in bed for several days before his approaching birthday, staring at the ceiling, trying to imagine where and when it had all started. From as early as he could recall, he had lived in the proximity of his annual tormentor. He often pictured in these foggy recollections that the Monster had been in the birthing room alongside his panting unwed mother, possibly beneath the gurney, sniffing the air for the first scent of evidence that he had arrived, delivered from his mother's womb in the wee hours of the morning, just as the sun was coming up over the horizon. Had the doctors and nurses seen him, anxiously awaiting the arrival of the Boy? In this fictional recreation of his genesis, Billy often pictured himself cuddled in a bassinet by the side of her bed, his blonde-haired blue-eyed beauty of a mother asleep after a tumultuous twenty hours of labor. And while she slept, he imagined, his Birthday Monster had snuck out from his hiding spot (beneath the bed, behind the curtains, in the closet, or directly through the window like a furry burglar), and cradled Billy in his long muscular arms, his infantile body burrowed into the deep thick brown fur of his someday-soon rival. The thing would then proceed to sniff the baby, to inhale from the diaper, to lick his tiny cherub face with his long slimy tongue. With its razor-sharp fingernails, the Monster would trim a lock of hair from the child's chaotic tuft of growth. Placing the boy back into his bassinet, the Monster would return when a full year had passed to spy on the young human a second time.

Of course, in reality, Billy could not remember any of the Monster's visits... that is, not until he was nearly six years of age. All memories from before that juncture were fuzzy glimpses of the awakening days of awareness. Slices and nuggets of his toddler years would rise to the surface, like the thick cream in milk. And when they surfaced, the Monster was never to be found. He existed only in his more formative memories of childhood. He could picture is mother's eyes from his earliest memories, but little else.

The thing ran its greasy claw along the front side of the garbage dumpster, digging into the surface with its thunderously powerful arms. A screech emitted that Billy immediately revolted. The sound sent jolts of terror through every nerve ending in Billy's shaky body. This night may very well end up being as close to a bad outcome as the two previous years combined. The Birthday Monster could smell his uncontrollable perspiration, of this Billy was sure. With only an hour until midnight, he wondered whether it would be possible to hold out. At midnight, when it was no longer his day of birth and the third day of May had come to an official close, the ghastly thing would return to whatever devious maw he had sprung from, to await another twelve months of plotting his next barrage through Billy's seemingly mundane life.

Friends and family had, through the years, given up on celebrating his birthday. At first he had seemed nothing more than shy about the whole affair, effectively sequestering himself from all that cared for him as the day approached on the calendar. Unknown to them, he did so for their very protection and not to offend their generous sensibilities. Were they around when the Birthday Monster came for him, it was quite possible that the beast would seek to harm them as well, and it was a chance that Billy refused to take. If it ever did harm to anybody but himself, then he would never be allowed his own forgiveness. In the past, it had unleashed its fury upon a house cat that had come too near, and in his path. On his twentieth birthday, while running through a football field behind the high school of his home town, the Monster had spied a small gallivanting kitten somewhere near the twenty yard line. He had subsequently altered his course (hot on Billy's scampering heels) towards the feline, gathering it up in his gnarled fist, without stopping his trudging pace.

As Billy listened behind him- the Monster gaining two steps, then losing three, then gaining four, then losing two- he could hear first the shriek of the dying cat as it begged the universe for its life, and then the gnashing teeth of the Birthday Monster, eviscerating and consuming his snack while still jogging at full pace. It had been done, without any doubt in Billy's racing mind, to set an example to him, to teach a lesson that nobody and nothing was safe if he disallowed the annual grumbling Monster his tender flesh for consumption.

Billy readied himself for action behind the dumpster, stretching the sleepiness out of his crouched legs, preparing for a new sprint that he had hoped to avoid with this ill-conceived hiding spot. With the dastardly thing only a few feet away, it was time to take action or become a cornered piece of buttered meat. *One more hour*, he told himself. *Keep out of reach for one more hour. Midnight comes, and he goes bye-bye like Cinderella's ball gown.*

The Monster's breath was so horribly festered that Billy could smell it from the hiding spot in which he crouched, even with a twenty foot wide steel dumpster between them. It seemed to sigh and clear its throat. He could picture its bright yellow eyes hoping to peer upon him, its claws growing stiff in reaction to the proximity of its prey, its wide black ears perking at the sound of Billy's own breathing patterns, slow and strangled by his deepest strangest fears. When his Birthday Monster moaned, it sounded off in a guttural nasal cleansing, readying its olfactory system for proper air sampling.

In his pre-pubescent years, before he had first made the decision to *run*, the Birthday Monster would simply lay in waiting. He would peek from the closet long enough to send Billy into gurgling hysterics, crying for his mother, running to her, and not allowing her to put him back in his room until several days had passed. Even sleeping in his mother's bed, he could have sworn that he had awoken from a sleepy dream to see the beast standing above him like an angel-gone-wrong, its frothing mouth and hideous neon yellow fangs tucked over his lower lip. Whenever the time came to reveal his Monster to his mother- pulling open the closet in a grand reveal of nothing but dirty socks, shoving his bed aside to expose hairballs and old comic books, pulling back the shower curtain to put on display the horrible mildew problem that his mother was so very embarrassed by- the thing would never be where he had insisted it would be. He was crafty in that way, always one step ahead of Billy, forever playing a chess game of cruel torment. "Every birthday, Billy. This is ridiculous, you know that? If your father had stuck around, he'd be tanning your hide as we speak," his mother would threaten. "Your imagination is getting the best of you... maybe you should go see a doctor about this ridiculous birthday monster."

And he had, for several years, visited a "doctor". This "doctor" had tried desperately to expose the underlying loss that came from his father's abandonment. He had "gone out for cigarettes" two months prior to Billy's birth, and the brilliant Dr. Gagne had thoroughly convinced himself that this was the root of young William's (he hated to be called William, but the good doctor seemed set on that nomenclature) supposed "Birthday Monster". When he had asked Billy what this horrid monster's name had been, Billy had responded that it did not speak, so he never thought to ask. Dr. Gagne had giggled, scribbling notes into his little binder, thinking smarmy thoughts that would have surely enraged Billy were they voiced aloud.

Billy took to his feet, choosing the western direction (from which he had originally come) as his escape route. Upon coming around the side of the dumpster, he grazed past his Monster, feeling a sense of idle dread in his skin as it met the coarse moistened hair of the thing. And in that fly-by of his arch nemesis, Billy's eyes met the Monster's... for but a nanosecond of time, but long enough that they connected souls, which unnerved Billy more than any physical contact ever could. It loathed him as much as he did it. At least they had *something* in common.

Pumping his knees in perfect rhythm, as he had been taught by his track coach so many years ago, Billy felt from the very start of his newest dash that he had gained a sufficient distance from his pursuer. He would only need to maintain this distance. It turned to look after Billy, sending off an awful howl into the night air, strained in the realization that the Boy had escaped him once again, and that the midnight deadline was within reach. The Boy would not escape this year. The Monster would not allow himself another failure.

The alley laid out before him, Billy scanned for debris that would slow down his trajectory. Garbage bags and rusted out shopping carts were strewn in erratic fashion through the path ahead, but he felt he could endure them without slipping up at all. Various vagrants slept in beds of newspaper on either side. Billy worried that the Monster would stop and snatch one of these unknowing victims up, as it had the kitten that one year. He considered, for a fleeting moment of time, informing each of the homeless men and women as he passed them, but kept the information to himself in the knowledge that the slobbering maniac would be upon him in only a moment were he to stop for any reason. He turned to see it lumbering after him, swinging its lengthy Wookie-like arms in his bouncing strides. It would, on occasion during their yearly pursuits, growl aloud, a snarling sort of catcall that would give Billy a shuddering sense of how far ahead his racing footsteps were.

In the twelfth year of his life, Billy had first run from the thing. It had taunted him on every birthday through his childhood, and on the precipice of his adulthood, he decided that the Birthday Monster was getting bold in its advances. In his tenth year, it had decided to sit outside of his closet hiding spot, snarling at Billy through the night. His mother refused to come console him in his bedroom anymore, claiming that he had "become a big boy." The Monster, somehow, knew this. In the eleventh year, it actually decided to stand over his bed, pushing his hot garbage breath on to Billy, who closed his eyes the whole evening through, bawling in terror, praying to God that the brutish thing would leave him be. And in the twelfth year, it had reached out and touched him for the first time, running its heavy paw along Billy's tear-stained cheek. And that, as they say, had been enough of *that*.

Leaping from his bed, Billy darted out the door, turning to catch a glimpse of the Birthday Monster's face, shocked at this new development. The Boy wanted to play a game of tag. How delightful! And so Billy had scuttled down the stairs and set off from his house, leaving the front door wide open behind him.

And the Monster chased him. Through the backyards of his neighbors, into the playground, up and down each and every street of his neighborhood. When midnight struck, though Billy would have never known the time since he never wore a watch back then, the Birthday Monster had evaporated into thin air, gone for three hundred and sixty four more days. His mother, of course, would scold him for both his late night traipse and his leaving the door ajar on his way out. When Billy had reentered the house she had slapped him firmly across the face, sending him into a new parade of salty tears. Though she had felt guilty for the act, his outbursts of insanity were becoming unbearable for a single mother like herself.

As Billy had feared, the Birthday Monster had decided to stop for an alley snack, even with the midnight hour fast approaching. Behind him, he could hear the temporary halt of the hairy ogre's pace. A yelp of agony came from the misty darkness behind him, where he had only just passed a middle aged man with a long beard, sitting inside of his sleeping bag drinking what had appeared to be a bottle of liquor. That man, Billy sadly thought to himself, had died as an indirect result of his scamper towards freedom. Billy paused in his spot, looking back down the alley, panting for the sweetness of lost breath. It roared in delight as it gutted the homeless man in the layers of darkness that confined them all, chewing him to bits with great speed. He took to his feet again, the end of the alley in his sight. It would spill out into Main Street, where he would expose more late night pedestrians to the Birthday Monster, but he would dart directly across the busy thoroughfare to an adjacent alleyway that he had previously taken note of in his travels.

Through middle and high school, Billy had fashioned himself into a running machine, a sort of expert at the art of moving one's body from one location to the other. With the acceptance, at the age of thirteen, that he may never rid himself of his Birthday Monster, it only made sense that he would teach his body to escape the thing on that yearly anniversary of cat and mouse pursuit. After shedding his baby fat in the eighth grade, he had blossomed into a speed demon nearly overnight. He joined the track team in the next year, and by high school was winning state competitions with ease. It was a sort of blessing that the Birthday Monster had been forever at his heels. Without that motivation, Billy often told himself, he could have ended up as one of those fat bloated beer-guzzling video gamers who rarely saw the light of day. Judge Judy and The Price Is Right. Welfare checks and obesity clinics.

Billy drifted into Main Street, slowing to look in both directions for approaching cars. In his scan of the usually hectic area of town, Billy discovered that there were almost no local citizens in the streets. A street vendor hocking sugared peanuts. A pug-faced hooker on the stroll. A man and his woman, walking with arms hooked together. Main Street was unseasonably dead to the world.

After slowing his pace to a slow crawl, he deemed the crossing to be safe enough, so Billy darted across the four lanes of bi-directional traffic. When he reached the opposing curb, he turned to observe his Birthday Monster, exiting the first alley. Billy took a deep breath and took to his running feet one more time, staring straight down the new alley, his exhausted lungs telling him to stop and give in. This new alley would lead him to the shopping mall on Franklin St., and so there he may put an inordinate number of people into harm's way. Billy would need to consider a double-back move on the Monster. It seemed reasonable that he could hide behind another dumpster in this alley, like the previous one before it.

As he took his first step into the alley, the wailing sound of horns filled his ears. A scream. A howl. Shattering glass and crumpled metal. When he turned to see the Birthday Monster sprawled out in the street, a deep sense of relief filled his gut with immediacy. Though he could not detect, with his initial viewing of the accident, what had happened, he was positive that the Monster was no longer in hot pursuit.

He jogged back towards the street which he had previously crossed in a desperate scramble, where he found a bright yellow cab several feet from where the Birthday Monster was huddled on the ground like a lump of discarded hair. It gave a low groan as Billy hovered above its body, observing what he hoped to be its final moments. The cabbie had now emerged from his destroyed vehicle, looking at the beast with his jaw agape, asking of Billy, "What the fuck is this?" Billy looked up to the man and saw that his forehead was bleeding, presumably from the unexpected wreck that he had just been an integral part of. "Is that guy dressed like Chewbacca?" the cabbie asked, and Billy could see the gears working in the man's head, trying to remember how many months had passed since Halloween.

The Birthday Monster turned on to its side, its glowing yellow eyes riddled with tears. It groaned in pain, reaching out its claw but finding insufficient energy to hold any of his limbs in place without the curse of gravity dragging them back to the ground. A long string of drool pooled on its heaving chest.

A sense of recognition filled Billy's mind and he leaned to one knee, staring for the first time into the eyes of the beast for longer than a passing moment of escape. For so many years, he had been stalked by this thing, and now he reveled in its final moments, both relieved and disgusted by the hideous thing. It now seemed so very obvious to him its intentions, the hellish thing ever in pursuit. Its elongated nose sent his heart into a whirlwind of emotions as he recalled himself, Billy, looking in the mirror every morning, wondering why he had ended up with such a terribly awkward and pointy nose. He reached down and took the Birthday Monster's hand in his own. The unwelcoming fur of the thing suddenly felt less rough than it had in the past.

As tears filled his eyes, Billy whispered in the thing's ear. Its expression changed, as the beast seemed to understand the words that Billy had spoken, scanning the Boy's face for something that he had lost. It lifted its massive furry head just enough to smell Billy's breath. Close enough to pull the Boy in closer. Billy's world went black after a short gasp, the Birthday Monster tearing his throat from his body in one lunging bite of his elongated fangs. The cab driver screamed in terror, running back to the comforts and safety of his cab, praying that it was still functional enough after the accident to get him away from the seven foot monster that had thoroughly ruined his day.

Billy's limp lifeless body lay next to his Birthday Monster's. As the hour struck midnight, The Birthday Monster pulled the Boy's body in close to his own, huddling them together in a deathly embrace. And the Birthday Monster closed his devilish eyes forevermore, finally at home and satisfied... for whatever value that had to a blood-thirsty animal such as himself.

The Birthday Monster evaporated, but the Boy's bloodless body remained.

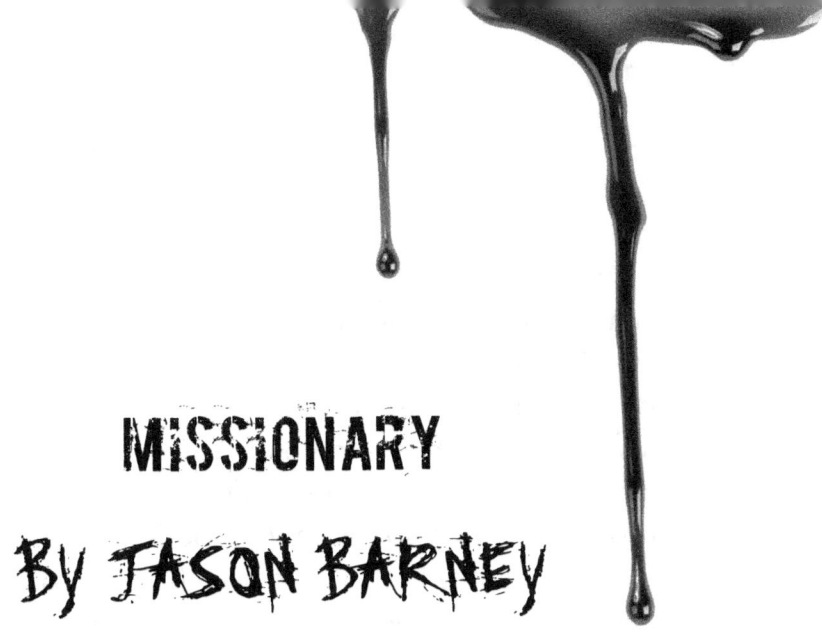

MISSIONARY

BY JASON BARNEY

Kon felt his aching joints protest as he pushed his body farther up the incline. He needed to bend over and lean forward to keep his balance. At times he was on his hands and knees as he navigated the steep mountain wall. He'd already jarred his back at one point, and he could still feel the dull twinge that made his spine feel as though two puzzle pieces no longer fit together.

He ran his open palm over the rough leather pouch he had over his shoulder, at times its contents where just bulky enough to prevent him from achieving a steady ascent. The added weight wasn't so heavy that he was struggling, but it redefined the pace and direction of his climb. At times his corrections and lurches made him feel like a drunken man stumbling away from his alcohol.

The terrain was rough, by far the most difficult part of the journey so far. The ground was strewn with boulders that denied him the benefit of hiking through the wild area in a straight line. Instead, he was traversing double or triple the distance because of all of the cuts and small angles that needed to be made.

Kon was being extremely careful. He was used to living in a city atmosphere, where families and merchants lived in homes constructed of mud huts and traveled on streets of sand brick. Here, weeks away from the comforts of civilization, he needed to concentrate just to avoid absent mindedly swiping a leg against a sharp rock or catching a tired foot on the bumpy earth. In all of his years, Kon had never seen such unfriendly ground.

He paused a moment and took in the desolate land around him. The countryside wasn't anything like what he had expected it to be. Home was flat and the sands were always golden brown. Here, the land was full of mountain passes, and the peaks were so high they were covered with white snow Kon had never seen before. The trees swayed in the strong winds, but they were sparse, scraggly and unhealthy, like a dying spider's twitching legs. He wondered how anyone could possibly live this far away from the great cities of his homeland and survive. He considered the type of people who would want to exist in such a barren and remote area, and he found himself questioning their belief system and values. Then he remembered the purpose of his trek, to spread the word, and he hoped he would come into contact with someone from this area soon.

His stretched his legs and back as much as he could, wishing the pain would go away, and wondered if he had done the right thing in leaving the city of Membo. While the intense heat of the desert back home was always uncomfortable, one earned to live with it over a lifetime. Here, the winds were sometimes cold and aloof, like a stranger on a street that stumbles into another's path and refuses to make eye contact. The ground was uneven and lumpy like swollen bruises on a person's skin.

Heavy clouds masked the sun. The light of the day was seeping away. He wasn't sure how far he'd gone today, he just knew that he was further away from his home, another day's march absent from the land, life, and belief system he was traveling to tell others about. It depressed him to think he may never see the people of his homeland again, but he comforted himself by restating the edict from that had come from the elders.

Word of their wonderful and high belief system needed to be spread. The facts of their culture and values must be broadened to the peoples of all lands. Kon believed enough in the sanctity of the gods to know heathens deserved to learn about them. Those who were not aware of the great advances the gods had bestowed on his people would get their chance to hear the words…through him and others on similar journeys.

Kon kept moving. There would not be much daylight left in a few hours. He was getting tired of loneliness as his only companion.

Hours later, when the night had washed over the land and Kon had set up camp for the evening; he performed the rituals, which kept him safe so far from home. Kon made sure to build his fire using the religious symbols carried down for generations. He bowed in each of the ceremonial directions, and prayed to the gods who would keep him safe. Whenever doubt entered his mind, he reminded himself he was doing their bidding.

The yellow and orange flames danced over the dry pieces of wood he'd piled in his fire pit. Every so often, when he doctored the fire, burning embers would drift upward with the smoke and join the stars high above. He looked for the gods and wondered how distant they were.

Kon relaxed next to the fire and carefully started to unpack some of his belongings. He placed one of his blankets under him to provide some protection between his body and bug infested sands below. He had another heavy cover to help keep him warm at night, and he had used it plenty of times while traveling through the mountainous regions. He drank from his flask of water, and snacked on his precious dried vegetables.

His meal complete, his belly full, and his mind at ease after the long day's journey, Kon set to giving proper respect to the gods.

His hands sifted through the remaining contents of his leather pouch and found the small wooden box he took out every night before going down going to bed. He opened it, grasped the small heavy idol of the goddess of war, and placed it in front of the flames. Kon watched as the gold and silver idol shined against the campfire's light. He thought the fire looked stronger and healthier now that the goddess was watching over it.

Kon's hands again descended to the pouch and he rummaged through different belongings until he found the scrolls. He pulled them out one at a time, as though he were carrying priceless jewels in front of a vengeful king. Kon unrolled each of them. He handled them gently, like a young mother cradling her first born, and for several hours he read them. He felt warmth and understanding from the gods bathe him in the chilly night air. He read the words and celebrated. The parchment couldn't have been wrenched from his hands by the worst storms or the fiercest armies. In those moments when he was alone with his deity, he was in love.

He thought back to the recent history that had allowed the word of the gods to spread so quickly. He'd seen the machine only once, but he'd seen the effects of it all over the cities of the Great River. For the longest time, only the educated and powerful had read the word of the gods and interpreted what the heavens desired for the world.

Now everyone was learning to read. Now the word of the religious leaders was spreading like smiles on a bright and shiny morning. Kon was a part of that effort.

Tomorrow morning he would resume his journey northwest.

He would go on as long as it took and reach the land of the godless.

Kon would spread the word. He thanked the gods for the printing press, and bowed to them for allowing him to journey and spread their teachings.

The trek continued for many more weeks. From the unexpected rains that drenched the lands and caused his feet to sink into the muddy ground, through the horrible cold snap that caused him to question his purpose, Kon kept moving. At times the feeling of God's presence was as obvious as the heat of the campfires he built every night. On other days, he felt like the worker who only goes to his job because he needs to feed his family. Through the aches and pains he went on.

Finally, one morning after he'd been walking for several hours, Kon detected the first signs he was nearing his goal. He had been approaching yet another mountainous region. Out of the corner of his eye, along a sandy section of unclaimed land, he saw a long stretch of pressed earth. It was a trail. He was so surprised by the discovery that he stopped walking and just stood for several moments. Evidence of other peoples was something he'd wanted to find, and now it seemed he'd achieved his goal.

The path was somewhat hidden by the patchy scrub brush and irregular rocks that littered the ground the way a windblown field of snow can create banks that cover a trail in the winter. As he studied it, part of him was surprised he'd been able to notice it all, but as he took in its length and direction, he felt embarrassed he hadn't seen it minutes before. Kon was forced to wonder if he'd missed any other signs of civilization at any point in his journey.

He quickly went to it, looking for information. He considered the implications of such a find. It must have been used often enough to prevent the violent weather of the desert from erasing it from existence, which meant there was likely a significant population in the region.

There were patches of plant life pushing up through some of the most well-traveled areas. He could see naked footprints where calloused feet had walked. There was evidence of sandals or boots, as some of the prints were too large to be unprotected. He couldn't identify the design, but there were indications of different sized wheels, as thin unbroken lines had pushed down the dirt and extended away in both directions. There were horse or camel tracks as well.

Kon wondered which way he should go. He could alter his course just a little and unite with the path. It wrapped around some of the rises in the distance. He couldn't tell if it turned into the mountains or if it went parallel to them. The other option was to drastically alter his course and turn completely away from his original course. If he did so, he'd be on the road, but the land in that direction looked ominously like the deserts he'd been through for countless days and nights.

He chose the way that led to the mountainous area.

Kon continued his journey and he couldn't help feeling excitement rush through his body, the way a child anticipates the arrival of a holiday. Since leaving his homeland he'd dreamed of reaching a foreign territory and teaching the primitives about the true nature of the universe. He also felt nervous, as he wondered how heretics would react to having the true gods revealed to them for the first time.

Thoughts of wandering nomads rushed into his mind. He couldn't help considering he'd run into a group of people and they would have their own incorrect belief system. Once the true vision's wondrous beauty and divine nature was revealed to them, all would be fine. The god of war had sent Kon a vision of peace.

He stepped with a little more energy, looking forward to his much anticipated contact with the unknown.

The trail was much less traveled than he had hoped. Kon didn't see a soul. At first he thought he might come across a band of merchants. He began to realize it was foolish for him to think of any people in this section of the world behaved or acted anything like the people in his homeland. He was just as likely to run into a hunters and gatherers as he was to locate a center of trade and commerce.

Kon found himself growing lonely and depressed. No other people were around. He tried to be with his god all of the time, but there were no other people. If he wasn't spreading the word, was he truly doing god's bidding?

The lone missionary continued on. Sometimes Kon felt he was walking in place, just lifting his feet up and down and not going anywhere.

He had decided to break with the road. Such a path along the Great River would have certainly led any traveler to at least a campsite, if not an entire village.

Here, out in the middle of a wild and abandoned land, the road only seemed to lead to further isolation.

Kon turned west, toward the mountains.

The swirling smoke funnel on the horizon didn't grab his attention until he realized he was looking right at it. It was brown, the color of moist dirt, and slowly reached up into the clouds. Kon wondered how long it had been in his field of vision before the reality of what he was looking at struck him.

He'd been cresting a small rise, searching for a favorable place to settle down for another night of solitude and prayer, when he'd stopped to take in the view. The frustrating experience of the road wasn't visible any longer. Trees and boulders surrounded him, and what he thought was virgin earth. Then, like a twister appearing in an unpredictable sky, the billowing smoke coalesced just beyond the next rise.

Kon tried to think of the last time he'd shared someone else's fire.

He smelled the smoke when he was still a good distance from his destination. The damp ashy smell had settled over the land near the source of the smoke, and it piqued his interest. With each step he felt his apprehension level rise. He put one foot in front of the other and continued his slow march across the valley. Kon kept his eyes on the thin cyclone of gray, but was attentive to anything that would indicate there were other people in the region. There were no scuffmarks in the dirt; he wasn't able to find any broken or bent blades of grass. There were no abandoned fire pits or charred pieces of wood to indicate anyone else had been through the area. Nothing else moved.

Finally, he reached the bottom of a hill that stretched far in either direction. The incline wasn't anything compared to the painful ledges and cliffs he'd been forced to deal with earlier in his journey. A few small trees with flaking bark sparsely populated the rise. They looked weak and close to death. Kon thought they were like old people who are forced to sit around and wait for the end of their lives. There were a few rocks but they didn't look like anything that would make the journey up any more difficult. The smoke continued to waft into sky, originating beyond the crest of the hill.

Kon couldn't help wondering what he would experience as he began the ascent. He estimated it would take him only a minute or two to reach the top, and he couldn't stop thinking about how his long journey would finally be fulfilled. He stopped twice on the way up and uttered a silent prayer thanking God for the chance to spread the word. It was impossible to know if he would be greeted warmly or if he'd be treated like an enemy.

He finally reached to top. There was a long flat field with copper colored grass. There were a few larger, sick looking trees in the distance.

There was a fairly good-sized campsite in the middle of the field. Bright orange flames reached above a well-placed circle of rocks like a mole poking its head above ground. The smoke floated away from the fire like ghosts leaving still warm bodies.

But there was no one in the field.

Kon kept a watchful eye on the horizon as he walked into the middle of the field and looked for information. He didn't see anyone, but the presence of the fire and the height of the burn meant someone had tended to it very recently. His heart rate increased with excitement as he realized there was a good chance the person who started the fire was probably within sight of the smoke. Whoever it was likely using it as a beacon; he could hunt or collect edible plants and just look back over his shoulder to find his way.

Kon stopped in mid stride as he realized there was a strong chance he was being watched. He knew enough about human nature to know people were very protective of their belongings. Back in the homeland he'd come in contact with enough foreigners to know fear of having possessions stolen was a universal concern. Kon raised his hands slowly above his head, to communicate to any observer that he was not a threat. He stopped just short of the fire pit.

There was little indication anyone had spent much time there. There was one area that looked like it was pressed against the ground, roughly the size of a bed. Someone had either rested or slept there. There were no footprints, supplies, or old scraps of wood. Kon's heart sank as his hope of spreading the word deflated like a balloon with a hole in it. On the small chance there was anyone watching him he kept his hands raised as he stepped closer to the fire.

He never saw the men who jumped him. One moment he was kneeling beside the unclaimed fire, asking the Lord for guidance. Next he felt something strike the back of his head and the weight of something big crushing him against the ground. His head immediately seared with pain. He felt wetness running down his face and neck. He was pinned against the grass and dirt, unable to move, with no way of defending himself. Terror erupted in his heart and chest as he realized he couldn't even struggle against whoever had attacked him. He tried to shift his weight, gain some advantage that would allow him to turn over, but powerful arms and a weighty form squashed him. He needed air, but his lungs were restricted. Kon wondered what had struck him, what object had delivered such a painful blow to his head.

The missionary tried to speak. He needed to try and reason with his assailants, show them he was not a threat. He tried to listen for the sounds of their tongue, but the scuffle was the only thing he heard. For the first time in his life, Kon wondered if he was going to die.

He felt the impact of the second blow to the head, but didn't feel the pain.

When Kon woke up his head hurt.

It felt like someone was pressing on both of his temples. The pain in the back of his head was so bad he thought his skull had been cracked. He slowly opened his eyes and saw that he was on the ground. When he tried to get up, he found that his arms were fastened behind his back. A quick adjustment of his weight allowed him to turn his hands, but he discovered his wrists were bound with something heavy and thick, probably leather. As his head cleared and his senses returned, he realized that his feet were bound together as well. He couldn't move.

He was greeted with a forceful blow to his stomach. Kon brought his knees up into the fetal position and gasped for air. Kon decided not to risk any further movements.

The fire was more alive than it had been before. He could see two forms moving around. He wasn't able to get much detail.

His stomach felt like it had caved in, and his breath was irregular.

"Hrin cikg tst fin golaksji vip-snop gle evans," he heard a voice say.

A second voice responded. Kon's purpose returned to him in a spark of inspiration and he realized that this was it. Despite the circumstances, he'd finally managed to make contact with the inhabitants of this part of the world. Admittedly, the first encounter didn't seem to be going so well, but he just needed the opportunity to speak to them. All he needed was one chance to deliver The Word, and all would be fine. Kon realized he was actually smiling.

He thought about the men who had done this too him and tried to put himself in their position. He imagined reacting very much like they had, with hostility and aggression to some random person poking around their campsite. He understood and accepted their violent reaction, but he knew his mission of peace would succeed. The Almighty willed it.

Kon remained silent for several minutes and tried to pick up any specifics of their dialogue, anything that would allow him to communicate. He'd held back, avoided speaking because he didn't want to alarm them. They'd already reacted in a negative way and he didn't want to do anything that would decrease his chances of success.

He watched as they roamed around the fire. They were restless, like cats deciding how to satisfy hunger. One walked in a half circle. The other was studying the darkening horizon line. Their language was abrupt and too foreign for him to recognize. Kon cursed fate and hoped he was able to use his hands to communicate at some point.

Excitement washed over him as he saw one of the two men reach for his leather pouch. He felt a little safer knowing they wanted to find out information about him.

The foreigner dumped the contents on the ground. Kon watched as all of his possessions landed on the dirt and stone. He was confident they would notice that he carried no sword, no knives, or anything that could be used as a weapon. They would understand his non-aggression. The man took his time and sifted through his things, like a detective searching for evidence.

Kon felt the excitement a child experiences when they look through wrapped birthday presents. When one of them lifted the scrolls and examined the papers he felt as though the Gods were with him, sitting on the edge of the fire, guiding the first meeting between distant peoples. Once they unrolled the parchments, they would recognize their religious significance and understand his peaceful journey. The man's look went from the religious texts, to the other man, and then to Kon.

The Word was being revealed. His work was being done.

Kon chose that moment to speak, to aid the meeting along.

"They are from one of our most special Gods," he said looking back and forth between the scrolls and the sky. "It is the word-"

The man dropped them into the fire. Kon's eyes widened and he struggled against the bonds that held him.

"No!" he yelled, not believing what he had just witnessed. "Those are the-

He was amazed at how quickly the distance between he and one of his attackers decreased. With the gracefulness and speed of a dancer, one of the men was standing over him faster than Kon would have thought possible.

"Please," Kon pleaded, "You must-"

Another kick into his ribs crushed his ability to speak. He was sure a few of his ribs snapped. He felt pain all across his mid-section.

Kon screamed in pain.

Several more blows landed over his body. Kon sensed he was about to pass out again. The fear he experienced was the most powerful sensation he'd ever dealt with. As blackness gripped him, he wondered if he were about to pass to the other side and how things had gone so horribly wrong.

When Kon awoke he was no longer on the ground. He was upright, his arms were still behind him, and he was moving. Vertigo gripped him and he almost wretched. His arms were still behind him, and his legs were bound together. He could feel something thin and solid directly against his back.

It was totally dark; accept for the light being thrown by the fire. The flames were much larger than they had been either of the previous times he'd seen them. Kon nervously glanced around and saw movement. He studied his surroundings and discovered he was tied to a post, which was leaning up against one of the dead looking trees.

Kon noticed one of the men was kneeling in front of the fire. He looked like he was praying. His head kept bobbing up and down. His shoulders and torso were moving back and forth, like old woman in a rocking chair.

He understood the men were practicing their own religion.

"I come in peace," he said. "I want to talk, to show you-"

Kon didn't see the other man, but he felt the cold sharp blade slice through the skin in his neck. He thought how odd it was; that he could consciously think that the knife hadn't really gone that deep, how it felt like there wasn't much damage to his throat. There was pain. He saw an arm arch upward into the blackness. Light from the flames glinted off the blade, and he saw the drops of dark redness fly into the night sky.

Kon instantly felt weak, and was surprised by how wet the front side of his body was. He could feel his own blood running down his chest and stomach like rain falling off a roof.

He tried to lift his head and failed.

His last vision was of two men in darkness.

ANGRY ARTIFACTS

By JEFFREY ANGUS

It was a hot wet August night in the city of Cordoba. Heavy rains in the early evening had soaked the city. The cleansing rain and the soft light from the streetlamp made the surface look smooth and shiny. The alley was quiet, the temperature in the high nineties keeping the residents of the city in and sheltered from the sticky heat. The downpour had cooled the asphalt just enough to cause wisps of steam to dance its way up into the star-filled night reaching for the full moon.

Gregg did his best to blend in with the shadows in the alley as he waited behind the rusty dumpster. He disliked Chinatown as well as the little people who resided here. This part of town was stuck in the past they lived with old traditions. *Get with the times*, he thought to himself, *its 2010 already*. A slight breeze brought with it the stench of rotting Chinese food, the heat helping the food reach a new level of disgusting. The smell helped to solidify his opinion of the entire area.

His turf was the docks; he was in control and ran the show at the pier. Greg preferred the smell of the sea and the sound of the waves to this stinky corner of Cordoba. He really didn't like scoring a hit when it wasn't on his turf. If it were not the chance of a big score, he would have stayed at the docks.

This was the location the fat little Asian man told him the goods would be stored. He reached into his shirt pocket and pulled out a blood stained folded scrap of paper. Gregg smiled when he looked at the scrap and unfolded the note. *This is the place.* Chang's Antiques and Collectibles: Your Place for the Unusual and Strange. Gregg held the note at an angle to catch the streetlamp's light. He was able to match what was on the paper with his surroundings and the Chinese characters that framed the English spelling that was in place for the tourists. Gregg looked at the sign above the door on the other side of the alley. It matched what was written on the paper, green and white letters and characters and the strange clock in the middle. Gregg was sure this was the location the delivery would be made to.

Earlier in the day, down by pier thirty-four, he had caught the little chubby Chinese man snooping around. Gregg saw him as an easy mark. He let the man nose around a bit and then made his move. The poor slob begged for mercy and give Gregg information he said would change his life forever. The idiot even drew him a map of the alley and a picture of the sign. Gregg smiled as he remembered the look on the poor wretches face as he watched the life flow out of the slit his knife created across his latest victim's throat.

"People need to stay on their own turf," Gregg snickered.

An engine and the squeak of springs from the entrance of the alley snapped Gregg out of his daydream. He saw that a small van that had just turned into the alley and was heading his way. He shrank back into the shadow as the headlights passed over the dumpster. The vehicle slowed and stopped a few feet from the door. The delivery person exited the vehicle and checked his clipboard. The driver was a small, chubby man, standing about five feet six inches. Gregg smiled; he liked when he could overpower his victims with ease. The driver made his way to the side door of the van and Gregg noticed the multi-colored clock logo on his jacket. The strange clock glowed and changed color much like the one on the sign. Everything was falling into place. This was definitely the location.

The man grabbed a few boxes from the side door of the van. He checked the clipboard again, made a few marks with his pen, and closed the side door of the vehicle. He whistled a happy tune as he made his way towards the door where Gregg lay in wait. He set down the boxes, fished out his keys, and unlocked the door of <u>Chang's Antiques</u>. With the door open and secure, he picked up the boxes and started to enter.

Gregg made his move and before the delivery person realized his peril, he was struck from behind. Gregg shoved his long-bladed knife deep into the courier's back, his hand clamped over the man's mouth to stifle any sound. The knife ripped through the internal organs on its way through and a good part of the blade came out the front side of the pour victim. The white delivery shirt changed to red as the blood seeped from the hole in his chest. Gregg slid the knife from the poor soul's back, the weapon making a sickening pop as it cleared the wound in his back. In a quick fluid motion, he brought the knife around and with a smirk, slit the dying man's throat.

Gregg smiled as he crouched down to look over his handy work. He wiped at his brow, more to remove spatters of blood then perspiration from the encounter. He smirked and nodded his head impressed with how easy this really had been. He noticed this chubby little Chinese man looked identical to the Asian guy he had removed from his turf earlier that day down by the docks. Gregg shrugged, thinking that they all looked alike, anyway, and dragged the body behind the dumpster.

Gregg paused, and turned back toward the body. His adrenalin tended to blind him whenever he made a kill. He took a minute to look around and make sure all was still clear. He was relieved to see that the attack had not brought unwanted attention to the location. The delivery van filled most of the alley and no one who might wander by would be able to see what was happening with in. He was satisfied that it was safe and relaxed a bit. Gregg bent over to check the pockets of the dead man and took anything of value or use. He then picked up the body and tossed it into the dumpster.

"More nasty Chinese won't make much difference." he snickered.

Satisfied with the scene, Gregg entered the shop and closed the door behind him. He paused long enough to let his eyes adjust to his new surroundings. When he was able to focus on the interior, he took a quick inventory of what lay before him. <u>Chang's Antiques and Collectibles</u> was larger than it appeared from the alley. The place was full of all kinds of boxes and crates. The interior had a strange feeling and smelled of spices and incense. Gregg had no need for any light do to the clock logo on each crate giving off a strange unearthly glow. Each box looked to have a date stenciled into the side just below the clock logo. Near the center of the room lay a few larger crates. The lids on them lay open and rested against the side of the wooden vessels. The floor of the warehouse had packing peanuts and a straw like material that must have come from the boxes strewn everyplace.

"So in these crates is what's supposed change my life," he whispered, making his way towards the center of the room where the crates lay. "We'll see about that."

He looked inside the nearest open crate and moved the remaining packing peanuts. On the side of this box was March 7th 2012. Gregg shrugged and set on his task. His hands made contact with something smooth and cold to the touch. He reached in with his other hand and pulled the item from the crate. It was a large music box, probably the biggest and most peculiar he had ever seen. The item design was that of a carousel horse. The excellent condition and the intricate workings of the piece astounded him. The color changed depending on how the light hit the piece of art. Even someone who wasn't an expert in antiques could appreciate a piece like this horse. Gregg was amazed at the detail of his newest acquisition. On the bottom again was the date of March 7th 2012. He wondered briefly at the significance of the identical dates. *Maybe it was shipped the exact day it was finished?*

He removed some of the packing in the crate and noticed a piece of paper. He picked it out of the packing material and unfolded it so he could read it. The writing looked to be Chinese and he couldn't make any sense of it. Gregg tossed the paper aside and continued looking around. His eye caught some writing on the back of the invoice he had tossed to the ground. He picked the discarded invoice back up and examined the back. Stamped in English were the words *Mystical Horse*, from the dig in Anyang, China. Gregg smiled and turned the horse over with joy like a child with a new toy. It was spectacular, and it was old and in great shape. It was inlayed with gold and what looked to be rubies, emeralds and garnets. This would be worth more than anything he had ever sold on the market. The horse itself seemed to be formed from a solid piece of obsidian. He was surprised it wound up in a dusty old antique shop and not in a museum.

Gregg set the horse on a nearby crate. He watched as the light from the clock logos glistened off the device. He sat and gazed at his new prize. He sat for a good amount of time and then the music box started to play a song all on its own. The strange music seemed to get louder and louder. Gregg started to panic and looked around. If someone found him here, all he had done would be for nothing. He clasped the device with both hands to see if he could muffle the sound or stop the music. Gregg was surprised to find the device was very warm to the touch. He felt very dizzy and just as he the world went black a felt a cold wind lifting him into the air.

Gregg regained consciousness some time later. He found himself to be back in the alley outside the shop. He rolled over on his side, wincing at a few scrapes on his face and arms. If anyone came past, they would have thought him just another bum sleeping off that night's binge. He lay still a few minutes and then propped himself up on his elbows. Sharp pain shot through his back, neck and head. He lay back down, brought his hands up to his head, and rubbed his temples.

"What the hell hit me?" Head pounding and in great pain, he leaned over and threw up.

"Much better now," he said, wiping vomit from his lips. He managed to get himself into a standing position and was able to take a good look at his surroundings. He started to get dizzy and felt like he was going to be sick again.

It took a minute for his eyes to focus and the feeling to pass. Gregg had a hard time standing and steadying himself. He leaned against a stack of wooden pallets that were gathered in the alley. He wiped his eyes to focus and clear his thoughts. Reaching a point that he didn't feel he was going to fall over, Gregg took a better look around.

"What happened in there??" He wiped his eyes again. "And how the hell did I get outside?"

He glanced above the nearby door and noticed the worn sign that read, Chang's Antiques and Collectibles: Your Place for the Unusual and Strange. He shook his head to get rid of the few remaining cobwebs. It started to come back to him. He was in an alley; he had just dispatched the courier and entered the door. He had found the music box...

Gregg got the strange feeling as if someone was watching him. He made his way towards the door; he turned the handle expecting it to be locked. The door swung open and he fell back onto the pavement. He maneuvered himself into a crouch behind the pallets. He stared in the dark portal the door revealed. A strange glow emitted from inside. His memory was starting to come back more clearly: the crates, the music box, feeling sick. The last thing he could remember was music playing from the ancient horse he had pulled from the crate. The sign out front was the same; the alley from what he could tell was the same, except the truck blocking the alley had a bit more rust then he had recalled. I must have slipped and hit my head and staggered back out the door.

"I don't remember that, though," he whispered to himself.

Gregg instinctively reached for his knife; it was not in its sheath. He was able to dislodge a board from one of the pallets and started towards the door. He peaked in and surveyed the area just inside.

Board at the ready, he continued into the dark. He closed the door behind him to prevent anyone looking his way from spotting his silhouette against the light from outside.

The room he entered was filled with broken crates that had the same markings as the sign outside. Most of the crates had either been broken into or disintegrated over time. Where once there were smells of spices and incense, now those of decay and mildew filled the room and water could be heard dripping somewhere in the distance. He wondered what had happened. This was obviously the same shop he'd been in not a few hours before. However, the smell and the conditions of the room had significantly changed.

Gregg made his way toward the stack of large crates in the center of the room. The lids on the crates were no longer resting on the floor and he was a bit puzzled. The last time he was there, the crates had been open and packing all over the floor. He was sure this was the same place he had found the musical horse.

"What the hell is this?" he whispered to himself. He took a look around trying to find the musical horse. It was nowhere to be found. He was sure he had set it near the entrance.

Gregg made his way around one of the boxes in the middle of the room and noticed the small musical horse sitting on the floor near the middle of the room. Gregg made his way toward the device. He didn't remember it being way over where it sat now. He decided he had enough of this strange place and grabbed for the horse. He looked it over and noticed it had a different date on it. On the bottom it had a number stenciled 10000 BCE. He felt warmth he did not expect. Gregg got very dizzy, he felt heavy, the warmth spreading through his body. His world went black.

It was a warm wet night on the mountain pass. The heavy rains that had soaked the rocky surroundings and the soft light from the moons made the wet rocks shine and sparkle like shards of glass. The path and its surrounding were very quiet. The heavy rains had cooled the area and steam from the days sun baked boulders made its way up into the black of the night.

Gregg, lay unconscious on the scree path. If anyone had come past, they would have thought him just another forsaken traveler unlucky enough to be caught by brigands or evildoers. Greg lay still a few minutes and then propped himself up on his elbows. The sharp fragments of rock cutting into his arms caused blood to run down his forearm. The look on his face showed the pain he was in. He lie back down and lay still except for rubbing his wounds. After a few minutes, he was able to sit back up and survey the area.

"What in the hell is going on?" Head pounding and in great pain, he leaned over and threw up.

He looked up into the starlit sky and the moon was full… wait, the moons. Gregg rubbed his eyes and looked back into the sky. He still could see two moons, one blue and one orange. Not far from where he lay was a small structure. It looked like a tool shack of some kind. Above the door he could see a sign. The sign was green and white with worn letters. A giant clock in the middle stood out and it would change colors as the hands slowly turned non-stop. He shook his head to get rid of the few remaining cobwebs, and thought to himself somehow that sign looked familiar. Along the cracks of the door seeped a strange light.

"You have to be freaking kidding me." Gregg mumbled in frustration.

He lay back on the path, closed his eyes, and tried to make sense of what was going on. Drifting off to sleep for a few minutes, he was startled awake by a loud shrieking cry. Something winged and large flew in front of the moons. What it was he was not sure but now it was heading towards him. Fear washed over him but he was able to shake it off and started to move. He couldn't believe what he was seeing. He jumped up and ran towards the structures door.

Behind him, where he had just been resting, the ground burst into flame as the dragon's breath hit its mark. Without a second thought he grabbed the lever on the door and rushed in. He tripped and landed hard, knocking the wind out of himself. He struggled to catch his breath. Out side he could hear the shrieking again and it was getting closer. He looked around and noticed a music box in the form of a horse. On the bottom was stenciled October 9th, 1964. The surface of the device was warm to his touch. He held the horse as the warmth spread through his body. A haunting music reached his ears. Gregg felt dizzy and everything went black.

It was a warm wet night in the jungle. The heavy rains that had soaked the foliage and the soft light from the sky made the surrounding high grass shimmer in the moons light. The path and its surrounding were very quiet. The heavy rains had cooled the area and steam made its way up into the black of the night.

Gregg was sprawled out, eyes closed on the grass path. He managed to get himself into a sitting position.

"What the hell is going on? Did I die or something?"

He propped himself up on his elbows and again the look on his face showed the pain. He lay back down and tried not to move. His memory came to him in a strong wave.

He struggled but managed to get into a crouch, and looked around. This was not an alley. He noticed barbwire and a bamboo tower of some kind. Gregg was very confused now. A loud thump could be heard and the sky lit up.

"What the hell?"

Someplace in the distance a voice could be heard, "Alarm, Alarm Enemy in the wire,"

Gunshots rang out in the air and Gregg felt a burn across his cheeks. He dove to the ground.

"What the hell." he felt his cheek and his hand came back with blood. He rolled into the brush that was along the path. Trying to understand what was going on. The crack of gunfire was strong and the weeds next to him danced as the bullets ripped through the underbrush. More instinct then anything Gregg took off heading towards a patch of trees.

He ran between the trees as his pursuers yelled and fired in his direction. He was being hunted and bit disoriented he didn't know which way to go. His legs burning and chest heavy from the pursuit, a panicked mad dash for survival he ran on. He broke through some heavy brush into thin air. He was airborne for a few seconds and then hit the ground and started to roll. Down he went for what felt like a lifetime and then the shock of cold water brought him out of his bad dream. Above him, the pursuers fired and shouted. He managed to get himself up again and running. He followed the river away from the shouting. Cold and disoriented he spotted a cave and without a second thought he entered. He sat in the dark and just listened. The sounds of the jungle were all Gregg could here. He was glad of that and not the voices of his pursuers.

He leaned back against the wall and felt something behind him. He felt around and his hands touched something wooden. As he felt around, he must have brushed some dirt away a faint glow came from what he was touching. It was some kind of box; he could feel the top slide off and his hand slip into something. He felt the smooth familiar surface. He pulled the musical horse out of the box and from the glow of the clock logo he could read July 8th 2010. He whispered to himself, that's today, or I think it is. Soft music, a familiar tune filled the air and a warm feeling ran through his body, then darkness.

Gregg was standing in an alley, facing an open door. He had some boxes in his hand. He looked up and noticed a sign that read, Chang's Antiques and Collectibles: Your Place for the Unusual and Strange. He glanced to his right and noticed the cargo van. He smiled with relief and was glad to see such familiar things. He looked at the boxes in his hands, thinking to himself, that's strange, they are the boxes the delivery guy had been carrying. Pain exploded through his body as he looked down he noticed a knife sticking out his chest. His white shirt turned red from the blood that was fast escaping the open wound. He then felt the knife across his neck and he started to fall. He glimpsed a small oriental face looking at him and thought he recognized where he was. He felt dizzy and all went black.

A small, chubby Asian man stood over Gregg's body smiling, "It will change your life forever."

THE SCARECROW MAN
BY DANIEL P. COUGHLIN

When I woke up that Saturday morning in late June, 1980, I knew something horrible had happened. I could hear my mom crying and when I went downstairs she was sitting at the kitchen table bawling her eyes out. She had a letter in her hand and I already knew what was written on it.

"Timmy?" my mother called when she heard my footsteps creaking toward the staircase. Her voice was coarse.

"Yes ma?" I responded as my throat started to burn from the grief I knew my mother was being forced to deal upon me. My father had left us and probably with nothing but a pot to pee in. I mean we lived in a fairly nice home and never went without food but we had no savings. My mother was a housewife and had never really worked a real job. Dad had always made the money and paid the bills. We weren't well off but we weren't starving.

My father was a likeable guy and he could make anyone laugh on a whim. He was the kind of guy that you wanted to show up at your Saturday night parties, he just kept social situations lively. I knew that he'd been cheating on my mother. Not that he didn't love mom, he was just the kind of guy that needed extracurricular activities in his life to prevent him from becoming bored. People just seem to have a sixth sense about these kinds of things and my mother knew it too. I don't know if she just didn't care or if she just didn't want to believe it was happening or maybe she tolerated it in order to maintain our family unity.

My father was a car dealer and darn good one. He was voted car salesman of year three times in the state of Wisconsin, which is where we lived. It was a quiet place where everyone knew everyone and one person's business was everyone's business. We liked living there, but after dad left us for some flaky California girl we had to move. Not that we couldn't afford to live in the small town anymore, it was just that my mother had too much dignity to deal with all the nasty rumors that would start circulating once the townsfolk found out about the affair and my father leaving. I also thought that without my father, my mother wouldn't have the same social status needed to keep up with the town's societal structure.

We moved to another small town, just me and mom and we were happy. There were days when I missed dad, but my sorrow would turn to anger and that would take care of me missing him, for a while. I could see that my mother wasn't the same woman anymore. She didn't sing while she was cleaning the house and the lines in her face began to deepen and this made me even angrier. I didn't care to see my father again.

It was the first day of summer vacation. I woke up from the sound of the neighbor's lawn mower and the fresh scent of cut grass seeping in through my bedroom window. My mother had gone to work at the bar down the street; she had the day shift. It was very convenient for her because she didn't have to use the car much, which meant we didn't have to spend too much money on gas. Mom liked the bar too, she was paid minimum wage and with tips we did just fine.

I walked outside and took in the summer air and it was refreshing. I got on my bicycle and went for a ride, a little tradition I did on the first day of summer vacation every year. I would ride for miles and miles and soak up the countryside. I took great pleasure in God's creation. Around these parts there was nothing but cornfields and forest. It was plain, but it was beautiful, to me.

About five miles down route 14 is where I saw him for the first time, the Scarecrow Man. He was hung up on a couple of four-by-fours and had the typical ratty blue jean-overalls and rustic flannel shirt on. I stopped, parked my bike, and went over to see him up close; I admire these kinds of things. That's just the kind of person I am.

When I got closer to him I realized that to the average person this man made of straw and rags could be very frightening, but I couldn't help but like the way he looked; silly. He had no heart and no soul, but he had a purpose. His job was to scare crows away from the field and protect his master's property. There was pride to be had in that.

"How are you today, sir?" I asked the scarecrow as if he'd respond back to me. He remained silent as he hung up there on his wood cross. There was something about the way he seemed to be looking at me, it wasn't quite scary but it was something other than comforting. It was as if he'd heard me and wanted to say something back. He understood something about me, or so I thought. We had a connection that I couldn't explain.

All I could think about on the ride home that day was the way the scarecrow looked at me through his scissor-hole-cut eyes. After thinking and digesting the way the scarecrow looked I couldn't help but feel sad for him. He seemed lonely up there by himself. As silly as it may sound, I decided to befriend my "scarecrow man" and made a promise to visit him at least three times a week that summer. It was crazy but it somehow brought a big smile to my face and if you're gonna do something, you might as well do something that's gonna make you happy, right?

That night when I got home there was a beat up truck parked in the driveway that I hadn't seen before. As I walked in the front door, my mom was sitting on our ratty old sofa drinking beer with a red-faced-fella wearing a mesh hat. They were laughing and having a good old time. I judged this by the twelve empty beer bottles sloppily set across the living room floor. My mother quickly got up and came to me with a genuine smile on her face.

"Timmy, this is my new good friend Wally Martin." she said to me. I could tell by the look on her face that she was hoping I wouldn't embarrass her by giving this man a scowl or turning my shoulder and running to my room.

"How do you do, sir?" I asked him as I made my way over to him with a smile. Heck, if somebody's going be making friends with my ma the way I know he's probably going be trying to make friends with her, I figured I'd best get to know him a little. To see if he was okay for her and all, you know?

"I'm Wally and I'm a new friend of your momma's. She sure is a pretty lady and we seem to get along good. That all right with you, boy?" he asked as he leaned forward and raised his eyebrows.

"I know sir. I mean I already know she's a good lady…the best" I responded quickly.

"Then I guess I'm preaching to the choir on that one, eh?" he said as he nudged my shoulder. He didn't nudge me hard though, it was real soft and it didn't make me budge too much. If he'd given me a good hit on the arm I would have immediately not liked him but he really wanted to make a good impression and so I let him have my approval, for now.

We sat around that night and Wally made jokes that weren't funny and my mother just died laughing at every one of them in the hopes that he would appreciate her. Around eleven o'clock Wally went home. I doubt that he was in any condition to drive but that was somewhat of a "norm" around these parts. After all, there isn't much to do around these parts except fill up at the local taverns.

After he'd left my mother that night, she came over to me and with beer stained breath she kissed me on the cheek and said, "Thank you."

I could tell by the tears welling up in her eyes that she needed this man for now. I could see the pain in her eyes and it broke my heart. She had been sad for so long and now she'd found someone who could make her happy, if not for just a short period of time. He had something that I couldn't give her and I knew she needed it, so I didn't make any stinks or stanks about him.

I went to see the scarecrow man the next day. I told him all about Wally and ma and how happy she seemed to have him around. He just looked down at me and I swear to *God the Almighty* he was happy for her the way I was happy for her too. I stayed with the scarecrow man for a few hours and looked at the field he was protecting and I admired its beauty. I said my peace with the man of hay before I rode home that night with the cool night breeze whizzing through my hair and I felt good. I hadn't felt this good in a long time. Ma had come into a bit of happiness and I liked seeing her like this.

Over the next few weeks Wally was over a lot but he would always leave at night. At first I thought maybe he was just being appropriate by not staying the night as it might not seem like the right thing to do with a young boy in the house, ma being a single mother and all. Even though I knew what they were doing in the bedroom during *private time*. I could see in my ma's eyes that she was starting to suspect something about Wally. Maybe he wasn't exactly the man she'd thought he was. Maybe he had some deep secret that he wasn't telling her or maybe I was just reading into things too much. I decided to ask the Scarecrow Man what he thought of the whole matter.

I rode out early the next morning and sat down in the dirt next to Scarecrow Man and asked him if I was being crazy for thinking that maybe Wally wasn't the man I'd thought he was. Scarecrow Man didn't seem to have an opinion. I sat and stared at him for a long while, studying the way he looked out at nothing. But there was something behind that clothe mask that I just couldn't explain. He seemed to be pondering the things I had told him and I appreciated it. I didn't get an answer from him that day and it bothered me some but I took it in stride. I rode home that afternoon and couldn't help but think about where Wally had come from. Why was he single? That night it came to me in a dream.

In my dream I was looking through the eyes of the scarecrow. My vision was somewhat hazy through the mesh netting of the potato sack he wore as a mask. I seemed to be moving about a hundred miles an hour through the cornfields and then I'd leap across the road and move swiftly through backyards and neighborhoods into another town not too far. I stopped in front of an old brick house where the lights were out and Wally's truck was in the driveway. I crept around the house slowly until I came to an open window where I snuck a peek inside. I saw Wally sound asleep next to a plump woman. They seemed peaceful in their slumber. I remember Wally snoring, it wasn't too loud but it seemed to annoy me. I watched them sleep for a while and then I left, back the same way I came.

The next morning I felt sore all over and I could barely move. I had a bad cough and when I sneezed I swear a cloud of dust extracted itself from my lungs. I went outside to my bike and rode out to the field, where Scarecrow Man resided. When I got there a farmer was stuffing him full of fresh hay, patting him down to smooth out the wrinkles. I approved of the way the farmer took care of my friend. He took pride in him. He pulled the rusty nails from the wood and hammered in new ones in.

I watched from afar until the farmer left and then I made my way over to Scarecrow Man. I told him about my dream and about how sore I was when I'd awoken that morning. He looked down at me from his post as if he'd already known. I was bewildered. There was something bigger than me *or him* going on here and it was special. My friend was showing me things that couldn't happen inside the realm of normality. The dream had not been a dream at all. It was a vision. I had asked the scarecrow man something the other day and he had shown me the answer in my dream.

"Will he hurt ma?" I asked him on this particular day. I was worried about her enough as it was and after the dream I had even more to worry about. I was sure, now, that Wally was a two-timer and that wasn't good enough for ma. I didn't want to see her get hurt again. That's understandable, right?

The scarecrow man seemed to smile at me in a menacing way that scared me to the bone. It was the smile of a madman. I sat quiet next to Scarecrow Man for a few more hours waiting for something, anything, but nothing came. I rode home that night and waited for sleep to come. I wanted the Scarecrow Man to show me something, I didn't know what but I needed something from him.

I drifted in and out of sleep that night as I waited for my dreams to come, but they never did and I didn't go and see the scarecrow man the next day either. I took the day to do my chores. I mowed the lawn and cleaned the house. I knew how ma always liked coming home to a clean house after work. I cleaned the place so spic'n'span that there was no way she wouldn't have a smile on her face when she came in through the door that evening. But when she arrived I was in for something I hadn't planned on.

When my father left us, he was with another woman and that was bad but he had never been violent and he had never drunken too much and said mean things. When ma came in the front door she was trying to smile at me but it was hard to tell at first because her eye was black and blue and blood had dried to her upper lip.

"Are you okay ma?" is all I could think to say. My heart dropped into the acid wash of my stomach. I knew what had happened and who had done it.

She couldn't look me in the eyes this particular night. She always looked me in the eye when she'd talk to me. She'd taught me to always look people in the eye if you wanted them to take you sincerely. This is something that always stuck with me. My heart began to drop even lower than my stomach. I'd never seen her like this. She was hurt in a way I hadn't seen before. I went to her and she embraced me. She held me so tight that it started to hurt. She went to bed early that night without telling me what had happened and I didn't ask. I didn't need her to feel humiliated by explaining herself.

I went to bed an hour or so later and got on my knees and prayed to God that he would keep my mother safe from this point on. I prayed that Wally would be out of her life.

Sleep came fast and my vision came shortly after. I was in the Scarecrow Man's mask again and I was pulling myself from the four-by-fours that bound me. Once I was down I seemed to be moving at superhuman speed again and before I knew it I was back at Wally's house and he was sleeping with the plump woman again. This time I snuck through the window and moved to the foot of the bed where

I was staring down at Wally. He was sleeping sound. I looked to his right hand and saw that it was bruised. The skin was cracked around his knuckles. Suddenly he awoke and looked at me with a fear that only God can put in a man's heart.

The next thing that happened was frightening. I tried to stop it but couldn't. I was pulling Wally from his bed so fast that it didn't even wake the plump woman. It was like I'd pulled a tablecloth out from underneath a dinner setting. I was dragging Wally through the living room of his house and then out through an open window. I could hear the skin come off his back as it caught on the splintered wood of the windowsill. He was trying to scream but I was stuffing hay into his mouth to muffle his cries. But it wasn't me stuffing his mouth with hay. It was Scarecrow Man. In my dreams we were one and he was powerful. His power frightened me but I trusted him, he gave me answers and peace of mind. I just assumed he was doing the right thing and being a friend to me in the process.

We carried Wally back through the cornfield to where Scarecrow Man held his post. When we got there, Scarecrow Man quickly dug a hole in the ground beneath his post. The hole was about six feet deep and three feet wide. Through the eyes of Scarecrow Man I could see the fear in Wally. He was choking and vomiting on the thick wads of straw that Scarecrow Man had stuffed in his mouth.

We were pushing Wally into the hole and he was fighting us. Scarecrow Man was too strong. I heard a guttural scream come from Wally as both of his arms snapped and Scarecrow Man forced him into the hole. Once at the bottom, we covered Wally with dirt.

The last thing I remember is Wally's right eye squinting before it disappeared into the dirt. There were some muffled cries but once the hole was filled there was nothing. It seemed as if this was some kind of sacrifice. After I'd stared at the ground where we'd buried Wally, Scarecrow Man mounted himself back up on his post and reinserted the nails.

I woke up the next morning with wild eyes. A rush of adrenaline surged through me as if I'd been hit by lightning. I checked on my mother briefly and saw that she was sleeping sound.

I got on my bike and rode out to see Scarecrow Man. I needed to know what he had shown me in the dream and if it had been real.

He was happy. The ground in front of him, as I suspected, looked like a fresh grave. But I didn't feel sad and I didn't feel guilt. All I felt was content. When I looked up at Scarecrow Man, to my amazement, he had real eyes. They were brown and yellow and tears rolled from them. I could tell that they were tears of happiness spilling down the cloth, making the dust turn a dark-muddy gray. I nodded at him in a pleasant fashion. The way old "war buddies" nod after they've saved each other in battle. There was nothing that needed to be said. I made eye contact and said, "Thank you."

He nodded back and then I watched as his eyes sunk back into the mesh of hay that made up his head.

I rode home that afternoon to console my mother. That was the last we'd ever see of Wally. There was an article in the paper explaining that he'd gone missing but even the plump woman who had turned out to be his wife didn't pursue it much. I guess they figured he'd run off, kind of like my dad.

Ma and I had a good summer and she wasn't upset for very long after Wally went missing. I went to see Scarecrow Man many times that summer. I was afraid to ask him questions about dad because I was afraid of the visions that he would show me if I did.

The night we took Wally was not the last vision that Scarecrow Man would show me.

A SECRET AMONGST BOYS

By Mason Ian Bundschuh

"Last one there's a rotten egg!"

Bobbie put all seventy pounds of himself into the pedals trying to catch up with Nathan. The two of them had only been friends since the beginning of summer but they were inseparable—especially after they both *knew*.

Though they were in the same grade, Nathan looked older. People sometimes thought he was already in high school. He was loud and brash and when he laughed his white teeth flashed as if in a dare. Not the sort of boy who usually befriended 'Baby' Bobbie. But Nathan had known, somehow he'd known before Bobbie knew it himself, and he'd shown Bobbie. And Bobbie wondered how he'd ever not known.

Their bikes flew down the old farm road, sending up dust and startled grasshoppers. The dry buffalo wheat on either side hummed with boisterous cicadas and Bobbie remembered that his mother'd asked him to take dinner over to Mr. Garritt, their cranky old neighbor. Bobbie wasn't sure which Mr. Garritt he disliked more, the one who used to threaten to loose his dogs on Bobbie for crossing his farm, or the new grieving one.

Nathan cast a glance back to Bobbie. His face was wild and beautiful—though Bobbie wouldn't have used those words to describe it. It was a hero's face, a face one was loyal to, but it was dangerous; like an angel with a secret.

For one second, with the sun hanging low over the dusty oak trees and the electric-blue sky careening overhead, Bobbie wished there was no secret. But once you knew you could never go back to not knowing.

Nathan laughed and pedaled harder, and the moment of Bobbie's doubt became the dead past. There was only the now, and now they were almost at the old run-down barn.

With a burst of energy Bobbie nearly caught up to Nathan, but the bigger boy leaned in and shot ahead. The monolithic barn door loomed in the ruddy light of failing day as the two boys slid to a stop in the weeds and dirt, letting bikes fall forgotten. As usual, Nathan slapped the paintless graying wood first. It rattled and boomed, startling doves roosting in the sagging eaves.

"You're a rotten egg," Nathan said perfunctorily, he was preoccupied with heaving the crooked door open.

"Only because my chain is loose." Bobbie knew it wasn't true; still he had to maintain his honor somehow.

Nathan had already squirmed his way into the dark interior but now his head popped out.

"You coming or what?"

Bobbie made a show of checking his bike chain. "Yeah, in a minute."

Nathan took a long look at the faltering sky and ducked back inside.

Bobbie squatted in the powdery dust and wiped his hands on his jeans. It was almost time again, and like every time he was afraid—just a little, but still afraid. Not the same sort of fear as running into Sam Carter and his dumb gang smoking down by the quarry, but still fear.

Bobbie stood. Startled cicadas made a sudden void of sound, almost as if he'd switched off a giant power transformer. They were afraid of him. Sure they were just bugs, but to them he was a monster. Bobbie the Monster. It made him feel strong and dangerous, and not afraid.

He faced the angular crack in the barn door. It waited to swallow him whole. But monsters aren't afraid, so he stepped forward. As his hands touched the rough, peeling wood he took one last look down the field. Nothing moved except the slowly settling dust of their arrival and the lengthening shadows of near dusk.

Nathan and Bobbie would be alone with their secret.

Bobbie entered the barn. It was dark and cool and smelled of mice and ancient hay. Nathan was already naked, clothes piled neatly on a barrel.

"Hurry, take your shirt off."

Bobbie did as he was told. The reddish light filtering through gaps in the walls dimmed noticeably. The sun had fallen behind the hills. An electric feeling raced along Bobbie's spine as he kicked off his jeans.

"Put'em up or the rats'll get'em." Nathan began pacing but his face was calm.

Bobbie hung his clothes on a peg. "Do you think there are any more besides us?"

Nathan didn't stop. "Maybe. Probably, somewhere."

The light was fading and Nathan was a pale ghost in the gloom. Gooseflesh prickled Bobbie's thighs as the evening breeze touched them tentatively.

"No old people this time," Bobbie said. "Mrs. Garritt was too tough."

"Ain't no more drifters." Nathan's voice was husky now.

"We could always just run."

Nathan grinned, his face hanging like a lantern before Bobbie. "We could. But there's always Sam Carter."

Bobbie thought of the senseless cruelty handed down by a kid who took three tries to pass 8th grade and nodded.

Nathan's teeth were white as the moon as he smiled. "Last one there is a rotten egg."

Bobbie only howled as the change came over him.

In the field, cicadas went silent in the wake of the two wolves. After a minute they turned back on like a swarm of power transformers.

JESSICA A. WEISS

MOTHER

Mother tried hard to raise us well
Punishing severely lest we failed
Constantly studied our every move
Wove evil plans dreamed with care
Used silken cords and silver shears
Amazing the moment of cutting her loose
We long to hear her screams again

GRAVEYARD QUEEN

By MARK ROLAND WILSON

Dean stood with his back against a crooked, gnarled tree that was hunched over in old age, and folded his arms in front of his chest, the leather of his jacket sleeves rubbing eerily against each other as he did so. He watched Glen's thin, weak figure dig with narrowed, bored eyes.

This was Glen's fault after all. None of this would have even happened if Glen could have kept his greedy hands to himself. They wouldn't be here tonight, freezing their Asses off in the mid-May chill. Because all of this was Glen's fault, he was the one doing the digging tonight.

It wasn't easy being the prom king without a queen, and Dean didn't plan on making his life anymore difficult than it already had become by digging up her grave. He had made this as easy on himself as he possibly could.

The six-pack Dean had managed to lift form the liquor store and the pack of Marlboro's in his jacket pocket should have been enough to last him the entirety of this endeavor. Funneling beer after beer and crushing the can with just one hand should be entertaining enough. But, if he became too bored, he could always force Glen to dig faster or something.

Suddenly, Glen ceased digging and leaned on the shovel for support. Dean raised a curious eyebrow at him, wondering what Glen thought he was doing. There were no breaks tonight. This wasn't going to be over until Dean had the king and queen dance with Patricia that he had so rightfully deserved two weeks ago; the dance that Glen had stolen from him.

Patricia Darling had been the most beautiful girl in the entire school. Everyone knew that she was going to be prom queen. It was a fact.

It was also a fact that whoever was going steady with her was going to be the prom king. And that was Dean Blake, the local rebel. He was the town's bad boy.

Dean is the kind of guy who went to school, but was never actually in his classes. He could be found smoking cigarettes in the boy's room while checking out his reflection in the mirror, making sure there was enough grease in his Elvis-like pompadour. Dean is the kind of guy who carried a switchblade in his pocket and took it out absentmindedly to play with while he bullied the underclassmen into handing over their homework and lunch money.

Dean Blake is also the kind of guy that Patricia Darling wanted to be with. And had been with.

Even though Dean never once bought her flowers, said he was sorry for making her cry when they argued, or even picked her up on time for a date at the drive-ins, he had made Patricia happy. It was a mystery as to how to everyone else, but Dean managed to be her beau for over two years.

Patricia and Dean were high school sweethearts. They were going to get married after high school and have children right away. Patricia would stay at home, take care of the children, cook and clean, and make her husband happy. Dean would work as a mechanic at his father's garage, one day take it over, and then hand it down to his son. They *were* going to have a son. A son named Teddy.

They would be that picture-perfect couple that made other couples sick, but at the same time, want to be even a fraction as happy as Dean and Patricia were.

That was only until prom, of course.

Dean arrived at Patricia's house in his baby blue Cadillac at seven-thirty the evening of prom, when he should have been there at seven. His reasoning for his lack of punctuality was that girls were never ready on time, so why should he have to be on time?

He came to a screeching halt in front of her driveway, rock 'n' roll blaring on the radio at seven-thirty, feeling a little uncomfortable in his rented tux. Uncomfortable was the nice way of putting it. When leaving the trailer he shared with his father, Dean looked over his shoulder at his old man, half-cocked already (and they hadn't even eaten dinner yet), chain-smoking at the kitchen table, and said, "I look like a goddamned penguin, Pop."

His father grunted, a cloud of smoke billowing out of each nostril. "They ain't gonna let you in lookin' the way you usually do."

Dean's normal attire consisted of blue jeans, a white t-shirt, and his leather jacket.

When Dean didn't reply, his father asked, "You don't want to look good for your girl?"

"Yeah, I guess," Dean replied, not exactly wanting to receive a lecture from his drunken father. He didn't sit through lectures at school, and he sure as hell wasn't going to sit through one at home.

Without giving his father the chance to make further conversation, Dean had disappeared, the screen door to the trailer slamming shut behind him.

Now, Dean was standing outside his car, assessing his reflection in the side-view mirror. Even though he had slipped his leather jacket on over the tux, he still felt like a total fool for being in the tux. It just... so wasn't him.

He made his way up the cobblestone walk way to the front door and rang the bell. A quaint little chiming sounded from inside the house, followed by Patricia's mother howling, "Pattie Cakes, Dean is here!"

Dean chuckled to himself, knowing how much Patricia absolutely *loathed* that childhood nickname of hers.

"Mother, don't call me that!" Patricia protested as she swung open the front door. When her crystal-blue eyes met with Dean's face, Patricia instantly began to glow.

"Hey, doll," Dean said, embracing her with a short hug and a quick kiss on her cheek.

Patricia ushered Dean inside and that is when he truly was able to see how beautiful she looked in her pink gown. It would have been outlandish had she been wearing the dress on any other occasion but since it was prom night, Dean could only describe her as perfect.

Of course Patricia and Dean were forced to go through the Hell that is having their photos' taken by Patricia's father as they stood at the foot of the staircase. And, finally, after a little small talk, Patricia and Dean were able to escape into Dean's awaiting baby blue Cadillac.

The night had gone off without a hitch. Really, no one could have hoped for a better prom. The class of 1956 was enjoying their final dance before graduation at the end of the month.

The only girls crying in the bathroom were the ones who didn't want to cry in front of their boyfriends as they reminisced with their best friends; best friends since meeting in the sand box in preschool.

Of course, a few of the guys from the football team had spiked the punch and got some of the school band guys high with a few tokes off a joint in the boys' room. There were no clicks tonight. Everyone was friends; everyone was perfect.

Dean stood off in the corner, tapping his foot to the Jerry Lee Lewis song playing in the background and twirling his switchblade between each finger of his fist. He had been standing there for over fifteen minutes, waiting for Patricia to return from the bathroom.

She had slipped off to 'freshen up' for a moment before the king and queen were named. Of course Patricia had known that she and Dean were going to win; she would have been daft to not know. And, in knowing that she was going to be crowned prom queen of the class of 1956, Patricia was obviously going to take her time to freshen up.

Dean knew this. He had expected her to be gone ten minutes at the most. But fifteen (now bordering twenty) was a little too much. He was horny and bored and just wanted to get this prom thing over with so he could take Patricia to the back of his Cadillac.

He left his post in the far back corner of the school's gymnasium and began to troll the hallways for her. He was hoping that he would bump into her on her way back from the bathroom so that he wouldn't have to enter the girls' room.

As Dean neared the bathrooms, he heard whispered conversation down a corridor to his left. He paused for a moment to listen in.

"Oh, please? Just one more kiss before you go?" It was the voice of a guy; one who hadn't quite hit puberty the right way. Dean didn't recognize his voice.

"No, Glen! I have to leave," the voice of a female giggled. "Dean will be looking for me soon!"

It was Patricia. Dean could literally feel his blood begin to boil as he rounded the corner. He was seething s he set eyes upon Patricia and this Glenn character embraced in a kiss.

"There you are," Dean said coolly, even though his head was heated. "I've been looking for you."

Patricia shrieked, however it had been muffled do to the fact that her lips had been attached to Glen, whom she pushed away.

She spun around, tears streaming down her face.

"Dean!" Patricia cried. "Oh, thank God you're here! Glen was trying to fore himself on me!"

Patricia began to charge for Dean, as fast as her outrageous dress would allow, with her arms open and ready for a hug.

"Don't lie to me," Dean said slowly, and she stopped dead. "I heard you two talking."

Patricia glanced the switchblade hanging dangerously open in Dean's hand and backed a few steps away from him.

It wasn't Dean's intention to kill Patricia. Not so much kill as slay, really. The knife was in his hand one moment, and then next it was in her chest, warm sticky blood spewing out like cherry filling from a pink pastry, staining its way down Patricia's gown in streaks.

In and out. In. And. Out. In. Out.

Dean didn't know how many times he plunged the blade of that knife into Patricia's chest, but he knew that he had stabbed her more than enough times to kill her. And he didn't even realize that she was dead until her screams had ceased, and she lay limp in his arms, her crystal blue eyes positively lifeless.

He was breathing heavily. He was covered in blood—sticky, warm, sweet blood. He could hear the announcement of prom Queen echoing down the halls from the gymnasium like a wailing, shrieking ghost.

"…The prom queen for the class of 1956 is…"

Dean froze, wanting to cover his ears, but he couldn't move. He was absolutely petrified.

There was that annoying break in the announcer's sentence, trying to cause a little bit of suspense. A little bit of excitement. But everyone knew who was going to be prom queen.

Or, would have been prom queen, rather.

"…Patricia Darling!"

Queue the applause.

That's when Dean dropped Patricia. She hit the floor with a thud, her dead eyes staring up at him, and he screamed.

Dean couldn't believe what he had done. He was angry, but he had no idea how angry he had been to do something as inhumane as butcher the prom queen. His girlfriend. His future wife. The mother of his children.

What was even worse, Dean couldn't see that red-haired, freckled bastard Glen anywhere.

That's when Dean decided to run. He ran until he had made it out of the building. He ran past his car. And he just ran.

No one knew that Dean had anything to do with it. Glen never spoke a word. Dean assumed it was out of fear, but one never really can tell.

When Patricia didn't take her place on stage that evening to accept her crown, teacher's chaperoning the event went searching. And they found her.

They found Patricia soaked in blood with the slightly mentally handicapped janitor on top of her, his pants at his ankles. There was a switchblade on the floor by his feet.

"Why the hell ain't you digging, boy?" Dean demanded of Glen, hurling an empty beer can at him, hitting him square on the forehead.

Glen retrieved the empty can from the half-dug up grave and tossed it back, missing miserably. "Why the hell *am* I digging anyway?" Glen retorted.

"Because, it's your fault she's dead," Dean replied simply. "Now, keep digging before I have to do you in, too."

It was a moment before Glen resumed digging. He had stared at dean intensely with his small brown eyes, like he was trying to burn holes through him. And, when it didn't work, that's when Glen turned around and continued to dig.

Dean cracked open another beer, drained it one large gulp and tossed it at Glen, hitting him in the back.

"Cut it out!" Glenn cried, wheeling his head around.

Dean, who was a little more than intoxicated, mimicked him with the voice of a young girl crying.

"Hey," Glen said, climbing out of the grave. He was sweaty and covered in dirt. He looked much like a freshly reborn zombie. "Why the hell weren't you at her funeral anyway?"

Dean narrowed his eyes. "What's it matter to you?" He lit a cigarette and blew smoke in Glen's direction, but the wind carried it away.

"Because, at her wake, you told me not to show up to her funeral," Glen replied. "But I went anyway, and you were nowhere to be seen."

Dean spat. "I was too busy with playing the devastated beau."

Glen rolled his eyes and continued digging.

"If you ask me one more goddamned question boy, you'll be in casket, too," Dean warned.

Dean didn't go to Patricia's funeral because he was too busy at the library: researching how to resurrect s lost loved one.

Every book he looked in said that it was highly unlikely that Patricia would come back as the same person she was. Dean could remember there being a quote somewhere along the lines of the corpse coming back "mean, vengeful, and downright *evil*."

That didn't matter to Dean. Patricia was Patricia. And, if she were to come back vengeful, she would kill Glen, not him. After all, it is all Glen's fault that Patricia was dead. It was, in no way, Dean's fault that this had happened.

The books also implied that Patricia wouldn't technically be alive. There wouldn't be a heartbeat. She wouldn't need to breathe or eat. She would be a rotting corpse that had the ability to speak and move.

This was of no importance to Dean either. He just wanted to be with her again. He just wanted her around long enough until he had the nerve to kill himself. Then, he would kill Patricia again and off himself. That's when they could be together forever.

One last bit of information that Dean found, and this time, it was crucial, was that he would need a sacrifice.

And who better to sacrifice than a weak, worn-out nerd like Glen who had just spent a good two hours digging up Patricia's grave?

Glen thrust the shovel into the overly green grass above him and then climbed his lanky body out of the grave. Just as he made his way completely out, the sky split and it began to rain, accompanied by a roll of thunder and a streak of lightning.

"I'm done," he panted, wiping raindrops from his glasses.

Dean walked hastily over to the grave and peered down inside. He could see the top of the casket.

"You're disgusting," Glen said. "You kill her before you get to pop her cherry and now you want to do it while she's dead. I heard that retarded janitor got to her—"

Dean's fist met with Glen's jaw creating a horrible cracking noise that resulted in Glen falling to the ground.

Dean jumped into the grave and embraced the soaking wet casket with a hug and a kiss. He was sinking into the mud but he didn't care. He was going to have Patricia back within a matter of minutes.

"I've missed you," Dean whispered to Patricia's casket.

The only thing standing in the way of Dean being reunited with Patricia was the fact that Glen was still alive and breathing.

When the head of the shovel met with Dean's skull it cracked. Blood, dark in the night (almost black) poured out his nose like the rain falling above his head.

Dean slumped over into a heap inside the grave, his blood mixing with the mud.

Glen jumped down onto the casket and bludgeoned Dean twice more to make sure that he was completely dead.

The twisted smile of a maniac spread across Glen's lips. He had never been so pleased with himself.

If anyone ever did find Dean's remains, there would be no way anyone would recognize that face. In fact, Glen didn't even recognize it.

"You stupid son of a bitch," Glen said to the dead body. "Don't you think I knew what you were up to? Of course you couldn't have known; I'm smarter than you are. The only sacrifice here tonight is you, buddy."

Glen wasn't exactly as smart as he had made himself out to be. When going through the notes that Dean had take on the process of resurrection, nowhere did he see a thing about how Patricia would come back as a corpse with half the motor skills and even less of the intelligence she had before.

No, Glen didn't know about that at all. He assumed that because Dean was so dead set on reviving Patricia, that the notes were trustworthy. How could he have known that Dean wouldn't have cared if she came back… as a zombie?

A zombie with an unquenchable thirst.

Half an hour later, Glen and Patricia were walking (well, Patricia staggering and limping) out of the graveyard, hand in hand. Finally, the two of them were going to be able to runaway together. It was something they had been planning to do for months.

Glen turned to kiss his future bride. It was then, in the moonlight, the rain clouds finally gone, that he saw Patricia for the last time.

Patricia's jaw had become completely unhinged. Her teeth were rotten, the color of Coca-Cola.

There wasn't even a chance for Glen to run—or, scream for that matter. Patricia had somehow acquired the strength of ten men and had him in an embrace that there was no escape from.

"Please don't," Glen whimpered. He was crying. "I love you!"

"And, I love…your brains," Patricia cackled, tearing apart his flesh. Her rotten teeth tore through Glen's skull, and her tongue wrapped around the warm brains hidden inside, like the cream filling at the center of a cupcake.

SITWAT GOES HOME

BY SARAH ISLAM

Two women hurried down the dirt road, heads bent bodies covered in large black cloths. Rain clawed at their faces and pricked their eyes. Around them the deserted village was already flooding and stalks of corn danced and clapped in the wind. The women had journeyed a great distance to reach this village somewhere in the heart of Pakistan. The vast stretch of land around them stood naked now, its robustness washed away exposing a more primal sinister character. Even the wind howled at the plight of the faithful who huddled behind closed doors.

The travelers reached a large iron latticed door through which a small courtyard could be seen. The older woman held her chaddar in her mouth and banged on the grille.

"Is anybody there?" she shouted. No answer. She slumped against the door shivering from the cold.

The girl, Sitwat, put her canvas bag on the ground and rattled the padlock chained to the door. She called loudly, "Brother? Brother!"

This time a door opened at the far end of the courtyard and a man hurried towards them, holding a plastic bag over his head. He peered enquiringly through the trellis.

"We have come from Lahore, son. For Sister Rukhsana…" the old woman said gratefully. He nodded, ran to a sentry's guard box next to the door and emerged with a large bunch of keys.

Fumbling to find the right one, he finally pushed the gates open. Behind them the corn whispered and a lone dog barked as lightening lit up the sky. He pointed to a huge wooden door and turned away. The visitors crossed the courtyard and entered a damp narrow corridor. They stood stomping the mud from their feet and shaking the rainwater out of their hair. It was a primitive hall with roughhewn walls and two dark rooms at the end. Sitwat peered at the rusted iron doors and smiled.

"Hello! My sister?" The old woman called shyly.

Out of the darkness a thin girl her head covered in a dupatta came towards them. She held an unlit gas lantern in her hand. They greeted her with a Salam.

"Wa Alaikum asalam," she said unhurriedly savouring the words and chewing on them.

The old woman, Sughra Bibi, told her who they were and why they had come. She had switched to the guttural Punjabi of her village and after she finished she looked almost embarrassed. The lantern girl smiled.

"This way, please," she said, turning around on her heel. They followed obediently.

She led them through a large room with a high ceiling. Sitwat saw that it was almost empty except for a string bed in the corner, an unlit fireplace and some cardboard cartons stacked on top of each other. Their cheap sandals rang out on the cold floor. Lantern girl stopped at a low brick arch with no door and stood aside.

They entered an archaic room with bare walls. Pigeons cooed in the vaulted ceiling and some women crouched on a thin rug around a kerosene stove. They watched the newcomers warily.

Rukhsana Bibi, one of the women, abandoned the peas she was shelling and got up with a smile. Sughra and Sitwat said a loud 'Salam!' and a murmur of voices rose in acknowledgment.

Sughra embraced Rukhsana who whispered "Welcome, welcome!" soothingly into her ear. Sughra pushed Sitwat towards her.

"This is the orphan girl I mentioned to you," she said in a hushed voice. Sitwat disappeared into her soaked shawl as Rukhsana Bibi touched her head with both hands.

"May God keep you," Rukhsana said gently.

The hostess now introduced the women on the floor. Two of them were distant relatives, the rest were village women who spent most of their time there cooking and cleaning, gossiping and being instructed in the word of God.

One of them, a woman named Zohra, a tall sharp looking woman with dark circles under her eyes, now bustled towards the Sughra.

"Bibi! You are soaked. You should change!"

Rukhsana nodded absentmindedly.

"Yes! Yes! You'll catch a cold." Zohra barked an order and a younger woman sprung into action. She ushered the women to a door at the far corner of the room and stood patiently as Sughra rummaged for fresh clothes in the canvas bag.

A few minutes later the old woman reappeared wearing a plain suit of thick velvet and a long rosary dangling from her fingers.

It was now Sitwat's turn. They pushed her gently into the room and closed the door behind her. She stood against the door rubbing her temples slowly. She opened her eyes and peered at the high ceiling. A bat that had been snoozing somewhere in the darkness fluttered to her feet and lay writhing. She kicked it out of the way. A single candle burnt on a chipped saucer on the floor and the smell of decay and mothballs hung thick.

It was a narrow space not much larger than a deep grave. Recesses had been cut into the crude walls to serve as shelves. She craned her neck and saw folded mattresses and large tin trunks stacked in a precarious heap almost touching the ceiling. A naked bulb hung cold and dusty, the only source of light present in the small room.

A spider scuttled on the ceiling his dry legs scraping against the coarse walls. Sitwat extended an arm and touched it with the tip of her index finger. It sizzled and fell to the ground in a fine powdery heap of dust.

She closed her eyes again and concentrated on the image of the women in the other room huddled around the lamp, their eyes wide as they listened.

"I would have kept her but she scares me..." Sughra sounded worried and kept looking over her shoulder.

"Don't worry, sister. Everything will be all right now. Peer Sahib will see to it," Rukhsana murmured.

Sitwat opened her eyes and hummed slowly to herself as she changed into a simple suit of homespun cotton. Then she put on a hand knitted sweater of coarse wool and wrapped a heavy chaddar around herself. She rummaged in the pocket of her sweater and took out a small dried doll that looked like it had been made of fresh fruit once but was now withered and shrunk.

She nudged it with a finger and the doll arched its back, got to its knees and crouched in the hollow of Sitwat's palm. She patted its head and pushed it onto its back with her finger. It lay there, panting. She put it back in her pocket and opened the door.

"It is so unfortunate! Now she only has Allah and you people to look after her..." Sughra trailed off as she watched Sitwat walking meekly towards the group in the middle of the room. After she had settled down on the floor Sughra turned back to Rukhsana Bibi.

"God alone knows what a shock it was for me when she landed on my doorstep just like that out of nowhere!" She snapped her fingers in the air. "She told me she had no one to give her shelter! What could I do? I am a God fearing widow so I took her in!"

The women made Tchk! Tchk! sounds with their mouths. Sitwat sat stoically staring into the fire.

The storm outside was getting stronger distracting the women with its force. It rattled the windows, knocked on the doors and seemed to stalk around the house trying to get in.

Rukhsana Bibi was a large woman. She sat still like a benevolent mother while her flock fidgeted around her. Her face was creased with laughing and her forehead was lined with sorrow. She owed the creases to her personality and the lines to her husband. She must have been a great beauty once but vanity had long since vanished leaving her barefaced and pure. She sighed often.

"I have grown so attached to her. God Knows that I always looked on her as my own daughter!" Sughra said squinting shortsightedly at the women around her. "But Allah has chosen your benevolent protection for her. We ourselves are struggling to eat twice daily how can we look after a girl of marriageable age?" she whined, putting her face in her hands.

Rukhsana touched her gently on the shoulder saying, "Don't worry! Don't worry!"

Sughra looked almost pacified. Rukhsana shifted her weight on the charpoy and said slowly, "Peer Sahib will make the final decision. Not that he will object, I'm sure," she added quickly as Sughra almost fell back on the floor deflated. "He is wise and I am positive he will take the right decision."

The wind howled. The women twitched and whispered on their rosaries. Someone brought out steaming cups of tea and salty biscuits. The tea was hot and sweet and the taste of the wood stove lingered in it, searing their tongues and scalding their throats.

"Very tasty!" Sughra said sipping loudly. "God is great!"

It was getting darker now and the women bustled around bringing out mattresses and dragging charpoys from other rooms. The kerosene stove had begun to smoke so Zohra stacked logs into the hearth and lit a fire. They stretched their legs and snuggled under warm quilts as the room began to glow with the bright fire. Outside the storm was getting worse.

The muezzin's thin voice rose above the storm and called the faithful to evening prayers. For a while the storm was forgotten as they prayed together. Afterwards a simple meal of dal, rotis and mutton cooked with potatoes was served. The potatoes were sandy with the ash of the woodstove and the rotis were thick and hot. Sitwat and her aunt ate like wolves and whispered to each other that they had never tasted such a delicious meal in their city homes.

It was now after nine and the electricity supply was still suspended. Rukhsana Bibi had sent a messenger girl to her husband to inform him of her visitors. This girl thin and shivering in her threadbare clothes returned from the men's quarters and whispered into Rukhsana's ear. She nodded and turned to Sughra.

"Peer sahib will see you now." She said. Sitwat and her aunt jumped to their feet and followed Rukhsana and the servant girl through a maze of narrow corridors towards the Peer's quarters by descending into the bowels of the house.

They came to an enclosed courtyard where a large pond lay deep and still in the near darkness. Ribbit! Ribbit! A frog sang and Sitwat laughed. Rukhsana pointed towards the water and said, "That is where Peer Sahib's grandfather fought a duel with the Djinn and captured him."

No one said anything so she stopped and lead them to the iron gate so they could take a closer look.

"Look!" She pointed. "It happened over there! Ever since that day every first born male child in our family inherits the power to use the vanquished Djinn in order to bring peace to the afflicted!" she said with a soft laugh. Sitwat's eyes glowed in the darkness.

"What Djinn?" she asked quietly.

Rukhsana smacked her lips. She was clearly enjoying showing off the family's special claim to fame.

"As God is our witness," she said, "a duel was fought between the evil djinn named Busa and my grandfather in-law to rid this village of his evil influence. His highness the Peer won the duel and the Djinn was banished to live at the bottom of that pond where he still lives bound with chains that he can't break. Your Peer Sahib always turns to him for counsel in times of need," she said serenely as if stating a fact of life to a slightly dim child.

"Can we see him?" Sitwat asked softly.

Rukhsana shook her head.

"No my child, only the very pious who have done suitable penance can see him. Like your Peer Sahib."

Sitwat's eyes burned and her cheeks glowed.

This one is certainly adventurous…, thought Rukhsana and put an arm around her.

"Come on!" she said. "Don't be curious. These things are beyond us mortal women. You are going to meet the master of the Djinn, Peer Sahib himself. God willing! You will no longer be helpless and unsafe in this world!"

Sitwat smiled and with a last look at the pond she hurried on after the others. They came to a blind alley and turned right to climb down a flight of uneven stone steps. In the small corridor Rukhsana adjusted the dupatta on her head and knocked on the door, which was thrown open immediately.

The strong smell of incense hit them first. They stood blinking in the dim light. Peer Sahib was sitting on a small wooden stool, his back to the door telling a rosary. In front was a small alcove where a raised grave stood covered with green cloth. Three men with long beards and black turbans sat against the wall beside him. One of them sucked on an orange noisily.

The women went to wait in a smaller room to the left and sat on the carpet. This room was stark except for a picture of the Ka'aba on the wall a bookcase in the corner and a large divan strewn with velvet cushions. A servant girl placed an electric lantern on a small stool and left.

Peer Sahib entered the room shortly after. Sitwat noticed that he was tall and well built. They stared at the great man in awe. He was surprisingly young with dark flashing eyes accentuated with a liberal dash of kohl, his beard black and well kept, his mouth moist and sensuous with unexpectedly red lips. He wore a flowing black robe made of well-spun cotton and his head was covered with a black turban. He sat on the divan and looked down at his guests.

"Yes, sister?" he said.

Sughra launched into confusing chatter. She told him of her husband's death, how she had been left penniless her two sons struggling to make a living and her problems as a single mother. The Peer listened and nodded.

"How can I help?" he said.

Sughra pointed towards Sitwat.

"She is an orphan. Poor unfortunate girl has no one to look after her and I can't keep her as I have two grown sons at home..." She paused unsure of how to proceed.

The Peer shifted his eyes to Sitwat who kept hers on the ground. He was silent for a moment. Her beauty illuminated the gloomy room and when the peer spoke his voice shook with excitement. He had not failed to notice her exquisiteness.

"God willing we will give her a home. My wife will teach her the Quran and give her a place in the ladies' quarters where she will be treated like a member of the family." Rukhsana nodded happily.

Gratitude struck Sughra dumb and she sat with a juvenile smile pasted on her face. To break the silence, Rukhsana started to recount stories of her husband's exploits against various supernatural creatures.

The Peer blushed modestly whenever his name was mentioned. He called for tea and sipped it loudly his eyes straying to Sitwat now and then. She looked up only when a sudden wailing rose in the main room next door.

He raised his eyebrows complacently as his assistant rushed inside and informed him that a group of women had brought a fourteen-year-old girl possessed by demons. The Peer handed his cup to his wife and wiped his fingers slowly with a snowy handkerchief. His nostrils quivered in anticipation and his feverish eyes met Sitwat's who bared her teeth in an unexpected smile. He was thrown off balance but recovered quickly.

"My people come to me when they are hounded by various afflictions sent to them by the Almighty. All this humble servant can do is to tackle them to the best of his capabilities." He stood up and began to shuffle out. He turned around at the door. "You can watch if you want." He willed himself not to look at her radiant face.

The women huddled closer to the door watching in anticipation as he prepared to work his miracle. Peasant women wailed and sobbed while a young girl lolled around on the floor, saliva dripping from her mouth.

The peer raised his hand for silence and a hush descended.

"Who are you?" he said in a loud voice.

"Shaitan!" said the afflicted girl in a guttural voice.

"You are unholy and unclean! Leave this girl!" He thundered.

"No! No! No!" She screamed, clawing at her clothes and tossing violently on the floor. The peer beckoned imperiously with his hand and two stout village women stepped forward to hold her down.

"Will you obey the word of God and leave this body or do you want me to use force on you, you filthy seducer of innocent souls?" He was shouting now and the veins in his neck were throbbing. The Devil in the girl merely grunted. "I will ask you one more time. Will you leave of your own volition?" he asked gravely.

The girl on the floor shook her head and screamed "No!"

"You have left me no choice but to call upon Busa, the master of lost iffrits and hunter of evil spirits!" he thundered and spread his arms. His assistant stepped forward and placed a long stake in his hand. A shrunken skull sat atop the stick and amulets hung from it. The congregation gasped and fell back.

The peer struck his staff on the ground three times and began to chant: *"In the name of Allah, get out, enemy of Allah! Get out!"*

They watched mesmerized by his performance and no one noticed when Sitwat reached into her pocket took out the shrunken figure set it on the ground and pointed towards the stricken girl.

The possessed girl sat swaying her head her arms held wide open by two women. The doll clawed its way up the girl's hip, ducked under her armpit and jumped into her lap.

As the peer's voice rose in a shrill falsetto "Allah! Allah!" the doll struck the girl's chest, reached into her and with one swift movement wrenched her heart out.

The girl stopped like she had been shot and fell back. Blood spurted out of the massive hole in her chest as the shrunken doll held up her beating heart in its hands tossing it from one hand to another and rolling its burning eyes. Its mouth was sewn shut and only the corner had come undone where a bloodied thread hung. The crowd wanted to scream, to get up run away but their bodies disobeyed and they sat horrified and rooted to their spots.

Sitwat whistled and caught the heart in her palm as the doll tossed it through the air. Then it jumped to the ground and ran towards its mistress who bent down and patted its head before returning it to her pocket. As the paralyzed crowd watched, Sitwat placed the heart to her ears and listened.

"Peer!" she called out. "There are no demons here. Only love…" she laughed. She turned to the dead girl's mother who shrank against the wall.

"You knew better than to pretend your daughter had anything but love for a married man in her heart!"

The woman sat frozen but her eyes rotated in their sockets trying to shut out the horror. Sitwat shook her head with a smile.

"Tchk! Tchk!" she said. She twisted her head to look at Sughra and pointed at her. "Go!" She said quietly. To the utter terror of the room's occupants the old woman withered and shrunk to the size of a pea, rolled away and fell through a crack on the floor.

The Iffrit now turned her attention to the holy man.

"Busa sends his regards from Basra, Peer Kalimuddin and trusts that you will stop using his name falsely for your nefarious means." She blew him a kiss, tossed the heart at him and vanished in a cloud of smoke.

THE MONSTER
BY CRYSTAL CONNOR

With every breath she took she inhaled fire. Both of her feet were swollen, cut, and bleeding, pain exploded from her feet to her jaw with each step. Her hands, arms, and face were scratched and cut. The pain in her side was so intense she might as well have been pierced by the Spear of Density. The trees blocked out the light of the moon, it was so dark she couldn't even see the tips of her fingers on her outstretched arms. She'd just returned home from the war, and was in excellent physical condition; otherwise she would have been caught two miles ago. She kept running. She ran faster.

After only 4 days of what was supposed to be a two-week visit Maleka Davidson was leaving Alabama. Maleka hated this place. She was disgusted by the ignorance of poverty. The stifling heat reduced her to the sin of sloth. Her head hurt from trying to decipher these coded southern sayings. Just last night she figured out that the word

"Bard" meant borrowed and southern translation for the State of Georgia was *"Jawjuh,"* and that she was from the *"Nawth"* as in, and I quote, "Ya' people from up Nawth sure do talk funny." It was almost as if she needed an English to Southern United States dictionary.

Maleka was tired of eating fried food and drinking either Grape or red Kool-Aid made with three cups of sugar, despite the directions clearly stating that only one cup was needed. Maleka was especially terrified of all the large and strange bugs in this state that could star in their own horror movies. Maleka took a break from packing, even the slightest of physical activities made her sweat profusely. She lay on the bed and smiled about the conversation she had had with her uncle this morning at breakfast, revolving around the apparently sacred origins of grits.

"Maleka, y'all eat grits up Nawth?" Bryannah asked.

"Of course we do," Maleka explained to her 12-year-old cousin. "There are quite a few farms within driving distance of Seattle that grow corn, but that…"

Bryannah looked puzzled and Uncle Emmitt angrily interjected before Maleka could continue.

"Ain't nothing as good as grits can be made from corn! Dontcha read yo' bible?"

"My bible?"

"Exodus 16:15. What poured down upon him's chirren when they was roamin' roun' in dem woods was grits. It says so right in da bible, *'it's the food the LORD has given you to eat!'*"

"So the manna that God rained on the Israelites on Mount Sinai was really grits?" Maleka asked slowly.

"Ain't dat what I said?"

Why not? Maleka had spent the last year fighting in the streets of a foreign country because someone had misinterpreted the holy writings of an ancient text, so why should it be any different right here at home. Using her toast as a spoon Maleka took another bite of the buttery, salted grits and smiled. It's no wonder her uncle had mistaken them for ambrosia. Uncle Emmitt went on to explain that after the miracle on Mount Sinai, there was no mention of grits for another 1000 years. Experts, he explained, found evidence that grits were only used during secret religious ceremonies, and were kept away from the public due to its rarity.

The next mention of grits, he continued, "Was found in all dem ashes over there in Pompell in a famous woman's diary."

"Do you mean the ruins of Pompeii? What famous woman?" Maleka inquired.

"Herculaneum Jemimaneus."

"Who?"

"Girl you just as slow as molasses running down hill in January. Aunt Jemima."

And if it wasn't Uncle Emmitt's wild stories that re-invented history it was her Auntie Tammy's constant complaint of how nothing made sense.

"Look at this damn blue bird sitting his ass upon that goddamned tree branch! Look at him, that's a damn shame. It just don't make no damn *sense*!" No one offered that birds were supposed to be in trees, everyone just chuckled and shook their heads and Maleka did the same.

Maleka knew she was going to miss them but she just couldn't stay in the South. She was mortified that her extended family members, their neighbors, and friends seemed to perpetuate the negative stereotypes of blacks in the South. In her family's defense the whites down here didn't seem much better. With their UFOs, swamp monsters, unfounded fear of the government, pickup trucks, and Confederate battle flags, Maleka couldn't help but hear that banjo song from the movie Deliverance every time she listened to them talk.

The most unsettling thing about being in the South for Maleka was everyone's devout belief in superstitions, and truth be told, this was the real reason she was leaving.

The woman who lived across the street from her grandmother's house always dragged a broom behind her wherever she walked when she left the house, even if it was only to check the mail. When Maleka asked her great grand aunt why she did that she was told, "Cuz she dohn wants deze fixuhs tuh git her foot track." Maleka knew what fixuhs were before she had a chance to unpack. Fixuhs were evil spirits and apparently they were everywhere.

The first night Maleka stayed in her grandmother's house she noticed a broom upside down by her bedroom door. When she took the broom into the kitchen to put it away, pandemonium broke out.

Her cousin Maybell explained that the broom was placed outside her door to protect her from the hags, and that this protection was necessary because she had seen a hag with her own two eyes. Maleka thought if she drank as much as her cousin did she would probably see things too. Not only were there hags but also there were signs, omens, dreams, mojo rings, witches, wearing a dime around your ankle, charms, talismans, myths and swamp monsters. Maleka's sleep was unrestful and during the day she was jumpy and on edge.

"You all packed and ready to go?"

Maleka jumped nearly five feet off the bed at the sound of Leticia's voice, and her cousin laughed until tears rain down her beautiful ebony face.

"Girl," Leticia said as soon as she caught her breath. "You is just as nervous as a long-tailed cat in a room full o' rocking chairs."

"I must have dozed off; I didn't hear you come in." Maleka said through her smile. "Yeah, I'm almost done. I really didn't have that much stuff to pack anyway."

Leticia sat on the bed next to Maleka and pushed herself back until she was resting against the wall. Maleka did the same.

"You really can't stay no longer?"

"Ticia, it's so hot down here I can barely think. Hey why don't you come up to Seattle? Once I get home and settled I can buy you a plane ticket. You can stay as long as you like, I think you'll like it, it's really pretty, there's lots of water and its cool."

"Girl I ain't never been on no airplane before."

Maleka could hear the fear in her cousin's voice. The two were the same age, 28, but her cousin had never traveled outside of her county.

"So? There's a first time for everything. You can catch the Greyhound … I know! What about Amtrak? That'll be cool to ride the train across the country; I can even get you your own private cabin!"

"I don't know."

"Well just think about it. Ok?"

"I will."

Both girls looked towards the door as their grandmother walked through it. Fat Mike was behind her carrying a large Styrofoam cooler that look heavy even for him. Her grandmother had packed a feast that would have fed an army for a month.

The cooler was filled with fried pork-chop sandwiches with mayo and hot-sauce, buttermilk fried chicken, scuppernongs, and Maypops, onion and tomato sandwiches, potato salad *and* macaroni salad, pork rinds and a half a dozen banana moon pies.

"Grandma, this is too much food. I'll be home in just a few days." Maleka really wasn't protesting because her grandmother packed all of her favorite food, even if it was more than she could eat in just a few days.

Fat Mike went to load her car and her grandmother sat on the edge of the rickety bed and touched her face before she started talking.

"Now don't you go wandering too far off de road, don't let darkness catch ya and stay out dem woods at all cost. If you hear a chain rattlin' on de tree you best be movin' along cuz it might be a plat-eye."

Great, Maleka thought. *Just what I need, another southern monster.* She had no idea what a plat-eye was and she wasn't going to ask. She didn't want to know. All she wanted was to be back in the Great Pacific Northwest where all she had to worry about was good old fashion ghosts, Bigfoot, and the occasional serial killer.

She handed Maleka a small burlap sack tied closed with a piece of twine. "Keep this wit' you' at all times no matter what happens."

Maleka took the little bag with trembling hands. She didn't want to take this with her; she didn't even want to touch it, this is what she wanted to get away from in the first place. Maleka dropped the amulet of protection into her handbag and gave her grandmother a big hug and kissed her goodbye.

On the winding road that seemed to stretch on forever, Maleka saw a filling station that looked like it hadn't been updated or remodeled in the last 100 years. She even heard the cheerful "ding-ding" as she pulled up to the pump. The breeze in the wake of a passing semi-truck felt good against her sticky skin. She was grateful for the cooler temperatures that were chasing the submerging rays of the sunset.

Maleka bought two bags of ice, a six-pack of coke, oil, and a road map she had GPS on her cell phone, but she hadn't had a signal in almost three hours. Maleka also bought $45.00 worth of gas and candy. The old man smiled at her as she dumped her stuff in front of him to ring up, Maleka returned his smile while looking away from his blue running eyes, wrinkled skin and broken teeth. As Maleka was rummaging through her purse for cash, because Visa wasn't really everywhere that she wanted to be, the charm her grandmother gave her tumbled out on to the vintage countertop. When Maleka left the store with her merchandise the charm was left behind.

Maleka had made it half way back to her car before the old attendant came chasing out behind her.

"Hey girl, wait a minute, you done left yo' charm."

Maleka turned to the sound of his voice and almost ran from the man who was holding the small bag her grandmother had given her. When he extended it for her to take she flinched away from it.

"Oh. Thank you sir, but I don't think I need it."

The man looked at Maleka with a flash of anger and it was clear that he was personally offended at Maleka's fear of it.

"Your peoples gave this to you for good reason. You need it for protection. I reckon you a long way from home so I suggest that you take this with you."

Maleka took a step away from the man and shook her head.

"I don't think it's a good idea to mess with stuff you don't understand."

"Girl you don't have to believe but you can't afford not to listen." The man warned as he walked up to her and dropped the charm into one of her bags.

Maleka slowly turned around and walked away from him, so shaken up that she almost forgot to pump her gas. She drained her cooler, crammed in the six cans of coke, and replaced the melted ice. She added oil to her car, opened the map, charted her course, and cursed the non-existent cell signal on her phone. As Maleka was placing the trash into the plastic bags her attention was once again drawn to the charm resting at the bottom. She threw all the trash on top, balled up the bags, and threw them away. As she sped away she noticed the old man watching her leave from the window.

Maleka had been driving in the dark for almost two hours. When she first learned how to drive the freeway scared her the most, but when her stepfather took her on her first night drive she was calm and confident.

When they drove at night there was really no need for his instructions so he just let her drive. The night lessons were Maleka's favorite time with her stepfather. He didn't warn her about the dangers of boys, drugs and alcohol, he did not bitch at her for not doing her chores or getting just a C on her math test, or quiz her about military terminology. It was just her and dad spending a few hours at night driving under a blanket of stars. Maleka had always enjoyed driving at night; she appreciated the solitude and welcomed the memories.

She could have shot herself for tilting her head all the way back to drink the last of the Coke. She looked back at the road in time to see a deer bolt out in front of her car and freeze just a few feet ahead of her. Despite everything she had been taught and had heard, Maleka slammed on the brakes and yanked her wheel heavily to the right. Her car slid off the pavement and lost traction in the gravel. She tried to right herself but overcorrected sending the vehicle over the yellow line. As she fought the car to avoid any oncoming traffic on the two lane stretch of road, the car returned to the correct lane before leaving the road, going into a ditch, and slamming into a tree.

"Goddamn it!"

Maleka put the car in park but left the engine running, afraid if she turned it off she wouldn't be able to restart it. The front of the car was damaged but not bad enough to deploy the airbags. She rubbed her head, unhooked her seat belt, and snatched her cell phone off the floor in front of the seat next to her. No service.

"Fuck!" Maleka threw the phone back on the floor with such force it bounced up and landed on the passenger seat. Maleka pounded on the steering wheel and looked into the rear view mirror.

The deer was still standing in the middle of the road. It turned its head as if to look in the direction behind them before returning its gaze to the car. The deer raised its head to the sky and Maleka watched the antlers of the large animal retract back into its head.

That's not what you saw, you hit your head pretty hard, and your vision is blurry. That isn't what you just saw.

Maleka watched the deer stand on its hind legs and take the form of a man. He started to walk slowly towards the car.

Don't let darkness catch ya and stay out dem woods at all cost.

Maleka grabbed the rear view mirror and moved it so that she could watch the man approaching as she reached beneath her seat for her gun. Without taking her eyes off of the man in the rear view mirror, Maleka put her car in reverse and then back in drive and back again until she gently rocked her car out of the ditch.

Only when she got the car back on the road did she take her eyes off the man. She pulled away slowly, but as she picked up speed the front bumper that was being dragged beneath the car punctured a tire. The car began to wobble before it took a nose dive to the right, the tire so damaged she was driving on the rim. She drove another

200 feet before the car died completely. She was on a slight decline so she let the car coast down a bit, then steered the car off to the side of the road when she felt it losing momentum.

"FUCK!"

A quick glance in both the side and rear view mirrors did not reveal the man's whereabouts, but she knew he was still coming.

Maleka took a deep breath and let her training take over. Her mother taught her how to shoot with a Smith and Wesson model 29-44 magnum, and her Uncle Sam had given her a badge marked expert.

The wonder nine that Maleka held in her hands was the Smith and Wesson's M&P. With a 17 round capacity, and a velocity 100 feet per second above what was advertised, Maleka had no doubt of the weapon's capability, but she couldn't shake the feeling that she needed something more.

Keep this wit yo' at all times no matter what happens.

"Fuck."

She pulled the lever on her seat until the headrest was laying on the back seat, then turned around, pressed her back into the steering wheel, and waited for the man, deer, or whatever the hell it was that caused this accident, to close the distance between them.

Maleka reached over, opened the glove box, and grabbed the four extra high capacity magazines. She grabbed the phone off of the passenger seat and shoved the clips and phone into the back pocket of her blue jeans. It wasn't long after when that she saw the top of the man's head crest the hill.

"Guard me, O Lord, from the hands of the wicked; protect me from the violent…" Maleka's prayer was interrupted by movement within the edges of her peripheral vision. Maleka was hesitant to take her eyes off of the approaching man, but whatever was on the other side of the road was closer to her than he was. Her eyes slowly traveled to the view outside of her driver's side window. Her eyes seemed to almost drag her head with them. Blurs of black and grey shapes became sharp lines, defined images…more deer, methodically taking the shape of man.

Don't panic.

"Deliver me from those who work evil; from the bloodthirsty save me." As if adding an exclamation point to her prayer, she pulled the trigger, killing a beast whose metamorphosis was nearly complete.

The rear window imploded. In the rain of broken glass and shadows Maleka fired six more rounds in rapid secession, crawled to the passenger side of her car and ran into the deep, tangled abyss that is the Alabama wilderness.

Don't let darkness catch ya and stay out dem woods at all cost.

The tree-lined paved road was lit by stars but Maleka was plunged into absolute darkness once she entered the forest. After nearly tripping and breaking her ankle, Maleka kicked off her flip-flops and immediately gained speed. It was a double-edged sword, as her tender spa-pampered feet quickly yielded to the unforgiving rough terrain of sharp rocks, jagged twigs, and tangled and knotted tree roots that carpeted the floor of the wilderness.

As she ran she unbuckled her belt and threaded her gun through it so that she wouldn't lose it. She refastened the belt loose; the gun beat against her thigh as she ran but she wanted to be able to maneuver her weapon freely when she needed to.

Instinctively she stopped running. Maleka slowly, blindingly, extended her hand out in front of her, and before her arm was fully outstretched her fingertips brushed against the rough bark of a large tree. Maleka stepped closer, put her cheek against the tree, and then extended her arms outward as if to give the tree a hug. With her arms fully extended the tips of her stretched and her exploring fingers still felt bark on both sides.

Maleka kept her right hand on the tree and used her left hand as a feeler to detect any other large objects in front of her, until the large timber that blocked her path was behind her.

Her fear heightened her sense of awareness and her deprivation of sight sharpened her ability to hear, Maleka found it easier to just close her eyes rather than peer into the darkness. She controlled her breathing, and concentrated on the muted sounds of the forest.

The terrain underfoot became soft. Instead of rocks, pinecones, and fallen branches the sensation Maleka felt against her feet were leaves, moss and mud. She stood still, cocked her head, and listened. The absence of sound alarmed her but continued to walk, slowly at first, then faster and faster until she was once again running at full tilt.

The ground was soft and soundless but as she picked up speed she heard branches snapping behind her to her left. Hoping to achieve the same level of strength, speed, and victory as the Greek Goddess Nike, Maleka ran. And ran, and ran…

…and slammed into a low hanging branch.

There was a flash of bright light around the edges of her vision, her feet swung out from under her and she landed on her back. Her lower back just above her tailbone exploded in pain as it came into contact with a fallen log, and as her head bounced off the ground Maleka bit her tongue. Running headlong into a thick branch had caused worse injuries than in her earlier car accident.

Maleka swallowed blood and listened to the sounds of the forest. Nothing. She performed a quick mental diagnostic of her body and categorized her injuries. She told herself she was fine and slowly sat up. Without warning it started raining, not the light misty drizzle she was accustomed to in Seattle, but a hard and heavy downpour of torrential rain in biblical proportions.

"Are you fucking kidding me?" Maleka screamed up to the heavens. "Is this your idea of a joke? Well I don't think it's funny! Didn't you hear me calling you for help?"

Maleka was standing though she did not remember the physical act of standing up. Her hands we're balled into tight fists, she was defiantly starring into the night sky and blinking away the rain. A voice in her head suggested that maybe this was not the way she should be talking to God, but she was so desperately angry and so terrified she couldn't stop herself.

"Give me a fucking break, answer my prayer, do something! I'm not asking you to part the sea I'm just asking for a little help. Is that asking for too much? Are you there?"

God did not answer her. She couldn't hear anything over the rain; she still couldn't see anything but she didn't want to just stand there, so despite nearly being decapitated Maleka started running. She counted her steps as she ran. There were 2,112 military steps in one mile with a 30-inch step; Maleka's running stride was 70-inches, so she knew she had run nearly two miles since plowing into that tree.

The soft mud that had padded Maleka's footfalls was now an enemy combatant. Encouraged by the rain the mud became thick and hostile, her feet were buried to her ankles with each step, she had to use force to wrangle her foot free and before she knew it she was calf deep in mud.

"This is fucking bullshit."

Maleka took a deep breath and turned around and slowly made her way out of the deep mud. A bolt of lightning arched across the sky. In the flash of light Maleka saw that she was in a small valley. It took Maleka almost a full minute to register what she had seen on the valley ridge.

Her pursuers had morphed themselves into one of the most feared and formidable canines on both the face of the planet and in the depths of nightmares; the wolf. Maleka now had to run from a pack of dogs that had the ability to run at speeds of at least 40 miles per hour and sustain those speeds for several miles at a time.

Though there was nothing remotely humorous in Maleka's situation she started laughing.

Maleka bolted away from the descending predators. It took her ninety steps to reach the slight incline that marked the valley wall. Digging in with hands, forearms, knees, and feet she scrambled up the hill. When she reached flat land she stood up and ran. Maleka counted sixty steps before she tripped over an exposed tree root. She reached out with her hands to break her fall but she kept falling.

Maleka slammed to the ground on her shoulder and began to tumble, roll and slide. Once again she was laughing, and received a mouthful of dirt, leaves, and, to her utter horror a bug. She hated watching the damsel in distress trip and fall in horror movies and yet here she was falling for the *second* time. Did she see lights? Maleka slid to a stop on her face, stood up, and ran. She did see lights. The lights that shone through the window of the cabin were like a beacon promising a safe haven from this storm.

She could hear the footsteps of the dogs behind her, she thought she heard them running past her as well, and knew that they were racing ahead to cut her off and surround her.

With every breath she took she inhaled fire. Both of her feet were swollen, cut, and bleeding, pain exploded from her feet to her jaw with each step she took. Her hands, arms, and face were scratched and cut. The pain in her side was so intense she might as well have been pierced by the Spear of Density. The trees blocked out the light of the moon, it was so dark she couldn't even see the tips of her fingers on her outstretched arms. She'd just returned home from the war and was in excellent physical condition; otherwise she would have been caught two miles ago. She kept running. She ran faster.

She was so close that the warm light glowing in the window offered her enough light to see the edges of her surroundings, but she didn't look at what was moving within the shadows. She jumped over the four steps of the cabin's patio and slammed her shoulder into the door expecting resistance but with one turn of the knob the door opened.

The rug slid under her feet and she almost fell…again. As Maleka regained her balance the only thing she saw was a pair of denim blue eyes. It took three seconds for Maleka's vision to pan out allowing the panoramic view of the inside of the cabin to come into focus.

The man she was looking at was shirtless, and tattooed. On his broad and chiseled chest was an eagle in flight and clutched within his mighty talons was a large swastika. The man was sitting in a chair, his foot on the edge of the table, and his chair was tipped back on the two hind legs. Covering the wall he was against was a large Confederate battle flag – an image that for the majority of black people living in the United States is a symbolism of racism. His hair might have been red or blond but his head was shaved. He wasn't alone. Another man was standing by the window and yet another was sitting on a small sofa directly in front of the man she had first seen.

Maleka spun around, slammed the door closed and engaged the deadbolt. Once the door was closed she saw a large chair, it was as heavy as it looked, and she had to use all her strength to drag it to the door and position the chair under the door handle. Maleka stumbled a few steps back and turned to face the men she had locked herself inside with.

For almost five minutes no one spoke.

She pressed her hand to pain in her side and took a closer look at the guy by the window. He wasn't standing as she first thought; he was sitting on top of some type of cabinet. He had a huge sucker in his mouth and she could smell the cherry scent of the candy from the other side of the room. He had the same denim blue colored eyes as the one leaning back in his chair. He wasn't completely bald because his red hair had grown out a little. It reminded Maleka of a peach. The thought of such a juicy fruit only served to underscore the dryness of her parched throat. As if reading her mind, he tightened the cap on his bottle of water and tossed it to Maleka. She drank it down greedily; cool water ran down the sides of her mouth, drinking as much as she could before she started coughing.

Both his arms from shoulder to wrist were covered in colorful, incredibly detailed tattoos, but what stood out the most were the flags. On the inside of his upper right arm near his chest was a tattoo of a red flag with a black swastika in the center, on the left the American flag. The man sitting on the couch was wearing a Dewalt wife beater style t-shirt and was wearing a ball cap that read, "The south shall rise again." At first she thought they all looked the same but it was clear to her that the one leaning back in his chair and the one in the window were related, possibly brothers.

The cabin was just one big square room, the kitchen was along the wall to her left, and the view from that window was of more woods. A large brick fireplace was in the center of the widest wall and there was a door off to the side that Maleka guessed to be a bathroom. There were three sleeping bags rolled up in the corner where there were three backpacks, and a slew of hunting rifles.

Along the wall above the couch hung pictures of Hitler standing in a moving jeep, bikini-clad blonde women displaying tools, and redheads posing with cars. There was also a poster of the University of Alabama football team running on the field. Maleka was surprised to see that poster hanging so proudly, as most of the players in the poster were black.

Finally the guy in the window swirled his candy to one side of his mouth and asked, "So what the fuck are you running from to make you think you're safer in here with us than out there with a gun strapped to your belt?"

"A pack of wolves." Maleka answered.

"No ma'am, you might wanna try that again, we ain't got no wolves down here." The candy man explained.

"I know but they weren't wolves at first." Maleka's thoughts were jumbled and confused and so were her words. She heard herself talking and was afraid that she wasn't making any sense.

"See, she told me to keep it with me. Then I didn't think I needed it, so I threw it away."

"You threw what away?"

"I really didn't think it would do any good, it's just a stupid superstition."

He slowly took the candy out of his mouth and asked again, "You threw what away?"

"The man at the gas station tried to give it back to me but I didn't take it."

"HEY!" He shouted, "Do you hear me fucking talking to you? I'm not going to ask you again. What did you throw away?"

"The charm."

"The charm?" He echoed.

"What charm, what was it for?"

Maleka noticed how his eyes lowered to the gold cross she was wearing around her neck as he asked the question.

"It was to protect me from the monster."

The man leaning in the chair slowly lowered it back on all four legs, and the one on the couch took off his ball cap and ran his hand through his thick blond hair. As his blond locks unraveled to fall against his sculpted shoulders, Maleka knew without a doubt that this man was a direct descendant of Thor.

Maleka could see the conversation the men were having with their eyes but she had no idea what they were saying.

"Travis she's high, she's probably from California, and they say they got some good ass weed out there."

The three of them shared a laugh as Travis put the candy back in his mouth and leaned against the window.

"I'm not high and I'm not from California." Maleka hissed.

Travis shrugged his shoulders, "That might be so girl, but you ain't from around here. You say you ain't high but your done spooked yourself so bad you ain't thinking straight and you ain't making no damn sense so I can't tell either way."

"I scared myself?" Maleka was furious.

"What you was running from was most likely coyotes."

"I know the fucking difference between a wolf and a coyote," she started, but the man in the chair interrupted her.

"Really, Big City? Because you said they weren't wolves at first, so what were they then, dingoes?"

More laughter.

"Fuck you!"

"Fuck you too you stupid fucking nigger cunt bitch! There ain't no fucking wolves down here. The only dogs we have out there in our woods are the coyote and maybe...*maybe* a pack of strays. You was running through the woods at night, it's dark out there and the woods got a way of playing tricks with your senses. You was just seeing things."

"Caleb's right," Travis explained. "You fucking people are all the same; you come down south and act like it's a trip to the fucking zoo. Y'all come down here so that you laugh at us ignorant, po' white trash, redneck hillbillies, and point at the dumb ass country niggers."

"Y'all watch movies like Deliverance and think we're just a bunch of inbreeds sitting down here making moonshine, playing banjos, eating fried chicken and spitting out watermelon seeds. Then the next thing you know y'all is running through the woods in the middle of the night shooting at shadows and running from dogs that are expecting to be hand fed."

More laughter. Maleka started to say something but stopped. She turned her head towards the door. The others heard it too. Scratching. The door shook gently. Something heavy landed on the roof and the ceiling creaked in protest under the weight of whatever was walking across it. Everyone looked up at once. The door shook again, forcefully this time. Travis tracked the footsteps on the roof his head, leaning further and further back until he was looking directly above him.

There was a long deep howl lasting almost 10 seconds before the others in the pack answered the call.

Everyone started moving at once. Maleka unhooked her gun from her belt and reached into her pockets for the extra clips. Without taking his eyes off the ceiling Travis stood, slowly turned around, and closed the interior shutters.

Caleb grabbed the hunting rifles that had been leaning against the fireplace. The man sitting on the couch flew past Maleka to close the shutters in the kitchen. He closed them in the nick of time. The glass in the kitchen window shattered but the shutter was not breached.

"Ryan." Caleb called and tossed a rifle to the man who now behind Maleka.

The silence that followed was deafening. With the enveloping hush everyone looked at Maleka, who was looking at Caleb with a look that said I told you so.

When Maleka had first tried to explain the night's events Travis thought it was a joke, now he thought it was her fault. He flew from the window to loom over her.

"You fucking threw the Goddamn charm away; you just fucking threw it away?"

Travis was a whole foot taller than Maleka, and as he screamed down at her she realized that the candy he had had in his mouth was not cherry flavored but in fact strawberry.

Neither his size nor proximity intimidated Maleka since both were to her advantage. Her situation awareness was acute. Maleka had mentally established that inside the cabin was her zone of security, and she knew where everything was.

From a very early age Caleb had developed a healthy fear of women; and learned to never underestimate their capacity for brutality nor be surprised with the vicious glee in which they carried out their monstrous deeds. Caleb did not like the way the girl's demeanor had changed, and though he couldn't pinpoint *what* had changed he just knew something had.

"Travis."

"If you knew it was to keep you safe why did you fucking throw it away?"

She knew how much room she had to maneuver. She knew how many steps it would take to reach Caleb, understood that he would have to be the next one neutralized because under no circumstances was she going back outside into unfamiliar terrain while it was dark.

With eight older sisters, a mother who was acquitted for the slaughter of his father, and having served a ten year prison sentence for killing a woman who was doing her best to kill him, Caleb had firsthand knowledge of how truly cruel and dangerous a woman could be, and he understood that they were in no way, shape, or form the weaker sex.

"Travis."

"Y'all think y'all so much better than us, so sophisticated and educated."

Maleka's breathing slowed. She was unprepared to deal with deer that changed themselves into people and then changed themselves into wolves, but fighting men was what she had been trained to do, and she had seventeen confirmed kills under her belt just this year alone. Her personal best so far.

That's what it was. She was calm, almost relaxed. Travis was a big guy. Most people who saw him coming would quickly look for the nearest exit, or cross the street. No one ever made eye contact with him, but this girl was looking him right in the eye and didn't even flinch, and Caleb didn't like that.

"Travis."

Maleka slowly slid one foot in front of the other, but kept her hands at her sides thus assuming a basic battle stance. Close quarters combat was Maleka's specialty. Because of her stealth, speed, agility, and ferocity in hand to hand combat, comrades in her unit started calling her "The black mamba." Most people didn't see her coming and those who did lacked the necessary training to defend themselves, and perished. And such would be the case with Travis.

Before he realized that he had even stood up, Caleb found himself by his brother's side. He gently pulled Travis away from Maleka and protectively stood between them.

"What the fuck were you doing out in the woods at night for anyway?" Travis demanded over Caleb's shoulder.

"They crashed my car."

"Of course they fucking crashed your car! Dumbass." Travis was furious and pacing back and forth.

"I don't understand why you're so upset Travis," Maleka taunted, "You said I was shooting at shadows and running from dogs that are expecting to be hand fed. Maybe we should open the door and give them some doggie treats and scratch their heads."

For a frightening second Caleb was unsure if he was going to be able to restrain his brother. He would have loved nothing more than to knock that smug smirk off her face but Caleb had a feeling that was exactly what she wanted and he refused to be baited.

"Travis, there are four of us in here and enough guns for us to have three each. We just have to maintain our zone of security until morning, and then we'll be able to offer adequate cover to reach the truck. The nearest town will be our extraction point."

Travis and Caleb looked at each other in astonishment and Maleka fought feelings of frustration.

"Extraction point?" Travis echoed. "Are you in the army?"

Something else jumped onto the roof, the door bulged in violently as if kicked, but the chair under the doorknob held.

"These ain't terrorist you was shooting at out there. There ain't no fucking extraction point and in case you haven't noticed we're surrounded. The Calvary ain't coming and you just fucking got us all killed."

Maleka was losing her patience with Travis.

"I killed two of them in the street."

"Did you kill them or did you just shoot them?"

The voice came from behind her. Maleka pivoted 180 degrees and took three steps back so that her back was towards the door and the three men were in view full.

"You said at first they weren't wolves, so then, what were they?"

Whatever was on the roof was now jumping, as if trying to stomp its way through. The door was kicked again and splintered along the hinges. The front room window shattered. The noise outside sounded like breaking tree branches, and a mixture of hyena calls and wolf howls. Ryan burst into hysterical laughter and Maleka decided it wasn't such a good idea to have her back to the door.

"Ok, Big-City girl, if you have a plan to get us all outta here alive you might want to tell us because that would be some pretty good fucking information to have right about now."

Before Maleka had the time to ignore Travis's hysteria, Ryan asked his question again.

"What were they at first?"

Before Maleka had a chance to answer, Caleb offered his hypothesis. "So what are we dealing with here, werewolves? Well, if that's the case we're all fucked because none of these bullets are silver."

"Can they fucking do that? The moon's not even full!"

As Travis's question drifted slowly towards silence, all of the men turned to Maleka for the answer. She thought that she was going to collapse as the heavy weight of how truly dire their situation was settled upon her shoulders. As if things were not challenging enough, unlike the men in her unit, these guys were not going to just do what they were told, and Travis was already becoming a problem.

Maleka's plan A was to stay inside the cabin until daylight, but whatever monster had chased her in here, and who had been kicking the door and jumping on the room, had a different idea. Maleka was going to have to come up with a plan "B" and "C" and a contingency plan and she should have done that 20 min. ago.

Maleka took Caleb's rifle to inspect it and was disappointed at her discovery. Caleb's weapon of choice was a Winchester Model 70. A bolt rifle. This was the perfect weapon for a sniper – and of course to use for hunting; but the mere seconds it took to reload this gun manually would cost someone their life in a combat situation. With a quick scan of all the weapons she knew she wouldn't find what she was looking for.

"What's the matter?"

Maleka handed Caleb his gun back.

"I was really hoping for a semi-automatic, or at least a gun that could have been converted. Even a revolver would be nice. Are there any handguns here?"

"Semi-automatic?" Caleb asked. "I guess if you're hunting people but we came out here to hunt elk. I got a colt .38 out in the truck."

"My state allows the use of semi-automatic for big game hunting." Maleka explained. "And the last thing anyone is doing right now is going outside."

"What's considered big game hunting in California…a Colombian Drug Lord?"

Maleka wanted nothing more than to knock Travis unconscious with the butt of his own gun, but as the best possible defense plan formulated in her mind she knew she was going to need him.

"I'm not from California Travis, I'm from Washington. Is there a window in the bathroom?"

"No." They all answered at once. Finally, God had answered her prayer. Maleka opened the door to the small bathroom and asked Ryan to drag over the chair that Caleb had been sitting in. She used the chair to hold the door open, and then lined the bathtub with sleeping bags.

Because Caleb was the tallest he was the one she put in the bathtub, and he was thankful for the padding of the sleeping bags, as he would be shooting from a knelling position directly over Maleka's head. Maleka wanted the gunfire aimed in such a way to produce highest the concentration of fatalities. It was one thing to shoot at the heads of unsuspecting elk. It was another thing entirely to be shooting at moving targets that had the ability to change from one creature to another, and whose sole purpose was your demise. Travis's position was on the ledge of the tub and Ryan sat on the toilet. They would surround her as she sat on the floor, and her goal was to provide them with enough automatic fire to give them enough time to reload their guns.

With the men in place Maleka moved the two floor lamps to each side of the bathroom door and used the outlets in the bathroom to plug them in. She directed the swivel heads of the lamps toward the cabin door and turned all the other lights in the cabin off. Just like a cop shining his light into your car window, not only would the bright lights of the 100watt bulb blind anyone, or anything, coming through the door, the intense white light directed outwards would provide a safe haven of darkness in which they could hide behind.

They sat in the silent dark for almost twenty minutes, and when Travis started talking it startled everyone.

"Caleb," he said. "I think you're the coolest mother-fucking man I ever met."

The iron shutters in both windows started to rattle. Caleb cleared his throat but when he started talking his voice was full of emotion.

"You've always followed me no matter where I went, I knew if I ever wanted my little brother all I had to do was turn around and you'd be there. In all my life this is the only time I wish you hadn't followed me."

Hearing Travis and Caleb say good-bye was more than Maleka could deal with. She had fought in four theaters in places that you would never be able to find on a map, just to be killed in her own country by a fiend that should not exist.

Keep this wit yo' at all times no matter what happens.

There was nothing she could do about it now, and Travis had been right all along. She indeed had killed them all. This was so unfair; it was just a stupid superstition, none of this was real. Except it was.

"I'm sorry."

Maleka wasn't just apologizing to Caleb, Travis, and Ryan. She was also apologizing to her cousin Maybell who put a broom by her bedroom door to keep her safe from the terrors that lurk in the night. She was apologizing to her grandmother, who had given her a gift that was meant to see her through on her journey, and to the gas station attendant, who knew how important it was when he tried to give it back after she left it on the counter. But more importantly, Maleka apologized to God for her earlier blasphemous display of disobedience.

With a final kick the door broke in half, flying inwards in two pieces, and as the wind and the monsters rushed in, everyone started shooting.

BIRDS OF A FEATHER

BY MATT NORD

"What more do you want from me?" Zach grumbled at the window. "I've given you everything I had."

Most of the crows simply stared at him. A few pecked at what remained of his cat, but most of the bones had already been picked clean. Other piles of bones lay strewn about the sidewalk, the street and his neighbors' yards. The black of the birds stood in stark contrast to the thin layer of snow that coated much of the ground. His front lawn was covered with garbage, remnants of the food items he'd thrown out the front door in an attempt to satisfy the ravenous birds. Unfortunately for him, for every crow that ate its fill, another two or three flew in to take its place.

The crows had been a problem in Auburn, New York for as long as he could remember. Every winter, tens of thousands of crows made their way to roost in Auburn. Steps were taken in an attempt to drive them away. Scarecrows, spotlights, fireworks, firecrackers; nothing seemed to work. In 2003, amidst much protest from PETA and other environmental agencies, the crow hunts started. This year, the crows were the hunters.

He thought of how ironic it was that a flock of crows should be called a murder, considering how fatally wrong this year's crow-hunt had gone.

Zach gazed out the front window, surveying a landscape covered with old food wrappings, bird shit and the bodies of the crows that he'd managed to kill with his pistol. The sight of the skeletal remains of animals and humans who had been unfortunate enough to be outdoors during the initial attack sickened him. It had reminded Zach of an old nature show he'd watched in which a swarm of piranha had stripped a cow to the bone.

His eyes glazed over, remembering the howls, hisses and screams. He shook his head at the memory.

Lucky bastards, he thought, looking out at the bones. *At least you don't have to starve to death.*

Zach regretted having to toss out his stock of food, but he had wasted almost all of his bullets trying to thin out the flock enough to make it to his car. He wasn't the greatest shot under the best circumstances, and the small moving targets didn't help matters. He'd only really succeeded in agitating the animals and had nearly gotten pecked to death in the process. If he had been wearing his contacts that morning instead of his glasses, he would have been screwed. He had used up a bottle of peroxide and two boxes of Band-Aids after that.

He stared at his car keys, which lay in a tiny, glittering pile, where he had dropped them halfway to the vehicle.

"Fucking crows," he mumbled. There had just been too many of them.

Several of the vermin hopped around the keys, pecking at them and cawing at each other, seemingly fighting over the prize.

What are they doing? he thought. The group continued to jump around the keys until one larger crow swooped in, scattering the rest of them. It picked at the keys, turning them over with its beak.

Zach watched the crow for a few minutes, unsure what to do next. *It's not like the stupid thing is going to…*

The crow finally found the hold it wanted, snatching the key ring up in its maw and taking off into the air.

He gasped and nearly ran out the front door to try to catch the bird, before remembering that he had another set of keys in the kitchen.

Why the fuck did I park on the street, anyway? he thought. If he'd parked in the car port, he probably could have made it.

When he tried to shoot his way through the crows, they went nuts and tried to break through his windows by flying directly into the glass, one bird after another. The only thing that had calmed them down had been to throw all of the food in the house out to them, seemingly satiating their hunger for the time being.

Now the birds simply perched on any open area outside... staring at him. He stood at the window, looking from crow to crow to crow, then down to the pistol he still held in his hand. He contemplated putting it to his head and pulling the trigger. That was why, even through the pain of the swarm of beaks piercing his skin, the thought of keeping a bullet had managed to remain in his brain.

He stared at the gun for what seemed like an eternity. *How long before help finally comes?* Zach thought. *Someone has to know we're in trouble here.*

He could hold out for a while, anyway. Why had thoughts of suicide jumped so quickly into his head? *Apparently, stressful circumstances can make a person go a little nuts. I just need to calm down. Not do something stupid.*

He started to feel a bit better about things, and even chuckled a bit at his own silliness. *Well, as good as I can feel considering my hot neighbor is now a pile of bones on my front sidewalk.*

He'd gotten so wrapped up in his thoughts that he jumped half a foot when the first crow flew into the window. The glass was already cracked from the initial round of birds that had tried to gain access into the house.

"What the fuck!" he shouted. "I don't have any more food!"

He could hear the windows upstairs getting attacked, as well. He knew what type of food they were looking for. More and more crows were crashing into the glass. He didn't know how much longer it would be before one of them shattered, allowing the murder of crows to reach him. He knew that inevitably they would.

Unless I do something.

He pulled his eyes from the mass of feathers that kept barreling into the window. He shoved his pistol in his rear waistband as he ran to the kitchen and snagged his spare set of car keys, tossing them in his jacket pocket. He then sprinted upstairs and into the bathroom. He threw open the cabinets and began tossing bottles, towels and boxes around, trying to find...

"Yes," he said, picking up the huge can of Aqua Net. "Thank God for ex-girlfriends with big hair."

Running from the bathroom, he patted his pockets with his free hand. He had only quit smoking recently and had forgotten that he'd stopped carrying a lighter.

So much for quitting being good for my health, he thought.

He ran down the hall to his bedroom, looking for a lighter. There, on his nightstand, sat a gleaming Zippo. As he reached for it, the window next to his bed shattered.

"No!" he screamed, as he grabbed the lighter. The room began to fill with the black birds. He gripped the two items tightly as he flailed his hands at the pecking creatures. He made his way back to the hall and slammed the door.

Luckily for him, most of the birds were still in the bedroom. One crow had not been so lucky. It squawked at Zach and flapped one wing wildly, the other caught between the door and the jamb. Zach glared down at the animal as he wiped some of the blood from his face. A multitude of cuts littered his face where the flying pests had attacked him.

"Little shit," he growled and brought the large aerosol can down, crushing the crow's skull against the wood of the door, bringing its thrashing to a quick end.

Zach glanced down at the blood on the bottom of the can. For some reason, this made him start to wonder about what, exactly, was making these animals go insane and attack… and if it was a virus or disease, whether or not it might be infectious to humans. He'd been pecked so many times that he couldn't imagine that he wouldn't have gotten infected if that were the case. With all the talk of bird flu, swine flu, the fucking platypus flu, his mind swam with visions of men in biohazard suits grabbing him and putting him in quarantine.

Well, anything is better than getting eaten by birds, he thought.

He ran back down the stairs, his pistol falling from his waistband halfway down as he did. It tumbled down the stairs, coming underfoot, nearly causing him to fall the rest of the way down.

"Shit," he yelled, catching his balance. He picked the gun back up and shoved it into the leg pocket of his cargo pants. He double checked the lighter to ensure it worked and shook the can of Aqua Net. It had to be half full. *I sure as hell hope this works,* he thought.

He had no chance to take stock of anything else before heading out the front door. He heard the window in the dining room implode, shattering under the weight of dozens upon dozens of the black birds that were rushing in through the portal. He burst out through the door and lifted up the aerosol can and lighter. Lighting the Zippo, he put it in front of the spray nozzle and pressed it down. The effect was better than he had hoped.

The flame shot out about two feet, roasting any crow unfortunate enough to fly into its path. He sprayed the fire in a small arc in front of him, slowly working his way toward his car keys. He was nearly to them when he was swarmed from behind by half a dozen birds. He let out a yelp and fell to the ground, rolling onto his back. The second set of keys fell out of his jacket pocket.

"Shit!" he screamed, knowing that if another crow got a hold of this set of keys, he'd be as good as dead. He didn't know if he could even make it back to the house. Luckily, if it could be called that, the crows seemed more interested in trying to peck his eyes out than in making off with the shining object.

The abrasions on his back screamed as dirt and gravel ground into them, but he knew he had more of a chance with his back away from those hungry beaks.

He flicked the Zippo again and torched the crows that tried to dive bomb him. After scattering the flock, he snatched up the keys from the ground, hit the automatic unlock and made for the passenger side door. He opened the door and dove in, turning around to slam the door shut. He let out a sigh of followed by a shriek of pain as a crow bit at the lobe of his right ear.

He smacked the bird away and grabbed his ear.

"Fuck!" he shouted. The crow flapped back up to the car seat and began pecking at the back of Zach's head. He tried to shield his head with his hands, but that just managed to get his fingers pecked instead. He continued slapping at the bird until finally landing a solid hit, knocking it onto the back seat.

He pressed his hand to his ruined ear. Warm blood seeped through his fingers. The pain reminded him of when he'd been a stupid teenager and he'd pierced his own ear. Only this time, instead of using a needle, it felt like he'd used a pair of dull scissors.

Before the thing could shake away the stupor of Zach's blow, he bent over the seat to try to finish it off. It flopped about on the floor like a trout on the bottom of a row boat. He snatched it up in one hand and it managed one last good peck before he grabbed its head with the other and snapped its neck. He dropped it back on the floor. He wiped his hands on his shirt and took a deep breath before moving over into the driver's seat.

He had been so focused on the crow inside the car that he hadn't noticed that the ones outside were now attempting to smash the car windows. One after another, the crows dive-bombed into the glass, no doubt sacrificing their lives for a chance that some of the others could feast on the moist flesh of the man inside. The web of the crack in the windshield spread with every bird that flew into it.

He had to get moving not only before they broke in, but before there was too much damage to the windshield for him to see out of it. He jammed the key into the ignition and turned it. The engine roared to life, and he threw the car into drive.

Thank God this isn't a fucking horror movie, he thought. He'd seen enough to know that now would be the time when his car wouldn't start, but he'd taken good care of it over the years, and never let the tank get much under half full.

He pulled away from the curb and sped away from the murder of crows that had bombarded his car. He ran the stop sign at the corner, taking a left on Hoopes Avenue, heading towards the college.

Unfortunately for Zach, the scene that spread before him was just a bleak as the destroyed neighborhood he'd left. All around, the bones of animals and humans littered the streets, sidewalks and yards. Thousands of crows perched on houses, telephone lines, cars, trees, and any other higher surface on which they could fit. They seemed to jockey for position as they pecked and squawked at one another.

He turned right on Franklin Street and passed East Middle School. The bodies of several dozen students and what must have been some parents were strewn about on the front terrace of the school. They were probably just getting there when the attacks began.

Driving past the college, he saw a similar scene. The parking lot was still nearly full, with dead bodies everywhere. Crows picked at the loose morsels of flesh on the few remaining corpses that had any left on them. Two cars appeared to have run into each other in an attempt to escape. The occupants were all dead, and he could see smoke coming from both engines. It appeared that the occupants had tried to make a break back to the school, because the doors hung wide open on both cars.

He slowed he car, hoping to avoid drawing attention to himself. He looked around and saw several shredded bodies lying right beyond reach of what he assumed to be their cars. A few of the crows hopped around them and picked casually at the remaining flesh. No doubt, they had attempted an escape just as he had.

Better them than me, he thought.

He also saw numerous faces staring out at him from house windows, most from behind curtains or between blinds, looking terrified and distraught. They must have kept a low enough profile to avoid attention.

"Sorry, but I can't hel..." he began to say out loud before being interrupted by two bloody hands banging on the driver's side window. The shock had caused him to jam on the brake, bringing the car to a halt.

"Please, help me!" the woman screamed. He could see the open door of the car in which she must have been trapped. Apparently she'd made it, but her...husband, or whoever, hadn't. She grabbed the door handle and pulled, but Zach muscled it shut again. She ran around to the other side of the car, chased by a multitude of the black birds. Zach hit the lock button before she reached the door. She pulled at it in vain.

"Please!" she screamed again, this time up an octave. She alternated between pounding on the door and swatting at the crows that pecked at her with machine gun speed. He paused for a second, and then simply shook his head. Her eyes widened at the realization that he had effectively condemned her to die.

"You son of a bitch!" she screamed before falling to the ground in a ball. Zach pulled away as she shrieked and bled, trying feebly to protect herself from the onslaught. It didn't last long. *It didn't last long. Keep telling yourself that,* he thought as his throat started to burn.

He looked back over his shoulder at the form in the road. The woman was completely obscured by thousands upon thousands of black feathers.

Nothing I can do about it now, anyway.

He continued driving down the street. Occasionally a crow or two would fly alongside or above the speeding vehicle, keeping pace for a while before falling back.

"Stupid birds," he mumbled to himself every time.

He continued down the road, taking turns without stopping, nearly losing control on a few occasions. He kept looking back over his shoulder, having a difficult time shaking the memory of the young woman's face just before the crows had engulfed her from his mind.

"What the fuck was I supposed to do?" he asked the steering wheel. "I'd have gotten fucking killed, too."

He couldn't shake the feeling of guilt, though. How could he have just left her to die? He'd made it into his car with only one crow managing to get in. His ear throbbed at the memory. He touched his ear where the lobe used to be.

"Fucking crows," he grumbled. He was getting close to 5 and 20, which would lead him out of Auburn, east toward Syracuse. "I never liked Auburn, anyway."

For some reason, he felt a sensation on the back of his neck, like one might get if they were being watched. He tried to shake the feeling but couldn't. He squirmed in his seat and the car swerved a bit for his efforts.

"Keep it together, man," he said to himself. "Just a little farther…"

He saw fewer crows the farther he drove, but noticed that the Seventh-Day Adventist Church on his left was covered with them. *Some sanctuary*, he mused.

Zach continued on down Prospect Street toward the Arterial. He only hoped that this was a local event, that the crows wouldn't follow him out of Auburn. This was their roost, now. Had it ever not been?

He nearly jumped out of his seat when he heard the loud caw from the back seat. *I killed that fucking thing*, he thought. *It couldn't be alive.*

He looked over his shoulder, jerking the wheel to the right. The passenger side headlight collided with a mailbox, shattering the light and destroying the box. He straightened the car out, getting back on the road. He hadn't seen any sign of the bird in the back seat. Maybe he'd just imagined it.

He ran a hand through his hair, taking a deep breath and trying to calm himself. The next thing he heard made the blood in his veins run cold as ice.

"Son of a bitch…"

His knuckles turned white as he applied a death grip to the steering wheel. He looked up into the rearview mirror. In the back seat sat the woman he had left behind on the street. Her face was covered with lacerations, and blood dripped onto her white blouse. A large black crow perched on her shoulder.

"You could have saved me," she said. The crow pecked at her face, snatching her right eye out of its socket and gobbling it up greedily.

Zach let out a scream and slammed on the brakes. He turned around. The apparitions of the woman and the bird were gone.

Turning back around, he ran a shaky hand through his hair. He grabbed the steering wheel with both hands and pressed his head against it, taking in a deep breath and letting it out in a long sigh.

"What was I supposed to do?" he asked the car horn. "I could've been killed, too."

As he played through the scenario in his mind's eye, he failed to realize that he had stopped in the middle of the main arterial heading out of Auburn. He heard the blare of the horn and looked up just in time to see the Dodge pickup slam into the side of his compact car. The smaller vehicle lurched, and he lost consciousness.

Zach awoke a few seconds later, the world upside down in his vision. His arms brushed the ceiling of the car, and he felt the pain of the seatbelt digging into his thighs. Looking around, trying to get his bearings, he saw the Dodge off to the side of the road, the front end bent in, smoke or steam coming from under the hood.

Another vehicle had pulled over next to it, the driver and passenger jumping from the car and pulling two injured, but apparently living, people from the truck. The four quickly made their way back to the car. A woman from the second vehicle looked over toward Zach and then scanned the sky, a terrified look on her face. He tried to call for help, but no sound came from his mouth as it filled with blood from some internal injury.

"Wh-what about him?" she stammered.

The driver popped his head back out and looked over at the destroyed car. They all heard the call and as one looked back toward the western sky. The black cloud of crows grew large as it moved towards them.

"Forget him," he said. "There's nothing we can do. Now get in!"

She did. Before she could slam her door shut the car peeled away, down 5 and 20, out of Auburn, New York.

Less than a minute later, the first crow landed near the upturned car. Hopping to the edge of the shattered driver's-side window, it cocked its head toward Zach and let out a shrill caw. Black, empty eyes stared at him as the next crow landed.

THE DEVILS ADVOCATES
BY C.D. REIMER

John Wormwood, a reporter for the free weekly tabloid called *The Silicon Valley Gazette*, hid himself in the underlit grove with his camcorder aimed at the illuminated 21-foot-tall bronze statue known as *The Gates of Hell*, mounted on a taller granite wall that dominated the Rodin Sculpture Garden of the Cantor Art Center at Stanford University. Twenty men in black-cowled robes had gathered here at midnight under a moonless sky.

Benedictine monks they were not.

After cutting the throat of a young goat that was bled dry into an orange bucket, three of them wrapped up the carcass in a tarp that they carried over to the old pickup truck parked on the street. Another took the bucket of blood and a bristle brush to paint a large pentacle on the concrete in front of the statue. Others set up and lit the five candles at the points of the pentacle that touched the circle. The three who carried the goat carcass returned with a struggling figure wrapped in a canvas sheet like a Turkish rug on their shoulders. The rest watched in silence with their arms folded into their sleeves, waiting for the *sabbat* to start.

Their leader threw back his cowl to reveal a clean-shaven young man that many people would mistake for a minister's son. He removed the canvas sheet from the struggling figure to reveal a blue-eyed, blond-haired woman who stood naked with a brilliant bikini tan. She was bound and gagged with a nylon cord, staring at him with wide-eyed terror. He kissed her gently on the lips like an old lover, and punched her in the face like a jealous lover. Blood squirted from her nose as the darkness took her. He swept her curvaceous body into his arms to lay her down in the center of the still wet pentacle. Being careful not to smear the circle with his boots, he stepped away to kneel before the pentagram. His followers kneeled behind him in a half-circle, where they chanted in a low murmur for ten minutes. He pulled out something from inside his robe that he held high above his head with both hands.

Wormwood zoomed in the lens of the camcorder.

The knife had an elaborately carved handle of a ruby-eyed goat head and curving ram horns. The wicked sharp blade glimmered in the light. The chanting continued until hitting a crescendo five minutes later. The knife plunged downward in both hands. A squirt of blood shot straight up to splatter on the leader's forehead, making him staggered backwards in either shock or surprise. The knife was buried into the woman's heart, nestled between her bloodied bosoms. Her fading eyes had shot open and were glazed over from tears running down her face. He stepped away to kneeled with the others, where they continued chanting for another ten minutes. The woman's naked body grew colder.

"Oh, God," Wormwood said, staring above his camcorder.

A piercing crack emanated from the bronze statue, where an orange line appeared in the seam between the two gates. They stopped chanting to wait. The gates were pulled back in a loud, rust-tinged squeal, revealing a luminous orange glow that filled the gateway. A wave of heat rushed over them like a baptism by fire, billowing their robes and Wormwood's gray hair, until the air shimmered around them from the heat furies.

A hunched figure in a tattered, cowled robe sat on the back of an ashen-gray horse that rode out from the orange glow to stop at the pentagram. Bony fingers threw off the cowl to reveal a goat head with glowing ruby eyes and curving ram horns. Looking down upon the sacrificial offering and at the kneeling men, an all too human smile appeared on that demonic face.

"I am the Horseman Death and the rider of the Pale Horse." The eerie voice was a whisper that thundered across the stillness. The Horseman Death got down from his steed and gestured a bony hand over the dead woman. "Your virginal sacrifice is appreciated."

"Dark Lord," the leader said in a loud, reverent voice. "How may your faithful servants serve you?"

"Your opening of the gates before the appointed time was a service not needed to be done." He gestured towards the kneeling men, and the Pale Horse snorted in eagerness. "More sacrifices are required."

The leader looked up in surprise. The Pale Horse stepped over the girl in the pentagram and reared up to strike a smoldering hoof mark on his forehead that killed him. His followers screamed and tried to flee from the trampling wrath that came at them.

The Horseman Death bent down to caress the face of the dead woman, pulled out the knife that left a gaping wound in her heart, and walked back into the orange glow. The gates slammed shut behind him with a resounding boom. The orange line between the gates disappeared.

Wormwood stepped out of the grove after the Pale Horse faded from existence a few minutes later, panning the camcorder over the twenty dead people lying on the ground with smoke curling up from the hoof print on their foreheads. They were all clean-shaven young men who belong to respectable families. He lingered the camcorder over the dead woman. Blood streaked from her bruised nose and the hole in her heart that pooled underneath her bosom.

The Pale Horse reared up in front of him from out of nowhere.

Wormwood fell on his ass with the camcorder pointing up at the demonic beast above him. Brimstone and hellfire washed over him like the sour breath of a homeless drunk in need of a new friend. He rolled out of the way before a searing hoof struck the ground where his head, crystallizing the sandy earth into black glass. He started running towards the side street where his car was parked.

The Pale Horse seemed slow to catch up with him. Perhaps it was only toying with the reporter. The cold asphalt of the street melted under its hoof steps that hissed steam in its wake.

Wormwood got into his car, a 1969 Dodge Charger that he got brand new when he started working as a reporter forty-two years ago. He threw the camcorder into the sheepskin passenger seat. The engine roared to life but not before the Pale Horse reared up behind the car. A pair of hoof prints blackened the cherry red paint job on the trunk lid that heated the metal underneath to a bright cherry red. The car shuddered from the impact. He put the pedal to the metal. An angry squeal left the Pale Horse in a cloud of vaporized rubber smoke. Looking through his rearview mirror, he saw the Pale Horse watching him before fading out again. He also saw the steam pouring off the back of his trunk. The resale value of his classic muscle car just went straight to hell.

"I don't get it," Sam Ferguson said, the editor of *The Silicon Valley Gazette*, shaking his bald head for the tenth time that afternoon. "No matter how many times I watch this video, none of it makes sense."

"I think the video speaks for itself." Wormwood used the remote to eject the videotape and turn off the VCR. When the cable news came back on, he muted the volume on the TV and put the remote down on the desk. "What part don't you understand?"

"You got a bunch of Stanford dummies running around in some kind of secret society."

"A *satanic* secret society."

"Is that the same thing as the Skulls and Bones society that former President George Bush attended at Yale?"

Wormwood grinned. "Similar but not the quite same."

"These Stanford dummies in robes are gathered at–what that's thing again?"

"Augusta Rodin's *The Gates of Hell*. A very famous statue by a very famous sculptor."

"Never heard of it."

"He's the same guy who did *The Thinker*." Wormwood gestured to the bookshelf behind the editor, who looked over his shoulder. "The same statue that your bookends are based on."

Ferguson grunted. "These Stanford dummies are at *The Gates of Hell*."

"Based on *The Divine Comedy* by Dante Alighieri."

"Which is what?"

"A famous poem by a famous poet that described all the levels of hell for which individual elements of the statue are based on." Wormwood paused. "How do you get to be editor of a weekly rag without having any culture?"

"My money, my press," Ferguson replied, sticking his chin out. "If you don't like that, go to hell."

"I keep forgetting you own this rat nest,"Wormwood said, laughing. "What's your beef with Stanford?"

"I went to Cal Berkeley."

"You went to Cal Berkeley without knowing either Rodin or Dante?"

"I dropped out of Cal Berkeley to become a newspaper man before you were born."

"You know, that saying only works when the other person isn't a few years younger than you,"Wormwood said.

"Quit being a smartass."

Wormwood shrugged. *It's always something with this guy.*

"Stanford dummies," Ferguson continued, as if that was his last word on a world-class university. "They painted this symbol in goat blood in front of this so called famous statue, and a naked tart was laid in the middle. Where she appeared to be–"

"She was sacrificed," Wormwood said, interrupting. "The blood squirt from the stabbing was quite visible on the videotape."

"The only thing that was quite visible on the videotape. This entire incident could've been an elaborate stunt to earn fleeting fame on the Internet."

"I know what I saw–this was real."

"How do you explain the electronic glitch?"

"I can't." Wormwood made the discovery while transferring the video from the camcorder to the VCR videotape. "There's an eighteen-and-a-half-minute gap if you watched the counter on the video. The videotape does show me falling down on my ass when the Pale Horse appears in front of me."

"You fell down on your ass, alright." Ferguson folded his arms. "There's no goddamn horse and no bodies when the camera panned around in your escape from your imaginary horse. The rest were gone."

"I got goddamn hoof prints in the back of my car. How do you explain that?"

"Mushrooms."

"What?"

"You heard me, John," Ferguson said, holding out his hand. "Give me the mushrooms. I can't have you reporting the news under the influence of a local delicacy."

"I haven't had mushrooms in years," Wormwood said, snorting. "The last batch of mushrooms I did have I got from you at a Christmas party. Anyway, I got a story here."

"You don't have a story."

"Twenty-one people were murdered last night–that's the story."

"Only <u>one</u> alleged murder was substantiated by your videotape–if the dead girl's body is ever found. Who are these guys? Who's the girl? Why haven't the police and the mainstream media been all over the museum since this morning? Oh, hell. Why did you wait until getting out of bed at noon to come into the office with this?"

"Okay," Wormwood said, sighing. "I'll get the devil in the details."

"Get the story while you're at it." Ferguson tapped his finger on his desk. "I want your story on Thursday afternoon. Otherwise, I'll go with Penny's story on Friday."

"What does Penny Alley have that's better than mine?"

"Besides steel balls, an actual story about pot farming by the Mexican Mafia on the slopes of Mount Umunhum in the Santa Cruz Mountains. Which happens to be a better story than your unsubstantiated mushroom-inspired fantasy."

"All she writes is crap."

"All her crap is better written, spell-checked, proofread and turned in on time. Something you used to be good at before you became a jaded news reporter trying to get the big story rather than the small story in front of your face."

"Fine, I'll get you the damn story," Wormwood groused, heading to the door. "Better written, spell-checked, proofread, and turned in on time."

"Just hand over the damn mushrooms."

Wormwood left the building and walked past his own car in the parking lot, ignoring the hoof marks burned into the upper half of the trunk lid. No amount of sanding at an auto body shop will remove that blemish. If he could prove that the Pale Horse was responsible for the mark, he might fetch a small fortune listing the car on Craig's List. Walking through downtown San Jose, he went over to Clark Hall at San Jose State University to visit associate faculty member Lawrence Singh in the Comparative Religion department. As the devil's luck would have it, the professor was having lunch in his office.

"Hey, doc." Wormwood entered the crowded office to drop his lanky body into the only chair that wasn't occupied by books and papers or a hungry professor. "Got a moment?"

Professor Singh shrugged, wiping his mouth with a napkin. "You don't mind if I eat my lunch?"

"I would never get between a man and his lunch."

"Unless, of course, the lunch gets in the way of the story." Professor Singh smiled and took a bite from his sandwich. "What earth shattering news do you have today?"

"I was wondering if you could give me some background information about the Apocalypse."

"Writing another 'end of times' story. A popular subject with the general public these days."

"Not exactly. The story I'm working is about the Four Horsemen in general and the Horseman Death in particular."

"Some people believe that the three of the Four Horsemen are already on the loose," Professor Singh said between bites. "The Horseman Conquest would be the New York Mets and Yankees, either one or both baseball teams dominating the World Series every year. The Horseman War is in Iraq, Afghanistan and all the other smaller conflicts around the world. The Horseman Famine is all of those unemployed Wall Street moneymakers collecting food stamps while checking their portfolios every five minutes. The last Horseman is Death who will open the gates of hell at the appointed time."

"When will that happen?"

"Only God knows for sure."

"If someone could open the gates of hell, would the Horseman Death and the Pale Horse ride out to kill them for opening the gates before the appointed time?"

Professor Singh held up his last bite of his sandwich with a raised eyebrow. "What kind of story you're working on?"

"I'm investigating a secret society at Stanford University who believe that Rodin's *The Gates of Hell* is a portal to hell that can be opened with a virginal sacrifice."

"Oh, that." The professor popped the last bite into his mouth. "What else is new?"

"You know about that?" Wormwood asked in surprise, having heard the rumor from a bunch of Stanford girls. "It is true?"

"Well, of course." The professor wiped his fingers with a napkin. "Every school has a secret society or two where students gather around this occult nonsense. Another excuse to hang out in the dark, listens to heavy metal music, smoke pot, and have unprotected premarital sex. A pentagram drawn in goat blood and wearing black robes make things even more atmospheric–or kinky."

"It is possible to open the gates of hell with a satanic ritual sacrifice then?"

"Oh, hell no. You can search the Internet for about anything, including satanic rituals for opening the gates of hell and manipulating the presidential election. Doesn't mean that any of that nonsense works. The occult–or any system of religion–requires faith to believe that something will happen. Most people who dabble in this stuff aren't serious enough to do diddly-squat with it."

"If they were serious about this particular ritual and did open the gates to hell, would the Horseman Death kill everyone and leave the Pale Horse to stand guard?"

"I'm not sure. Our knowledge about these theological characters are based on the writings of people who had divine visions, drunk too much wine, smoke weed or manure, or sampled the local mushrooms." Wormwood groaned inward about the last item. "The horses, for example. Some people believe that the horses play no role other than being horses. While others believe that the horses may serve as a guardian of a place."

"If the Horseman Death and the Pale Horse were in our world, would I be able to take a picture of them with a digital camera?"

"I believe you may find a film-based camera to be more reliable than a digital-based camera for recording unexplained phenomena." Professor Singh gave him a discerning look. "Don't quote me on that in the paper. The occult and paranormal research is outside my role as a comparative religion professor. I'm still a few years away from getting tenure."

Wormwood returned to the offices of *The Silicon Valley Gazette*, ducking under the windows of the editor's office that looked out on the floor. He went to the photography department down the hall. Although the news desk was fully modernized with computers to enter the story and print out the tabloid, the photography department was still old school with 35mm cameras that use film and a dark room to develop the pictures. Getting one of those non-digital cameras out of the hands of a graying hippie with braided long hair and a wild beard was a different story.

"Why in God's name do you need a *film* camera for?" Crazy Larry demanded, folding his arms from behind his desk. "Didn't we provide you with an expensive digital camcorder to take still pictures and videos of naked Stanford girls?"

Wormwood flushed. "What gave you that idea?"

"The last camcorder you turned in."

"Didn't I erase all the pictures?"

"Not all the interesting pictures with the naughty bits."

"Which you have added to your own private collection?"

Crazy Larry grinned. "Ferguson's been screaming about your cockamamie videotape with the naked girl on it."

"The *dead* naked girl was bonus material. The *digital* camcorder failed to do the job."

"The bikini tan wasn't bright enough for you?"

"Not that. Didn't record the supernatural phenomena that well. I got a glitch that equals the gap on the Watergate tapes. Isn't film supposed to be more reliable than digital?"

"For supernatural phenomena?" Crazy Larry asked, laughing. "The newer digital cameras are starting to beat film. If you're in doubt about what you're taking a picture of, a film camera would be better."

"Which is why I need to check one out."

"No."

"But I'm working on a story!"

"Ferguson has a very low opinion of your story."

"What he's too old, too dumb and too blind to realize is that this is a Pulitzer Prize winning story."

"A Pulitzer Prize winner… you?" Crazy Larry laughed again. "Have you been hitting the mushrooms again?"

"I haven't," Wormwood said, annoyed by this mushroom business. "Can I have a film camera?"

"Film you can have in abundance." Crazy Larry got up and unlocked the cabinet behind his desk. "The paper overstocked for the Year 2000 scare that didn't happen like all the naysayers said it would. Now they say 2012 will be the mother of all endings. Not that I'm betting on it."

"Doesn't film have an expiration date?"

"That's why you can have it." Crazy Larry laid down ten boxes of 35mm film on his desk, each one with an expiration date of December 31, 1999. "The cameras, however, are my babies. They don't belong to the paper. I'm planning to sell them on eBay when I retire from this hellhole."

"If you bought less pot–"

"Prescription medical marijuana."

"–you would have a lot more money for your retirement account. What's your medical condition again? Oh, yeah. The '1960s went away and all I got was this lousy beard' denial syndrome. Insurance doesn't cover that?"

"That's rich coming from a mushroom head." Crazy Larry handed over a recent vintage 35mm camera. "Do I need to show you how to load the film and press the button?"

"Nope."

"Watch out for Penny Alley."

"What the hell for?"

"Ferguson sent her out to background check your story by finding your naked girl. If you're full of crap, she's going to be pissed at you. You know, hell hath no fury like a woman reporter scorned."

Wormwood arrived at the museum shortly before sunset, parking his car on the same side street as before. Walking through the museum to kill time, he saw Penny Alley talking to a museum official in the Rodin exhibit hall. He went upstairs to look at the landscape paintings, angry that he might be forced to share his byline with his longtime rival, a young upstart who never had to hustled for her stories like he did before the Internet came along to provide everyone with instant news coverage that meant nothing special. This was *his* Pulitzer Prize winning story.

After the museum closed down for the night, he spent his time outside trying to avoid the security guards, teenagers making out and old people walking their piddling dogs. He added a theological beast to his avoidance list when the gates were opened at midnight. A long night since the Pale Horse faded in and out from existence that made it difficult for him to keep tabs on the demonic beast. He waited for the perfect moment to take his pictures.

When the Pale Horse stood at the gates before dawn, Wormwood hid back in the unlit grove. An orange line appeared between the gates before they opened with a loud crack and pulled back into the luminous orange glow that filled the gateway. Fiery heat washed over the sculpture garden. The Horseman Death came out with a cherry red apple in his bony hand that he held out to the Pale Horse, who it ate with great relish.

Wormwood snapped his pictures. The clicking and film advancing mechanisms were loud in the stillness, where both the Horseman

Death and the Pale Horse turned to his direction. He got off one more shot before he started running for his life with both legs pumping and the camera clutched in his elbow like a football. If he needed the old college try, now was the time.

The Pale Horse came charging after him.

He got into his car, throwing the camera down on the sheepskin passenger seat and fiddling with his car keys into the ignition switch. The engine got started and the Pale Horse reared up behind the car. He screamed from the shuddering impact of another pair of hoof marks on the trunk lid. The car leaped down the road in a roar of raw speed and furious smoke. Looking in his rearview mirror at the rising steam and the retreating road, the Pale Horse had already faded out of sight.

Everyone was assembled in the editor's office after lunch the next day. Wormwood's two pictures were blown up to poster board size and taped up on the interior windows. Ferguson, Crazy Larry, and the young Penny Alley stared wide-eyed at the pictures. Although the bronze statue and the granite wall in the background appeared sharp and distinctive in the background, everything else was a blurry mix of black and orange that it looked like a rotten pumpkin a week after Halloween.

"This is the Horseman Death and the Pale Horse," Wormwood said, using a red laser pointer to point them out. "Here's the proof that Rodin's *The Gates of Hell* is an actual portal to hell."

Ferguson snorted. "You seriously want us to believe that these two blurry pictures represent the Horseman Death and the Pale Horse of the Apocalypse fame that a bunch of Stanford dummies initiated with a virginal sacrifice?"

"Yes."

"Larry, what's your take on these pictures?"

"John took pictures of something," Crazy Larry said, looking at Wormwood while scratching his forehead with his middle finger. "I developed the film from the roll. There was no tampering but the film stock was quite old. That could account for the blurriness in the middle of each picture. Or he left a thumbprint on the lens. Of course, it could be supernatural phenomena."

"Supernatural phenomena," Ferguson repeated slowly, looking at the two men. "You are two *fairies* been sharing mushrooms?"

The two men shook their heads.

"Penny, what did you find yesterday?"

"Local police found the girl's body in a nearby dumpster," Alley said, brushing back a raven lock of hair. "She was bound, gagged and naked. No name until next of kin has been notified. The cause of death was a puncture wound to the heart by a sharp object, possibly a knife. The murder weapon hasn't been found yet. The knife design from the videotape is based on a medieval manuscript illustration of a sacrificial knife used to summon the devil. No real knife of that design has ever turned up. Replicas are available on the Internet for D.I.Y. virginal sacrifices.

"A source at Stanford University told me that her boyfriend and nineteen of his friends are missing. No one knows where they all went. The guys are all members of a Stanford debating club called–"

"Let me guess," Wormwood spoke up, waving his hand like an impatient schoolboy needing to go wee-wee really bad. "The Devil's Advocates."

"That's correct," Alley said, conceding with an annoyed frown. "How did you know?"

"It's a bit obvious."

"It's not obvious to me," Ferguson said, disgruntled. "What's a devil's advocate?"

Wormwood rolled his eyes.

"A devil's advocate," Alley said, glancing at her notes, "was traditionally a church lawyer who would argue against the qualifications of a candidate nominated for canonization. The term today means someone who is able to debate the opposite point of view, whether they believe that point of view or not. These boys were all pre-law students and past members of debate clubs in high school. No solid evidence of any past dealings with the occult. No missing person report has been filed yet for anyone. The police are being unusually tight lipped about this one. The mainstream media haven't caught on yet."

"There's my story," Wormwood said, smiling like the devil. "This is what I been trying to prove."

"This is not your story," Ferguson said, smacking his hand against his desk. "This is Penny's story that's backed up with hard facts. These pictures represent a mushroom-inspired fantasy not supported by any facts whatsoever."

"Are you out of your mind?" Wormwood asked, waving the laser pointer. Their eyes followed the red dot that danced back and forth across the blurry pictures. "This. Is. My. Story."

"We're running with Penny's story this Friday. The first half of your videotape will go up on the website on Thursday as a teaser. Larry will process the videotape."

"I can't believe this."

Alley smiled sweetly at him on the way out, clasping her notebook to her bosom like an innocent schoolgirl. Larry picked up the videotape from the VCR and took back the laser pointer back from Wormwood, smiling like a not so innocent pothead.

"Sorry to do this, John," Ferguson said, shaking his head. "Next time get some harder information."

"Fine," Wormwood said, pulling down the pictures. "I'll interview Death at the gates of hell. That should count for something."

"Only if you get an interview with Osama bin Laden, too."

Wormwood returned to the museum later that night, earning a quick run in with the Pale Horse that left a third pair of hoof marks on the back of his car. Parking his car on a different side street, he hiked over to the museum and managed to avoid the Pale Horse for the rest of the night. When the gates cracked open again before dawn and after the Pale Horse went through, he turned on the voice-activated mini cassette recorder in his coat pocket and ran over to stick his foot into the closing gates. He screamed from the intense heat that engulfed his foot, hopping up and down on his good foot while cradling his hurt foot. The burning sensation from the invisible fire dissipated when he noticed Death staring down at him with an expression reserved for a cable representative trying to sign up people for their expensive televisions service.

"Who the hell are you?" the Horseman Death asked, placidly.

"I'm John Wormwood," he announced in a loud squeal. "I'm from The Silicon Valley Gazette and I would like to have an interview."

"You want to interview Richard Nixon?"

"Uh, no. I'm not Bob Woodward from <u>The Washington Post</u>. I don't want talk to Nixon. Maybe later."

"Are you trying to sell something, Avon maybe?"

"I just wanted to ask you about what happened a few nights ago."

"You want an official statement then?"

"If you don't mind."

The Horseman Death snorted, almost as loud as the Pale Horse—or Wormwood's editor. "Some dumb asses thought this statue was the real thing and I had to correct their fatal assumption. No one opens the gates of hell before the appointed time."

"Do you know when that might be?"

"No comment."

The gates of hell were slammed in his face. He had plenty of doors slammed in his face over the years but none as special as this one. The orange line between the gates didn't disappear. He turned around to take out the mini cassette recorder and rewind the audiotape. When he heard the Horseman Death's voice on the tiny speaker, he started screaming in excitement.

The gates opened silently behind him. The luminous orange glow that cast his shadow was overwhelmed by a larger shadow on the ground. He looked over his shoulder to see the Pale Horse leaning through the gates with its lips pulled back to expose maggot-covered teeth in a grotesque mockery of Mr. Ed's smile. The pungent smell of his own urine wetting his pants caused the Pale Horse to snort derisively.

"I'm leaving," Wormwood whispered, taking a step forward. "I'm leaving right now."

The Pale Horse bit the back of his shirt and coat with its mouth to hurl him backwards through the gates before he could even scream. The mini cassette recorder fell to the concrete floor outside of the gates, shattering into pieces that melted into sticky goo from the intense heat. The only recording of the Horseman Death's voice was forever lost. The gates slammed shut with the orange line disappearing for good. The famous bronze statue by the famous sculptor returned to what it has always been and nothing more than that.

The newest issue of *The Silicon Valley Gazette* featured the lead story written by Penny Alley that broke open a bizarre murder-suicide pact at Stanford University. Twenty male members of a debating club called "The Devil's Advocates" killed a nineteen-year-old female student—a former girlfriend to the club's leader who refused to give up her virginity to him—in a satanic ritual. The club members were found dead in their locked clubroom, each one bearing a hoof-shaped mark on their foreheads and died from ingesting sulfur that was stolen from a chemistry lab. The beaten up truck with the dead goat was found abandoned in a nearby shopping center parking lot. The alleged murder weapon and hoof-shaped branding iron were never recovered. Authorities speculated that the murder took place in the surrounding hills. Both Penny Alley and *The Silicon Valley Gazette* were later nominated for the Pulitzer Prize in journalism.

The same issue also reported that John Wormwood, aged sixty, a veteran newspaper reporter who broke many significant stories over a forty-two year career, was found dead in his car near the Cantor Art Center at Stanford University. Police had ruled his death as a drug overdose from ingesting lethal quantities of hallucinogenic mushrooms. No mention was made of Wormwood's contribution to the lead cover story or the three pairs of hoof marks found on the back of his car.

HALL OF TWELVE

BY REBECCA BESSER

Jack Henderson was driving home from work when he noticed that something was different. At first, he couldn't place what exactly the difference was, but that it was there. By the time he reached his street the feeling started to turn into dread. Where there were normally children playing and elderly neighbors working in their yards, there was silence–no movement, no sound, and no people.

Fear for his wife and daughter caused him to accelerate. His dark-blue luxury sedan slid sideways with a squeal of tires as he maneuvered into his driveway. He jumped out of the car, leaving it running as he banged his way through the open front door.

"Maggie!" he yelled. "Regan!"

He slid in something slick and wet on the floor of the foyer, falling and landing on his back. The marble tiles almost knocked him out as his head made contact with the hard stone.

Groaning, Jack rolled onto his side and up, onto his knees. He stayed that way for a moment with his eyes closed, trying to remain conscious. When he finally opened his eyes, he instantly wished he hadn't. The foyer floor was covered in blood and it was now all over him.

Slipping and sliding, he forced himself to his feet, gripping the banister of the stair railing to hold himself upright while the world spun.

"Maggie!" he bellowed again. "Regan! Answer me!"

Silence.

He closed his eyes and took a couple of deep breaths before letting go of the banister. When he opened his eyes, he was looking at the floor. While the world had stopped spinning moments ago, it began again as his stomach lurched.

Lying on the bottom step was his daughter's tennis shoe with a bloody bone protruding out of it, into the corner. Blood dripped from the leg onto the tile of the foyer, and strips of muscle and skin hung from bone.

Jack bent over as he lost the contents of his stomach, adding color and acidity to the already wet floor. He fell to his knees, and that's when he saw Regan's head. It was sitting in the potted fern by the door. Her eyes were gone, and the flesh was torn from her face.

Slowly, he crawled over to her, envisioning her beautiful face and her bright smile. But when his hand came in contact with slick, rough skull, he knew that what he was seeing was reality. He cupped the head of his daughter in his hand and drew it close into the crook of his arm–his mind and body numb with shock and grief.

Jack's hand absently caressed the top of the bloody skull, his fingers becoming entangled in the few scraps of scalp and clinging hairs that were left. With disgust he shook them off, and as they landed in the blood and vomit mixture with a *plop*, he noticed for the first time that there was a hole in the back and the brains were missing. Around the hole, there were deep groves that looked like they had been made with something long and sharp. The only thing his brain could come up with was tooth marks, but he couldn't think of anything that would be that large and have teeth that big. Now curious, he looked over at the leg that was only a few feet from him. He could also see the grooves on it.

Suddenly, Jack's brain cleared a bit and he remembered his wife. He'd been so shocked at finding the severed pieces of his daughter, he'd forgotten all about her.

"Maggie," he whispered and looked around frantically, but he didn't see any of her lying in the entranceway of their home.

Setting Regan's skull down on the step beside her leg, Jack stood, slipping slightly but righting himself before he fell again. For a moment he stood undecided, looking up the stairs and then down the hall, wondering which way he should go and what horrors might be awaiting him.

Cautiously, he moved through the rooms on the first floor, but found absolutely nothing else alarming. The backyard looked normal, and he even went half way down the basement steps to check if anyone or anything was down there. Nothing was moved or missing.

Again he stood at the bottom of the stairs, tears returning to his eyes as he looked down at the remains of his little girl. She'd only been six years old.

Trudging up the stairs, he gripped the banister once again for balance. As he ascended each step, his heart sank lower. There was still no sound coming from anywhere. If his wife was upstairs, he expected her to be dead.

Jack searched all the rooms, ending in the master bedroom. He was almost surprised to see that the covers of the bed and all of the pillows were shredded–some of them streaked with blood. He examined them more closely and noted that there wasn't enough of the red liquid for it to have been a fatal wound. There was a streak here, a small puddle there, but nothing significant.

He sat down on the bed, letting his head fall forward into his hands. The only thing he could think of was that she'd been kidnapped–by who or what, he didn't know.

In a daze he reached for the handset of the phone that had been knocked out of its cradle and now lay on the floor–assumable by the struggle that had resulted in the appearance of the bed.

His brain was in a fog, but he managed to dial 9-1-1. There was no answer. He frowned down at the phone for a moment and then threw it across the room as hard as he could. Satisfaction ran through him as it shattered the mirror it collided with.

He jumped when a loud booming voice yelled from downstairs.

"Hello? Is anyone here?"

For a split second Jack panicked, thinking he should hide, but he realized that he had nothing to lose. At that moment, he didn't care if he lived or died.

Stumbling like a drunk as his head wound pulsed painfully, Jack made his way downstairs. Just as he turned toward the living room, a burly man appeared in the doorway. They both jumped at the site of each other. The larger man raised a rifle, aiming it at Jack's mid-section.

"If you're robbing me, I don't care," Jack said with a smirk. "Shit, take everything. It means nothing to me."

The large man opened his mouth, but shut it again, lowering his gun. He looked Jack over. He was quite a sight covered in dried blood and vomit. His gray eyes held a hollow sadness and tears quivered on his lashes. But at the same time, his countenance held defiance and strength–his clenched jaw, ridged stance, and harsh tone proved that he was a fighter at heart.

"We aren't here to rob you," the burly man said with surprising gentleness. "We're here to see if there were any survivors, and we found you."

Jack sighed heavily and looked down, the tears finally falling free to wash streaks down his face.

"My name's Ben. Do you have any family? Is there anyone else here? We need to get moving and find somewhere safe. Those . . . things might come back."

Jack's head shot up and a berserk desperation replaced his sadness. "Things? What things? Have you seen them? I think whoever was here took my wife!" He darted forward and gripped the front of Ben's shirt, half dragging the much larger man down to his level. "Tell me, damn you!"

Ben would have laughed at the crazy behavior if it hadn't been warranted. "Calm down, calm down. I don't know exactly what they are yet–I haven't seen them myself. My daughter caught a glimpse of them before she managed to hide."

At the word daughter Jack groaned and released Ben. Going limp, he slid to the floor, sitting with his back against the doorjamb.

"We have to get what supplies we can, and move out. George there, he has a cabin in the woods we can hide in for a while."

Jack glanced to the entrance of the house to see a small group of men standing outside. One nodded at him, Jack assumed he was George. Having been so focused on Ben, he was surprised to see the others.

"What's going on?" Jack said, dragging his hands through his blood crusted hair. "I don't understand any of this. Why do we have to leave? What's happening? Why aren't they answering emergency calls?"

Ben sighed, and squatted down beside Jack. "We aren't entirely sure. We can't reach any emergency personnel. Hank saw something on the news before everything went crazy, he can tell you more than I can."

He looked outside at the group of men who were milling around the yard, waiting to see what they would be doing next. He scanned them with his eyes, not finding the one he wanted.

"Hey!" he yelled. "Has anyone seen Hank?"

A young man, who couldn't have been more than twenty years old, stuck his head in through the door.

"He took a small group and went to the next house," he said. "I guess he figured you had things handled and wanted to check the last few houses before dark."

Ben nodded. "Thanks, Xavier."

The young man nodded and ducked back outside after his eyes darted to Jack briefly.

"So," Ben said. "Are you going to come with us? Or stay here and try to sort things out on your own?"

Jack turned toward the stairs, his eyes falling on what was left of his daughter.

"I'll come with you," he said. "If nothing else, I want to pay those bastards back for what they did to my little girl."

Ben followed his line of vision and saw the skull and leg lying on the step. His jaw tightened in contempt for whoever would do such a thing to anyone, much less a child.

"I have some debts to settle with them as well," Ben said, thinking back to the carnage he'd found in his own home. "Let's get your daughter buried in the backyard while the guys get supplies. We're loading up as many trucks as possible with food and anything else we might need. Oh, I don't think I caught your name."

"Jack," he said standing and nodding. "Jack Henderson." He walked over and gently lifted what was left of Regan into his arms and carried the pieces out to the backyard without another word. From the shed he retrieved a shovel and started digging.

Ben followed him out, stood his rifle against the privacy fence close to the gravesite, and found another shovel in the shed. He too started digging.

It didn't take them long to bury what was left of the girl.

They stood over the small grave, not saying a word. The clangs and bangs of the men gathering food and supplies from the house echoed out to them.

Jack sighed. "Could I have a minute, please?"

Ben nodded, put his shovel away, collected his rifle, and went back into the house.

Jack knelt down and caressed the loose brown dirt with his hand, tears once again springing to his eyes as a lump formed in his throat. For a few moments he had a hard time breathing, but finally he was able to speak.

"I know how much you loved to play out here, so I know you'll be happy to stay. When I think of you, I'll always remember the sound of your laughter and the sight of the sun shining in your golden hair as you ran and played. I'll always love you, and I'll always remember you. I promise that I'll find Mommy and make sure she's okay. And I'll make whoever hurt you suffer for what they did. I love you, Regan. Daddy will always love you."

Bending forward, Jack rested his forehead on the grave and sobbed.

Two hours later, twenty men, three women, and one child journeyed to George's cabin. Jack fell asleep soon after they started out. He was spent physically and emotionally, but he soon woke up when shooting started.

Reaching for the 9mm pistol one of the men had given him, he looked around wildly. It was now dark, and he couldn't see anything beyond the truck windows.

"What's going on?" he asked the driver and felt bad that he couldn't remember his name.

"Don't know," the man said, spitting out the window, the juice from his chewing tobacco hitting the asphalt with a sickening splash. "Sounds like we're in for a little bit of excitement. Maybe we'll get to plug a couple of those murdering freaks."

The man opened his door and climbed out, taking his pump, 12-gauge shotgun with him. The *click-click* of the shotgun's slide echoed through the night, causing Jack to shudder as he too exited the vehicle, gripping the 9 in his sweaty palm.

Another spray of gunfire blasted from the lead truck. Its shiny red paint reflected the flares from the muzzles, creating split second flashes of blinding light. In those brief seconds Jack saw what they were firing at and his blood went cold.

 Five tall figures shrouded in black cloaks were standing on top of a grass-covered hill. Two of the Beings were holding leashes of grotesque monsters. Brief glimpses of the creatures revealed images reserved for the worst of nightmares.

One of the monsters was as big as a bull, with a head and mouth similar to a bear's, but with a longer snout and teeth that were as long as a grown man's arm. Blood dripped from its jaws as it roared and snarled, its own teeth cutting into its flesh. Prancing on six legs that were nothing but muscle under translucent skin, it strained the chain that its master held.

The other monster was smaller, more worm like, with a giant centipede body that wriggled as its numerous talon tipped legs pawed at the soft brown earth–it too strained for release. Its entire face seemed to unfold into a huge mouth with multiple rows of blood stained teeth, and even over the gunshots Jack could hear it making sucking noises.

With eardrum straining shrill cries, the Beings released the monsters. They advanced toward the string of humanity on the road, the bullets not deterring them at all.

The bull creature slammed head first into the lead truck, which could barely be seen around a slight bend in the road. Roaring ferociously, it ripped the door of the truck open and pulled out the occupants with its teeth and claws while they continued to shoot blindly into the air. Soon screams and the crunching of bones were the only things that could be heard from ahead.

The worm creature was stealthier. It attacked the people in the second truck, slinking behind them as they aimed their guns at the bull-beast. Quickly crawling up their backs, it latched its huge mouth around their heads. With a sharp snapping noise, it pulverized their skulls and sucked out their brains.

Jack was in shock at how quickly it moved. He also noticed that bullets were having no effect on the monsters. They bounced off the almost armor like plating of the worm's body, and the bull just seemed too thick with muscle to even feel them, as if the bullets were nothing more than mosquitoes.

After the bull had finished its meal of the occupants of the lead truck, it turned its attention to Jack and the man with him. They stood slack jawed and paralyzed with fear as they were targeted.

Jack was the first to recover. His arm shot up and he fired the 9 as fast as he could, emptying the clip at them. They kept coming, ready to make the men the next course of their meal.

BOOM!

A shotgun blasted so close to Jack's head that he thought he would be deaf for the rest of his life. But luckily, the shot had been true, and had blown half of the worm's legs off on one side, the hollow point shredding flesh as it moved through.

It fell to the ground, squealing like a pig, but in a much higher pitch. The bull, having only been a few steps behind, came to a sudden halt and sniffed the injured creature. Its long tongue snaked out and licked at the worm's brilliant orange blood. Seeming to like what it tasted, its tongue shot out again and wrapped around the squirming, squealing, injured creature, trapping it between its jaws with an audible crunch. Blood gushed out of the bull's mouth while it snacked on its dinner companion.

Jack nudged the driver. "I think we should get out of here while we still have a chance."

The driver nodded and they backed up the couple of steps to the truck, not taking their eyes off of the devouring monster. The truck was still running. They climbed in slowly and closed the doors behind them, locking them securely, although they would have no effect on keeping the beast out if it decided to attack. Ripping the gearshift into reverse and pressed on the accelerator hard, the driver took off at a speed that caused Jack's head to slam against the dashboard.

"Hold on!" the man yelled, as he jerked the wheel and spun the truck around, slamming into drive.

"Holy shit, man!" Jack exclaimed, gripping the seat and the door.

"Better reload," was all the man said in response.

Jack looked up to see the bull running after them at full speed, with some of the worm's legs dangling from its gaping mouth. Slick orange goo dripped from the appendages onto the asphalt, causing the giant monster to slip. It slid sideways and went down on its stomach once, before getting back up and continuing its pursuit.

He hurriedly reloaded the shotgun, and leaned out the window to take a shot. The recoil of the shotgun slammed into his shoulder, nearly throwing him out of the truck window and into the monster's path. But just at the moment he was sure his life was at an end, the driver of the truck swerved and righted Jack before he fell.

Once he had his equilibrium back, he saw that his shot had been a good one. He'd hit the beast in the eye. It stumbled, growled deep in its throat, and fell to the ground, pawing at its eye. A watery green substance gushed from the wound, bathing the ground with slick monster blood.

"Got it!" Jack yelled, climbing back into the cab of the truck.

The other man grunted and kept his eyes on the road in front of them.

The caravan drove with no real direction, following one road after another. The blackness of night gradually gave way to purple, and before they knew it, the sun was peeking over the horizon. Feeling safer in the light, they stopped to regroup and decide how to proceed.

Hank, the one who seemed to know the most about the Beings, came up with a plan. They would now be going straight into the woods, and hiding off the main roads. He believed the Beings were watching the roads and waiting for what he called, 'Meals on Wheels,' to come along so they could feed their pets.

Starting out once again, they turned onto the first dirt road they passed. It didn't take long before they were deep in the woods. Everyone was tired and hungry when they finally stopped again around midday. It was almost like a picnic as they sat in the shade, under the bright green leaves of the trees as the sun shone above them in a bright blue sky, but the armed guards that kept watch and switched out to take their turn to eat dispelled whatever pleasant picnic atmosphere they could have mustered.

For the next two days they traversed the countryside looking for a place that was safe, and only spied a small group of Beings in the distance once. They were now down to fifteen men and two women, after the attack on the road. Some wished that they hadn't decided on quad cab trucks; then there wouldn't have been so many lost at one time. Everyone was sad over the loss of the only child that had been traveling with them. Ben's ten-year-old daughter. She'd been in the first truck, and so had Ben. Since he'd been lost, Hank was now in charge.

It was by accident that they finally found a place to stay. Xavier had wandered a little way off over a hill to relieve himself and had stumbled upon an old farm. The house was in shambles, but he decided to take a closer look to see if there was anything they could salvage. Going around to the far side of the house, to find a safe place to enter the abandoned dwelling, he spied a small wooden door set low in the side of the hill. Curious, he went over and opened it. A musty smell emanated from the depths of a dark cave like opening. The angle of the sun did little to dispel the gloom more than a foot or two, so he came back to the group and a couple of men went with him to explore, while the rest stayed behind with the trucks.

Moral was low. Everyone was scared. They didn't talk much about the creatures or the attack on the road. Not knowing what would happen from day to day, and not knowing if something was waiting around the next corner to devour them was taking its toll.

Everyone was silent as they watched the hill and the sun that was setting behind it. Anxious glances were cast at the shadows of the forest that surrounded them. Every sound, every breeze that rustled leaves, made them more nervous. When a shriek and angry, excited yelling broke through the quietness of dusk, hands flew to guns that were never far from reach, and they all backed up against trucks or trees, or anything else solid they were close to.

"No! Leave! Get away! They'll find us! You'll lead them to me again! I can't go back there!"

Two men hauled a half-naked, crazed old man over the hill. Xavier followed a couple of steps behind, rubbing his head and frowning.

"Calm down, you old coot," Mark, one of the haulers, snapped. "You're gonna' draw more attention with your mouth than we ever did with the trucks."

Will, the other hauler, huffed and tried to keep the man under control. "You're damn lucky we didn't shoot you. I'm still tempted, so don't push me too far!"

The old man went limp and had to be dragged along the ground as he whimpered and pleaded pathetically.

Hank met the men when they were half way down the hill. He spoke to Mark and Will quietly, glancing down at the old man. Nodding and listening to what the men told him, he got excited.

Grinning from ear to ear, Hank turned and announced that they'd found somewhere to stay. Apparently the cave that Xavier found was a large fruit cellar with a tunnel that led all the way through the hill to come up in the hatch of a barn. It would be the perfect place for them. It would hide them, and it had an alternate entrance in case they needed a way out.

That was where they found the old man. He'd heard someone open the door and had scurried through the tunnel and out into the barn. When Xavier had stuck his head through to check the place out, the old man had slammed the heavy wooden door down on him and tried to run for it, thinking he was in danger from the Beings. Will and Mark had chased the old man down and tackled him, bringing him back to get some answers.

Everyone was excited and grins spread across every face at the prospect of having a permanent, safe home. They felt exposed and vulnerable being out in the open all the time. Quickly they set up camp on the other side of the hill, using wood from the old farmhouse for firewood. Most everyone went to bed early. Stress made everyone tired, but Hank, Jack, and a few others wanted to find out more about the ranting of the crazy old man. They'd had to tie him up and gag him just to keep him still and quiet.

Venturing deep into the tunnel with flashlights, Hank laid down the law.

"Don't try anything, you crazy bastard," he said, pulling the gag from the man's mouth. "We just want to talk. If you get squirrelly we'll shoot you. We don't want to be found by those creatures any more than you do. First off, what's your name?"

"Earl," he said, swallowing and stretching his mouth. "My name is Earl James. You don't understand what you are dealing with."

He looked up at the men surrounding him with a wild look in his eyes, fed off of fear and desperation.

Hank squatted down in front of Earl. "That's why we wanted to talk to you. Can you tell us more about the Beings? We want to understand what those *things* are, so we can figure out how to deal with them and stay alive."

Earl laughed. The sound was void of mirth and made the other men shift uncomfortably. "You can't understand them. No one can understand Hell incarnate."

Hank didn't reply, he just watched Earl and waited.

"We tried to run from them, but they were too fast," Earl finally said with a sigh. "My family and I. Someone said something about an announcement on the news about some scientific experiment gone wrong. They were trying to create a portal to an alternate universe or some shit. Who knows! Those scientific people are crazy!"

Hank looked down at his hands and stood. "Yes, I saw that broadcast."

"Wait," Jack said, stepping forward. "You mean these things are from an alternate dimension or universe? That's just crazy! There's no such thing!"

"Jack," Hank said. "Calm down. It was all over the news. It's legit, or at least it's the closet explanation we have." He paused and put his hands on Jack's shoulders, looking him straight in the eyes. "You saw those monsters when we were attacked on the road. Where would you say they came from? Nowhere I know of, or have ever heard of, has creatures like that. Unless you want to take a trip to Hell, and I don't think you need to, because it's here."

Jack clenched his jaw. "What does that mean for my wife? Where is she? Gone to another universe?"

"The Hall of Twelve."

Both men turned back to look down at Earl. "Where?" they asked in unison.

Earl leaned forward. Spit was collecting in the corners of his mouth, making it appear as if he were rapid and mad.

"The Hall of Twelve," he whispered and cackled dementedly.

"That's where they took us. Took us all . . . Roll the dice . . . See if you live . . ."

Hank stepped back from Jack and glanced at each man in turn. They all shrugged.

"What's the Hall of Twelve? What are you talking about? Dice? Roll?"

Earl started to shake and rock back and forth. "It's a place of evil, of death. They take you there. They make you to roll the dice. Only one number will set you free. The rest lead to your doom." He cackled again and started mumbling to himself. "I rolled free . . . I rolled free . . . I rolled free . . ."

A chill went down Jack's spine, adding credence to what the old man said. He wanted to believe Earl was just insane and none of it was true. But something deep inside his soul said the place existed and it was where he would find his wife.

Hank couldn't get any more information out of Earl. In the end they let him go. He ran out of the tunnel like Hounds of Hell were chasing him, and in his mind, they were.

The men left the tunnel and joined the rest of the survivors in the camp. Hank and Jack decided to keep watch, since both of them had too much on their minds to sleep.

Hours passed as the two men sat by the fire, staring into the flames, each lost in their own thoughts. Just before dawn they heard a distant howl. They jumped, ripped from their reverie. Looking at each other they picked up and readied their guns, standing.

"Should we put out the fire?" Jack asked in an urgent whisper.

Hank shook his head no.

They waited.

The howl sounded again, closer.

"What should we *do*?" Jack asked again, panic edging into his voice.

Hank didn't answer right away, but seemed to think about his response. "Wake everyone. If they come here, everyone needs to be ready to move."

As quietly as possible they woke one person after another, who in turn, woke someone else, until they were all awake. By that time Hank had decided they should hide in the tunnel, so they did.

Everyone funneled in as the howling grew increasingly closer and louder, with shrieks joining in. Shaking with fear, everyone stood in the darkness waiting to see what was going to happen next.

The howls suddenly ceased and everyone breathed a silent sigh of relief, only to scream when something large attacked the door to the cave that lead to the tunnel. Giant claws splintered the rotting wood of the door. The beast roared menacingly as two noses on long appendages similar to large fingers, reached through the opening and caught their scent. It ripped the door off to get to them. Luckily for the people hiding inside, the beast was too large to fit through the opening.

"Run!" Hank screamed, firing at the creature, blowing one of its noses off. It roared in pain and anger. Attacking again, it used its huge paws to dig out the opening, making it larger.

Rushing through the tunnel in the blackness caused many of the people to fall, tripping others, causing injuries and drawing blood. It seemed like forever before they reached the barn, and they couldn't get out fast enough. In their panic they hurt each other further.

Behind them the beast had gotten into the tunnel. They could hear it thumping and growling as it followed. As they fought to get out, a woman tripped and knocked herself and another woman down the hole. Their screams of pain as they were eaten alive echoed out of the hatch. Hank and Will slammed it shut and rolled a heavy, metal fifty-five gallon drum over it and sat it up, hoping against all odds that it would slow the creature down.

No one stayed together; they scattered across the countryside.

Jack headed west, away from the sun, seeking darkness to hide him. Not knowing the region hurt him badly. He found himself in a swamp. Falling forward in the deep, silty mud, he lost his gun, leaving him defenseless.

He could hear someone coming behind him and crawled over to a small pond. He broke off a reed, stuck it in his mouth, and lay face down in the water behind a fallen log, hoping the Beings would pass him by.

The roar of the giant, digging monster was getting further and further away. Jack figured it was going after the smell of blood from one of the injured people. He didn't know if there were Beings with the creature, but he assumed there were. It was better to err on the side of caution in his opinion.

Lying completely still, he focused on slowing his breathing to become as invisible as possible. He heard someone or *something* coming. Silently, he prayed they wouldn't be able to find him and would pass by.

Branches snapped and he heard hissing. Whatever was there advanced closer and closer to his hiding place. Still, he held himself immobile. Chirping and buzzing followed the hissing and it sounded like there was more than one of them.

Jack thought about lifting his head and peeking over the log, but he was too scared to risk it. Time passed slowly as he waited. Finally he heard noises that told him they were moving away. With a sigh of relief when he could no longer hear anything and thought he was alone, he lifted his face from the water and took the reed out of his mouth.

Suddenly he caught movement out of the corner of his eye and felt intense pain in his back and shoulder when a dark cloaked figure landed on his back with a threatening hiss. The six-inch claws that adorned its huge foot dug into his flesh, one curled around his shoulder and stabbed into his chest, while the rest sunk deep into his spine.

Jack screamed, his body jerking in utter agony. He tried to turn and fight the Being off, but he realized that it had severed his spine, leaving his body useless. As he fought and cried out, he was forced to swallow mouthful after mouthful of the water he was pinned down in, choking him and almost drowning him. But, just before the mercy of death took him from the horror that had attacked him, the Being removed its claws, gripped his neck, and lifted him from the quagmire.

He was held, dangling over the ground, blood and water dripping from him, while the Being inspected him.

Looking down at the Being, he wished it had killed him and gotten it over with. The creature scared him. Deep violet eyes stared back at him. They glowed with hate and malice. He could feel the Beings consciousness violating his whenever he looked directly into them. It made him feel dirty as it slithered through his mind with the sneakiness of a snake. Closing his eyes, he denied the Being access. It shrieked and shook him, trying to make him open his eyes again, but Jack refused. The three fingered, smooth hand that gripped his throat tightened, but still he didn't comply.

Now angry, the Being slammed him down on the ground violently.

The last thing Jack saw before he lost consciousness was other survivors that had been captured being chained together by more of the Beings.

The old man's words, *'Hall of Twelve . . .'* echoed through his head as the blessed blackness of oblivion overtook him.

When Jack awoke, he was laying on a filthy cement floor. Feces and urine were intermixed with decaying straw and mud, supplying him with a disgusting pillow. Spitting he tried to sit up, only to wince and cry out in pain. Everything came back in a flash, and he knew his body no longer worked. He was doomed. Slowly, he looked around, noticing for the first time that he wasn't alone.

There were ten other people crammed into the barn stall with him. There were bars running vertically up the top half and the bottom consisted of rough, thick wooden boards. Everyone was quiet and watching the door, dreading that it would open at any moment and something horrible would be standing there, ready to torture them. They all knew it would happen. It was just a matter of when. The waiting caused the fear to grow and build inside the minds of the humans awaiting their fate.

Distantly, Jack could hear the opening and closing of a heavy door, followed by screaming. All around them were sounds of other people packed too close together, weeping, mumbling, and shuffling about.

"Still alive, huh?"

Jack looked to his left and saw Xavier sitting in the opposite corner, almost hidden from view by others.

"Yeah, unfortunately," Jack said, hissing in pain as someone accidentally bumped into him, trying to make themselves more comfortable.

They didn't get the opportunity to speak further, as the door was yanked open and three Beings hissed at the captives inside. They freaked out and started trying to press themselves against the back wall. They trampled on the old, young, and wounded.

The Beings chirped at each other and started dragging people out, shoving them into a cattle shoot with a barbed wire roof, forcing them to squat down and shuffle forward if they didn't want to get cut. Fear lead to panic, panic lead to shoving, and shoving lead to a few people running face first into the barbed wire.

Jack cringed as a young woman lost both of her eyes to the sharp metal. She screamed as blood ran down her face, her eyeballs now shredded. Without thinking she stood up and tried to run, wrapping more of the wire around her neck. No one tried to help her. They just pushed past as she struggled–slicing her throat and strangling herself to death.

When everyone was out except for Jack, one of the Beings grabbed a hold of one of his legs and dragged him out. Knowing there was no way he could traverse the shoot, they continued to drag him to where it led. Cement steps, uneven floors, and drainage ditches battered him relentlessly. He blacked out a couple of times because of the pain, only to regain awareness and be beaten back into unconsciousness.

They arrived at a table set between two doors. One was off to the right, and lead into a cement block building. The other was behind the table, set into the wooded wall of the barn they were in.

One of the Beings lumbered over and sat behind the table. Its clawed feet clicked on the floor while it waited, like a human would drum their nails on a table top in a show of boredom.

Jack forced himself to blink rapidly and began looking for his wife, hoping to see her one last time. He knew that in his current state he couldn't save her, and that brought tears to his eyes. He felt weak and worthless. What kind of man was he? He couldn't save himself, much less his wife, even if he did find her.

He was watching the Beings empty more stalls of people into the shoot, and each time someone was pulled out and shoved into the narrow passage his heart jumped with the hope of seeing the woman he loved. She never appeared.

A movement to Jack's right alerted him that something was happening. A young man was pulled from the shoot and shoved over to the table. The Being sitting behind the table and under the only light in the room–a bare bulb hanging from a wire–nudged a set of dice toward the man. Jack could see the dice clearly from where he sat, and a chill ran down his spine. They were made of bone, and the dots were made of dried blood. He was betting that it was human bone and blood that made up the squares of chance.

The Being nudged the dice toward the man again, hissing loudly. He glanced up at the Being that stood beside him and then at the one sitting behind the table. Slowly and reluctantly, he reached forward and gripped the small objects in his hand. Swallowing hard, he dropped them back onto the table. Both of the Beings leaned forward and examined the dice, chirping and clicking to each other.

Roughly, the Being standing beside the man gripped his arm and dragged him to the door on the right, the one that lead into another building, or part of the building they were in. The heavy, metal door was pulled open. Roaring and growls could be heard coming from what appeared to be a brightly lit tunnel. The man screamed and tried to fight, but the Being was too strong for him. The door was closed behind them, but everyone could still hear the screams of the man. A sudden loud and particularly menacing growl made everyone jump. It was followed by more of the man's screams, which quickly fell silent.

The door opened again, and the Being stepped out, closing the door. A middle-aged woman was pulled from the shoot next. She knew what she was supposed to do and apparently wanted it over with quickly. Without prompting, she picked up the dice and threw them back onto the table, staring straight ahead at the wall. The Beings hissed, and the one sitting at the table slammed its hand down roughly.

The woman was forcefully pushed toward the door behind the table. The Being opened it. Bright sunshine flooded the barn. Birds sang merrily outside and green grass shone brightly. The smell of fresh air stirred the people in the shoot. They started shaking the sides, trying to get free, but it was no use.

The woman was shoved outside and the door was slammed shut behind her. Jack wondered what she had rolled. Earl's words, *'Roll the dice . . . See if you live . . .'* echoed through his head. The crazy bastard had been right.

The handler Being reached into the shoot to pull out their next victim, but the one at the table hissed and pointed at Jack.

He shuddered and gulped. It was his turn.

The Being lifted him off the floor and held him up high enough that he could see the table. The dice were nudged toward him. Jack picked them up, his right hand the only part of his body that he could move other than his head, and examined them as they lay in his palm. He rolled them around and noticed that one of the dice didn't have a three on it. It was blank. That's when it hit him. With normal dice you couldn't roll a one. But, with one of the numbers missing from one of the dice, then it became possible to roll a one and every other number adding up to twelve. To roll a one had to be the first door, the one that lead to the outside and freedom.

His chances were slim, but with a deep breath he threw down the squares of bone and prayed that he would roll a one. It didn't happen.

Frowning down at the dice, Jack added them up. Ten. He'd rolled a ten. The Beings chirped and clicked happily again, and he was carried to the door on the right. He flinched as the entrance was opened and he was momentarily blinded by the bright light.

He clung to the Being that carried him, fearing what might be awaiting him. The roaring and growls were intensely loud in the hallway. Each door they passed had a number on it. He noted fresh, red blood was running freely from beneath door number four and into the drainage ditch in the center of the hall floor.

That must have been the first man, Jack thought shuddering.

Before he was ready, they were standing in front of door number ten. There was a heavy metal bar across it, to keep whatever was inside from getting out. Jack could hear whatever was in there moving around and sniffing at the door.

The Being removed the bar, opened the door, and threw him inside. The door was slammed shut and he heard the scrap of metal on metal as the bar was put back into place.

The room was gloomy and void of any furniture. There was one window high in the wall. It had bars and no glass. Sunshine beamed down from that single opening, lighting a patch of the brick floor. Dried blood and small pieces of bone scattered the bare surface, an ominous sign of what was to become of Jack.

A purring growl from the far dark corner alerted Jack to the creature's whereabouts.

Shuffling and sniffing got closer and closer to the center of the room where the sunny patch was. Jack watched in morbid fascination as a creature like none he'd ever seen before stepped into the light and showed itself.

It looked almost human in some ways. Its face was similar, but its head was mounted upside down. The entire top of its head was its mouth, with long sharp teeth waiting to eat. Hair hung from its chin like a beard, but was brunette, lustrous, and curly like those women's he'd seen on hair color commercials. Its skin color was almost white it was so pale. Its arms, legs, and torso, were also similar to a humans, except they were three times as long and very skinny. On each hand it had four extremely long fingers that had suction cups instead of pads.

It stood watching Jack, while he sat watching it. Stepping forward slowly, it purred again, licking its upside down mouth, its tongue swirled around the top of its head.

Jack gasped as he saw something moving in the creature's mid-section. The face of a human pressed against the skin, stretching it. Something about the face was familiar to Jack, and after a moment of shocked disbelief, he knew it was his wife.

When Jack gasped, the creature growled and leapt forward, going down on all fours, opening its mouth wide.

Jack was unable to defend himself.

The monster bit off Jack's right arm, spraying blood all over itself and Jack in the process. Quickly swallowing the limb whole, it came back for more, biting off Jack's other arm, tugging violently to severe skin and bone.

Screams, wild, terrified screams almost deafened Jack. It took him a moment to realize they were his. He lay on his side, his blood gushing out of him to fill the cracks between the bricks; he realized that no one stood a chance. Even if his wife had been alive, he couldn't have saved her. No one was safe.

The beast quickly bit off and ate his legs, leaving nothing more than a torso with a head bleeding on the floor. Jack could feel the darkness of death coming for him. He welcomed it, knowing death was better than living in this new world where the Beings reigned, where pain and torture were the only options.

"Maggie . . . Regan . . . I'm sorry I couldn't save you," Jack whispered with his last breath, as the monster ripped off his head with a liquid crunch.

EDEN ROYCE

DEVILS PLAYGROUND

Night is the time when
Yellow Sun becomes Blood Moon
Evil comes to play

Darkness hosts the game
Tree branches like dried fingers
Indicate the starting line

There are no time outs
While you live you must join in
Last hope for this race

Come! Sit in the swing
When he pushes your back, feel
Breath full of cold heat

Leap off and tumble
Run and hide He is counting
The time you have left

Cold hands Touch of ice
He's found you Game over
Until tomorrow…

ALL YOUR FLESH ARE BELONG TO US: A ZOMBIE TALE

By JASON M. BLOOM

He had been playing for over three straight hours now, and was working up a powerful thirst. After waking up from a fitful dream, peppered with images and sounds from the last bloody skirmish, Jonathan Goldman had shot up in bed, a line of sweat just under his jagged hairline. The dream had barely even registered; he couldn't even remember a time when he didn't wake up like that. He just sort of shrugged it off, his focus reserved for something else, something more important to him than dreams, or even breakfast.

He pushed the tip of his dirty sock outward from his seat, using his toes to wedge open the mini-fridge enough to get one hand in while he continued to use the other one to click the mouse. He felt around for another can of Gamer Power Juice, the last word thrown in by marketers to ensure the beverage sounded like it was not entirely made of sugar and water, which was clever but not altogether the truth. As far as Jonathan was concerned, it was just the fuel he needed to get through. There was also a leftover bowl of instant noodles, a thin film of oil coating the surface, but to Jonathan, although he had been playing for hours, he had just woken up, and it was not yet time for breakfast. Not that food was his primary motivation. He had other needs to feed; other desires more pressing than shoveling gobs of sustenance into his maw.

He was currently logged in to his favorite game, the only thing that truly kept him going, the sole thing on his mind; the addiction from those rushing endorphins made each victory that much sweeter, it was as if he could barely control himself. The game even followed him into his dreams, playing over and over again while his eyeballs worked overtime, pulsing back and forth under his fleshy lids. He had spent endless hours working on intricate strategies, marking up detailed maps, annotating moves and analyzing data, simply to keep ahead of the other players.

It wasn't always like this. Once upon a time, Jonathan was enrolled in a University, he took online courses in Computer Design and Programming, with a minor in creative writing, you know, to help with game content. He spent nights filling freelance gigs, working on websites for chefs and musicians, lawyers and small companies that deposited cash in his bank account, which he dutifully used to order things he needed, like pizzas and Chinese food, and occasionally a new game or piece of equipment for his Media Lab, or Studio Apartment, depending on who you asked.

Plopping the Gamer Power Juice can down onto the desk, he ran his free hand through his thick, greasy mop as the bluish light flickered across his eyeballs. They moved back and forth across the screen, checking his reserves, studying his defenses, positioning his troops, ready to make his move. He glanced at his currently opponent, logged in as De@thde@ler11, and the corners of his mouth twitched. Suddenly Jonathan got curious about the online queue, and flipped open a second screen to peer at the list of other players logged in. There was necrotix69, tehShamblerr, Gr@veW@lker2 and fle$hbot. These appeared to be the best of the best, the most highly ranked around, and Jonathan was right up there. He was currently ranked number five in the Americas, and number seventeen in the world, which wasn't too bad, considering he had only gotten into this game over the past six months. Before this, he spent far too much time working on projects or schoolwork, but all that changed when the dead began to roam the streets, stalking the living and devouring their flesh.

To Jonathan, the changes were minimal. He already spend the majority of his time indoors, so he proceeded to board up the windows and doors in the downstairs entryway, and barricaded himself on the second floor. He was able to use the fire escape to forage for supplies with no problems, glad for the fact that reanimated corpses found coordinating ladders quite impossible. He blacked out his windows so the pulsing of computer screens would not attract any undue attention, and found that buckets worked just fine for collecting rainwater from the roof and waste from himself, which he dutifully emptied each day into the narrow alley on one side of his apartment building.

He had never known his neighbors, and probably never would now that they had all been turned into shambling zombies. The once-bustling city was the first place to be overpowered by the endless hordes of teeming, rotting husks as they ate their way through the streets with a fury. A sturdy pair of noise-canceling headphones kept the screams at bay, shrieks of anguish and howls of despair from the living and dying, sounds which ripped and clawed their way through his thick curtains. The grunting and growling from the dead did not bother him, it became like white noise now, as they shuffled aimlessly through the ruined city streets, occasionally banging against doors and windows in their endless search for a tasty meal. As for Jonathan, he had no more responsibilities, no more homework, no more clients, and all the time in the world.

A gamer for most of his life, Jonathan relished his time unwinding, although to the uninitiated, the game itself seemed more like work than actual work. Carefully balancing resource management, military strategy, offense, defense and chat appeared overwhelming, but was all easily monitored by Jonathan. Compared to deadlines and difficult coding exercises, micromanagement in gaming was relaxing and even cathartic. He allowed his brain to shut down and go on autopilot, empty himself of the daily stresses as his eyes and hands moved mechanically, fluidly moving and rearranging pixels and manipulating his opponents. But this game session was different.

His current opponent was not playing this match like he usually did; Jonathan had played against this guy many times before, both before the dead stalked the streets and many times afterwards. Fortunately, the Internet itself did not shut down, which made sense; it wasn't centrally located, and there certainly was no OFF switch. As long as electricity could be generated, and the lines stayed intact, it was viable, even though most everything else was kaput. Phone lines, televisions, radios, and most satellites stopped broadcasting, leaving many of the survivors bereft. Small personal generators helped immensely; Jonathan had one that he had liberated from a local hardware store and hauled into the small attic space above his apartment, nestled safely from the weather and insulated so that the noise was buffered by the walls and the thick pink insulation. Electricity was necessary for running monitors and hard drives, the CPU could not work without the life-giving volts that ran through its circuits.

But Jonathan himself needed very little: his small refrigerator, a few lamps, the buckets, and his computer. He cooked with a small gas stove, fueled by propane tanks pilfered from around town, and his appetite reflected a simplistic palette; food was simply funneled into his body to keep him going, and he often ate without thinking about it, shoveling with one hand. He used bottled drinks to stay hydrated, and washed up with the collected water from the buckets and pots and pans scattered on the roof. Lucky for Jonathan the weather had been cooperative, he wasn't sure what he would do when the rain stopped falling and snowflakes took its place, probably melt the snow into water, he supposed, but that was a few months away.

But the thought that warmed him was the simple fact that the Internet was not something so easily dispatched as a single television, or even a radio station. It was more like a super-organism, a living being, its hydra-like heads represented by the multitudes of monitors blanketing the world, its reach poking like tentacles into every wired house, every connected business, each hot spot and cafe from Montreal to Tokyo. It was ubiquitous, and simply impossible to terminate. Sever one connection, and two more would spring up in its place. Well, not exactly, but to Jonathan, its' very survival was linked to his own; it was his lifeline, his connection. Many servers were already down, most of the internet at this point was simply the cached pages of out of date websites, message boards looking for help with missing people, stuffed with threads for survival tips, theories on the outbreak, and recipes for painless suicides. Not all areas appeared to be connected, but the servers Jonathan tapped into for his gaming needs apparently remained untouched, connecting users from across the states and even various points overseas: Brazil, Hong Kong, Australia, Korea.

His current opponent was logging in from a server, which connected him to Seoul in South Korea, and the program that ran the chat script translated his keystrokes into US English, so Jonathan could read it easily. It was the only human communication he had had for over three months now; the city had gone mute around him, all except for the constant moans of the dead. But up until today, it had mostly been leetspeak.

"lol u got pwn3d!", "OMFG killsh0t is t3h r0xx0rz", "pew pew ftw!!1!", and "QQ n00b, kekeke!" Only once did someone type "l@ym in pr0n" which was not very troubling to Jonathan, since he knew for certain that both his parents were dead long before the zombie uprising began.

But today there was no chat at all, and his opponent certainly wasn't playing like his usual self. His troops were disorganized, his strategy embarrassing, his defense a Swiss cheese-like mess of holes. Jonathan easily swept in and destroyed an entire civilization, razing the whole city, leveling buildings and massacring citizen after citizen; this one taken down while mining for gold, that one shot in the back while cutting some lumber. Innocent civilian and veteran soldier alike, Jonathan mercilessly destroyed them, detachedly snuffing each one out of existence. Devoid of feeling, he was a like killing machine, which incidentally was his screen name, K1llMach1n3.

The match ended quickly and the stats screen popped up. Jonathan's fingers quickly skimmed across his keyboard, entering a quip into the chat box. "GG. ur teh suck!! i haz mad skillz." Then, nothing. He expected a quick reply, but the chat simply hung there, unanswered, not even a simple O RLY? to continue the berating. He tried again. "u suk b1g t1m3." Nothing. Jonathan was about to switch back over to the main screen again when "rgheksl sjfierongnxl;knvfjpkjffffffffffffff" crawled across the screen, filling up the small chat box with nonsense. It was almost like his opponent, thousands of miles away, was leaning on the keyboard.

Jonathan lost interest and switched to the menu screen, selecting the multiplayer option and waited for his next opponent to join the game. Maybe he would have better luck in another part of the world, since Korea was such a disappointment this morning. The computer made the ding noise that meant a player had been selected and they were set to play a match. He glanced at the screen, it read: br@ine@ ter4U. Jonathan didn't even smirk, even though the previous time he had seen this moniker he nearly snorted Gamer Power Juice through his nose. He just wanted to play, the jokes were growing stale and he was getting hungry and cranky.

The game started and he found his new opponent no better than the last; sluggish play, slow to adapt, he practically walked around his enemy and destroyed them. He was confused. It seemed everyone was having an off day. He opened the chat and typed rapidly. "WTF? I'm liek a N00BC4NN0N!" The reply he got back was a new one for him.

"go ez plz, n00b tryin 2 lern gmae."

Jonathan sat in stunned silence for a moment. This wasn't right, he had played this particular opponent numerous times, and his stats were far better than his own. He rightfully should have been owned, but this guy barely put up a fight. *What gives?* he thought. Could this be another player, masquerading with someone else's screen name? Possible, but highly doubtful, as this game site was very particular about that, and so Jonathan responded.

"wut giv3z? i played u l@st w33k! y do u suk so much n0w?" he typed, then sat back and waited. There was such a significant gap between chats that Jonathan thought maybe the connection might have been lost. He had reached into the fridge and retrieved another can to drink, and he was contemplating firing up the stove to heat up something to eat when the chat window came back with a response.

"jsut turn3d, having tr0ubl3 adjusting." Jonathan rubbed his eyes in disbelief. Did this guy really expect him to swallow that whopper? After all he had gone through, all he did on a daily basis just to survive, and this guy a world away was busting his chops about turning into a member of the living dead? And that was his excuse for a crappy game? Now, fully annoyed, Jonathan's fingers flew as he typed a response. "St0p scr3wing around! u suk!!1! ur not ded, u ju3t suk @ this gmae."

The reply was quicker this time. "NO, i am ded. no 1 el3e aliv3 h3r3." But that couldn't be, Jonathan thought feverishly. Then it dawned on him, he couldn't recall the last time he saw another living person in the past four months. In all of his recent memory, and during all of his latest foraging expeditions, he had not seen another living soul, only the remains of humanity; scattered, lost, shambling around looking to finish the last of his doomed race. Apparently, that inevitability may be closer than he had thought.

"wh3r3 RU?" The chat box popped into view, the short query burning into Jonathan's eyeballs, although rightfully it could have been all of the excessive screen time. "rite h3r3," he typed, and the query came back again. "wh3r3 RU?!" it screamed in his brain.

"@mer1c@."

"w@t c1ty?"

"Y?"

"w@t c1ty?" the chat was insistent, and Jonathan fought his reservations with a terse reply.

"s3@tt13." He thought better of it, and added "Y???"

"1 h@v3 c0nt@ctz th3r3. i'll s3nd sum1 2 u."

Decisively, Jonathan clicked out of the chat screen, then out of the menu and the game altogether. His skin burned, felt prickly, the back of his neck was burning up and his head was swimming. He tried to stand up, and he nearly fell down again. He felt nauseous, and decided he should really eat something. But tears started to come to the corners of his eyes. *"What was happening?!"* he thought furiously, on the verge of losing it entirely. He was on the edge of freaking out as he sat back on his mattress, clutching his stomach and rocking slightly back and forth, which he did only when he was in a really bad place. Had that guy been telling the truth? Could Jonathan really be it, the last living person in a land filled with the undead? His head felt very light, as if it were filled with helium and about to lift off from his shoulders and float away. His room started to look fuzzy around the edges, as if seeing everything from beneath the surface of water, and all of a sudden, everything went dark.

Jonathan awoke to the sounds of banging outside of his building. His head was pounding, but he could still hear the muffled noise in the streets below clearly; a cacophony of trash cans smashing, wooden planks tearing free from their moorings, glass tinkling as it hit the cracked asphalt and was crunched to a fine dust underfoot. He got up, slowly, and headed over to the window, tugging the dark curtain aside ever so slightly, just enough to peer at the scene below. He gasped.

It was dusk, and even though he had a decent view of the entire length of the street, all he could see were the rotting tops of zombie heads. He stared at the partially exposed cranium bones, flaps of torn scalp, muscle and tissue, gray bits of rotting skin and strands of hair hanging limply as the area teemed with the walking dead, searching, moving with a single purpose, and hungry for him. Releasing the blackout curtain he swiftly ducked back, toppling over the chair behind him and falling hard on his tailbone. A sharp jolt of pain shot through his body, and he could feel the spot throbbing, but upon further inspection nothing seemed broken. For a brief moment, a thought raced through Jonathan's mind. Well, not a thought exactly, more of a series of intertwining images: he was standing on the rooftop, wrapping a thick cord around his neck and about to jump, then a flash and he was in a large bath about to drop his computer, still plugged in, right into the tepid water, then a scene of his bloody wrists, large vertical slits gaping open and spilling their crimson contents onto the carpet under his bare feet.

But they were only fleeting images, disappearing from his mind just as soon as they entered and not worth devoting any real attention to. Jonathan was not the type, because if he were he would have long since checked out of this city, out of this world, this entire existence. The sounds from outside were getting louder now, insistent, frantic, closer. He nudged the fridge open and snatched up another can, not as cold as he would have liked, but oh well. He pulled out his chair and sat down in front of his computer. The light flickered over his eyes, mesmerizing him with a hypnotic calm as he logged into his game. On the other end of the world, his opponent, d3@d4U2, grinned, his yellow, cracked teeth showing through the gaping hole where his cheek had once been.

THE NIGHT VISITOR
BY LORRAINE HORRELL

As she stepped into the cold dark room, it sent a shiver down her spine.

"Here you go Jess, this is going to be your room for the next two years. I hope you settle in well," said the nurse who was showing her around.

"If you need anything don't be afraid to ask, okay?" she said grabbing onto her hand and squeezing it tight.

"There is just one thing," said Jess through her chattering teeth. "How do I turn the heating on? It's freezing in here?" Jess shuffled around trying to get some heat back into her body.

The nurse went over to the radiator and stuck her chubby hand on it.

"Well the radiators on, but it is very cold in here. I'll have someone come look at it for you!" she assured her as she continued to stride out the door. The stocky nurse backed up and shouted, "You are extremely lucky to get a place this late in the year you know"

Right so, thought Jess, *I am not supposed to complain about anything, or I will have that thrown in my face.* Jess was a quick learner.

She unpacked all her stuff, having nowhere to put it. It was the smallest, pokiest room she had ever seen. It had a single bed, a radiator that was obviously not working, one set of drawers and a modest desk to study at.

Even though it had a large window overlooking the hospital grounds, not a lot of light entered the room. The hospital grounds were kept immaculate. There was a beautiful oak tree right outside her window. The sound of the wind sweeping through the leaves made Jess shiver even more.

Jess tried to make it as homely as possible but it was still cold and dismal and far from her luxurious room at home. She could just hear her mothers voice, "You're not there for luxury Jess; you're there to learn."

She finished putting her clothes away when there was a gentle knock on her door. It was the girl from one door down; she had come to introduce herself.

"Hi, I'm Susan but you can call me Susie. All my friends do." She had a smile that lit up like a thousand fireworks. Her eyes twinkled and her teeth were shimmered. Just looking at her smile made Jess feel at home already.

"Nice to meet you Susie, I'm Jess. Come on in! You will have to excuse all the mess, I am still shifting stuff around trying to make the place feel more homely." Jess stood back from the door to let her in.

Susie did not go into the room, though. She looked around the small room but didn't enter.

"Oh actually it's okay, I have to be somewhere. I just wanted to pop in and introduce myself," replied Susie, turning to walk back down the hallway.

On second thought, maybe she isn't very friendly, thought Jess. She looked kind of pale; maybe she wasn't well. Jess couldn't wait to start on the wards and start her training, she was so eager. All the excitement had built up in her and was ready to explode.

Jess thought no more of Susie. When she turned around she noticed her lace curtains were blowing gently as if from a breeze. She checked the window. It was closed tight and there was absolutely no sign of any draft coming in. The building was old and decrepit in parts. There were probably drafts and leaks all over the place, but...

Jess had arrived on Saturday and that night a big gala ball was being held for the all of the student nurses. Jess didn't have tickets. Everyone else had started their training back in September. It was now January. The hospital had rang Jess last week, offering her a place.

She didn't ask any questions. She accepted on the spot. This was what she had wanted to do; she had always wanted to care for others. The nurse, Sister Margaret, that had shown her around earlier, had told her about the ball.

"Everyone got their tickets for the ball in November and unfortunately there are none left. So you will be all on your own tonight, dear. The corridor will be quiet. Give you a chance to catch up on your studying."

Jess heard the music from Susie's room and the clatter of heel's heading down the hall. Doors slammed and voices shouted and laughed until there was nothing but an echo, which faded shortly after. The silence hurt. She felt isolated and very alone. Jess always had someone around at home; her parents, brothers and sisters, always someone to look after.

She was all alone, and shivered from the cold, both physical and emotional. Jess threw on two jumpers, gloves and three pairs of socks and buried herself under her blankets. She still couldn't heat up.

All the lights down the corridor were out. She picked up a book and got to the second page before drifting off to sleep.

She was awakened later by the sound of footsteps coming down the hall. She checked her watch. It was just after eleven. Way too early for anyone to be back yet! The footsteps stopped outside her door, but she could see underneath; no feet or shadows.

A knock came at her door. The hairs on the back of Jess's neck stood up.

"Hello!" she replied. Nothing, no answer and no sound.

Her heart was fluttering around inside her chest. Jess could only hear the sound of her quickened breath; it was sharp and raspy. The footsteps started again, they were coming closer now. She looked around to try to figure out where the sound was coming from. It was very dark. She couldn't even remember where the light switch was and there was no way Jess was getting out of the bed.

She thought maybe this was the wards' idea of playing a joke on the new girl on the block.

"Very funny!" said Jess desperately hoping her suspicions were true. "Jokes over; you had your laugh."

The footsteps were still approaching. Jess could see the outline of a black shadow coming towards her bed. It had to be a bad dream or somebody messing with her. The door never opened. Had someone been in her room all along without her knowing it? Jess was petrified at the thought of some creep watching her change and settle into bed.

She tried to scream but nothing came out, her throat was dry and tight. The blood rushed frantically around her body, her heart beating out of control. She could feel the blankets rising and lowering rapidly as she breathed in and out.

The footsteps stopped right beside her bed. The cold air had frozen her throat. Her mouth moved, but it was as if someone had put a plug in her throat to silence her.

In her head she was screaming. She told herself to calm down, that it was only a dream.

Something pressed on her chest as if holding her down. It was so strong and over powering. She tried to get up, but the force was too strong. A million thoughts floated around in her mind, none of them making any sense. Something brushed her fringe off her face. She was completely frozen with fear. The touch was icy cold, the touch of death. She could hear the slight sound of breathing, a hoarse breath, short and quick but struggling.

Jess felt the breath on her face. She tried to move again, but it was no use; her whole body was numb. Her muscles were useless, her limbs limp and still. She didn't like this feeling of no control. It terrified her.

She wanted to cry but her face wouldn't even move. She tried to close her eyes. They too were stiff. She just wished it, whatever it was, would go. She felt her blankets unfold off her body as the little heat she had managed to accumulate escaped. Her body trembled, as the presence pushed harder on her chest. Something grabbed her throat and tightened its clutches. It was as if it was trying to strangle her. Jess had never been so scared in her entire life. The icy hands clasped her neck as she gasped for air. She coughed and spluttered, fighting for her life. The movement came back to her face.

Jess closed her eyes. She couldn't see anything but she didn't want to see anything either.

A knock on her door woke her the next morning; it was Susie.

"Hey Jess. God you look awful! Are you ok?" she said, her eyes wide with concern.

Jess didn't want to cry, but she couldn't help it. Her tears flowed freely.

Susie hugged her.

"Its okay, Jess. I missed home too when I started. We will all be here tonight and we will go out, okay?" she promised. "It was just because you were all on your own last night, I'm sure. This place can be daunting at the best of times, especially when you spend the first night alone."

Jess wanted to open up and tell her everything, right then and there, but she knew Susie would think she was crazy.

"I was just so isolated last night," she lied. Jess was shaking all over, her teeth still chattering away. She was pale and sick looking.

Susie stepped back from the door.

"Jesus Christ, its freezing in there. It's colder then the North Pole in there!"

Jess started laughing, something she hadn't in a while and it felt good. She felt herself perk up a bit; it's amazing what a smile can do. She had heard laughing was infectious before. Now she knew why. It was all just a bad dream last night. She would put it down to being alone in an old building for the first time, her imagination was powerful. She told herself all of that, but she knew what she felt; that horrible feeling of someone watching you, someone violating your privacy, and those cold icy hands clasping around her neck, that couldn't be her imagination.

"Did you tell Nurse Bloody Ratchet about your heating not working?"

Jess laughed again.

"Nurse Ratchet?" She had to think for a minute. "Yeah she told me she would have someone look at it, and then quickly said I was lucky just to be here." They both burst into fits of giggles.

"Come on, get ready. We're going down town today. Nurse Ratchet is Nurse Margaret. We call her that because she is a little psychotic and lives for the hospital" explained Susie; her smile sent happy chemicals to Jess's brain again.

It took Jess half an hour to get ready. She forgot about last night. She put on her best clothes and straightened her hair and squirted herself with her favourite perfume and she felt better already.

The girls had fun in town. They went shopping and had lunch. Over lunch they chatted as if they had been best friends forever. Never once was there an awkward silence. Time flew by and Jess didn't think about the prior night's events.

It was getting late when the girls decided to call it a day. The dark clouds in the horizon had rolled over town, relentless and unforgiving.

"Looks like it's gonna lash," stated Jess.

"Yeah, we better get going."

They called a taxi and made the short journey back to the hospital. As they drove up the long and meandering drive surrounded by shaped bushes and beautiful old trees, Jess thought how creepy it looked. It was more like an asylum then a public hospital.

The building was hundreds of years old, practically crumbling down around them. It was painted white and the windows were all barred up. Jess wondered was that to stop people from jumping or to stop people from getting in through the windows. Either way the windows added to the hospitals eerie exterior. As the taxi drove around the side to their quarters, the rain fell. It fell in big splashes as the skies opened and the clouds turned black and bellowed as the thunder rolled in. Jess could see her bedroom window from the taxi. The light was on.

"That's weird. My light is on. I didn't even have it on this morning," proclaimed Jess.

"Don't worry, it's probably Ratchet. The old bag checks our rooms regularly to make sure we don't have any illegal substances." Susie winked cheekily at Jess.

"Oh right," said Jess. She wasn't convinced though. The air had changed from cool to humid. It was hot now. Jess was delighted maybe some heat would stay in her room.

They stepped out of the taxi just as a flash of lightening streamed past. It was extremely close. Jess's bedroom light had now been turned off, but the lightening lit her window enough for Jess to see a dark shadow in it. The figure wasn't moving, just staring out towards them. The hair on Jess's neck pricked up again, the memories of last nights horrific ordeal came flooding back.

"That's Nurse Marg... I mean Ratchet... she gives me the creeps," Jess declared as they made their way into the large building.

They parted outside Jess's room, the cold breeze still blowing from the closed door.

Jess turned her keys slowly. She didn't want to go in there all alone, but she couldn't make a big deal about it, people would think she was a wimp. Jess thought of Ratchet lurking around her room, it sent a shiver down her spine.

There had been no sign of old Ratchet roaming around the corridors. She fumbled around the doorway looking for the light, eventually finding it. Two pairs of socks were thrown on her bed and her underwear drawer was wide open.

"I could have sworn I closed those drawers and put my socks away last night," mumbled Jess.

Jess locked the door behind her. It had been a long day and she needed a bath. She went to the bathroom and began to run the hot tap. Jess went to her bed to get her bedclothes, which she had always left tucked under her pillow. They weren't there. Instead they were thrown in a pile on the ground.

Okay, someone has definitely been in my room, she thought.

Jess ran back to the bathroom. She had forgotten about her bath running. She glanced into the bath as she turned off the taps. It was stained a red colour and the water was thick and murky looking.

Jess's gut wrenched as she did a double-take. It hadn't been like that when she started to run the bath. What the hell was going on? Her heart started to race again. She felt like she was going to throw up to throw up, but there was nothing in her stomach. Her room light started to flicker on and off. The bulb flew out of the socket and brushed pass Jess's nose before it hit the wall and smashed on impact.

Jess jumped. She couldn't be imagining this, the evidence was there as clear as day. She left the bath full and ran up the white and cold corridor to Nurse Margaret's room. She banged on the door until she got an answer.

"I'm coming," came the reply. Nurse Margaret, or Ratchet as the girls called her, came to the door solemnly.

"Yes? You are aware it is after nine o'clock," she said, her face barely moving from the permanent frown she wore.

"There is something wrong in my room, Nurse Ratch... I mean Margaret," began Jess.

Nurse Ratchet dragged her out of the corridor and into her mouldy old room, which was extremely warm, sickly hot almost.

"Shusshhh. You don't want to make a scene of yourself, do you?" She continued sternly, "Tell me what happened?"

She grabbed Jess by the shoulders and pulled her over to an old chair in the middle of her messy room. There were medical books and dictionaries all over her bed and floor. Empty cups decorated the debilitated chest of drawers. Jess told her everything; she didn't leave out any details as she sobbed.

Nurse Ratchet was surprisingly sympathetic. She listened intently and never judged or offered any explanation. She agreed to go down to Jess's room with her and check out her tub. When they got back to the room, the water in the tub was as clear as crystal and there weren't eve n any red stains around the sides. Jess had never felt so foolish. She felt her jaw drop, like some silly children's cartoon.

She couldn't believe it. Nurse Ratchet didn't mind, she assured her. It was probably her way of adjusting to her new surroundings. A lot of girls had trouble when they moved away from home.

Jess felt relieved after her talk with Ratchet. Jess decided she wasn't that bad after all. She was very compassionate and understanding given the unusual circumstances. Nurse Ratchet even changed the bulb in her bathroom for her. It was all just a trick of her mind. She noticed a slight drop in temperature again after the older woman left her room and goose bumps rose on her arm.

Jess was tired. She just needed a good night's sleep. She felt as though she could sleep forever. Her bedclothes weren't on the ground where they had been last. Instead they were tucked neatly under her pillow, as they should have been.

Maybe she was getting Dementia or Alzheimer's she thought. She was a bit young but it was possible. She wrapped her arms around herself and rubbed, trying to heat up.

She started to undress. It was freezing. The cold had sunk deep into her body and settled in her bones, it was relentless. She had never been so scared before. She thought about ringing her parents but they would only worry.

Jess stepped on a piece of glass that was hidden on the floor, and the shard cut open the bottom of her foot. The pain shot up through her leg and throbbed. She lifted her foot up to the sink and inspected her wound; it was pretty bad. She washed the glass out and put a plaster on it. As she left the bathroom she glanced over at the tub and again it was full of murky water, the stench was unbearable. The sides of the tub stained red again.

I am losing my mind, thought Jess. She turned off the light, afraid of what she might see if she left it on.

Jess woke in the middle of the night again. Something was forcing her down.

Her heart was thumping, she pleaded in her head for it to end. Her mouth closed tight and wouldn't open. Nothing was happening; the shadow was just pushing her down, forcing her to stay, and not letting her move. Why? Jess didn't know. The force swept her hair back and breathed on her face. Jess felt the deathly cold breeze. Her body was in shock and the pain from her foot was throbbing.

Why is this happening to me?

Jess was finally able to open her mouth but nothing came out. She tried to lift herself off the bed, but she wasn't able. She couldn't explain what was happening.

Nurse Ratchet had said it was probably stress, but that certainly wasn't it. Jess had been stressed before, but nothing like this had ever happened. It was like a deja vu of last night's escapade. The weight got heavier on her breastbone. She felt like her chest would cave in at any minute. There was no rational explanation for any of it.

She breathed in a deeply as she could and let out a chilling scream that could have woken the dead. Immediately the pressing weight stopped and she gulped at the air to catch her breath.

Her strength returned and she was able to move. Jumping out of her bed, she quickly threw on her dressing gown and ran down Susie's door.

"Susie, Susie.... wake up, I need to talk to you!" she yelled, banging loudly on the door.

Susie came to the door in a tee shirt. Her hair was a mess. As soon as she opened her door, a burst of heat met Jess. She rubbed her eyes sleepily. A couple other doors along the hallway opened as heads popped out to see what the commotion was.

"Jess, what the fuck is going on? What happened?" her speech was very strained and barely audible. She seemed to be half asleep.

Jess pushed past her and continued into her room, taking a seat on her bed. She didn't get any bad feelings in Susie's room and the chills from the cold began to dissipate slightly.

"Susie, there is something wrong with my room!" she stated "I think you know that already though, because you never want to come in…" there was a long silence. She hoped Susie would cut in and start explaining, but she didn't. "What happened to the last girl that was here?"

Susie's face changed from sleepy to wide awake. She could see how upset Jess was. The tears were streaming down her face and she was trembling like a blob of jelly. Susie didn't want to lie to her, but she was ordered by Ratchet not to tell the new girl.

Susie thought long and hard before she said anything, and decided she wouldn't like to be lied to, if the roles were reversed. After a long, uncomfortable silence she was ready to confess.

"About three months ago, a girl…" she began.

"What girl?" asked Jess.

"Please Jess, just listen ok!" She took a deep breath and continued, "The girl who used to stay in you room, well, she was caught trying to strangle one of the elderly patients."

Jess's face slumped. She was all agitated, knowing something worse was coming but couldn't wait. She had to know. She twiddled her fingers while Susie continued.

"By the time Nurse Ratchet caught her, the girl had already strangled three patients that were. We were all being watched. The police questioned everyone; no one was exempt. I was questioned three times because we used to work the same shifts on the same ward. We both started at the same time and became close friends. I really liked her, but then she changed. She became a recluse, hiding in her bedroom and avoiding any contact. She didn't even want to talk to anyone. The girl was messed up, big time. She was really weird, Jess. No one liked her anymore. Ratchet eventually caught her with her arms around a patient's neck. The poor old lady couldn't breathe or scream for help. Becky, the girl, sat on her chest as she strangled her. Ratchet called the cops on her. she was told to go to her room and gather her things. When Ratchet and the cops came for her, well, they found a blood bath; it wasn't pretty. The girl had slit her throat and wrists and was lying in the tub dead."

Jess was speechless; she sat dumbfounded as Susie finished.

"I don't believe in ghosts," said Jess, *but that room is haunted.*

"There have been two girls that stayed in that room since then. One lasted an hour before running down the corridors screaming, the other was admitted to the psychiatric ward the following day."

Jess stood up, her emotions running riot. The anger flowed through her veins before finally erupting.

"I can't believe no one told me about this!" she said looking directly at Susie. Jess didn't want to accuse Susie of anything, but she should have told her. It all made sense now: why she checked up on her regularly but never wanted to come into her room.

"I couldn't tell you, Ratchet threatened me," Susie said. She had tears in her eyes, "She threatened to throw me out if I told you."

Jess's face looked demented as the news hit her like a blow to the chest.

"She was so nice to me earlier, I can't believe that woman," shouted Jess. "She told me I was stressed, made me feel as if I was going crazy."

"I told you she was a bitch," said Susie.

Lights started to switch on in the corridor, and it wasn't long before Ratchet came knocking on the door.

"Girls, what is going on? Let me in!" Susie reluctantly let her in, Ratchet was frothing at the mouth with anger, her grey hair tossed and mangled.

Jess didn't know what came over her but she lunged at nurse Ratchet, knocking her to the floor as Ratchet screamed and pleaded for help.

Jess repeated over and over, "Why didn't you tell me?" before being pulled off by Susie. Jess fell to the floor. She was an emotional wreck, tired and weeping.

Ratchet rang her parents; they would come collect her and be there by the morning.

Jess stayed with Susie that night. She was afraid to sleep, feeling tired and violated by the malevolent spirit. When her parents arrived the next morning she had never been so glad to see them. Their daughter was reduced to a trembling mess. Her mom burst into tears when she witnessed what a wreck her daughter was, tired and emotional.

Nurse Ratchet had some explaining to do, but at that moment the concerned parents just wanted to get their daughter home. Jess jumped at the slightest little sound. She watched her back continuously. All she wanted to do was get as far away from there as possible.

Maybe nursing wasn't the profession for her after all.

HANGING BY A THREAD

BY JEREMY BUSH

"Where am I?" I say out loud, but to myself. I have just awoken, and can't remember at all where I am. I can't feel anything—any part of my body. I want to move myself, but can't. I try to, but I can't feel anything. I can't see anything at all either. I think I have my eyes open, but it is still all blackness…I can't be sure if I have my eyes open or not. I concentrate and tell myself to open my eyes. I think about my eyelids and nothing else…I think I can start to feel them…I'm almost sure I can feel them now. I try to open them. I don't know if I have…it is still all darkness. I blink my eyes for a minute…there is light starting to come. I keep blinking. It is getting brighter and brighter. I can't make anything out—there is only light…I still can't feel the rest of me.

I am starting to see things—nothing distinct—just blurry shapes. Now there is movement…constant movement…and things are getting sharper and sharper by the second. I keep looking and blinking. I still can't feel anything… I am beginning to make out colors now. I can see something distinctly. It is brown and round… not perfectly round, but more of an oval shape. It is moving across my field of vision from top to bottom, at a steady rate…It has left my range of sight. I keep blinking. I see another brown oval come into my field of vision—my eyesight has improved enough so that I can see its outline and shape clearly. I think it is a hat…a brown hat…a derby or a fedora…*I must be mad*…It is floating across in front of me, a hat flying through the air. It also disappears.

I begin to notice something…feeling…sensation…a strange tingling. It is my cheek (my right cheek) that is tingling. I try to move again, but no luck. My cheek is still tingling. It feels like something is on it, resting on it, pressing down on it. I lay here blinking, wondering if another magical hat will come. I blink just my left eye. What is that? What am I seeing? The view through my left eye is slightly distorted. I can see through it, but not like my right eye (or is it my right eye that is seeing distorted?); it is almost like there is something between my left eye and what I am seeing.

I keep blinking my eyes. Another hat (this one is black) comes into view and then quickly disappears. I close my right eye… yes, there *is* something in front of my left eye. I keep my right eye closed, and blink only my left eye. I can't tell what it is. I can't quite make it out. I blink and blink and blink. It is almost as if there is another eye in front of my left eye. Like a faint, translucent eye is looking back at mine— blinking when I blink, squinting when I squint. It is the reflection of my eye…in water? No, that can't be. It is too faint for a mirror. Maybe it is glass…yes, I think it is glass. Why only over my left eye?

I can feel my cheek fully now. There *is* something pressing against it. I can see what it is—glass pressed down on my cheek. I can see it with my left eye, but not the right. The right eye is too close. It sees directly through without noticing it. So there is glass pressed down on my face…at least on my face, if not more of me…and there are flying hats above me. But I don't feel like I am looking up into the air. My head (my equilibrium) is telling me I am looking down.

I can just start to feel my toes and fingers…the very ends of them…the tips. I try to wiggle them—no dice. I am able to focus my eyes better now. I think I can see something. It is gray, thin and long. There is green on either side of this gray. I think it is a path or sidewalk…yes…yes, it is. A path made of grayish-white stones…with grass on each side of it. The feeling is slowly coming back into the rest of me. I can feel all of my arms and legs…and I can just start to feel my torso. It is odd—to not have any sensation in your body, then start to get it back—it is an odd, odd feeling.

I am lying down…I can tell that now. I am lying stretched out. I try to move again, but still I can't…I am almost certain now that I am laying face-down on my stomach. And my face must be pressed down against glass…ah, movement below me again…another floating hat traveling along the stone pathway. I can now see that there is a man underneath this hat, walking along the path, traveling across it. I can't see his face or much of his body. I can see his shoulders mostly. I am looking down on him, and can see his hat-covered head and his shoulders. This is *another* brown hat. And a brown coat (I presume) is on his shoulders.

I try to move, but still I can't. I can tell for certain (almost for certain), that I am lying completely stretched out, with the right side of my face being pressed down onto glass… maybe my face is just *lying* on glass, not being pressed down… yes, it just felt like that at first. My face is resting on glass, maybe on a window of some sort.

There is something else besides the path and the grass; a different green, mixed with brown here and there…ah yes, I can see it now: it is a tree. I can see others by it as well. I try to move my head, but I can't even move—what is that? It is gray, like the stone sidewalk. It isn't flat though. I can tell it is closer to me than the sidewalk. It is higher…a building? Yes, it is a building…a small building—or does it just look that way from up here? I can't tell yet. But it *does* appear to be made from the same type of stones as the pathway. Ah, here comes another floating hat. Now I might be able to tell. Yes, it is a small building. It looks like it is hardly bigger than the man; like it could hardly hold four of him in it. What kind of a building could it be? I think it is a cube-shaped building—it looks like a square from up here. Why would there be a cube-shaped building?

I try to move again…still nothing. Now I try to just concentrate on my finger, just one finger, and move that…I can't. I don't know how I can feel all of my body and not be able to move. How can I feel all of me, and not be able to move any of me? Maybe if I yell for someone to help me…maybe someone is near me…maybe someone will help me.

"Help me!" I yell out. "Help me!" I don't hear any response…no one is coming for me. I start to yell out again and realize that my mouth won't move, nor my tongue. I can feel my lips pressed together and my tongue resting on the bottom of my mouth. I have sensation in them, so why won't they work? I try again. Still I lie on my stomach, no movement, no words coming from me. I thought I had yelled out loud (just now and when I first awoke), but now I know I haven't. It had only happened in my head. The sound was only in my head. My voice had only been in my head.

How can I have feeling in all of my being, but only be able to move my eyelids and eyes? I strain—I attempt to strain—trying with my all to move…

Now what is that? What is that?! Something has shot across my field of vision, too fast for me to make out what it was…there is another…if only it would go slower. Here are more…many, many more…thousands of them…large black specks flying in front of me. Now some are slowing down…they are swirling around in circles, over and over again. They suddenly stop. They have all landed on the trees. I can now see that these large black specks are birds (many of them), covering the branches of the trees, turning them black…from green to black. They stay but for a minute—sitting on the branches, cleaning, flapping—until something startles them and they all soar into the air and away from me.

I see what it is that startled them… A man is walking (strolling is closer to it) along the path. This one is hatless, unlike the others. He is going slowly, walking a couple of steps and then stopping; turning his head to look everywhere and at everything. He shuffles along and stops by the trees. He looks up at them. I can actually see his face… Can he see me? Maybe he will see me! No…I don't think he has. He is already looking away at something else, something down on the ground this time…I did see his face though…for a few seconds anyway. He has the head and face and walk of an old man: no hair (or almost no hair), big bushy white eyebrows, wrinkles, and a stooping gait to go with his shuffling walk. I follow this man with my eyes everywhere he goes. I can see now he has a stick or a cane that he is using to steady himself as he walks.

The old man walks over to the stone building. He circles it twice, and then stops beside it. He is holding his cane in the air, pointing and shaking it at the building. A hand comes out from the building and tries to grab at the cane, but can't reach it. The old man strikes at this hand, hitting it several times with his stick, until it disappears again. The old man circles the building again, waving his cane and his arms at it the entire time. He then walks past the building to a large block…I think it is a large stone block…it looks like a large stone block—like the stones the building and pathway are made of, but much bigger. It isn't high…I don't think it is high (it is hard to gauge distance and depth from my vantage point). It is a rectangular shape; about the size of our old man if he was laid down on his side. The old man stops by this stone and taps it with his cane, while looking in the direction of the building…I wonder if he is saying something…and what? The old man gives one last shake of his cane at the building and shuffles off, out of my line of vision.

I wonder…who is in that building? Who was the owner of that mysterious hand? What kind of a building is it? Maybe it—what is that down there? A small animal of some kind (most would look small from up here…where ever 'up here' is). Is it a squirrel? No… no big bushy tail twitching behind it. It's not a groundhog…is it? No, it just hopped, and now I see those ears sticking up at me. The rabbit hops along the ground, nibbling at the grass occasionally. I see him hop near the stone building. Like the old man, he circles around it. He stops, standing up on his hind legs, with his front paws together in the air, and his nose twitching. Then he turns and sprints, hopping here and there, back to the trees—I see him no more.

I strain my eyes to see if I am missing anything—if there is anything I can't see or haven't seen yet. I tell myself to move my head…but still I can't. So I concentrate on moving my eyes. I don't think there is anything more I can see: There is the stone path, going in a straight line, for the most part, from bottom to top (or north to south, to put it another way). There is grass on either side of this path. On the right side (or east) of the stone walkway are the trees—not many of them (not a forest), but a few trees. On the left side (or west) is the stone square building. The stone block is also on this side, but slightly to the north and west of the building. As to anything else…I just can't see it, if it is out there.

It is getting brighter outside…isn't it? It seems like it is getting brighter out there. I am feeling a little hotter than I was…Why can't I move?! Why can't I—what is that? It looks like a horse…yes, being led by two men…no, wait…one is a woman—or is it a man…? It is so hard to tell from up here. Yes, now I can see. It is a man and woman leading the horse…with a small child on its back…a small boy I think. There is no saddle on the horse—the boy is riding bareback, holding onto the horse's mane, leaning against its neck. I can't see the faces of the man and woman. They appear to be middle-aged from the little I can see of them. This man is also hatless, but he has a full head of orange-red hair. The woman has long hair. I can see that it covers her shoulders and goes down her back. It is also reddish, but darker than the man's. Their son (I assume it is their son) has orange hair as well. I wonder how old he is. He looks not even half the size of the grown-ups.

The parents lead the horse, with their boy on its back, down the path, then over to the grass near the trees. They stop under the trees. I can't see the parents or the child. Only the back end of the horse is sticking out far enough from under the branches of the trees for me to see. They stay there awhile (doing what, I don't know, I can't see). All is still below me except the tail of the horse flicking back and forth. They start moving again, and now the horse is gone from my sight as well…there they are—I can see the man and woman through the trees. They are walking hand-in-hand. They have stopped and I can see everyone now, including the horse. The man steps to the side of the horse. He is lifting the boy down to the ground. The boy runs away, running through the grass and under the trees. The man is holding out his hand to the woman. She takes it in hers, and he leads her toward one of the trees. They have disappeared from sight… there they are again. The woman steps next to a tree and leans with her back against its trunk. The man moves close to the woman and he brings his head toward hers…

The boy has moved from the trees and grass to the pathway. He is running up and down it. Now he is slowing down, his head turned toward the building. He stops. He is watching the building intently. He walks toward the stone building, stopping every few feet, his gaze never wandering from it. As he approaches within a foot, the hand jumps out from the building and grasps the boy. It grabs him around the neck and starts shaking him. The boy is hitting the hand with his tiny arms, flailing them about in the air. The hand isn't letting go. It lifts the boy up in the air.

The man is running, his wife close behind him. The man is swinging his fists furiously at the hand and at the building. The woman is holding onto her boy, trying to pull him from the grip of the hand. The man runs to the path and pulls a stone from it. He is holding it in his hand and striking the hand over and over again. The hand has let go and is pulled back into the stone building. The man and his wife carry their son to the other side of the path and lay him on the grass. They are both kneeling next to him. The woman is waving her hands in the air. She grabs the boy and hugs him to her chest…Tell me he's okay! *The hand has killed a small child!* Who is that in the building? The man jumps to his feet. He is frantically turning this way and that. He brings his hands up, cupping his mouth… he must be yelling. The mother is still holding her boy to her chest, rocking him. My God! He must be dead—no! He just sat up! The husband and wife are both hugging him now…he has broken free and jumped to his feet… he is running around on the grass again, running toward the trees. The man and woman are still kneeling on the ground, watching him run. The man gets up and helps his wife to her feet, leading her toward the trees. The boy is running from the trees to his parents, back and forth, over and over again. The man grabs the boy as he and the woman reach the trees, and sets him on his shoulders. I see him walking toward the horse... the three of them have disappeared from sight—the trees are blocking them...

I am even hotter now! I'm starting to sweat. Why can't I move? Where the hell am I? And why—ah, they have reached their horse. The father sets his son on it, and grabs hold of the rope around its neck. He is leading the horse while supporting the woman with his other, free arm. They walk through the grass under the trees, disappearing and reappearing through the branches and leaves. After they come out at the end of the trees I see them veer back onto the stone walkway... they have walked out of my field of vision....I wonder...who is in that stone house?

It is *so* hot! I can feel my feet and the palms of my hands sweating... I try to move... I concentrate on every part of me, telling myself to move that part of my body, but still I can move nothing. There is no one to see under me anymore. Now that the man and woman with the boy and his horse have gone, there is no one. I look over every part of what I can see... I look at everything over and over again. I study the leaves on the trees intently, and try to count the number of stones in the pathway and the number of stones in the roof of the stone house. What is that on top of the stone block? On each side of it there is something... it is too far away for me to tell... they are thin... from here, they look like thin dark lines sticking up slightly...

I try to move again... *My God! It is hot!* I lay here looking down, only able to blink my eyes, and there isn't anything moving at all... not even a bird or a squirrel...

If I could have slept I would, but I have just been laying here for what seems like hours, unable to move; getting hotter by the minute. I have only seen two birds and a squirrel in that time, and nothing else—but wait... here is something... one of my floating hats again... this man is walking briskly—with purpose... he walks up the path past the stone house, then crosses the grass to the stone block and stops beside it. He takes off his hat and wipes his head with a handkerchief from his jacket. He is dressed nicely—his Sunday finest, I think. He circles the stone block, bending down and studying it intently, even touching it several times. He steps back to the side of it, puts his hat (which is a tan color) back on, and stands there with his hands in his jacket. He appears to be waiting for someone. He stands there in the same spot, unmoving, looking only at the stone block. Who is he waiting for…? Maybe for him… here is another man coming down the stone path, but not nearly as briskly. In fact, he stops several times and looks back the way he came from. He walks to the stone building. He stops. He looks around and then hurriedly walks on down the path beyond it. He stops again. He turns about, and with a more determined gait walks back to the building and then around it, to the stone block. His head doesn't turn to the man already waiting there, and the man already waiting doesn't turn his head either. This new man reaches his hand out to touch the stone, but quickly brings it back. He nearly runs—he scampers from it, stopping a short distance away. He turns back toward the block and stands there. He appears to also be waiting, but for what? He is fidgeting—standing on one foot, then the other—twiddling his thumbs, then clasping his hands behind his back. The two men still haven't looked at one another.

I am so hot! My neck, under my chin, is sweating. I can feel the sweat drops rolling down from the back and sides of my neck, and collecting under my chin and the right side of my neck. That part of my neck feels like it could be pressed against the glass as well… I can't tell what kind of shoes I have on my feet, but I can sense that I have a pair on… and they are enclosing my feet and making them sweat even more…

Ah, here are two men walking together… strolling along the path—conversing with one another, I would guess. It is hard to tell the height of the people from up here. I mostly see their head and shoulders. Not unless they sprawled out on the ground would I be able to see their bodies, and even then it would be hard to determine their height for sure. But these two men give the impression of being tall. They stroll around the stone house. The hand flies out to strike at them, but they pay it no heed. They keep walking, without turning their heads from looking at one another. They walk to the block. They appear to greet the other two men, but with no response from either. They walk a few feet beyond the stone block and stop there, still talking together. These four men all stand facing toward the stone block, with the house behind it, waiting…

The men are still standing and waiting. The two friends have stopped talking and are looking down at the ground and at the stone block… Now I see a woman running, her long hair flying out behind her. Her hands are out at her sides, grasping onto her dress, holding it up so she can run. When she sees the stone house she stops running. She holds one hand in the other, behind her back, and slowly walks around the building toward the stone block. I think her head is down—she might be trying to avoid the men's gazes. She slowly walks past the block, stopping behind the two friends. She looks to see whether she has a good view of the stone block, and then lowers her gaze again. Here is someone else coming… no, it is a family, I think. Yes, a man with seven—no, eight—kids… and here comes his wife, holding another child by the hand, with one in her arms. They are herding their brood down the path… across the grass… and to the back of the crowd gathering by the stone block. The kids are well behaved for the most part, not running around. Here are more people coming down the path… a man and woman walking side by side, and behind them is another man. And coming up the pathway from the other direction is another man. And here comes another and another… I even see some are coming in from the grass by the trees, walking across the grass and under the trees in the direction of the stone structure. There are more and more—men alone, men with their wives, men with their families, men with their friends—from all directions now, it seems. They are all dressed in what appear to be their best clothes. They are filling in all the space around the stone block, gathering around it, facing it. They are still coming—some running to get a place; others trying not to run, but still walking swiftly…

There are still people joining the crowd, but the rush is over. It is only the stragglers who are left, trickling in one at a time. It is a large crowd now—mostly men, but still many women and some children mixed in. For the most part they have all found where they would like to stand to get a view of the stone block and are standing there waiting, staring toward the block…

The crowd is waiting… I try to count how many people are in this crowd, but I am distracted… there are more people coming up the stone pathway. I see two men. One is holding what looks like a thick chain in his arms. Both are in dark blue—I think dark blue uniforms, but I can't tell for certain. They have identical hats, also dark blue and very military-looking. Both have something on their left side… I think attached to their uniforms… it looks like it might be hanging from their belts or something…ah, I can see now—they are sheathed swords hanging down. These men are walking in step with one another, their legs swinging at the same time…Here is another… just behind the soldiers is a man in all black from head to feet. He has a shroud over his head, also of black. In his arms he is carrying a large axe—a large double-headed axe. The three are making their way up the pathway at a slow and solemn pace.

I see a woman running out from the trees. I hadn't seen her go into them. I wonder if she has been hiding in them. She is running wildly, her arms gesturing violently. She runs straight toward the soldiers— she is darting back and forth between them and all around them, clasping her hands together in a pleading manner and thrusting them in the air toward heaven. She has just noticed the man covered in black… she appears to be shaking. She throws herself at his feet, lying prostrate before him. He steps over her and starts to walk by. She lunges and grasps onto his legs, hugging them and trembling all over. The soldier not carrying the chain has stopped and turned around. The man in all black motions with his black-gloved hand, and the soldier comes back. He is bending down… he must be saying something to her… he is grabbing her hands, trying to wrestle her from the man's legs. He is trying to pry off her fingers. She is stubbornly holding on. The soldier's hat has fallen off—he appears to be getting frustrated…he has just hit the woman's arm—still she hangs on. He is kicking her in the stomach and chest—still she hangs on. He punches her in the head repeatedly—she finally lets go. The soldier shoves her over on her stomach and jerks her hands behind her… he is tying them together. He pulls her up from the ground. She can't keep her feet, so the soldier is dragging her by her tied hands. She stumbles a few steps, then trips and is dragged along—her feet scraping the ground, her body at an angle, the soldier pulling her behind him. I see blood flowing down the woman's head, down her neck and onto her yellow dress.

The soldier (with his hat now back on) returns to the side of his fellow soldier. They proceed as before—steps in line with each other, slow and solemn. The man in all black hasn't moved the entire time, other than to motion to the soldier. He follows the soldiers, keeping the same distance as before. This procession marches around the stone house to the stone block. The woman has stopped trying to walk on her own… I don't see her moving at all—she has gone limp. The soldiers stop at the stone block. The one dragging the woman lets her fall to the ground. The man in all black stops near the side of the stone block, and he remains there with the double-headed axe resting in his arms, facing toward the crowd. The soldiers go back to the stone building. I see one pulling something off his person as they reach it. He holds it in his hand and moves it toward the building, while both stand there. They step forward and disappear into the stone house… The crowd is waiting—the man in all black, as well. The woman with her hands tied has come out of her stupor and has managed to work her way up onto her knees…

My God it is hot! It feels like my entire body is sweating now. I can feel the beads of sweat standing on my forehead and face. If only I could move and get out of this place! Here come the soldiers, out of the building. Between them is another man…they have him by the arms. The thick chain the one soldier was carrying is now wrapped around the man: around his wrists and chest, up around his neck, and down around his legs. The man can only take small steps with the chain around his legs—he has to shuffle along. As they move him away from the stone house I am able to see him better. This man is in tattered rags—he has nothing on his feet at all; his pants are so worn, they appear to be half-gone; his shirt has lost any sleeves it might have had, and has holes big enough for me to pick out from up here. I can also see the grime and dirt on his clothes, and on him, even from my vantage point. They slowly and solemnly lead him, the soldiers still in step with one another, over to the stone block and the waiting crowd. The woman with her hands tied behind her back sees the man in chains. She tries to get up from her knees, but slips and falls to the ground again. The man in chains has his head turned toward the woman, unmoving. He appears not to be resisting or struggling— the guards have him tightly by the arms. They stop directly in front of the stone block. The chained man is now trying to struggle. They push him down onto his knees. They are taking the chain and each is pulling on an end. They are putting the chain through the dark lines I saw on each end of the block…it must be a ring or something. Each guard pulls hard on the chain, forcing the man's head and neck down onto the stone block. It also pulls his arms straight out from his sides and down flat onto the stone block. They are doing something with the chain by the rings… they must be fastening them somehow— they are bent over them and I can't see that well… they stand up… the chain is wrapped around each ring several times… it looks like each end is… I think each end is spiked into the ground—has a stake through it into the ground. The chained man tries to struggle loose, but he can barely move at all… he tries again, but quickly loses strength and stops. I see him arching his back—he must be testing the chains. He pushes until his muscles start trembling, and then he collapses back down. He is breathing hard. He tries again to break free, but quickly begins quivering and again collapses.

One of the guards steps in front of the stone block and pulls something out of his uniform. He is holding it in front of him, up by his head. It looks like paper. He appears to be talking while looking at this paper...I wish I knew what he was saying. The crowd is all looking toward him—all heads are turned in his direction. Even the children are standing still... they must be listening. The guard finishes and puts the paper back in his uniform. He moves back around the stone block and places himself behind the chained man. As he stops, the other soldier starts marching and takes a position beside him, behind the chained man.

The man in all black, who hasn't moved since he took his place, slowly walks the three steps to the side of the stone block. The woman is still lying on the ground, her body shaking. She forces herself back up onto her knees. I can see the streams of tears on her cheeks from up here. Blood is still trickling down her face. The man in all black takes the handle of the axe in both hands. He extends it out full length over the chained man, so that the head of the axe is directly over the chained man's neck. He slowly brings the axe back up and over his head. The woman is trembling and trying to get up on her feet. The man in all black spreads his feet apart. He is starting his downward swing. The woman is on her feet—she lunges and falls on top of the chained man. The axe blade hits... *My God! It is horrible!* The woman has taken the blow intended for the chained man! It has struck her neck! There is blood everywhere. Her body is sliding down to the ground. Her severed head is falling down after the body, still attached by a tendon or skin. It lands, resting on her back so that her face is staring straight up at me—eyes wide and tongue hanging out of the side of her mouth. Blood is streaming out onto the ground, soaking the grass around her neck.

Those in the crowd are horrified. Most look away, covering their eyes with their hands. I see a few people who turn away and vomit on the ground. The children are all screaming and crying. The chained man appears to be convulsing and he also vomits—onto the stone block. The soldiers are keeping their faces staring straight ahead of them, not looking anyway (especially not down) but straight ahead. The executioner lets the axe head rest on the ground by his feet. He bows his head and leans against the end of the handle of his axe.

I feel sick—my stomach—I feel like I also could vomit. *My God! I am so hot!* The sweat is dripping off my nose onto the glass, distorting the view in my left eye even more.

The executioner is straightening himself back up. He is again extending the axe over the man in chains, the axe shaking in his hands. He brings it up over his head. He is swinging the axe down to its mark. It strikes the man's neck, and blood is spilling from him all over the block and flowing down the sides of it. The man is twitching and convulsing—his neck is cut, but still intact. The executioner raises the axe over his head again. He swings it down. The head falls off and lands beside the woman. The body goes limp. Sweat is still dripping from my nose—pooling on the glass—distorting my view further and further… blood is flooding out from the neck of the man. The stone block is completely covered by it. The blood is moving out from the block on all sides, soaking the ground even more. I almost vomit, but luckily don't. I think I would choke on it since I can't move at all.

I focus my eyes on the crowd. Some have turned away or covered their eyes with their hands, but most are staring straight ahead at the execution—at the effects of the execution. Looking straight down on this scene it is hard to see any of the faces of those in the crowd, or the expressions on the faces. One of the soldiers walks to the executioner. He reaches inside his uniform coat and pulls out a white cloth. He extends it to the executioner, who takes it and wipes off the head of his axe. *My God! The woman's head is still staring up at me! Her eyes are staring into mine!* The executioner is handing the cloth back to the soldier. He faces toward the bodies, bows his head slightly, and then lifts his axe up into his arms. He turns around and slowly walks past the stone block and bodies, past the stone house, to the pathway. The soldier with the white cloth is unfurling it to its full length. He kneels beside the bodies. He is wrapping the head of the man up in this cloth. He stands up, the bundled head in his hands. He steps back to the side of the other soldier. They also bow their heads slightly toward the bodies, and then start marching in step. They proceed past the bodies… past the building… they are marching down the stone path, following after the executioner.

The woman's head is still staring up at me! I must look at something else… the executioner has disappeared from my sight. The soldiers, who are marching swiftly, are almost out of my range… they also are now gone. A man in the crowd is slowly making his way toward the bodies. He stops and takes off his coat. He lays it over the woman; over her head… thank God it is no longer staring into my eyes… Look at the crowd—there are so many people—how can no one see me? If only I could move at all! If only I could shout!

The crowd appears to be breaking apart. Many are already starting to leave… *My God! I am so hot!* I feel like I'm afire… I have shut my left eye. The pool of sweat has grown so that I can't see from that eye—it is too distorted. If only someone in the crowd could see me and help me… I must try to move—why can't I move?! I must concentrate on just one part of me at first… I will try to move my lips… they won't move…but my tongue is! I can move my tongue… the crowd is still dispersing. Many are pushing closer to the stone block, to look at the bodies…if I can just get their attention. Oh no! The sweat is starting to block the view from my right eye as well… Ah, my lips just twitched! Concentrate! I can move them now… why can I not speak? What if they all leave before I can? Wait…here it comes, "Help me! Help me!"

They are looking around at one another and every which way. They must hear me. "Help me! Help me!" I yell out. Someone is finally looking up. He is pointing his arm up at me. The others around him are looking up and pointing now…"Help me!" Those in the back of the crowd are looking up at me…the whole crowd sees me now. *I am saved!*

I must try to move… I focus on my toes—they are moving now… now my fingers—I can curl them into a fist… now my head and neck. I move my head, pulling my cheek up off the glass. I can finally look directly down with both eyes. The people in the crowd are moving toward me. As a mass they are pushing their way to the path, getting closer and closer to being directly under me. "Help me!" I shout again. Some in the crowd are frantic, running this way and that, pointing up at me… I can move my legs… now my arms can move as well… I must try to get up. I am pushing up with my arms. I will push my body up—I will force it to move. What is that noise? *My God! The glass is cracking right under my arms!* The ground is rushing up at me…

I hit the stone pathway. My entire body is in pain. I try to move, but I can't move anything. And I can't yell out. *Oh, how I want to scream out in pain.* I can only see—the stones of the pathway, the grass next to it, and feet running toward me. There is red running out in front of my eyes. It is spreading, covering the stones… now covering the grass… now it is all I can see—only red. It is getting darker—a darker and darker red. The pain isn't as sharp now…as the red grows darker, the pain lessens. It is almost black now, and the pain is nearly gone… I can see nothing. Even the red is gone—but the pain is gone as well. I am starting to lose all feeling in my toes and fingers… it is spreading down my arms and legs, this numbness. Now it is crawling up my body… I can no longer feel my chest…it is moving up towards my head. It has taken my shoulders…and my neck… this is it… I can feel it in my head…the numbness is starting…

"Where am I?" I say out loud, but to myself. I have just awoken, and can't remember at all where I am. I can't feel anything—any part of my body. I want to move myself, but can't…

WHAT SHE SAW

BY DARREN GALLAGHER

"Excuse me sir," Joanne said raising her hand, her little legs shook back and forth as she sat there waiting for him to look up.

"Yes Joanne."

"I really need to go to the bathroom," she said desperately.

"Okay, go on," he said and lowered his head back to correcting homework.

Joanne got up so fast that she stumbled getting out of the chair. Most of the others kids laughed at her, the teacher never reprimanded them. She picked herself up embarrassed and ran out of the class.

She hurried down the corridor, her small legs over working to get her to the bathroom before her bladder gave out.

As she was passing the teachers' lounge she heard a woman scream; the pain she heard in her voice made her stop and listen. It came again; Joanne knew she couldn't pass by without seeing if the person was okay. She desperately had to pee but she was always told to help people, even if it was just telling someone else that something bad had happened. She was going to check on this woman; if something did happen then she would go back and tell her teacher. She figured she could hold it for now.

Joanne walked to the door and reached for the handle and started to turn it. As she did another scream came towards her, it startled her and she almost released the handle. Suddenly a man's voice began to talk to the woman, he sounded angry. Joanne wondered what was going on and she started to feel afraid. Slowly her small hand turned the knob fully and pushed the door open gently. Standing across the room with his back to her was Mr. Sweeney, Miss McCallion was lying tied up on a table before him. Her white blouse lay open beside her, her skirt was pulled up almost to her waist, and there was something covering her mouth.

Joanne didn't know what was happening but she knew it was wrong. Mr Sweeney's right hand fell by his side; Joanne saw light reflecting off something he was holding. Suddenly he moved his arms out and in an arch motion and positioned his hands above his head. Joanne could see quite clearly now that the object in his hand was a dagger; her eyes widened, and she could hear muffled sounds coming from Miss McCallion.

Mr Sweeney started to talk, but she couldn't understand him, he was talking in a different language. Suddenly he brought the dagger directly down onto the chest of Miss McCallion and a muffled but loud scream came from her. Joanne was horrified, she wanted to scream; she resisted it while something warm flowed down her legs.

The blood poured out of Miss McCallion, it ran down her ribs and stained her perfect white blouse. Mr Sweeney started to dig the dagger around inside her chest, which released a flurry of blood up into the air. This time Joanne did scream. She released the handle and ran back down the corridor to her class.

She opened the door so fast that it slammed back into the wall. Her teacher looked around angry, and then softened once he saw her. Joanne skin had faded to a pale white, and her eyes bulged out, tears where beginning to form.

He crossed the room to her quickly, knelt beside her and asked what was wrong; he could see she was also still leaking onto the floor.

"He killed her," she sniffled out.

"What?" he asked shocked.

"Mr Sweeney... He tied her to a table and killed her." Tears rolled faster now.

"Joanne, I don't know what you're talking about? Killed who?"

"Miss McCallion, he killed her down there." She pointed down the corridor.

"Show me," he said urgently, unsure of what had happened.

They walked down the corridor as fast as she allowed; she was still frightened. He didn't need her to show him, there was a path of water leading down to where she had stopped. He felt sorry for her, wetting oneself in school was never an easy thing to live down, students could be mean. He just hoped this was a story she made up to hide the fact that she did.

He went to open the door, but Joanne stopped him. "Be careful, he has a knife, that's how he killed her."

He looked down at her puzzled and alarmed, and then opened the door slowly. Laughter flowed out of the room. Mr Sweeney and Miss McCallion were sitting at the table drinking coffee; there were even a few buns between them.

"Everything okay in here?" he asked them.

"Yeah, why?" Mr Sweeney asked puzzled.

"Doesn't matter," he said and looked down at Joanne. "Did you make something up to cover the fact you peed yourself?" He asked quietly kneeling beside her.

"No, I saw it. I promise!" she said confused while she stared at them.

"Okay then, let's go call your mother and get you cleaned up," he said walking away from the door, it swung closed slowly while Joanne continued to stare at them.

Just then the room flickered and the two happy teachers disappeared to reveal the image she'd begun to see earlier, only now there was blood everywhere, all over the table and the floor. What remained of Miss McCallion's body was still tied to the table; the skin had been torn away from her ribs and her legs. Mr Sweeney was standing pulling clumps of flesh from her arms, the dagger still moving swiftly in his hand. Suddenly he moved towards the bottom of the table; Joanne couldn't believe her eyes. Miss McCallion was staring at her; all of her skin, hair, and even her eyes were gone from her head. Two black holes peered at her from the blood stained skull of Miss McCallion as the door closed.

THE PIT

BY DARREN GALLAGHER

Zach was seven years old. He lived with his parents and two older sisters. He was small and thin for his age, with quite a round face, making him an easy target for his siblings.

Sharon was the eldest; she was thirteen. She was a plump girl, with long brown hair. Annie was eleven; she looked like Sharon, a smaller, slightly thinner version. Annie always did what Sharon told her to.

They were always mean to Zach, always picking on him, calling him names, beating him up, anything really they could do for *fun* as they called it. Zach never said anything to his parents; they were always too busy with other things to listen.

Whenever their parents went out they left Sharon in charge. "She was old enough now to look after everything," they said. When they were gone that's when Zach's nightmare would start, or sometimes even when the parents weren't looking, any chance they got really, they tormented little Zach.

One night their parents went out, and as always left Sharon in charge. At first nothing happened. Zach thought it was because they wanted to make sure their parents wouldn't come back, and catch them being mean to their little brother. They were devils but acted like angels when their parents were around.

They were all sitting in the living room. It was a small room, but big enough for a three piece suite, coffee table and a unit in the corner; one which Zach had spent countless hours in because of his two loving sisters. There was a big fire place with a mirror on the wall above it. The fire looked lovely on this cold winter's night.

They sat watching TV peacefully, but Zach knew it was too good to be true. Any second now they would start, and it wouldn't end until their parents came home, or they got tired and went to bed. Zach decided to leave now before they did. He got up and started to walk towards the door.

"Where do you think you're going, fat-face?" Sharon snarled at him.

"Yea, sit down shorty," Annie shouted.

Zach wished he'd just sat there until they actually had started.

"I'm going to get some food," Zach answered, wishing he didn't have to explain everything to them.

"No you're not, sit your fat ass down," Sharon barked again.

Zach reluctantly sat back down on the seat. He sat waiting, he knew any minute now they would attack.

He was right. Within a few moments after having sat down, Zach saw Sharon turn and look at Annie; he saw the glint in her eye. He knew it was coming; and it was coming now.

Annie smiled back at Sharon and they both started to get up. Zach launched himself off the seat and made for the door; he wasn't going to sit there and wait for them to get him. He was just beginning to turn the handle when he felt something hit him on the back of the leg. Annie was faster than him; she kicked him before he could open the door. The pain was so immense that Zach's leg buckled. He fell against the door, and before he could regain his balance someone had grabbed his hair and was pulling him back. Sharon's grip dug deep, and she ripped out at least half a dozen hairs in the process. She decided she'd like to take him for a walk. She stepped back, pulling Zach onto the floor. She never released her grip as he fell. She held it, deciding which way he'd fall, and which way he'd land; she loved it. No sooner was he lying on the ground with his scalp on fire than Sharon started to pull again.

"Come on boy," she said as she dragged him along the floor. Zach could do nothing but turn around and go with her; she had such a strong grip.

"Come on boy," she said again, laughing and smiling at Annie while walking around the coffee table.

Annie stood at the door laughing as she watched Sharon pull Zach around the room like he was their little dog. He held in his screams, he didn't want to give them the satisfaction, they fed on that, and he knew it.

"Make him bark," Annie shouted and laughed harder.

Sharon bent over laughing, and then looked down at Zach. "Did ya hear that boy? Bark!" she demanded.

Zach didn't do anything; he didn't want to be their dog.

"Bark!" she said again, this time anger was present in her voice. She didn't like it when he didn't listen.

"Did ya hear me? Bark!" she roared. Fury had replaced her laughter, and she no longer smiled.

"No," Zach said.

"What?" Rage overwhelmed her voice. "If I say bark, you bark! Ya hear me?"

"No," Zach repeated terrified, knowing quite well that he'd pay for it, but he wasn't going to satisfy her.

"BARK!" she roared at him; but got only silence.

"BARK!" she roared again; this time brining the heel of her shoe down on Zach's left hand.

Zach screamed; the pain was unbearable, his hand felt like it was broken. He rolled around on the floor holding his hand; he felt like he was going to throw up.

"I told you to bark," she said again still furious. But he was in so much pain that he wasn't even listening to her. She kicked him in the stomach and walked off.

"Come on Annie let's leave the cry baby alone."

They left the room and when into the kitchen. Zach lay on the floor curled up in a ball, clutching his hand. The pain from both his hand and stomach was so excruciating that he couldn't move.

Zach didn't know how long he was lying there and he didn't care. He could hear them laughing and joking about it in the other room. He wished he could kill them and lay thinking about different ways they could die.

He wanted to get up; wanted to hide, before they came back. Zach got to his feet and straightened up; the pain in his stomach wasn't too bad now, but his hand was still throbbing. He walked to the door; he could still hear them talking about him, laughing at him. He stood at the door listening, and looked out into the hallway; planning his escape.

The hallway was narrow; just to the left of the living room was the main door to the house, straight across was the stairway, and to the right was the kitchen; where the two devils sat.

He knew he'd have to be quick, straight across the hallway and up the stairs, into his bedroom. He was just about to go when he heard them saying there were coming back to kick his ass again. "Oh no," he thought, "they're gonna catch me before I get across." Zach made a run for it, but they saw him as they were coming out of the kitchen.

"Get him," Sharon shouted.

Annie ran towards him, but he made it onto the stairs before she got there. He thought he'd gotten a life line, "just don't mess it up now," he thought, "get up there before they do." He was looking up the stairs and never saw Sharon stick her hands through the rungs on the stairwell; she got the slightest grip of his jeans and pulled. Zach lost his footing and fell forwards. He reached out to save himself; but when his left hand grasped the stair, the pain was too intense and he had to let go; his head walloped off the stairs.

"Get him down here," Sharon said to Annie.

Annie obeyed and grabbed Zach's feet, and pulled him down the stairs. Zach's head hit every stair on the way down.

"Where ya think you're going?" Annie said, pulling him to his feet. Zach's forehead was slightly cut, and had already swollen.

"Trying to get away from us were ya?" Sharon asked. "You know what happens when ya try and get away from us, don't ya?" she said smiling at Annie.

"The pit?" Annie asked, with a wide grin on her face.

"Yeah," Sharon answered. "The pit."

"NO!" Zach shouted desperately. "I'm not going in there. NO!"

He struggled to get free, but they were too strong. The harder he struggled, the harder they laughed. They dragged him down the hall towards the kitchen, and stopped at the door under the stairs.

"Open it," Sharon ordered.

Annie let go of Zach and reached for the lock on the door, as she did Zach tried to get away, but Sharon slapped him hard on the back of the head. Annie opened the door and grabbed Zach, and then they forced him in. Zach didn't want to be put in there; he was screaming and struggling to get free.

They got him in and shut the door. It was dark in there; Zach could see nothing except for the little stream of light from the doors edge. He started hammering on the door and it rattled furiously against the frame.

"Let me out!" he shouted over and over again, but only heard laughter.

"Enjoy the pit; don't let any monsters eat ya," they shouted into to him as they walked away. He heard their voices diminishing as they went into the living room, ignoring his screams to be let out. He didn't like being in the pit, he hated it most of all, it frightened him.

Zach sat for ages listening to them talk and laugh, hoping they would come back and let him out. He hated them so much for everything they did and for putting him in here. He wished they were dead.

"Hello there little boy," a soft cool voice said. It sounded like it came from inside the pit.

"Who's there?" Zach asked nervously.

"Those are two lovely sisters ya have there, little boy," that soft cool voice said.

"Who are you?" Zach asked getting to his feet, as fear ran throughout his body.

"I can help you with them."

"Who's there?" Zach said, raising his voice a little, he was beginning to panic.

"Relax; I'm here to help you."

"Help me with what?"

"To kill you're sisters." That soft cool voice said; it sounded as if it was grinning when it said it.

"I can't kill them." Zach snapped back.

"Yes you can. You want to don't you? You want them dead. Don't you?" The voice asked.

"Yes. But I can't; they're my sisters."

"Well why do they do those horrible things to you then, little boy?" It asked, pressing the question on him.

"I dunno." Zach said sorrowfully.

"They're not your sisters; real sisters wouldn't treat you like that."

"Who are you? Show me who you are?" Zach demanded.

"Ok then little boy," the soft cool voice responded.

Suddenly two red slanted eyes appeared in the dark in front of him; they frightened Zach so much that his legs almost buckled.

"Don't be afraid," the voice said; but it was too late.

"Wh... What are you?" Zach asked, his voice trembling.

"I'm your friend, I'm here to help you Zachie." Those red eyes said cunningly.

"Help me do what?" Zach asked nervously.

"To kill your sisters."

"But I can't." Zach said quickly.

"Yes you can." That soft cool voice pressed on him. "Look into my eyes Zachie, you will see that you can."

Zach looked into those slanted red eyes and felt determined to agree with them; suddenly he felt relaxed.

"Are you ready?" The voice asked.

"I can't get out."

"The door's open Zachie-boy," the voice said slyly. "Take a knife from the kitchen; then kill them!" It demanded.

Zach pushed the door gently and it was open, he felt relief at being able to leave the pit.

"Wait, Zachie-boy," the voice said, while a small, cold, black hand grabbed his arm. Zach turned around to look at it; as he did those slanted red eyes came rushing at him. Zach felt his body move backwards like he had been pushed by a gust of wind. The red eyes were gone, and no voice was speaking to him, but Zach was free and he was going to the kitchen.

Just as that little black hand grabbed Zach, Annie had left the living room and went upstairs. Zach slowly pushed the door forward and came out of the pit. He carefully closed the door behind him, and walked into the kitchen. He went directly over to the knife drawer, opened it slowly, and took out the biggest knife. He held it in front of his face, and smiled fondly at it.

"Annie, hurry up," Sharon called from the living room.

"I'll be down in a minute," Annie called back.

Zach knew this was his perfect chance; he turned around and walked out of the kitchen. When he reached the living room door, it was slightly ajar. He reached out his left hand; it didn't hurting anymore, and pushed the door gently as he slowly walked forward. Sharon was sitting on the chair closest to the TV, and was absorbed by it. Zach crept up behind her; she was totally unaware of him. She just sat there and laughed at what she thought was funny. Zach remembered all the times she had laughed at him; his heart filled with hate. "No more," he thought.

Zach lifted the knife high above his head and brought it down forcefully on her shoulder. The knife went deep, hitting bone and bouncing awkwardly off it. Blood came gushing out in all directions, some even squirted onto Zach. She screamed horrendously and jumped away from him. "That scream was nowhere near the screams I'd done because of her," Zach thought, as she scrambled to the other side of the chair. She looked at Zach terrified; shocked at what he had just done. Zach smiled at her, and then lashed out with the knife. She reached out to save herself; but the blade tore deep into her hands and forearms. Blood sprayed everywhere and dripped all over her, the chair, and Zach. She screamed and screamed but it had no effect on him; he just lashed out harder and faster, like she had done when he had screamed.

Upstairs Annie heard Sharon screaming, she didn't know what was happening, and it frightened her. She didn't want to go down, but Sharon was all alone; she couldn't leave her by herself.

She started down the stairs. As she did, she heard Sharon screaming louder and louder. She was really scared. She didn't know what was happening to her sister, but she went down anyway.

When she reached the bottom; she looked directly into the living room, she saw Sharon lying on the chair. Everything was red; her body, her clothes, even the chair. She saw Zach standing over her, "How'd he get out she thought." Then she saw the knife in his hand, and she realised what had happened.

"Zach... No!" she cried out, as she ran into the living room. Zach smiled at her as she came towards him; it was her turn now.

Annie ran to Sharon, but she knew by the way she was lying, that she was already dead. She was horrified but still she came, she wanted to be with her sister.

Before she got anywhere near Sharon or the chair, Zach launched forward and stabbed her in the stomach; the blade almost came out the other side. Annie bent forward onto the knife, and towards Zach. She didn't scream; she couldn't. The feeling went in her legs and she fell onto her knees. On her way down she saw Zach smiling at her, but there was something different about his eyes; it looked like they were glowing. Zach pulled the knife out when her knees touched the floor.

"Zach no!" she managed to splutter out.

Zach smiled at her. "Not this time fatty," he said and swung the knife at her.

The knife caught her on the throat, and it cut clean through with ease. Annie fell forward clutching at her neck; gurgling rapidly as she tried to breathe. Zach continued to smile as he looked down at her. He was happy; he'd never have to take any more from them ever again.

Zach stepped over Annie's body and walked towards the living room door. When he got there he looked back. Sharon lay dead on the chair, and everything was covered in blood. Annie lay on the floor; a huge pool of blood continued to flow out of her body, she no longer was trying to breathe. Bloody footsteps followed him across the floor, as he stood there looking back on what he'd done, he felt happy.

Zach walked back to the pit, opened the door, went inside, and sat down. He had closed the door behind him and sat there in the dark. There was nothing but silence and darkness; he felt alone.

Some time passed and Zach felt more and more alone, then suddenly that soft cool voice spoke again.

"Very good Zachie boy... Very good."

Zach smiled. He was happy again; and no longer alone. His new friend was still with him.

IAN D.G. SANDUSKY

SHOTGUN

Heavy in my hands,
Their rotting frames break the hill.
Quick trigger, swift death.

SMOKE

If the dark has mass,
It is something far stronger
Something fingers touch

THE HUNGER OF SHADOWS
BY ROBERT FREESE

"I don't wanna go, daddy." The five year old squirmed in her car seat while her father unlatched the chair's safety belt.

"Why not, sweetheart?" Jason was tired. After driving for more than ten hours straight, they were only halfway to Kim's parent's house. He always hated the drive up to Presque Isle. It was a grueling twelve hundred mile trek. It seemed like half the vacation was spent in the car.

Dunsmore was just a little past the halfway point. For as long as they had been taking the trip from Columbus to Presque Isle they always stayed the night in Dunsmore.

Both the girls were restless from being crammed in the car for so long. He felt bad for Callie, the little one, being strapped into the hard plastic seat for the duration. If she wanted to be a little crabby he was not going to challenge her.

"She's just a fraidy cat," Taryn offered sliding out the opposite door. Although the thirteen year old was plugged into her iPod and simultaneously texting on her cell phone, she never seemed to shy away from an opportunity to tease her little sister.

"I am not! You're a fraidy cat," Callie said defensively. Her lower lip pouched out. Jason thought she looked exactly like her mother when she did that.

"Enough, Taryn Amanda Barnes," her mother said. Kim was out of the car and stretching. Her legs felt numb. It was wonderful to finally stand and move around. Feeling was slowly creeping back into her legs.

"I'm just saying," the older girl said, never looking up from her phone. "Besides, why are we here? I'm hungry."

"I'm hungry too, daddy." Callie was starting to whine, which meant she was getting tired.

"Do I have a mutiny on my hands? We're going to eat when we get to the hotel. I just thought this would be fun. We always pass this place and say we should stop but we never do." He kissed his youngest daughter on her forehead.

"Really, Jason, we can just eat and turn in early." Kim looked as tired as the girls.

"It's not that late," he said, taking his youngest daughter's hand and then his wife's. "I hate being cooped up in the car all day long and then going to the hotel without doing anything. It's not even dark yet. We got a heck of a jump on the drive leaving as early as we did."

"It's probably just a tourist trap."

"So let it be. I'm tired of being in the car and I'm not ready to be cooped up in the hotel room with the girls just yet. After this we'll eat and get over to the hotel. If there's time you can take the girls to the pool."

"Fair enough." Smiling, she kissed his cheek.

"Keep up, Taryn," he called over to the teenager. She had a defiant attitude about everything she did these days. Every comment could possibly lead to a conflict of some sort. She was just barely a teenager and already she was pushing them away. She hardly acknowledged her father, but she followed a short distance behind.

It just dawned on him there were no other cars in the parking lot. They approached the entrance of the two-story building, the front of which looked like an old-fashioned movie theater. There was a three-sided marquee that was missing more bulbs than it had. None of the marquee lights were on. It looked like the Dunsmore Wax Museum had been closed for ages.

"Is it even open?" Kim squinted to see through the dirty windowpanes of the circular box office.

"It says they're open until eight. It's only," he looked at his watch, "six thirty."

"I'm starving," Taryn said, prompting her little sister to chime in with a "Me too."

Suddenly, a man appeared behind the box office window. Jason had no idea how long he had been there. He seemed to just appear from the darkness.

"Welcome to the Dunsmore Wax Museum, the oldest waxworks in all of Massachusetts." His voice was low and scratchy. He wore granny style round sunglasses, a black suit with cape and top hat and a black leather glove on his left hand. It was impossible to tell how old he was, but Jason felt like he was an old man.

"Four tickets," Jason said when he finally found his voice. "Two adults and two children." Taryn rolled her eyes, agitated at being referred to as a child.

"Tickets are two dollars apiece, sir, regardless of age. Eight dollars total, please."

"I'm sorry, did you say eight?" Since the moment Kim had given birth to their first, he had resigned himself to a lifetime of paying out the nose for family entertainment, regardless what they did. Somehow it didn't seem right to pay only eight dollars to do anything.

"Yes, sir." The man just stared at him through the dirty box office glass. It was impossible to tell where he was looking behind the dark shades.

Jason pushed a twenty under the half circle cut in the box office glass. The old man passed a ten, two ones and four brightly colored tickets back to him.

"You folks from out of town?"

"Yeah," Jason answered, tucking the change back into his wallet. "We're headed up to visit my wife's parents for the week."

"Very good. You folks take your time and visit all the exhibits. We've got rooms upstairs and down. Some of them are new. Stay as long as you like."

"Thank you, Mister…" Jason looked for a name badge but saw none.

"Moon. Keivert Moon. I've been curator here for a long, long time." He offered a slight grin then nodded his head. With that he took a step backwards and the darkness behind him seemed to swallow him whole. He was gone.

"Weird," Kim said looking at her husband.

"Yeah. I bet it's just part of the show. Besides, it was only eight bucks."

"I don't want to go in, daddy." The little girl tugged at the hem of his shorts.

"Come on, sweetheart. Let's go in and see some of the displays and then we'll go get something to eat."

"Chicken nuggets," Callie said excitedly.

"Sure, chicken nuggets." Jason led his family into the waxworks.

Upon entering, they walked into a large front room called The Presidential Suite. They were greeted by the wax likenesses of nearly every president from Washington on up to the current administration. At the cast of John F. Kennedy, motion sensors activated snippets of his famous "Ask not what your country can do for you" speech that played over speakers hidden behind the figure. The sound was tinny sounding and metallic, like the sound from an old drive-in movie speaker.

"I don't like these," Callie said, clutching her mother's leg.

"Don't be silly. They're just wax figures." She caressed the side of her daughter's face.

"No they're not," Taryn countered. "They're really people that creepy old guy froze forever in wax. They're trying to get out, but they can't. They're stuck here forever. But if they ever get out they'll come and get you for not helping them escape."

"No!" The five year old buried her head into her mother's leg.

"Give it a rest, Taryn," Jason said. Why was there never a moment's peace? "Callie acts better than you do and she's only five."

His older daughter stuck her tongue out then turned the music on her iPod up loud enough for her parents to hear it. She went back to texting her friends.

Room after room took them into different worlds. They explored one after another, marveling at the wonderful details in the wax images. For such a run-down building on the outside, the inside was impeccably clean. They saw kings and queens, famous inventors and criminals, politicians, rulers and dictators. In one room dedicated to the exploration of space, they encountered astronauts from numerous space missions and even listened to Neil Armstrong's famous, "One small step" speech.

"This place is huge," Kim said after getting pictures of Jason and the girls next to Buzz Aldridge.

"Way bigger than it looks from outside," he added, looking around. "There're still a couple more rooms we haven't seen down here, or we can go upstairs and check out the Rock 'n Roll Hall of Fame, Sports Heroes and the Golden Age of Hollywood." He was looking at a map on the wall. "What do you say?"

"I just want to go," Taryn said, not looking up from her phone. "This place is lame."

"I want to go too, daddy," Callie whined.

Kissing him on his cheek, Kim whispered, "And you wanted daughters because you thought they would be sweeter than sons."

"I say we go up, check out a couple more rooms, then get out of here and find some food before we crash at the hotel."

Both girls made faces like they had just been told they were going to have to get jobs for the summer instead of having it off. Jason took Kim's hand and led them up the stairs.

Upstairs, in the Rock 'n Roll Hall of Fame, they took pictures with some of the biggest hit makers that ever topped the charts. Taryn was interested enough to take pictures alongside some of the current pop stars with the camera on her phone, which she immediately began sending to her friends. They went through the Sports displays and then visited the wax figures of Marilyn Monroe, Humphrey Bogart and dozens more. As they came out the other side of the Hollywood display, the hallway narrowed and led toward a display room called the Chamber of Horrors.

"Can we just go back, daddy," Callie whined beside him as they approached the open doorway into the new display.

"No, we'll just go through here and then go back down. This is the way out."

"I don't want to go in there, daddy."

"Fraidy cat," her big sister teased from behind.

"I am not!" She turned and slapped Taryn on her bare leg.

"Hey, squirt! Mom, Callie hit me!"

"Stop it the two of you." Kim was losing her patience. "We're going to be done in a minute. Just follow your father and don't make another sound."

This is great, Jason thought. Now his kids are being punished by having to follow me through the wax museum. Everyone was just tired. Maybe this wasn't the best idea.

Strobe lights mimicking lightning blasted across figures being tortured in racks, iron maidens and hanging by chains on the walls. Some of the displays were quite graphic. Victims were frozen in scenes of various tortures. Some were being burned with irons and brands. In one it showed a witch being burned at the stake.

"That reminds me of Mrs. Whateley, my science teacher," Taryn said at the display of the burning witch. She took a picture of it with her phone and sent it to her friends.

"This is a bit much," Kim whispered to Jason. "Callie is terrified."

"I didn't know it was going to have this kind of stuff." Jason was leading them through the darkness, going from one display to the next. "Besides, this is the way out." He nodded up to an Exit sign pointing into another room.

When they entered they found themselves in an oversized graveyard scene. They stopped to take it all in. In addition to the gravestones, there was a wax figure dressed up in a hooded cloak wearing a pentagram on a chain around its neck. The figure was holding a book. It was standing off to the side of the numerous grave markers and monuments. Walking by the figure activated a light show of different colored beams and a strobe effect that simulated lightning.

A spotlight of red fell on the figure. Crackling sound erupted through the ancient sound system.

At the far end of the display was a blinking Exit sign.

"I am a necromancer. The dead I shall raise with words from this ancient text. Older than time itself, these words will awaken the elder gods who lived in this world billions of years before man. Older than history, they are the darkness, the shadows behind every living being. Soon their day to arise will come again."

A peal of booming thunder struck again and a wind machine began blowing.

"I think I've had enough," Kim said, picking up her youngest daughter. The little girl clung to her, practically shaking with fright.

"I want to see what it does," Taryn said.

Of course, Jason thought, now that Kim said it was time to go, Taryn was interested in the displays. He reached out and took the teenager's hand. She instantly pulled away from him.

The words booming from the speakers were in Latin.

"Consurgo vetus ones quod cubo vestri per. Nutritor super pallens they es vobis. Totus es vitualamen vobis. Isest leviculus, EGO teneo, tamen is est quis has ut venio in a fibula super umbra everto epulum in populus."

Blowing more ferociously, the wind machine whipped dust and pieces of the display into the air. The particles seemed to form a small twister. Flashing lights cast dark shadows and seemed to form a whirling vortex near the display's center.

"Daddy, I want to go!" Callie squirmed in her mother's arms until Kim put her down. The little girl pulled on her father's arm.

"Look at that." Jason couldn't take his eyes off the swirling vortex. Whatever the trick was, he couldn't figure it out. Dark shapes seemed to fly out of the blackness.

Taryn was trying to take a picture of it when one of the shadows jumped from the vortex, snapping at her. She screamed when the pain exploded throughout her body. The cell phone was gone. Her hands were gone. In their place were bloody stumps. She screamed hysterically as blood pumped from where her hands had been bitten off.

"Taryn!" Kim went to her daughter, but a shadow swooped down, picking her up off the floor. Several more seemed to dive into her, taking bites from her flesh, ripping her body to pieces. The woman's blood rained down upon her family.

A shadow clawed at Jason's face and then poured down his throat. Choking, he finally screamed as the shadow ate its way through his stomach, exposing itself with a flash of blood and innards. He lived long enough to hear his older daughter scream for help as the shadows converged on her. She sounded like a little girl again.

Callie ran to the exit sign. She knew what it said, that it was a way out. When she pushed the door open, the man in the suit, top hat and sunglasses was there.

"Where are you going little one?" Snatching her by the arm, he jerked her off her feet and slung her back into the display where the shadows were feeding. Keivert Moon pulled the little girl's arm right out of its socket, but there had been no time for the pain to register before the shadows had completely consumed her.

Josh Reinhart flipped a couple switches and plugged in the show's intro to the new webisode. The screen came alive with Dave Merwyn screaming on a roller coaster and then participating in a little urban bungee jumping off a city bridge. Why people wanted to watch this was beyond him, but each new webisode took the Internet by storm and that was what the sponsors wanted. It was easier to sell body spray and pizza pockets when half the world was watching.

"Okay, guys. We've got just over one hundred and sixty thousand people logged on and ready to watch. Let's make this happen."

Watching the monitors Josh witnesses Dave, the loud mouth host of Virtual Vacations, put his game face on, snapping instantly into character. This is what Dave was born to do. He knew it when he was on that ridiculous reality show about the people living together in the high rise. More than two million people followed his daily blog until he was voted off the show, then his readership doubled as he continued blogging about the other contestants. The show's numbers dropped significantly when he was off and the producers used any excuse to bring him back. Dave was hot, the current "in thing" and he was going to milk his fifteen minutes of fame for all it was worth.

The camera showed Dave standing just outside the Dunsmore Wax Museum. The sun is shining behind the building. There is no traffic passing by and nobody on the streets. In fact, the rest of the town appears deserted. Josh wonders about this but as soon as Dave addresses the camera, like all the other viewers, he's glued to his seat. That's why the website's sponsors pay him all the money; people were just attracted to Dave Merwyn.

Tapping the microphone on his chest and giving the biggest, cheesiest smile his face could accommodate he goes into his regular spiel. "This thing is on and you've got me, Dave Merwyn, taking you on another virtual journey to find more of the coolest places on planet earth. Today we're in Dunsmore, Massachusetts at the Dunsmore Wax Museum. This is the oldest, and one of the last, wax museums in the entire state of Massachusetts. Its curator, Keivert Moon, claims it offers more than four dozen rooms filled with some of the most extravagant displays in the world. Check it out, gang. The building doesn't look big enough to house almost fifty rooms, but amazingly, it does. Let's go inside and see if Mr. Moon will give us a tour. Come on."

With the camera operator and soundman following, Dave turns, crosses the road and then opens the double glass doors leading into the waxworks.

"Stay with him." From the van, Josh watches to make sure the camera picks up everything. "Good." With Clint on camera and Bill on sound, there are no worries about the quality of the work. Watching the various monitors in the van's mobile studio he keeps track of the people logging on for the show, which is streaming live. "We're up on two hundred thousand people logged onto the site," he says for Clint to hear. "Stay with him."

The camera follows Dave as he enters the Presidential Suite. Standing in the center of the room is the museum's curator. He looks old and fragile but he stands erect and tall. He seems especially tall and lanky in the top hat.

"Mr. Moon, how long have run the wax museum and where do you get your displays?" The camera focuses on the old man. Light from the camera can be seen in the reflection of the man's sunglasses.

"Sometimes I feel like I have been here forever. As for the displays, we have artists all over the world that we commission for certain works. They are true artists, as you can tell." He waves his hand around the assembled presidents. The camera goes into a tight close-up of the wax visage of Bill Clinton. Doing a bad impersonation, Dave can be heard saying, "I did not have sex with that woman. I just put my penis in her mouth."

The camera swirls back to the host, who smiles and says, "Come on. Let's take a look at everything else the Dunsmore Wax Museum has to offer."

From the cramped confines of the van, Josh keeps vigil before the bank of monitors as the camera picks out various displays to highlight. Already he is thinking ahead of how he is going to edit the new episode for the short attention span viewers.

"Everything is looking really good. You're getting some great stuff, Clint. Make sure Bill gets in there whenever Dave goes off on his shtick and does the voices and stuff. People love that crap."

One of the monitors flashes, showing a stream of incoming emails. People were already writing in. Dave's three second impression of Clinton was already being circulated throughout the web, going viral less than a minute after it happened. That clip would be file shared nearly half a million times before the show was even over.

"Let's go up here and see what we can find." The camera follows as Dave ascends the steps to the museum's second level. All of a sudden the camera pans away from the host to another set of stairs going up.

"What the hell?" It was Clint, panning all around to show the second set of stairs.

"That can't be right." Bill moves slightly and the audio equipment picks up his movement.

"Guys, I can hear you. I don't want to hear you. Where's Dave?" Josh watches as the camera moves to find Dave. The host is standing near the top of the stairs and looking up.

"I don't know if you remember from outside but this building is only two stories tall. It does have a basement with more displays, but there is a second set of stairs just over here, going up to a third story. Take a look."

The camera pans away from the host to show the stairs. Clint captures it all while Dave talks. "I don't know where it goes, but there should not be another set of stairs here. It's weird. But we'll check it out in a couple minutes." The camera moves back on him and then moves in for a close up. "Let's check out some Hollywood starlets." Dave wiggles his eyebrows before entering the Golden Age of Hollywood display.

Reading some of the comments coming through the instant messaging, Josh looks up in time to see Dave groping the wax image of Rita Hayworth. He goes on to violate the Judy Garland figure that is dressed to look like Dorothy from the Wizard of Oz.

It would be mere moments before both snippets of Dave's rude humor were running wild through cyberspace. There were more than a three hundred and forty thousand people logged on and watching, which was a good audience for the live show.

Sometimes it was too much. Josh had conflicting thoughts as to his contribution to the world, driving around the country and directing the show. There were dozens of fan sites where kids posted videos of themselves doing asinine things on vacation with their parents because they had seen Dave do the same thing on the show. Sometimes it seemed like such a waste of talent.

Josh didn't get it. Kids were different today. Everything happened in front of a computer screen for them. When he was their age he was out in the world, with his friends, hanging out and having fun, not logged on to a computer for endless hours getting absolutely nothing done.

Now he spent too much time in front of a computer. He hated it sometimes. After they were done filming they'd go back to the hotel for the night. He would stay up most of the night with Clint editing the footage into a nine-minute show that could be downloaded whenever viewers wanted to watch it. They would post it on certain sites but it would not take long for the show to be all over the world, showing up on tens of thousands of websites.

When he looks back at the monitor Dave is entering the Chamber of Horrors.

Immediately the host goes to a display depicting a witch being tortured on a rack and puts his hand under her dress. It is nothing too vulgar, but enough for the audience for this kind of stuff.

"You are such an idiot," Josh mumbles as he continues to read more comments from viewers. Most of the people writing in think his antics are funny.

"How about a little head," Dave says at the display of a guillotine victim. He reaches into the display basket and pulls out the severed wax head. Holding it close in an extreme close-up, he licks the wax head's nose and nostrils.

"A complete idiot," Josh mumbles. His stomach grumbles. He is hungry. They spent half the day driving to this location from the last. He hopes they will be done soon so they can grab a bite to eat. His mind is wandering, watching between the messages and the show.

The camera follows as Dave enters the graveyard. He gives the display an enthusiastic, "Wicked cool," and a thumb's up. The cameraman catches the activation of the lightshow and warlock's monologue. Mock lightning blasts all around them. Then the Latin incantation plays through the popping, hissing speakers.

"*Consurgo vetus ones quod cubo vestri per. Nutritor super pallens they es vobis. Totus es vitualamen vobis. Isest leviculus, EGO teneo,* tamen is est quis has ut venio in a fibula super umbra everto epulum in populus."

"Whoa!" It was Clint again and Josh reminds him again to keep quiet. Then the director sees what the cameraman sees. Incredibly, he is able to focus in and capture both the swirling vortex with the host in the foreground in the same scene.

"This has got to be one of the coolest things I've ever seen," Dave says, turning towards the camera. "Like I always say, you find the coolest stuff in the most out of the way places. In fact…"

He is suddenly cut off. In the blink of an eye one of the shadows had swooped down upon him and bit off his head.

"Jesus Christ!" Josh was instantly at attention. "What the hell just happened?"

The camera shows Dave's body going limp, but before it falls it is snatched up in the clawed tentacles of another shadow. Several shadows feast on the body, ripping and tearing it to shreds.

All at once the camera and sound equipment are shed, dropped and forgotten. At the angle the camera falls, Josh can see Clint and Bill sprinting toward the Exit. They push and shove but the door will not budge.

From beyond the view of the camera's lens, a giant shadow tentacle whips out and wraps around Bill. The soundman struggles and thrashes about trying to break free from the grip holding him, but the tentacle holds tight. He is pulled out of the camera's sight. His screaming is cut short and replaced with the sound of snapping bones.

Beating wildly on the door, Clint screams over and over to be let free. When a shadow flies past him he screams in agonizing pain. The camera reveals a giant chunk of his flesh missing from his back. Blood pours out of the wound, which exposes parts of his spine. Another shadow dives in close and bites a portion from his skull. His body falls and lies still only a moment before another shadow drags it from the camera's range.

"What the hell?" Josh feels flush and sick. The website was ablaze with viewers wanting to know what was going on. Snippets of Dave and his crew's deaths were already being downloaded, shared and emailed faster than a lightning strike.

At last the camera is consumed. Picked up, it spins wildly in the air. Still connected to the live feed, the images it is recording are still streaming live. Sucked into the whirling vortex the camera vanishes. Nothing but overwhelming darkness shows on the screen.

When he thinks the connection has finally been broken, Josh reaches for the keyboard. When he does, the monitors' screens crack and shatter. A solid blackness starts pouring from the screens. A tiny shadow finger falls onto his arm and bites deep into his flesh. Screaming, he falls backwards, hitting his head against the van's door as more of the inky shadow pours from the ruined screens.

Struggling to find his balance, Josh throws the van's door open and falls out onto the parking lot's hot macadam. Quickly he slams the sliding door shut. The van shakes where it is parked, rocking on its suspension. Something is beating wildly from within. Quickly he scoots away from the vehicle. All of a sudden, there is laughter in the air.

Keivert Moon is standing outside the museum. He is laughing and clapping his hands. The sun is hot and heat waves seem to make Moon appear apparition-like. Taking off the glove covering his left hand he reveals a hand as black as the shadow creatures. When he takes off his sunglasses, his eyes reveal burned out pits aglow with the shadows from beyond.

"I've served them my whole life. More than two hundred years. You start to become like them, the old ones. They're coming to reclaim what is rightfully theirs. They will claim the darkness once again and rule the earth. The light will be dead." Laughing, his image shimmers where he is standing, the heat waves seemingly erasing him from the landscape. There is a brilliant flash of light and then a booming crack of thunder and the old man is gone.

The van's windshield shatters and the shadows start pouring out like thick tentacles made of black jam.

He begins to run. There is no destination in his mind. Josh just has to get away. He has to escape. Leaving the shadows behind him, he runs as fast as he can.

The sunlight is slowly ebbing away, giving way to an all-encompassing darkness.

The road was getting to him. Ric Armitage had been driving for hours. For whatever reason, it had gotten darker sooner than usual, and he hated night driving. He needed to find a hotel somewhere and get some sleep. If he got up a little early and pushed it, he could get to Boston in the morning before the meeting.

The stretch of Interstate he was traveling was barren. He had not passed another car in hours. The regular drives to Boston were getting to be a real pain.

Ahead, he saw there was an upcoming exit. It offered a couple eateries, gas stations and a hotel. Ric took the exit as soon as he came upon it.

Circling around, he drove past two service stations and a number of fast food places. None of them looked open. There were a couple lights on, but for the most part all of them looked deserted.

Driving a little farther, he found the Wagner Inn. It was a tiny motel off to the side of the road that looked to have thirteen rooms to rent. Even though it was not that late, there was not a soul around. He pulled into the lot, parking next to the office.

Dim lights flickered behind the curtains in the couple of rooms that had cars parked in front of them. The air was warm and humid like it was going to rain, but there hadn't been a cloud in the sky for days.

Entering the office, a little bell above the door rang. Everything was quiet inside the office. It smelled of dust and cheap disinfectant.

"Hello?" He hoped whoever ran the place could recommend a place where he could grab a bite to eat. There was another bell on the desk. He tapped it a couple times. Nothing rude, just enough to let the proprietor know he was waiting to rent a room.

Nothing stirred. The place seemed abandoned.

"Hey, is there anyone here? Hello?"

When he got no response he went around the desk. There was a doorway into a backroom. He opened the door a crack and said, "Hello? Customer here, I'd like to rent a room."

Silence greeted him. Ric pushed the door all the way open. The room was dark except for a desk lamp on a nearby table. On the table was a computer. Its screen was smashed.

"Not good," he said quietly, looking around. "Hey, are you all right? Do I need to call an ambulance?"

When he went out into the office, a loud boom shook the building and rattled all the windowpanes.

"What the hell?"

Again the boom and the shaking. The way they came, one after the other, they made him think of stomping of feet.

Outside he looked to see if there had been an accident. Another boom rocked the air. It was coming from just down the dark roadway. Leaning on his car, he peered into the night to see what it was.

The shadows had been feeding and now they were taking definite shape, forming bodies. What he saw seared into his mind and fried every nerve ending in his body. The body was as big as a house. Fear froze him as the giant creature continued its stroll down the roadway. Each booming of its giant clawed feet resonated with the power of a tremor. It seemed to notice Armitage just standing there. The body was alive with a multitude of whipping tentacles flailing about.

He had no more strength to scream than he did to run away as the giant talons reached down to grab him. The stench of the creature's fetid breath overwhelmed him. Before he could even understand what was happening, dagger-like teeth came down upon him and began grinding his body into a pulpy wad. In an instant he was swallowed into the darkness.

And the shadows continued feeding.

THE DEVIL, YOU SAY

BY KEN GOLDMAN

*"Sway down Mama, sway down low.
They gonna know me wherever I go ..."*

Bruce Springsteen
"A Night with the Jersey Devil"

Professor Marcus Suthers with twenty of his intrepid young followers got a good-sized fire started near the students' tents. He knew these Pine Barrens would provide the necessary backdrop for the folklore shared by some of his invited locals from the nearby towns of Ong's Hat and Mount Misery. With something like a million acres of South Jersey forests, the area boasted its share of legend going back almost three centuries to the American Indians who called themselves the Lenni Lenape. Throughout the years these whispering pines had accumulated many voices, and tonight some of those voices would share their stories among the maze of the forest's white sand trails. By the crackling flames, warming themselves against the autumn chill, a legend's believers sat alongside his skeptics.

Professor Suthers felt uncertain under which category he fell, but as a Rutgers University biology instructor and a member of the

Pinelands Field Research Station he felt obliged to keep an open mind pertaining to the tales of the Garden State's alleged ghosts and demons, but especially regarding tonight's in absentia guest of honor. Of course, this campfire scene would add a little flair to the mythology surrounding the celebrated Jersey Devil, and Suthers saw nothing wrong with that. The creature's unique mythos was right up there with 'Nessie and Sasquatch, his reputation easily lending itself to some modern day theatrics along with some good old homespun creepiness. Suthers warmed his hands near the fire, the dancing flames causing a 'now-you see it, now you don't' effect on the man's face as he began.

"The Dutch explorers had it right when they named this place the Barrens. Although the Cedar trees along the riverbanks provide some blood red color to the region, the sugary white land soil here was never meant for farming. The Lenape tribe used to refer to these parts as 'the place of dragons,' so maybe the locals felt the need to create a monster or two. Here – right here in these woods is where many of the Devil sightings took place, you know. Pretty dark and somber around here, eh?"

Suthers lit his Meerschaum, hoping the image of a pipe-puffing professor might add credence to his words, although he knew his youthful appearance probably undercut that perception. "Of course, many locals insist those encounters were only with the area's natural creatures, and the Barrens certainly contain enough of them. Residents of Ong's Hat often claim they hear shrieks and howls coming from these pines, but wild forest animals make noise, and the occasional cougar has been spotted around this particular campsite. However, those cougar sightings have been few for many years because most of those larger cats have been hunted out. The Barrens are extensive, so no one really knows what's out here any more. But some of tonight's guests claim they know. And perhaps during tonight's little field trip we may be fortunate enough to witness what they claim they have seen."

A few invited area residents managed a perfunctory smile. Most didn't. As if on cue a hoot owl bellowed out her healthy howl into the night air. That merited a laugh from the circle of young campers, and one wiseass student provided an additional "Whoooo-ooooo" to supply the nocturnal creature a little backup.

Suthers enjoyed another puff. "Legend has it that Mrs. Deborah Leeds - the locals call her Mother Leeds – had twelve children. I guess that would make her the Octomom of her day. After giving birth to her twelfth child, the woman complained 'Let it be the Devil!' if she had a thirteenth – and during one stormy night in 1735 her unintentional curse bore some nasty fruit. She went into a painful labor, screaming her guts out. Some say Mother Leeds was a witch and the child's father was rumored to be the Devil himself, although records suggest the man was Japhet Leeds, a hard drinking pioneer trying to feed a large family and hardly the demon type."

Taking another draw from his pipe, Suthers managed a toothy smile that emerged Cheshire-like through the billows of smoke. "Yeah, I know, I know. It's tacky stuff born of much simpler times. Anyway, the Leeds woman gave birth to a normal child, but then it supposedly changed form, morphed into some kind of beast with hooves and a horse's head or some kind of goat's, then sprouted bat wings and a forked tail. Breathed fire too, yada yada and yada. Moments after its birth the infant growled and screamed like any respectable monster would – then sank its teeth into Mother Leeds' midwife's throat and killed his twelve siblings too. Scarfed down their flesh right in front of mom, then killed her also and flew up the chimney. Circling the villages to give their residents a good peek, he headed toward these pines. And here he stayed, dining on livestock, occasionally reemerging in nearby towns or on some back road or farm to perform a little of the ol' Booga-Booga. And thus, as they say, the legend was born."

No hoot owl bellowed to fill the momentary silence this time, but the professor had made his point. Suthers directed his students' attention to the elderly man who chose not to sit very close to the flames.

"Class, here on my left is Mr. J.T. Russel, a farmer from the happy little town of Mount Misery to fill you in. Mr. Russel claims he's a first hand observer of the notorious Devil from New Jersey." Polite applause followed, a reaction the old man chose to ignore. With some difficulty he stood up from his tree log with the aid of a crooked cane. Clearing his throat the grizzled local seemed as if he could have come from backwoods central casting. His face clearly had not seen a razor in weeks and his matted white hair looked as if it had been pissed into. With no trace of a smile he eyed his audience, then sat.

"Let me get one thing straight from the start with you young people. I don't see tonight's gathering as no picnic, no ma'am. So if you intend to heat your franks and s'mores over this fire while I'm speaking, I'll be taking my leave – although I'm fairly certain the last thing you'll be wanting to do after hearing my story will be to roast some dumb ass marshmallows."

The man's prologue provided a nice touch of local color, Suthers thought. Realizing J.T. Russel was deadly serious the professor didn't hold that opinion very long. The old coot seemed set on scaring the bejeezus out of everyone present.

"Don't matter whether that Devil creature hails from Jersey or Hell, since to my mind they're both pretty much the same place. I'm a farmer. Not much else a man can do with the land 'round these parts 'cept stare at it, not if he wants to put food on his table. There're only two real decisions a farmer's got to make 'round Leeds Point. One is the woman he selects to share his bed with, and the other is what kind of livestock he intends to raise. Both better be good choices, 'cause you're goin' to be stuck with your selection for the rest of your days, that's a damned fact. Lucky for me I selected chicken farming, 'cause them egg-laying chickens just like to eat and make more chickens. As for the woman in my bed – well, let's just say one of my two selections weren't bad, and my Stella weren't it."

Some of the students laughed, but old man Russel never cracked a smile. He stared at the crowd of young faces like a stern parent, waited for the mumbling to go silent.

"Jersey Devil, my ass. That's just some idiot name for the tourists to swallow, like we got some fucking kiddie cartoon stalking these woods. Well, let me tell you, that chicken killing offspring of Mother Leeds ain't no cartoon – he's some goddamned monster, and a hungry one at that. People 'round here average maybe ten sightings a year of that beast, and there's the zoo in Philadelphia what's got a million dollar reward for his head to this very day. He sure as hell may be a devil considerin' the destruction he brung to my life…

"Bout five years ago I'm going into the hen houses and I'm findin' half my chickens with their heads chomped clean off. I'm thinking it's got to be some fox come in the night, maybe a whole family of 'em because the chicken killin' is so complete and efficient. A fox hunting inside a hen house ain't no cliché to a man who's raisin' livestock for his living, and a hundred dead chickens forces a working man to take some drastic measures, to hell with the law."

The old guy lowered his voice. Maybe he did it for effect, but to Suthers it seemed J.T. Russel was sharing some sort of secret, maybe unloading something heavy he had grown weary of carrying.

"I set some metal traps all 'round them coops strong enough to bring down a goddamn bear. Yeah, sure, I known them animal traps was illegal, nor did I give a rat's turd. I figure in the morning I'll have me at least one fat and very dead fox caught in the teeth of one of them traps. If I'm lucky, I'm thinking maybe I'll find that bushy tailed bastard still alive so's I can have some satisfaction breaking his fuckin' neck with my bare hands."

Suthers' ecological considerations kicked in. "A fox has to eat too, Mr. Russel. I'm not saying it was right some creature killed your chickens, but nature tells an animal he has to hunt to survive and that's all he knows to do, so you can't blame–"

The old man shot the instructor a look that suggested he would tolerate no fools tonight. "A man's got to eat too, Mr. Suthers. And it weren't no fox, Professor. It weren't nothing even closely resemblin' no fox, no ma'am. I could see that 'count of the sheer number of dead poultry he's leavin' behind. Some of my fattest chickens was still in their coops minus their heads but uneaten, as if this damned creature is toying with me, challengin' me to catch his wily ass. Or maybe it was just his sheer joy of killin'. He missed the traps, the lucky bastard, but footprints I found the next mornin' inside the chickens' coop was clear proof it weren't no fox. See, I spread sawdust all 'round them hen house floors just to discover what bloodthirsty beast might be dining so often on my livelihood. I been in these Barrens my whole life, and I can tell you I ain't never seen no fox had hooves. This weren't nothing that went on all fours neither. Them sawdust prints showed this fucker walked like a man!"

A disquieting silence followed, a long one. Samantha Winoker raised her head from the shoulder of her male classmate. The pretty blonde student stood up.

"Excuse me, Mr. Russel, but that isn't very much for us to go on. I mean no disrespect, but just because you're saying it, don't make it so. Many people claim to see flying saucers too, you know, and for some reason it's always people who live in secluded places like these Barrens. I read somewhere there are sandhill cranes in this area with wingspans something like seven feet, and they screech too, so maybe –"

The sophomore coed had touched a raw nerve, and Mr. J.T. Russel beaded in on her like a man transformed into a hawk. "Sandhill cranes don't hunt livestock. Girlie, you say you want some proof we got something more substantial than some dumb ass bird in these Barrens? Well, I intend to show you that proof, if you'll just shut that pretty little yapper for a moment."

The kid sitting next to her quickly pulled Samantha's hand and whispered something to her that evidently echoed the old man's words. She looked over at Suthers who nodded his agreement and added a finger to his lips. Samantha sat down and said nothing, but J.T. Russel's eyes stayed on her as he spoke.

"I may not look book learned to you young folks, but I'm no fool neither. While countin' my dead poultry I weren't about to lose my head like one of my chickens. So I'm decided this next night after lights out I'm going to keep guard of my coops, and not with my shotgun, nuh uh. I'm graspin' my woodsman's axe because I want that bastard's blood spilled close up where I can smell it. But he was a smart fuck, he was. Three nights I'm waitin' for his return, and by the time he finally comes back I'm half asleep against the wall in the dark. Well past midnight I see this shadowy figure skulking among the coops, and my blood just run to ice. He was long and lean like some huge bird, but movin' with the stealth of a lizard, and his wings, they're flapping at the sawdust so as not to leave no trace this time. I got to my feet praying the bastard was too chicken-hungered to hear me."

The pines rustled, and several of Suthers' students looked around. The professor took a quick glance over his shoulder too. T. J. Russel had worked some wicked magic on everyone and he didn't intend to let the moment slip away. The old man approached the flickering fire, warmed his hands over it.

"I'm creepin' in the gray dark behind that bastard, close as I can allow myself. And my brain, it's just racing, racing . . . but I'm not a man who's thinking one hun'red percent, see, 'cause I'm so bent on killing this fucker I'm forgetting something, something important. I realize what I'm overlooking only a moment before it's too late . . .

"The goddamned traps! I still had them set all over the coop! In that darkness near the biggest paddock I stepped into one of those steel toothed mothers, and *Ka- chomp!* Damn near tore my foot clear off! Them teeth cut right through my flesh and I hear this terrible crunch like dried wood, and I know that's my own anklebone I'm hearing. That trap brings me down to the floor in this red agony, and – *I can't help myself!* – I'm screaming, screaming like there's this buzz saw chewing my foot into tatters of raw meat! But then I realize that none of this agony is the worst of it. Because that bastard Devil, he's standin' right over me, and he's near enough that I see he's got teeth longer and sharper than the metal trap what's got me in its death grip. His mouth, it's open and dripping like he's preparin' himself for the gourmet meal of his life. So I quit my screaming, fearful my Stella might come running to provide that winged fiend with two meals 'stead of one. Clear thinking took a moment or two, but then I 'membered I still held that axe and there's but one way I'm goin' to walk away from this horned fucker – or, at least hobble away. I screwed up whatever fortitude remained after havin' the hot piss scared outa me, and then I done what I hadda do . . ."

Here Russel backed off from the flickering flame as if the man wanted no one to see his face during his telling of the next part.

"One savage chop, that's how I figured I'd do 'er, and I brung that axe down full force on my own limb maybe three inches 'bove my foot. Hardest thing I ever done was keeping myself silent while enduring the worst pain of my life, and I had to bite down on my hand to do it. But I needed to go for another three hits to hack through some thick bone before I pulled myself free of that metal snare – and free of what remained of my right foot that still lay bleeding in its teeth. And that whole time the creature – your fucking Devil - he's just staring down on me, enjoyin' every moment of my misery. Even in that gray dark I can see his goat horns, smell the fetid stink of his breath.

"Well, I got free, all right, just in time to see him seize my foot from the trap, then gnaw on it like he's havin' his goddamned midnight snack. Ate the boot right off, shoelaces danglin' from his fucking maw like spaghetti. I swear he was grinnin' while he chewed through to my toes, though those five little piggies no longer belonged to me. But I didn't intend to wait around for him to finish. Dragging the stump of what remained of my mangled limb I managed to limp outside to the barnyard before I saw that bastard lappin' up the blood trail behind me like some starved mongrel. I felt certain he would follow my own blood right back to the ragged stump I was tugging behind me like some useless pine log. Instead I watched him take to the sky and disappear 'neath a dull moon. But he left me with this to make sure I didn't forget our encounter, no ma'am . . ."

The old farmer pulled up his pants leg to reveal in the firelight the raw stub of meaty flesh where his foot should have been.

For a long while no one said a word. Suthers spoke to break the silence.

"The place of dragons. Not entirely an inaccurate description for these parts. Thank you, Mr. Russel."

A girl's sudden giggle from the circle of students caused everyone to look. It seemed an inappropriate interruption, but Suthers felt the proceedings had grown a little too heavy and maybe required some levity. Doreen Slevan's embarrassment showed in the dancing light.

Some guy called out, "Did Cliff's hand slip in the dark again, Doreen?"

Clifford Boornsteen gave an unconvincing laugh that only his girl Doreen seemed to find funny while she buttoned her sweater. "This might be a good time for me to pee on a tree," Boornsteen said. The student managed an awkward exit from the group and disappeared into the forest. The moment of comic relief over, Suthers planned to introduce another storyteller, but the old woman named Eunice McClellan spoke first.

"Mr. Russel, may I say I certainly found your story captivating? Colorful, dramatic in all the right spots, and appropriately spooky. My goodness, you almost had me believing every word of it. Except for the simple fact that none of it is true. You old fool, ever' one in a twenty mile radius of Mt. Misery knows you lost that foot to the gangrene years ago! Your Stella told me so herself! The only Jersey Devil I see here is holding onto a cane!"

J.T. Russel was not about to allow the old woman to paint him as a liar. "Some stories a man keeps to himself and maybe his wife, Eunice, so his neighbors don't point at him while whisperin' the word 'crazy,' you drunken whore!"

Suthers knew he had best transition to another tale. "Mrs. McClellan, how about sharing your story with us?" He expected the old man to pull himself to his remaining foot and hobble off cursing into the woods, but Mr. Russel remained seated on the log and kept his eyes fixed on Eunice. This seemed to please the old woman. She rose, all smiles, and approached the fire in the circle's center.

"Oh yes, I have a story to tell, all right. One I doubt even Mr. J.T. Russel here will disbelieve." She looked right at him. "Because ever' one in these parts knows it's true . . .

"'Course my story goes back a few more years than Mr. Russel's. Difficult as it may seem to believe, I was a young woman once, and not hard on the eyes either if you ask any of the local men from Ong's Hat that aren't in the ground. Walter, my late husband, he didn't have very much beyond the money he carried in his pocket, but on our wedding day he rented this fine car.   Spent almost every penny he had on it, too. An Oldsmobile, I believe it was, and this was in '46 when the back roads 'round here was mostly mud. Atlantic City is but a stone's toss from these Barrens, and Walter intended to treat me to a weekend at the Traymore, this luxurious hotel along the boardwalk. Why, that place seemed just about the most beautiful sight I'd ever seen. But the fancy brochures was as close to the Traymore as we got on that rainy June evening. On my wedding night I learned quite a bit concerning the portals of evil 'round these Barrens. I believe Mr. Suthers will corroborate what I'm about to say, won't you, Professor?"

Marcus Suthers had done his homework. He had been aware of those reputed portals for a long time. "What Mrs. McClellan is referring to, is – well, shamans of that period studied the Barrens and believed the area contained powerful portals to the spirit world. They claimed that lust . . . any form of lust, whether for power or money or sex, invited destruction and evil to pass through those portals into the world. It's just legend and hearsay about this area, of course, something the local priests are rumored to have kept among themselves for years." His students listened politely, although Suthers heard someone mumble 'Bullshit.'

Eunice McClellan did not miss a beat. "Don't matter if you young people disbelieve. Can't say I blame you. Over sixty years, and it's been hard for me to believe myself. But that don't mean what happened to me didn't, because on my wedding night I swear pure evil from Hell spurt from those portals.

"After our wedding ceremony we were just outside Woodstown when Walter's Oldsmobile got stuck in thick mud. It was a real gully washer that night, and the rain was just relentless. Walter, he's spinning and spinning those wheels, but them tires was just digging in deeper. He finally decided to get out and push, but that did nothing but soak my new husband head to toe. Walter comes back into the car and turns to me. 'Eunice, sweetheart, I think we may have to forego our night at the Traymore 'till someone comes along here can pull us out...'. I took one look at my groom all covered in filth like he's some poor fool who's fallen into a vat of chocolate, and I 'most laughed myself sick. Walter, bless his soul, he managed to find humor in our situation too, and before long we're both inside that Oldsmobile laughing like a pair of magpies. Then Walter comes up with an idea.

"'You feelin' a little chilly, are you, sweetheart?' he asks.

"'Why, yes, I am feeling a little cold,' I tell him, certain I know what's coming next.

"'It's our wedding night, Eunice. And from the looks of things I think we're going to be spending this night right here. So I'm thinking, considerin' we're now man and wife with all the proper papers signed, maybe we don't need no fancy Traymore Hotel to consummate our nuptials. I'm thinking, with a little squeezing together in such tight quarters, maybe me and my lovely virgin bride, well, maybe we can do our consummatin' right here and now – and keep ourselves warm in the bargain.'

"All right, so maybe I blushed for a moment or two. What virtuous young girl wouldn't? But when I looked into my new husband's eyes I'm thinking, why hell, maybe Walter's suggestion didn't seem such a bad idea, and it would certainly make for one memorable wedding night to last us into our old age. Walter steps out into the downpour to wash off all that mud, and before another few minutes go by, we two are holding on to each other with most of our new clothing tossed into the back seat. During those precious moments I'm not 'shamed to tell you young people the last thing I was feeling was cold...

"Until that night I'd never given much thought to the rumors of no Jersey Devil comin' through some portal of evil 'cause of the smell of pure lust. But I learned quick that wherever that devil calls home, for certain he's got no sense of what's romantic and personal to a young bride making love for her first time. Walter and me, we're in the throes of a young couple's bliss when we hear something heavy what sounds like a bag of rocks thump down on the roof of that

Oldsmobile. Stopped us clear dead in the middle of – well, I needn't go into detail about that 'cept to say that 'till that moment neither of us had paid much attention to what was outside. Couldn't have seen much anyway, 'count of all the rain. But we sure as hell heard something . . .

"'Screeeeeeeeeee! *SCREEEEEEEEEEEEEE!!!!*' That's about the best I can imitate the sound we heard, like some madman's violin – but whatever it was, he was shrieking from right on top of us! Walter and me, we just looked at each other and froze. And that creature, he's pounding on the roof with arms that sound like he's carrying two mallets, and one snake-like arm reaches down the windshield like he's trying to bust right through the glass hopin' to snatch one of us. A moment later that glass just shatters, and what I see is this long limb covered in scales with twisted claws that grab my Walter by his neck and lift him clear out of his seat.

"*'Eunice, go into my coat pocket right now!'* he yells. I have no time to ask what for, so I crawl into the back seat and rifle through his pocket like he tol' me. It's then I discover my new husband has been totin' this pistol he never bothered tellin' me about. It didn't seem very big, probably some low caliber job, but for one sickening moment I had to ask.

"'Walter, what is this–?'

"I could see the question was foolish, given the circumstances.

"'Shoot him, Eunice! Shoot this fucker right now!' That screeching Devil, he's already tryin' to drag my groom through the shattered windshield, and Walter, he's going *'ARRGH!! ARRGH!!'* so I really have no choice, even though I never shot a gun in my entire life and I'm scared to death my first bullet will find its way into my new husband.

"I'm screaming, 'I can't get a clear shot! Walter, what is this creature?' But Walter, he's in no position for discussion. I see I have to take matters into my own hands, or come morning there's going to be the bloody remains of two people found near this Oldsmobile. So I throw open the door and tumble out into the pouring rain. I'm covered in sludge, but even with my eyes caked with muck through that misty darkness I see a sight what for sixty years I still wish I could forget. This man-sized lizard is laying belly down on the Olds' roof, his long forked tail whippin' at the sky. And his claws are around my husband's throat!

"'Kill him! Kill him!!' Walter is screaming, and with one hand steadying the other I take aim, intendin' to do just that. I swear, when I pulled the trigger that little gun hardly made a pop, like it was some child's toy. But then I hear that devil-thing screech louder than before, and I know it's because this time he's shrieking with pain. The creature drops Walter back into the Oldsmobile and turns quick to look at me, and only then do I realize I'm standing out there in the rain dripping with mud, just as naked as the day I was born. I'm certain death is coming for me in the next minute so I fire again, but this time the pistol just clicks. I'm thinking maybe I water soaked the damn thing, or maybe Walter didn't feel the need for more than one bullet in the chamber. But none of that mattered one bit because that Devil, he'd lost interest in my husband and now turned all his attention on me. I'm holding this worthless weapon while watchin' that lizard thing slink from the roof toward me. I tossed the gun at him, as if that would do any good and I can't think to do nothing better than shut my eyes tight hoping for a quick death, holy virgin full of grace . . .

"Well, death didn't come for me, as you can see. But something crazy certainly did . . .

"I can feel that Devil crouchin' near me, feel the heat from his breath even in the cold rain. He's making this strange sound like a moan, but when I squint open my eyes I can see just how huge this Devil-man stands and that his groan ain't no cry of pain like before, even though blood is dripping through the scales of his shoulder. But he's paying no mind to that, and whatever rage he's shown before is gone. Instead, he's sniffin' my flesh like he's some sort of hound, and he's paying special 'tention to the scent of my private places because the storm has washed my naked flesh clean and all my womanhood is out there big and bold for the takin.' I'm frozen like a statue, not knowin' whether that's thunder grumbles I'm hearin' or the beating of my own heart, and I'm thinking, 'Oh Jesus! Oh merciful Jesus! This creature intends to have his way with me right now!'"

J.T. Russel leaned towards Suthers, whispered to him. "Every man in Ong's Hat intended to have their way with that whore too. And most did. Ain't no Devil made her do it, neither. Virgin, my ass!"

If Eunice overheard the old man's comment she chose to ignore it. "Well, my Walter, I guess he must have known that Devil beast's intents 'cause I see my man sneaking from the Olds and carefully openin' the trunk, just as devious as that damned Devil whose attention remained on me and not on my husband. Walter comes sneaking up from behind holding a tire iron held high and aimed square at that monster's ugly goat head. And he would have smashed that thing's brains back to hell had not the lightning struck that very second and cracked the sky in two. I swear everywhere just lit up like a Christmas tree. Walter dropped the tire iron, and that abhorrent brute spun 'round like a whirlin' dervish. And I'm thinkin' we're both dead for sure now . . .

"But on this night we had one more shock comin'. The Devil just stares, first at Walter, then back to me. He sees that tire iron in the mud and he hadda known Walter meant to use it. That beast, he lets forth this shriek that I know can't be anything but laughter, and he keeps it up for the longest minute I've ever experienced, clearly savoring every moment of our terror. Then he pushes me into the mud and just takes off for the sky like he's had his fill of entertainment for this night. We watch him disappear into the storm clouds, then Walter and me, we practically crawl back inside that Oldsmobile shaking with both terror and the cold, refusin' to let go of each other 'till morning."

Eunice McClellan took a moment for some composure. "See, people from 'round here know that story's just as true as the rain. That's 'cause on the same night when my husband found the Devil, I believe he also found God. Maybe there was something of the divine light in that lightning strike because Walter became the pastor of Leeds Point during that same year. Stayed with the church 'till the day he died, too, now twenty years past." Eunice turned and locked eyes with J.T.

Russel. "And a man of the cloth, he isn't known for tellin' tall tales, is he?" Pleased with herself, the woman took her place on her log.

Old Russel had no immediate comeback except to grumble something containing the words "shriveled-titted whore." Marcus Suthers thanked the pastor's widow for her enlightening tale and recognized that as his moment to move things along, but Doreen Slevan again beat him to it.

"Professor Suthers, Clifford hasn't come back. He's been gone fifteen minutes."

Another guy suggested, "Maybe Boornsteen needed to do more than pee on a tree. Idle hands are the devil's work! Hoo Hah!!" Doreen shot the kid a look, turned back to Suthers.

"Cliff doesn't know his way around these woods, and I don't think he even brought a flashlight. He's out there somewhere and it's pretty dark."

Twenty students gave the shadowy pines a quick once-over. A chorus of shouts followed.'

"CLIFFORD! CLIFFORD!!"

"CAN YOU HEAR US?"

"WHERE ARE YOU? ARE YOU ALL RIGHT?"

"CLIFF? *CLI-IFF-FFFF!!!*"

Some girl suggested Boornsteen was just being the jerk he always was, probably smoking weed among the pines and yanking everyone's chain for a laugh. But Suthers didn't buy that. He managed to keep his voice calm. "I don't think it's a good idea we all go scattering through these Barrens at this hour. I'll look for him just around the periphery of the campsite. I won't be long." Someone offered him a flashlight and Suthers got to his feet, but before he took a step another voice spoke.

"I wouldn't do that, Professor."

The voice belonged to Frederick Conners, a retired History professor from some small Atlantic County undergraduate college. Suthers had met the silver haired widower during a Jersey shore vacation, and following their tipping a few beers inside Stone Harbor's more upscale pubs they talked through the night. Conners proved an excellent authority regarding the history surrounding Leeds Point. He knew many of the area's residents and had been instrumental in locating tonight's speakers.

"Marcus, it isn't safe out in those Barrens. Hear my story before you venture out there, okay?"

"The boy might be lost," Suthers said, then spoke so only Conners heard. "These kids, they're my responsibility, Fred."

"I'll search for your student with you. I know these parts better than anyone, and these footpaths are tricky at night. I promise I'll keep my story brief, Marcus. Sit. Please."

Suthers practically whispered to him, "You said the Barrens weren't safe."

Professor Conners fished out his cellular, punched in a number. "Jamie, this is Fred Conners. I'm out in the Barrens at the Decatur campsite. We may have a lost student. Kid's name is Clifford Boornsteen, about nineteen years old. I don't think he could have gone far. Will you send out a couple of rangers to have a look? Thanks, Jamie." He turned back to Suthers. "Sit, Marcus."

Suthers sat. Professor Frederick Conners clearly wanted the floor, and he wanted it now. The man stood as if he were still addressing a lecture hall.

"You see, I know a bit of this Jersey Devil's legend too. Quite a lot, actually. He's the main reason I retired to Leeds Point, you know. I wanted to learn as much about him as I could, and I believe I have. I take my research seriously because many folks claim to have seen this Devil thing, even a few historical figures. Commodore Steven Decatur, a naval hero for whom this campsite is named, is said to have hit the creature with a cannonball. And Joseph Bonaparte, former King of Spain and brother to Emperor Napoleon, swore he spotted him while hunting in these parts. Yes, some big names from all over the world have given this Devil his due. Gunners, fisherman, bird watchers, even the occasional priest – all insisted having met New Jersey's scandalous demon, and their descriptions of him are both consistent and convincing. So Mr. Russel and the widow McClellan here are in very good company, as I'm certain are Professor Suthers' other guests tonight who have their personal stories. And, of course, I have some information of my own to add to tonight's narratives. But I promised my good friend Marcus I would be brief . . ."

The elderly professor looked as if he were about to let a wildcat out of a paper bag. Suthers relit his pipe and waited for the old guy to drop his other shoe. Turning first to Eunice McClellan, Frederick Conners did just that.

"Eunice, I mean no offense. I understand the loneliness one feels after the passing of a beloved mate. As you know, cancer took my wife ten years ago. I've seen you at the old Leeds Tavern on more than one occasion since your husband passed away, and often you stay until closing. Hell, I know a bottle is a poor substitute for a loved one, but it sure helps to drown that loneliness, doesn't it? We all fight our own demons, Eunice. Your neighbors tell me that your version of your encounter with that Jersey demon becomes somewhat embellished when it's soaked in alcohol. I believe that part you added tonight about your firing Walter's pistol is the latest version, am I right?"

J.T. Russel laughed long and hard at that one. His reaction got Frederick Conners' attention.

"And Mr. James Thomas Russel, let's talk about you for a moment. I'm told you've stretched a tale or two yourself. I've spoken to a few of your fishing companions. Bill Peters is with us tonight and I'm certain your close friend here will confirm that he's not much of a believer in that Jersey Devil stuff, are you Mr. Peters?"

Russel's old pal looked like a man who had just been ambushed. "Not the way James Thomas tells it, no . . . I guess not." He turned to Russel. "I'm sorry, J.T. I've heard about ten different versions of that Devil story from you along with maybe a hundred other fish tales. I come here tonight on Professor Conners' invitation 'cause I always enjoy a good yarn from you even knowing it ain't fact. Understand, it's nothing personal 'gainst you."

Suthers could see from J.T. Russel's expression that it was plenty personal. Fred Conners' accusations had turned embarrassing, and Marcus had to say something before some nasty words flew.

"Frederick, you said you had a story for us?"

Conners flashed a smile that bordered on smug. The man demonstrated a surprising flair for the dramatic.

"I've got maybe a hundred of them, Marcus. That's right, kids. I've read the books, done the research, experienced first hand for a full ten years just what walks among these Jersey pines. I've searched for that damned Leeds Devil almost every day, taken copious notes, followed trails and rumors, and I've come to but one conclusion, campers. I'm sorry to disappoint you young people, but there are no portals of evil in these Barrens, folks. No Devils from Hell, no Devils from Jersey, unless you're counting those that carry hockey sticks. Earlier I heard one of you students whisper the word 'Bullshit' regarding the Leeds mythology. Well, that pretty much sums up the legend for me too . . . Now, Marcus, let's go search for that missing student of yours before the poor kid steps on a snake." He lowered his voice for Suthers as if he were scolding a child. "Might be a good idea to put out that pipe. There's dry timber out there."

In record time Professor Frederick Conners had managed to punch one cavernous hole into the Jersey Devil legend while humiliating two of Suthers' guests, making Suthers feel a bit like a smacked ass. He forced an unconvincing grin, grabbed a flashlight, and went for the save.

"Okay gang, Dr. Conners and I are heading into those nasty woods now. Maybe we'll uncover a witches' coven instead. Keep an eye on the fire, will you?"

Conners was already on the move. Suthers rushed to catch up with the robust old guy on the twisted path. In under a minute the campsite disappeared among the cedars, swallowed by the forest's darkness; in under two minutes no sound remained excepting the whispered rustling of trees and the crunch of dried sand beneath the feet of the two men.

"Easy to see how my student could get lost out here, Fred. This path twists in a dozen different directions."

"There are lots of footpaths in the Barrens, Marcus. With no flashlight the kid could have picked the wrong one in the dark, then got disoriented. People occasionally disappear among these pines. It's not exactly an open plain out here, and these trees can absorb shouts. But he hasn't been gone long. We'll find him."

Aiming a light beam in several directions, Suthers called out Cliff's name a few times. His own voice seemed muffled among the Barren's pines but he heard no response. Conners had gone strangely silent, maybe too silent. For a long while he walked so fast Suthers double-timed to keep up with him and his lungs felt ready to bust.

"Jesus, Fred. Are you going for the three minute mile?"

Conners seemed more interested in putting distance between themselves and the campsite than in locating Clifford Boornsteen. He stopped in his tracks, turned to his companion. He wasn't even breathing hard. The two men shone light beams on each other's faces, looking at one another as if each expected the other to speak.

"You're not fooling me, you know, Marcus. You've been a member of the Pinelands Field Research Station for some time now, haven't you? You believe in that Leeds Devil, don't you?"

"Would it matter if I did? You clearly don't, and you made certain to discredit enough of tonight's storytellers to assure no one else believes either. But I'll tell you something I don't believe, Fred. See, I don't believe you made any call to a Ranger station to report Clifford Boornsteen missing. I know there's no woman named Jamie in any Pine Barrens stations near this place. Care to show me your cell phone so's I can have a look at the record of that call you never made?"

"No need for that. Cell phone doesn't even have any batteries. Found it at some campsite. Wouldn't matter anyway. There's no reception out here. The trees, you know."

"I'm not playing Twenty Questions with you. Fred. Just tell me what's going on here."

Conners' smile grew wider and somehow uglier. "Did you ever hear that old saying about the Devil, Marcus? The one about the real Devil, not the one from Jersey. People say the best trick that Devil ever performed was to convince mankind he doesn't exist. Well, hundreds of men have actively searched for that Jersey demon as far back as the early 1900's when entire towns claimed to have seen him. But back then he wasn't as careful, and he got spotted a lot more than now. So if there is a Jersey Devil, he would have to be one clever bastard to roam these Barrens for over three hundred years without getting caught, wouldn't you say? You see, Marcus, old man Russel and that pitiful Eunice McClellan, their stories were exaggerated, all right. But they also were true. They met that Jersey Devil face to face, just like they said."

Suthers had to laugh. "And you know this how? You went to some trouble to prove they were liars."

Frederick Conners offered only another broad smile. "A devil is crafty, Marcus. It's what makes him a devil. He creates confusion, doubt. That's what keeps his celebrity alive."

"You spoke of the Jersey Devil as a lie to keep the myth going?"

"Speak of the Devil and the Devil appears, Marcus. You ever hear that one?"

The old man took Suthers' pipe from the professor's breast pocket, breathed on the ashes inside its bowl. A surge of flame jetted from the Meerschaum. "Care for a smoke, Professor Suthers? I'm thinking during these next few moments you may be needing one. Shame you didn't bring something stronger." He crushed the pipe in his hands and grabbed Suthers' throat. His flashlight fell to the ground still lit, throwing the two men into ghostly silhouettes.

"What the hell–?"

In the dull illumination Suthers watched the smile melt from the old man's face, although his teeth still showed. "I killed Frederick Conners ten years ago, Marcus. Occasionally I climb into the old guy's skin when I'm feeling sociable. But your flesh is so much younger and will be easier to slip into. I'm feeling like a new man already! Your name – Marcus Suthers – well, it could use some panache. But I think I can live with it. At least for a few years."

Conners tossed his own flashlight aside, but the moon allowed enough light to see purple veins emerge near his temples. With sudden force he tightened his grip. This wasn't the strength of an older man.

"Have you gone fucking crazy? What are you talking about?"

"Your students hang onto your every word about the Devil from Jersey, don't they? Call it ego, but I enjoy the attention. Love to keep the enthusiasts guessing! Is he real, is he not? They'll be arguing about it for centuries!"

Suthers struggled to breathe, but the old guy just held tighter, squeezing his throat with both hands now. He heard a thick tearing sound, saw Conners' clothing stretched to its seams, but that tearing; it was also something else . . .

. . . something else . . .

"Watch closely, Marcus. Not many get to see this."

The seams of Conners' flap jacket ripped open. His flannel shirt split. Falling in pieces, clothing shredded and dropped to the ground leaving Frederick Conners stripped bare. The old guy no longer seemed raw boned. He appeared larger . . .

No, he *was* larger. Some eruption seemed to be occurring inside him. His skin bubbled with lumps, his body blotched, veins pulsed through flesh.

Flesh tearing through more flesh . . . raw flesh turning itself inside out . . . shaping, then reshaping . . .

. . . into something malleable, a huge lump of clay-like matter that refused to remain in one shape, a reptile one moment, a bird the next, a creature incapable of standing straight even as it lifted the younger man from the sand path.

"I'm real, Marcus!"

Teeth like twisted nails sprouted from purple gums. Something foul smelling drooled thick from the mouth. The reptilian thing tossed Suthers to the ground, twisted claws swiping the air inches from his throat. Then came a sound he had never in his life heard.

"Screeeeeeeeeeeeeeeeeee!!! SCREEEEEEEEEEEEEEEEEEEEEEEE!!!"

Suthers could only watch the flesh fold over on itself, then turn into something else. Dark scales separated then split wide like torn fruit, a pulsating bleeding tumor sprouting weed-like from behind and mutating into membranous wings snapping like leather straps at the forest air. Forked tail pointing to the night sky, the creature snatched the squirming man from the ground, studied Marcus Suthers as if trying to memorize what it held in its claws, sniggering to itself the whole time.

Then it ate him.

"Boornsteen! Hey, Boornsteen, you wandering prick! Welcome back, jerk off!"

"Did you bring enough weed for the rest of us?"

Doreen Slevan heard the greeting and turned to see Clifford step from the shadows of the forest.

"Christ, Cliff. You had me worried to death."

"You had us all worried, you stupid shit," another girl said. "Just how high did you get during your sojourn to the enchanted forest?"

Doreen rushed to him. "What happened to you? Were you lost? We heard some sound, some awful screeching coming from the woods. Did you see anything?"

Boornsteen seemed a man who had swallowed his tongue. He managed some words.

"I saw something ... yes ... I saw something terrible, man. I mean, something really terrible in the forest. I had to hide I was so fucking scared. I'm not sure I can describe–"

"SCREEEEEEEEEEEEEEEEEEEE!! SCREEEEEEEEEEEEEEEEEEEEEEEE!!!"

Doreen looked upwards. "That's the sound, Cliff! That's what we heard earlier! Look!"

Silhouetted against the hazy backdrop of the moon flew something huge. All around the campsite heads turned upwards, arms pointed. Whatever the thing was, it disappeared in the dark sky.

"It's one of those big cranes," Samantha Winoker said. "Just like I told you. It had to be."

Old man Russel and Eunice McClellan saw the thing too. They looked at each other, and then looked away. Seated on his log Russel said to no one in particular, "I think that young professor is overdue." Reaching for his cane, he hobbled over to Boornsteen. "Tell me, just what did you see in them pines, young man?"

The moment had attracted everyone's attention. Boornsteen looked the elderly chicken farmer in the eye and practically spoke right into his face.

"I saw that old guy with Professor Suthers grow wings and turn into the Jersey Devil."

That got a laugh all around. But Mr. James Thomas Russel was not a man to be made a fool of.

"Drugged out ass hole," he muttered, and hobbled off.

THE EYES THAT WATCH
BY A.J. FRENCH

He had lived on the eyes for a long, long time. They nourished him. People say that the eyes are the windows to the soul. At least they had that much correct. But there was more. The eyes weren't just windows; they were repositories. They housed the very essence of the soul.

It was once a village, a collection of thatched huts surrounded by woods. At the time he had dwelled in the trees, in the shade between the trunks, in the shadows. He had captured many hunters and the occasional lost girl. He would watch their eyes as they died, the slow encroachment of dread, the growing panic, the fear.

The fear was always the strongest. At the precise moment when they realized they were going to die, a surge of paralyzing terror ran through them. They shrank, growing smaller and smaller, while their eyes bulged out. And he would watch, eager to catch the final glimpse as their soul was annihilated.

Afterwards, the cutting, the tearing...

... and the removing of the eyes.

In such a way he had sustained his unnaturally long life, by feeding on the souls of his victims and devouring their eyes. But times had changed. The village had become a metropolis, with fewer places to hide. The trees were replaced by concrete buildings, the dirt roads by asphalt, the shadows by artificial lights.

He was forced to retreat to the rooftops and alleyways. There, he had built a nest in the ruinous wreckage of an old opera house in a room filled with dust and shadows and sunlight. Nobody came around the opera house anymore. It had been condemned for a hundred years but had somehow managed to avoid the wreaking ball.

The room was also filled with myriad eyes, each plucked from the skulls of his many victims, festooning the walls and ceiling like macabre party decorations.

They weren't living eyes. No. He had long ago sucked the souls out of them. Now they were fossilized relics, glass things, souvenirs, reminders of how he had survived for so long, and how he would continue to survive. He sometimes rolled one across his bony fingers, relishing how it felt and the memories of the anguish he had caused.

The days of hunters and farmers and wandering soldiers were behind him. Now everyone rode around in horrific metal contraptions called automobiles. He had trouble catching these technological monstrosities, for they moved much faster than any horse.

He was growing weak. There were less available victims, which meant less available souls. The metropolis did not cater to eaters of eyes, such as him. It made things very difficult for them.

But occasionally luck would send him some clueless female victim, some vestige of the damsel in distress of old, and he would be revitalized. This usually occurred around the colleges and schools, and also outside of bars. He hung around these places, perched in dark trusses and shadowy eaves, watching the street below like a hawk in search of prey. And sometimes, he got lucky.

His patience paid off that night, for there she was now, heading out of the bar and down the street, her eyes wide with wonder, her soul beckoning to be drained.

Oh, how he would get her attention . . . when the moment was right . . .

Alice stepped out into the night. After a few paces, she turned and saw somebody following her. He was keeping to the shadows, hugging the buildings, with darkness concealing his face.

She should've taken a cab. Maybe she still could. She glanced at her wristwatch: a full hour before the bars closed. Streets would be empty till then.

She stopped, glanced back again. There he was. He'd sidestepped into an alley. Only his left flank was visible, arm hanging out of the wall. The hand was strange: bony and misshapen.

Did it clutch something, a knife perhaps?

That's just your imagination, she told herself. You've been watching too many TV crime dramas.

And yet, it definitely had its knuckles wrapped around something.

Shivering, she hastened through the downtown streets, heading for home.

He kept up with her, his footsteps mirroring hers. She felt lightheaded, indecisive: she shouldn't have had that fourth margarita. Damn Cassandra, peer-pressuring her. She had a psychology paper due tomorrow, for God's sake. It was so like her to procrastinate. And now she was too buzzed to work and would have to finish the paper in the morning. And meanwhile, Cassandra had hit it off with that gorgeous frat boy. Thanks a lot, BFF.

She passed a brightly lit bar and peered into the window; people hunkered around tables with pint glasses. Maybe she should go in, wait for the creep to pass her by. Yeah, that sounded like a good idea.

She went in, the atmosphere one of loud music and conversation. She stood by the window, watching, waiting. The creep never appeared.

After ten minutes she went out and looked around, saw nothing, then continued toward home.

Then the footsteps were back. She heard them swishing on the sidewalk behind her. She turned, staring into the gloom, resolving to confront the man before this went any further. Just because she was an out-of-town college student didn't mean she had to put up with this crap. Sure, she'd read the articles in the newspaper about missing girls, had heard the stories of serial rapists roaming the campus.

But that was kid's stuff compared to back home. Back in Brooklyn nearly every man you passed had a snide remark or a knife to flash you; or a dick. So she wasn't about to let this asshole intimidate her.

"Hey," she yelled, "quit following me!" Her voice carried down the street and the man stopped. Watched her for a moment, then sort of bent to the side and vanished into the shadows. Then, gone.

"Trouble?" said someone.

She wheeled, fists raised, heart pounding in her chest, but it was only an old man standing with an old woman, arms linked. "I said, are you in trouble?"

She caught her breath. "No—I mean yes. Some creep was tailing me, but I think he's gone."

The couple leaned to the side, glancing over her shoulder. "Down that way?" the man said.

She nodded. "Looked like he went into the alley."

"Oh my," said the woman.

The man eyed her solemnly. "Perhaps you'd better get home, young lady."

She turned and watched them go, waiting until they passed the alley, wondering if they would stop to check things out. They did. She heard voices. It sounded like the old man was speaking to someone.

In the next instant hands came out of the shadows and snatched the couple away. The woman shrieked. Leaden thumps echoed through the buildings.

Then, silence.

What the hell happened, did that creep attack them?

No. They're going to come back out any second… any second, now.

They never did.

She stepped cautiously toward the alley. She wanted to help them—shit, it was practically her fault. But she'd warned them. Even if she hadn't spoken to them, they still would've gotten nabbed.

That creep is only here because he's following you. They would have passed by unscathed if you hadn't brought your nasty friend along.

"Shut up," she muttered.

She was halfway to the alley now; a car cruised by, its headlights cutting into the night. Twin blades of gold ran along the sidewalk, up the building, and down the alley. A flickering of disjointed shapes moved as the car sped away.

Christ, what was that? Horrible shadows in there—like giant winged insects.

Her heart began to flutter; gooseflesh rose on her arms; and a cool, moist hand clamped down on her thighs.

I have to help them.

Don't lose your nerve now. Her mother's voice. Where's that tough New York broad I raised? Where's the ten-year-old who tackled my boyfriend the night he was beatin' on me?

"She's right here," Alice said . . . and stepped into the alley.

The scene confused her. Too dark to make much out, but she sensed repetitive movement, and she could see glowing lights—hundreds of them—stretching back into the distance. There were sounds: sucks and slurps and smacks.

Another car roared past, illuminating the alley. Her throat closed and she nearly swallowed her tongue. Fear, wider than an elephant's foot, pressed down on her chest.

She saw them in one blinding flash. Crouching, winged, multitudinous bodies like charred bacon, hands like daggers, mouths cavernous and ringed with teeth.

All at once they turned and glared at her, chunks of meat half raised to their lips. They had dismantled the couple, ripped them apart, divvied up the pieces and were now consuming them. Blood decorated the walls in long fanning arcs.

As the headlights receded, the creatures came together in a burst of flight, interlocking and fitting into one another like puzzlework, shrinking down until they resembled a man; pants, hat, coat—all leaping out of the darkness.

Alice suddenly realized it was the creep who'd been following her.

Screaming, she turned and fled the alley.

God, this wasn't real, wasn't real, couldn't be real. She'd had too much to drink. Maybe one of those rotten frat boys had laced her margarita. She just had to forget about it and get home. Nothing was happening. It was only a dream.

One of her heels broke and she went sprawling onto the concrete. Goddamn it, she was usually such a pro when it came to high heels. She could run a marathon in them without getting a blister.

She sat on the sidewalk, crossing her legs. Empty black tarmac ran alongside her and away from her. Closed-up shop fronts, protected by metal awnings, lined the street.

Turning the shoe over in her hands, she thought, There goes fifty bucks.

She glanced back the way she'd come but there was no one, no winged horrors or strange men in brimmed hats.

"Goddam frat boys," she muttered, rising to her feet and brushing herself off. "Drug my margarita, will you? Why do they even bother looking for rapists in this town, when half the student body already fits the mold? Men."

She took off her other shoe and carried them both, her bare feet pressing against the concrete. Luckily she hadn't lost her Prada handbag. That would've really spoiler her night.

Hey, Cassandra. Had a real nice time with you last night. Didja get that hottie's number? Oh, btw: you owe me eight hundred bucks.

She stepped on a splinter of glass and cursed, picked up her foot. A small trickle of blood ran down her heel.

Great, just what I need: an open wound as I walk through downtown.

She smeared away the blood with two fingers and continued walking. She glanced back, but there was only the empty street.

Soon the row of dorm rooms rose up ahead. She crossed the last section of asphalt and cooed as her toes reached the grass.

All she had to do was get to the other side of campus, and then she'd be home and could forget about this.

The image came to her again: a long row of nattering imps, winged and devouring flesh. God, what a nightmare. Maybe she should quit drinking. It could only improve her schoolwork.

Halfway across campus. Dim green grass surrounded her, interspersed with parking lots and concrete pathways. To her right, the planetarium—doomed like some ancient cathedral—glittered in the moonlight. To her left, a matrix of buildings and stairwells seeming to crawl toward the sky. The dorms, which she thought resembled housing projects when she first arrived in town, lay directly before her. Another five minutes and she'd be home.

The campus was quiet. Usually there were people around—even this late. Always some couple necking in the grass or some random kid on his laptop.

But not that night.

She glimpsed movement at the top of the Commons building. Someone was up there, some black ominous thing.

She knew immediately who it was.

Get a grip, girl, she told herself. It's just the drug, that—what do they call it out here—that roofie. Some frat boy probably slipped it in your drink. Get home, get to bed, and it'll wear off.

Yeah, okay, sure. But if I ever see those douche bags hanging around campus I'm gonna kick their balls in. That's a promise.

She glanced toward the rooftop. There he was, standing with arms akimbo, like he was goddamn superman or something.

Feeling a rush of power, she halted in place and gave him the finger. Stayed that way for a long time, back arched, forearm raised. But he didn't move. Finally, when she was ready to give up and head for the dorm, he started crawling down the wall.

She was reminded of the old Spiderman movie—not the one Sam Raimi directed, but the crappy Technicolor one from the 1980s. Eric and her saw it together, back when they were still "Eric and her."

The man coming down the Commons building moved like Spiderman did—clutching the wall, hands and feet cupped, spine bent. When he reached the bottom, he sprang to the grass and started toward her.

Now she had to make a choice. Keep telling herself she'd been drugged and wait for the man to disappear, or cut the bullshit and run for her life.

She ran.

Across the grass, past the auditorium, the glittering planetarium stood. As she reached the dorms she hurtled the length of chain separating the grass from the pavement. She made it but somehow dropper her shoes; they clattered noisily on the concrete.

To hell with 'em.

She yelled, "Hello, is anybody there?!"

Her words bounded through the brick hallways, and now she was running along the promenade with countless black classrooms flying by. All she had to do was make it past these, and she'd be at the dorms.

The entire left half of her body got snagged. Her shoulder jerked painfully and she spun around on her feet. She kept going. Only then did she realize she'd dropped her handbag, too.

"Shit!" she cried, skidding to a halt. She wheeled back and took a few steps, her eyes searching the ground. There it was. It had gotten caught on the metal railing. She had to go back: her building key was in there. Without it, she—

The man emerged from the shadows. He stooped to pick up the gold bag. A glow came from somewhere—from overhead—from everywhere. She couldn't really tell. All she could do was watch in horror as he brought the bag to his face . . . and devoured it.

She fled through the halls, too terrified to scream.

Then suddenly she'd made it. The buildings petered out and she found herself in the open space of the parking lot. Rows of cars, streets, houses, wind, dust and air, even a couple of trees. And people—oh yes, lovely, lovely people—getting things out the trunks of their cars, chatting, heading up to their dorms.

She slowed to a walk so as not to appear insane. She caught up to a group of Asian kids in white button-down shirts.

"Can I walk inside with you guys?" she said. She was breathless, and her words came out in rapidly. "I forgot my key."

"Sure," one of them said.

She looked back but saw no one. The hallway was empty save for blackness.

When she got up to her room, her head was spinning. Her roommate, Jane, was still out partying. She was glad. She didn't want anyone seeing her in this condition.

What a crazy walk home. I must be out of my mind. I hope it's nothing serious. Maybe I should see a doctor.

What she decided to do was call her mother. There was a three-hour time difference—which meant it was five o'clock in Brooklyn—but her mother answered the phone anyway.

She wasn't pleased. Alice explained that she'd had a scare on the way home, that someone had followed her. This news had a mollifying effect.

"Did he see which building you live in?" she asked.

"No, I don't think so. It's probably nothing. I just got scared, you know? I don't have anyone to talk to out here. Sorry again for waking you."

"There's no problem, sweetheart, you can call any time."

After speaking for thirty minutes, Alice hung up. She turned off everything except her desk lamp, which painted the room with mellow light. She needed things calm. Her heart was racing. She hadn't come to terms with what had happened—if anything had happened. Her worst fear was that she'd fled from something solely in her mind. She didn't want to think about the implications of that.

She went into the bathroom and flipped on the light. She slipped off her top, stepped out of the skirt, and unclasped her bra. She stood looking at herself in the mirror; the slender arch of her back, the curve of her breasts, the heart-shaped bowl of her hips.

She ran a hand up her thigh, pausing at the cleft of her vagina. Goosebumps patterned out across her body, and her nipples hardened. She felt slightly horny, a feeling that always made her think of Eric. She missed him, but was also just plain lonely. It was a shame that a body as nice as hers was going to waste.

Sighing, she stepped out of her panties, set them on the clothes pile, and got into the shower

An hour later she was lying beneath the covers in nothing but a T-shirt. She'd left the desk lamp on. She was tired—hell, exhausted—but she couldn't seem to sleep. The events of the night kept replaying themselves in her head. Each time she recalled the scene in the alley, it gave her chills.

"God, enough already," she said, and switched off the light.

The darkness was sudden and absolute. A familiar terror gripped her soul and she tried to make it go away. Everything's okay, she told herself. You're home, safe, so stop acting like a frightened child.

As her eyes adjusted to the blackness, shapes swam out of the gloom: her desk, the rack of clothes, Jane's bed and chest of drawers… and something else, something standing in the corner, something wearing a coat and hat.

The man stepped over to the bed. He looked like a cardboard cutout, the faintest suggestion of a man, only a shadow. He didn't even have a face.

Alice began to convulse, her breath stopping and starting, her nails digging into her palms. Her whole body trembled and she was paralyzed.

Get up! her mind raged. Get out of here; he's going to kill you!

Oh that's silly, she thought. He's only a figment of my imagination. My hectic schedule's been making me crazy lately. Nothing to worry about. Semester will be over soon.

The shadow fell forward, bringing his knees onto the bed. He put his weight on her legs, and the mattress seemed to bow. He was crawling toward her now, like a cat stalking its prey.

Oh God, I can feel him! I can feel him! This is really happening! It really is! Oh God, what is he? Please, somebody help!

He scuttled forward, collapsing on her chest, knocking the wind from her lungs. In the darkness—somehow she sensed this—he began to strip.

"Get off me," she whispered. She tried fighting him, tried kicking with her legs and batting with her arms, but her body wouldn't obey her commands. She felt like a bowl of soup. He was holding her down, without even using his hands.

"Look at me," he said. "Look—look into my eyes."

And then she was. His face was all darkness, but deep-set in that darkness was a pair of white, bulging eyes. They seemed to throb, to draw her inward, and the longer she stared at them, the paralyzed she became. It was like staring at the sun.

She could tell he was naked now, could smell the strange musk of his sex. She knew she should say something, and the words came out of her mouth before she could arrange them.

"You're responsible all of those missing girls aren't you? You're the one who's been… raping them."

His chuckle sent a vibration through her body. She felt her skin quicken.

"Rape is such a shallow word. I do so much more than . . . rape. I fill, I engorge, and then I release. And then . . . I absorb, I swallow, I consume—"

She waited for him to say more, but after a moment he split into a dozen different pieces. She was broken down, deflated, and then sucked dry. In the room, flittering above the bed like luminous butterflies, were hundreds and perhaps thousands of cold watching eyes, and before she knew what was happening, her own eyes had joined in the swarm.

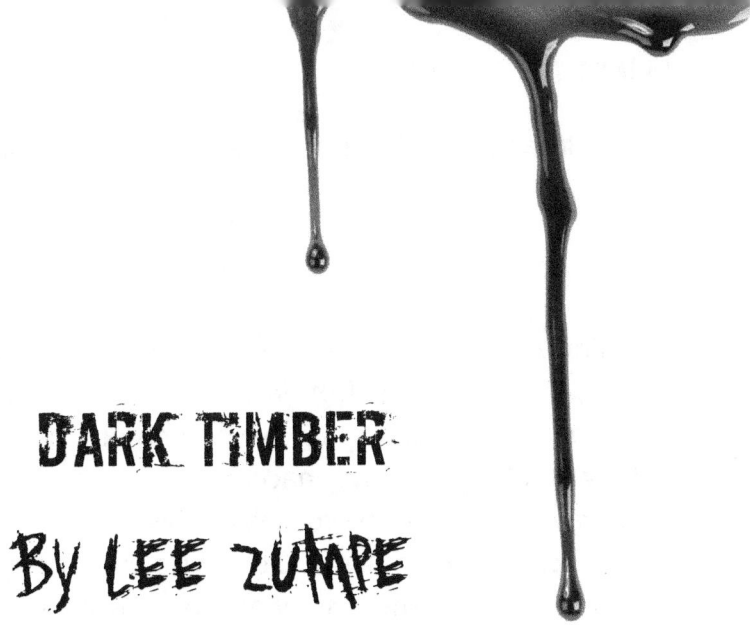

DARK TIMBER

BY LEE ZUMPE

1.

The narrow road wound through primeval spruce and birch forests, along crystal blue lakes and streams and by floodplain meadows dotted with rowan bushes and lingonberries.

A modern, air-conditioned motor coach raced along this rustic route, heading north through idyllic countryside. Earlier in the day, the occupants had noticed dairy farms, textiles factories and aquaculture centers dotting the landscape. As their trek took them farther from Sheremetyevo International Airport, they found fewer traces of civilization in the vast woodlands racing by outside the windows. In its enormity, its murkiness and its capacity to give refuge to both primitive horrors and the blackest secrets of the Soviet era, the seemingly impenetrable and ancient wilderness had no true counterpart in North America.

Somewhere in the darkest of the shadow-plagued Russian thickets, one of the planet's most endangered species endured, surviving in a vast, clandestine game preserve. That these beasts had staved off extinction at all seemed miraculous, particularly in light of humanity's centuries-old war against them.

Their salvation, though, came with a substantial price.

2.

Clint McCormick watched as the old man glared at the blaze in the hearth, a tankard of ale frothing on the discolored table before him.

Grigory Rodchenko may have been old, but to describe him as elderly would be a grave inaccuracy. His age showed mainly in his iron-gray hair and in the furrows of his solemn expression, an equal mix of scars and wrinkles. Otherwise, his sinewy leanness and his somber industriousness showed no outward signs of deteriorating health or failing faculties.

For a man well into his 80s, Rodchenko proved an intimidating figure. Of course, to make a living breeding and maintaining an ample supply of *vlkodlaci* on more than 80,000 hectares of land, one had to be intimidating.

In stark contrast, several of the men gathered in the Russian hunting lodge appeared to be in less-than-perfect shape. The exclusive club catered mainly to wealthy Americans, and these particular individuals personified some of the worst characteristics of the country's affluent.

Benson Kaiser, for instance, had seen far better days. Stocky and august-looking, he displayed the hallmarks of a 19th century patrician – decked out in overpriced 21st century fashions that barely fit his plump frame. While a series of medical procedures had veiled much of the oilman's gluttonous nature, his pallid and puffy face betrayed his fading fitness.

A venture capitalist that had survived the recent economic downturn at the expense of others, Godfrey Meadows' gaunt and ashen countenance hinted at malnutrition. His emaciation, however, stemmed from a string of communicable diseases – all treatable, though some incurable. The decadence and depravity of his youth haunted him in middle age.

Spencer Woodruff, a real estate tycoon whose dwindling assets still amounted to nearly a billion in U.S. dollars, prided himself on a healthy lifestyle. At 55, he jogged 20 miles a day and ate only vegetarian dishes. Still, a lifetime of uncontrolled hypertension had taken its toll. Between the chronic migraines and his ever-worsening eyesight, Woodruff surmised his best days were behind him.

William Whitney, the biotech mastermind and owner of GenEnergy Research, seemed untouched by greed, excess and anxiety. The light of the fire illuminated his expression: His cheeks were half-covered with black whiskers, his eyes were deep-set and full of inquisitiveness. Long-limbed, slender and youthful, McCormick judged his age at no more than 35.

McCormick himself was a wiry man of 40 years with a sandy, petit goatee, sideburns and short hair. Tall, willowy and symmetrical, he possessed a singularly aristocratic face anchored by piercing emerald eyes. Unlike the others, he had inherited his fortune. His family's wealth went back generations and through careful investment and management, their prosperity had continued to expand.

Hale and hearty or flabby and feeble, they had all traveled to this remote location to join in an extraordinarily expensive, private hunt.

Set in the deep, thick forests of the Tver Oblast north of Moscow, the hunting lodge dated back to the 1950s. Built from rough sawmill lumber, it featured a large common room with plenty of wooden chairs and benches as well as a few scruffy recliners; a modest table capable of accommodating eight people; a wood-burning stove in addition to the oversized fireplace; and an old console television that clearly hadn't been used in at least a decade.

The lodge boasted eight double-occupancy rooms and four small, unheated bathrooms.

"I trust your bellies are full." Lazar Lavrovitch, a Russian-born American citizen, served as the group's translator. Rodchenko did not speak English; in fact, Rodchenko rarely spoke at all. "Grigory suggests you all retire to your rooms for a few hours of slumber," he continued, though McCormick hadn't noticed the old man dictating any orders. "We will meet here in this room at midnight for the hunt."

Most participants, weary from jet lag and overstuffed on sturgeon in aspic, solyanka, caviar, pirozhki and khachapuri, eagerly embraced the suggestion and shambled off down darkened corridors to collapse on lumpy mattresses in small but tidy bedchambers. Rodchenko drained his tankard, stood, spit into the fire and walked out onto the front porch. Moments later, McCormick, still sitting in the great room, caught the scent of a Cuban cigar.

"Not tired, Mr. McCormick?" Lavrovitch lingered in the great room, flipping through the pages of "Ogoniok," a weekly-illustrated magazine produced by Kommersant Publishing Group. "It will be a long night, you know. Russian winters can be merciless, and late November offers a taste of what's to come."

"I don't sleep much," McCormick said. "Insomnia."

"What do you think of our facilities?" Raised in a New England enclave of Russian expatriates, Lavrovitch had taken care to conceal his accent. Still, after a few beers, its ghost emerged, all but imperceptible to most. "Do the grounds meet your expectations?"

"So far," McCormick said. "I'm mainly interested in seeing the game."

"I have to say, you don't much strike me as a Wolfer," Lavrovitch said. He swung about in his chair so he could face McCormick. "Not like the type we usually see here," he said, gesturing toward the other men in the sleeping quarters. "Not like them. They join the hunt because they can afford it. Another way to flaunt their wealth."

"One of the most exclusive clubs around, I gather."

"Absolutely," Lavrovitch said. "We receive hundreds of inquiries every year, but we screen each candidate. We only admit a few dozen each hunting cycle."

"I was surprised at the low turnout." From what McCormick had heard, the hunt – offered twice annually – usually attracted a throng of Wolfers, enough to fill all the beds. "Why all the vacancies?"

"The economy," Lavrovitch said. "Fewer applications – and fewer individuals made it through the evaluation. Too many people of questionable backgrounds; too many people who might – what's the phrase? 'Spill the beans,' you know?"

"No one has ever broken the code of silence? Seems hard to believe."

"A handful have tried," Lavrovitch admitted, the corners of his mouth turning upwards to form an indecent grin. "I'm sure you know what became of them."

"I know they disappeared," McCormick said. "That much was explained in the orientation." All of the participants had been subjected to a three-hour lecture upon their arrival. Having spent the better part of the day traveling by motor coach, none of them had the energy to show much enthusiasm. "I think it's best if I don't ask for specifics."

"You're a wise man, Mr. McCormick." Lavrovitch leaned forward in his chair and lowered his voice. "The truth is, it doesn't matter who they might be. Reclusive billionaires or publicity-hungry public figures – if they so much as mention the word 'werewolves' in connection with this establishment, our agents will ..." He paused, easing back into the recliner. "Let's just say that it always works out in the end."

"What I don't get is how you can keep them confined over long periods of time." McCormick noticed a subtle change in his host's demeanor and immediately regretted his phrasing. He felt like he had just stuck his arm elbow-deep into a snake sack filled with Eastern Diamondbacks. "What I mean," he quickly said, "is that even though they're animals, don't they have a human component – and doesn't that make them more difficult to control?"

"Well," Lavrovitch said, his suspicion allayed for the time being, "the 'human component,' as you refer to it, doesn't manifest itself in our animals. It's a common misconception that these beasts are even remotely civilized, in fact."

"Really?"

"Absolutely. All the stories you grew up on, all the movies you've seen – they're all completely false." Lavrovitch shook his head emphatically and waved his hands as if dismissing all the phony legends. "All backward, they are. How does that old saying go, 'Even a man who is pure in heart and says his prayers by night, may become a wolf when the wolfsbane blooms and the autumn moon is bright.' Preposterous!"

"I'm not sure I understand," McCormick said. "Are you saying that the werewolves – the *vlkodlaci* – don't actually transform?"

"Not at all," Lavrovitch said. "I'm saying that they aren't people who turn into wolves because of some ancient curse. They're wolves who, over thousands of years, developed an ability to temporarily transform themselves into humans."

3.

Clint McCormick eyed the U-shaped, boggy grassland beneath the twilight, flustered by the uncanny absence of sound. The unsettling silence suggested an exodus of native fauna, as if lesser beasts had long ago ceded the territory to a dominant carnivore.

The narrow strip of man-made prairie was no more than 400 meters wide, though it stretched several kilometers in length – so far that even in daylight, McCormick doubted he could see the distant tree line. Somewhere in that dusky sylvan hinterland, McCormick knew he would find a sprawling confinement facility serving as both a feedlot and a factory-farming production system. He had personally surveyed top-secret satellite images: The entire area had been blurred in photographs available in public forums, a legacy of the Cold War.

A decade of exhaustive investigation had led McCormick to the Oboroten Complex and the adjoining Rodchenko Hunt Club. What began as a passing interest in folklore relating to werewolves and other shape-shifting creatures had blossomed into a 10-year obsession to locate the only surviving members of the endangered species – even if it was a captive breeding population.

While he knew enough to expect appalling conditions at the facility, his painstaking research ultimately revealed only abstractions and conjecture. The cloak of secrecy constructed by Grigory Rodchenko and his former KGB cronies proved as impassable as the 325-kilometer high-tech security barricade that surrounded the most sensitive area of the complex.

Tonight, McCormick hoped to resolve his lingering doubts.

Each Wolfer had been positioned in the dark timber encircling the meadow at 30-meter intervals. The men waited on steel tree stands equipped with nylon web-strap fasteners and optional full-body harnesses and drop blinds. Some of them employed the gun rests – another luxury for the pampered, wealthy Wolfers.

Most of the hunters brought Winchesters and Remingtons. For show, McCormick flaunted a CZ 550 Classic Safari chambered in .375 H&H Magnum cartridges. He also carried a Barrett M98B, a bolt-action sniper rifle – a weapon he trusted implicitly and a perfect choice for the task at hand.

Before striking out into the Russian wilderness, Lazar Lavrovitch drew names from a wooden bowl, assigning the order in which the participants would engage the prey. He recapped the rules of the hunt: A total of five *vlkodlaci* would be released, one at a time; each Wolfer would be allocated a specific beast along with two opportunities for a kill shot. Should the Wolfer fail to fall the werewolf in two shots, the other participants could then engage the prey.

A feeder, strategically located in the middle of the meadow, drew the game in close to the hunters. McCormick saw little challenge in the contest – luring half-starved *vlkodlaci* to a bucket of blood and guts surrounded by languid Wolfers seemed somewhat less than sporting.

The appearance of the first beast beneath the cloudless night skies validated McCormick's speculation.

It lumbered awkwardly across the grassland, its hunger eclipsing any remnant of stealth once ingrained in its species. At first glance, the individual could have been mistaken for a very large gray wolf: Its smooth, furred legs, narrow muzzle and massive shoulders attested to its predatory nature without revealing the genetic anomaly brought about by rapid evolutionary change during the Ice Age.

Long before the other Wolfers noticed the telltale biological variations that differentiated the animal, McCormick saw its anatomical aberrations. It had a much shorter neck than common wolves, though it easily measured 2.5 meters from nose to the tip of its tail. Its coat lacked a layer of guard hairs, consisting mainly of a dense undercoat – though in this example, the beast's fur appeared sparse due to poor living conditions. It boasted a larger skull than the common wolf, suggesting the creature possessed a more highly developed brain.

Having covered most of the ground on all four paw pads, the werewolf stood nearly erect as it neared the feeder.

It scanned the woods with golden-brown eyes. While it may well have sensed danger, its hunger pushed it to accept the risk.

Unlike the others, McCormick could smell its emptiness. It had not been fed for days, and, prior to that, it had lived on the brink of starvation all of its life. Moreover, it reeked of another kind of deficiency: It lacked purpose and instinct, bearing and reasoning. The Oboroten Complex had reduced it to little more than a mindless devourer.

McCormick pitied the solitary *vlkodlak* as much as he lamented the fate of its ancestors: Hunted to the brink of extinction long after their kind presented any real threat to humanity, the last few centuries had seen them endlessly hounded, exploited and abused. The Nazis sought to exterminate them; the French tried to incarcerate them in deplorable conditions and the Soviets tried to enslave them as dogs of war in various military campaigns. The disastrous 1984 Kabul massacre in Afghanistan forced Konstantin Chernenko to eliminate his government's clandestine program.

At that time, the entire Oboroten Complex was handed over to Rodchenko to utilize as he saw fit. McCormick knew the old man represented only one small link in a chain of atrocities that stretched back centuries; still, he looked forward to settling the score with him.

A single shot from Benson Kaiser's rifle struck the werewolf an inch below the sagittal crest of its skull, instantly ending its pathetic existence.

McCormick winced, knowing he could not act quickly enough to save every creature imprisoned in the complex. More blood would be spilled in the coming hours.

If he acted quickly, McCormick hoped most of it would be human blood.

4.

In one regard, Lazar Lavrovitch's comments earlier in the evening had been correct: The *vlkodlaci* confined in the Oboroten Complex were evolutionary throwbacks. They represented the last specimens of a branch of the Canidae family that emerged during the last Ice Age. Competing with humans during the Late Pleistocene, *canis erectus* evolved initially as a bipedal beast of prey, enabling them to rival the hunter-gatherers spreading across the globe.

Then, one of those unconventional leaps in biology occurred – and Canis erectus developed the ability to mimic the physical traits of its primary adversaries.

Modern textbooks had erased all mention of the species in the mid-20th century. Academicians routinely rejected its very existence, quickly debunking any credible evidence by crying *werewolf* – equating convincing claims with centuries of myths and fables.

For the scientific community, the inability to adequately address the genetic anomaly that created the real werewolf proved an embarrassment best swept under the carpet. For the descendants of politicians who endorsed centuries of genocide, the pogroms were best veiled from a new wave of environmentally conscious citizens.

For a wealthy man like Clint McCormick, though, information on the subject was easy to obtain. Aside from his affluence, his unique heritage offered opportunities to delve deeper into the secret history.

Lavrovitch erred in claiming that people do not transform into wolves.

Whether he intentionally suppressed the truth or he really believed that all of history's purported sightings could be attributed to a strain of prehistoric full-blooded *vlkodlaci*, McCormick did not know. McCormick did know that in the shadowy centuries before civilization materialized, interbreeding had taken place between Canis erectus and Homo sapiens. The resulting hybridization, a recessive genetic trait, continued to manifest itself in a small number of families around the world, including McCormick's line.

In the distance, he heard a metallic clanging as a massive gate swung on its hinges. He heard a second *vlkodlak* plunge headlong into the night, a congenial full moon teetering above the treetops. Like its predecessor, its hunger defined it.

McCormick estimated the distance to the facility at just under three kilometers. The time had come.

He used a night vision spotting scope to target his first victim. He had already determined each marksman's general location using his acute sense of smell. Grigory Rodchenko believed in redundancy, stationing as many sharpshooters in the field as he had Wolfers, presumably to maintain order. Fortunately, Rodchenko's hired guns had been plucked from the dregs of the Russian military.

Targets No. 1 and 2 both reeked of cheap vodka and cigarettes. McCormick pegged them both with one shot each, killing them before they could utter a sound. Target No. 3 slumped over in his tree stand, the nylon harness cutting into his flabby midsection. Asleep, his rasping and wheezing had been a minor aggravation for the last hour. The bullet burrowed into his skull, cutting him off in mid-snore.

Target No. 4 proved more elusive. At first, McCormick feared that he had been alerted to the attack. After all, the custom-made suppressor on his Barrett M98B didn't completely muffle the noise. Each of Rodchenko's mercenaries may have been under surveillance, too – monitored from a central locale capable of warning others of an assault.

An instant later, McCormick's fears evaporated: He located the target on the ground near his tree stand, relieving himself.

Turing his sites on Target No. 5, McCormick found himself looking down the shortened barrel of a Dragunov SVU sniper rifle.

He instinctively rolled, allowing himself to fall several meters to the ground where he scrambled for cover.

His momentary panic faded when he relocated the marksman: He remained frozen in the same position. At first glance, McCormick had not noticed the peculiar angle of his neck or the thin trail of blood running down his chin.

Target No. 5 had already been neutralized.

McCormick met William Whitney, the biotech wizard, over the werewolf carcass in the middle of the meadow.

"There's another one approaching," Whitney said. While McCormick had been eliminating the marksmen, the owner of GenEnergy Research had used a specially made tranquilizer gun to subdue the other Wolfers. "I need to get back to my position. I'd prefer not to have to kill it, but I will if the sedative doesn't work."

"It will work," McCormick said. "Just make sure you get these people out of here alive." McCormick eyed the dark timber anxiously, anticipating a second wave of sharpshooters. His senses, though, told him the woods concealed no more mercenaries. "I don't like them, but I don't want their blood on my hands."

"Neither do I," Whitney said. "In a few minutes, I'll have what I came for." Their alliance had been provisional. McCormick didn't approve of Whitney's plans to return to the United States with a live specimen for experimentation, but he needed his cooperation on site as well as a critical key code that would power down the containment system at the complex. "I'll have them out of the country before they wake up."

"What about your prize?"

"He'll go back to a holding facility in Germany, first," Whitney said. "Then I'll have him transferred to a GenEnergy lab in the Midwest."

"He won't be harmed, physically," McCormick said.

"I gave my word," Whitney answered, visibly annoyed. Both men knew the *vlkodlak* would be closing on the feeder in a few minutes. Either one, fully transformed, would have been capable of deflecting its onslaught, likely killing it in the process. Whitney needed a live specimen. "If I can unlock its secrets, map its genome, I may be able to help those who share our condition – the ones who can't control it like we can. You know that it's worth it."

"I know that it's lived its entire life in a prison, like the others," McCormick said. "It deserves freedom. You're just liberating it from one jail and putting it into another. You're not offering it a choice."

"It will be cared for, I promise you," Whitney said. "Now go – there are others you can help. Get them out before Rodchenko realizes what's happening."

McCormick handed his weapons and his gear to Whitney.

A moment later, he had transformed.

5.

Heart hammering in his chest, McCormick sped across the meadow. His nails had hardened, sharpened, reformed into claws. His teeth and jaws had realigned, his tongue danced over sharp fangs. His bones had shifted, his muscles thickened. A tail extended from his backbone.

The moon-swabbed forests and the starry twilight became a dark blur as he raced toward the Oboroten Complex. He dared not speculate about the scope of atrocities committed in the covert facility over the years. He tried to steel himself for the misery he anticipated.

Gunfire erupted less than a kilometer in front of him: His team had arrived on the scene.

They had explicit instructions to eradicate the perimeter defenses and create a breach in the exterior wall. Under no circumstances were they to enter the facility before dawn.

An explosion took down the main gate. Inadequately trained sentries fell back, many fleeing into the forest – fearful, perhaps, that the *vlkodlaci* might break free. By the time McCormick arrived, the facility's outer defenses had been obliterated. He counted the corpses by the stench hovering in the air – at least 22 had been killed in the daring raid on Russian soil.

That he did not count among the dead either Grigory Rodchenko or Lazar Lavrovitch aggravated him.

As a werewolf, McCormick's feet steered him effortlessly around obstacles, both animate and inanimate. In the thickest tangle of dense woods, he could maneuver through thickets of trees without moderating his speed. In the dank corridors of the Oboroten Complex, his progress was no less nimble.

The few defenders who remained, sheltered behind makeshift barricades, marveled at the grace with which the invader advanced – and trembled at the ease with which he butchered their cohorts. A fusion of elegant action and shocking fury, McCormick mauled the soldiers mercilessly.

With the swipe of an arm, his claws ripped throats, opened chests and severed limbs. Those foolish enough to thrust themselves in his path met a ghastly end: He snapped hungrily, his jaws closing on their necks, whipping them side to side before flinging them away like tattered vermin.

McCormick felt a sharp sting in his left shoulder as he approached what appeared to be the facility's command center. He shrugged off the pain as a minor nuisance at first.

"He's not one of ours," he heard Lavrovitch say. Both he and Rodchenko stood close to the back of the room, a bank of monitors behind him. The screens cycled through countless images depicting the inhabitants of the complex. Most appeared restless. Some, in wolf form, howled angrily. Others, in human form, pounded on the doors of their cells. "A fine specimen, though."

Had there been others in the control room, they had either been dismissed or had abandoned their posts.

Rodchenko muttered something in Russian. He held an OTs-38 Stechkin silent revolver, a five-shot double-action revolver. He let the weapon rest at his side, confident that he would not need to take a second shot.

McCormick felt a burning sensation in his abdomen. He staggered forward, his legs wobbling beneath him. He felt his bones starting to shift, his internal organs migrating painfully. He tried to prevent the transformation but found his will power insufficient.

The transformation complete, he collapsed to the floor.

"Mr. McCormick," Lavrovitch said, feigning surprise. "I should have known. Grigory will probably cut my salary for letting you slip through the screening process."

"What did you do to me?" McCormick struggled to get back on his feet. The pain in his shoulder had increased to levels he had never experienced previously. His genetic condition generally muted the effects of such wounds and provided enhanced regenerative properties.

"Kind of like a silver bullet, eh?" Lavrovitch showed off that depraved grin again – the kind of smirk that only materializes when someone takes pleasure in another's suffering. "Actually, it's a special cartridge, coated with a toxin that inhibits the part of your brain that controls your *vlkodlak*. Makes you, you know, more manageable."

"Fine," McCormick said, swallowing his pain. "Doesn't change the outcome. I have a team outside that will storm the building at dawn. They'll end this, with or without me."

"Yes, you have a team of 20 commandos," Lavrovitch said. "And we have a contingent of 100 Russian troops en route as we speak. Call it our 'cavalry,' coming to save the day."

"Bastards." McCormick moved forward, faltering before taking three steps. "They should be free."

"Sorry, Mr. McCormick," Lavrovitch said. "That's not an option."

Something silvery and black surged through the shadows along the perimeter of the room, moving so swiftly even McCormick could not identify it. It brushed Lavrovitch as it pounced on Rodchenko. The old Russian disappeared behind a control booth, a geyser of blood erupting from the darkness.

Lavrovitch's eyes widened in horror and he bolted for the door. A bullet struck him in the lower back, shattering his spine. McCormick looked over his shoulder. William Whitney stood in the corridor carrying the Barrett M98B.

"Wasn't expecting backup," McCormick said, his breath growing ragged. He leaned against a nearby desk. "Glad you brought a friend."

The *vlkodlak* had already finished off Rodchenko and was eyeing Lavrovitch. Whitney had only spared the translator's life to give the werewolf a chance at vengeance.

"Poetic justice," Whitney said, scarcely flinching as Lavrovitch screamed. "How many *vlkodlaci* do you think he's sent to their death over the years?"

"You were supposed to clear out as soon as you had him," McCormick said. "Don't get me wrong, I'm glad to see you … but what made you come here?"

"He did," Whitney said, nodding toward the *vlkodlak*. "I gave him a choice. He wanted to come help you, make sure you freed the others."

"He can talk?"

"He's no Shakespeare," Whitney said. "But he knows a smattering of Russian and French."

Pleased with his disembowelment of Lavrovitch, the *vlkodlak* cautiously joined his new friends. He transformed into a human-like form that more closely resembled a Neanderthal than Homo sapiens.

"Merci beaucoup," he said, bowing courteously. "Nous vous sommes extrêmement reconnaissants." Seeing the lack of comprehension in McCormick's eyes, the *vlkodlak* apparently realized that he didn't speak French. Turning to Whitney, he said, "Remerciez-le de ma part."

"He wants to thank you," Whitney said. He was busy studying the control panel, searching for a way to release the werewolves.

"I gathered that," McCormick said. "Sounds like he has a pretty extensive vocabulary to me." The sound of gunfire outside reminded McCormick that they weren't out of the woodlands of Tver Oblast yet. "Company," he said, pain still darkening his eyes. "Lavrovitch called in a hundred soldiers. We're outnumbered."

"Not really," Whitney said, keying in a code he his corporation's hackers had provided. "If this works, we'll outnumber them ten to one."

An infinitely long moment passed as the Oboroten Complex's obsolete computer systems processed and validated the code. An override protocol written decades earlier, Whitney's hackers believed it had never been erased from the core mainframe. They believed it would open every cellblock, remove every mobile confinement wall, and unlock every gate within the compound.

As the doors opened, a cacophony of howls flooded the night.

The starving *vlkodlaci* streamed into the dark timber, hungry for revenge.

DIANA

BY CATHERINE SISSON

How voluptuous she sits on her pedestal
looking down on all the racing and chasing we do.
Her beaming charms entice courageous efforts.
Brightest in the box she sits in the corner as if it were possible to
ignore her.

Mad Woman,
conducting the seas
you are less whole these days.
Has the darkness taken hold of you too?
The waning of your stolen light holds the solace
of this weighted soul.

THE SHADOW BEAST
By ANTHONY BELL

Remember, as a child, passing your reflection in a window at night? Did you ever stop and try to stare through the reflections? The lights would get brighter the longer you looked because your curiosity was turning into fear, and you realized how vulnerable the blind were in that moment. Did your breathing slow as you tried to limit the noise you made?

Anything could've been out there in that cold night, staring back at you. Anything as in everything. The worst creatures your imagination could conceive of; the monsters from the nightmares you'd woken from that your mother cooed weren't real. The nameless, unspecified beast in the forest that broke your composure and caused your walk to evolve into a panicked run that threatened to upset your balance and force you to scream like a little girl.

Have you ever felt this way when staring back at yourself in an unyielding window at night? Have you ever been magically regressed to a child in such an instance, too scared to move, afraid to breathe?

It's strange, isn't it, how a childhood situation that one immobilized you with fear can have that same effect, if for only an instant, now that you're an adult? How walking across that dimly lit parking lot at night after the horror flick gives you a reason to look back once, twice, fucking five times, sure that some faceless man will be running at you with a knife held high.

True, it's strange, but there's got to be some rationale, right? There's a reason why we as people sometimes have the feeling of being watched; a sharp fear of danger that gives us pause; an essence of vulnerability that quickens our pace and observance of our surroundings. With all the reason and sophistication in the world, instinct still commands our minds. Instinct knows the truth about things, even if we, however, do not.

Sometimes it was logical to have the closet door shut before you were tucked in at night.

Sometimes, when looking over a dock at your wavy face on the surface of the water, it was prudent to pull back as the murky depths swished and swayed beneath, because maybe a second later something would've shot up from those depths, making that the last time you ever looked over a dock.

I was eleven years old when I stood before a dark window at night, staring back at myself. Since that night I've always kept my shades drawn. There is no other way.

I had a mom and a dad. We all do; I know that, but I mean that I lived with mine. They still enjoyed each other's company and wrestled at night behind a closed door. We ate dinner at a table together and weren't short on laughter, although I wasn't always able to understand the reason for our laughing. We lived in a two-story house in a nice neighborhood, which made what happened when I was eight even more unbelievable. We had a dog, Bear. He was a big mutt, but I didn't care; my parents picked him up from the pound when he was just a puppy for my fifth birthday. I loved that dog.

When I was eight-years-old, the Shadow Beast set Bear on fire.

It was the first time I'd ever seen it. It's hard to explain. It was like a shadow and yet at the same time like a full, fleshy thing, something with substance and shape. Almost as though it could shape itself at will. I first saw it while playing war with some army men action figures. There was a noise and I looked up to see the Shadow Beast standing in the doorway of my room. It was like a very thin black sheet, maybe made of silk, and before I had time to more than register its presence, it dashed to the other end of the hall, quick as if teleporting. I took a step forward, unaware of its menace. It slithered down the stairs and I followed because, well, I was eight.

When it reached the garage, I knew something was wrong because it held my dad's gasoline can. It seemed it shouldn't be able to, as insubstantial as it looked. At this point it appeared almost wolf-like, or werewolf-like. Maybe a werewolf wearing a cape. At times the werewolf shape of it—the hair, teeth, evil eyes—was visible as if illuminated by the brief, bright emission of lightning.

Gasoline spilled from the can and splashed across the floor as though the Shadow Beast weren't quite strong enough to hold steady the five-gallon can. It was strong enough, however. Trust me, if you'd seen some of the stuff it did later on, you would know it was strong enough. It did it on purpose, for fun.

Some gasoline even splashed on me. It wouldn't have been that bad if it had stopped then. I could have washed the gasoline off. No problem. But it didn't stop then. Right then, Bear ambled into the garage, big paws swinging with each step.

The Shadow Beast turned and raised the gas can. Bear approached as if it was a familiar person. His big tail was swishing through the air and he looked up at the Shadow Beast and the can it was holding as though anticipating a treat. He didn't get a treat, though. He got a face full of gasoline. The Shadow Beast poured the entire can on my dog. His thick coat was dripping with the stuff and he was using his paws to try and wipe it from his eyes.

I didn't know what to do. It happened so fast that I don't think I could have moved quickly enough, anyway. The next instant, the Shadow Beast dropped the empty can and produced from nowhere—inside of itself, maybe?—a lit match. The flame was so tiny, a yellow teardrop. So tiny, and yet I knew what it could do, how bad it could be. The Shadow Beast looked directly at me, as if we were two conspirators sharing a secret. And this was one of the instances when its wolf-like appearance was visible. It glided toward Bear like a skater on ice.

And dropped the match.

I lunged toward my dog, hoping against hope that I would somehow be able to catch the match. Hoping that maybe God would give me a boost of superhuman speed necessary to save my dog from the fate that was so obvious. But God didn't. And Bear was engulfed in fire. The initial contact and explosion of flame knocked me off my feet. The heat was intense. I was so close that it felt a though I'd stuck my head in an oven. Bear ran outside, yelping. Hearing that hurt my heart, physically and emotionally. I couldn't breathe and my entire chest seemed to shrink into itself.

I stumbled after. The yelping, my god, the sound was so horrible. I remember my heartbeat escalating to a dangerous rate as I ran toward the sound of my dog. Tears blurred my vision and I couldn't run fast enough. I slipped and fell; got back up with dirt under my nails. I rounded the corner of my house and at first wasn't sure what I was seeing.

It wasn't Bear. It couldn't be. It was a fireball. A stinking, blazing fireball running in circles. But it was Bear, I couldn't deny it. I began to sway, then cried and turned to run, went smack into my mother. She screamed. Bear still yelped, a banshee escaping him.

I fainted.

When I woke, I thought it had been a nightmare, but my mom was beside me. Her eyes were watery and her cheeks were wet. More than her eyes, it was the stench that told me it was no nightmare. She helped me to my feet and I started to turn because I couldn't write

Bear off so easily. She maneuvered around me and began to usher me toward the house, but too late; I saw my dog, a tangled mass of burnt hair and skin, looking nothing like my Bear. He was a good dog, had never even bit anyone. So why? I asked my mom and she could only cry and held me against her. I tried to tell her about the Shadow Beast, but she told me in a gentle voice to shh, it would be okay, everything would be okay. Just shhh, darling.

I never forgot about Bear.

About a year later my mom and dad asked me if I would like another puppy. They weren't so direct, though, because they knew how I felt about replacing Bear. No, they were good parents. Subtle and attentive. We were walking by a pet store one day after having finished some other errands and my mom and dad met eyes. They thought I didn't see, but I could also be subtle and attentive. Mom said something like, *Oh, look at those cockatoos; they're so cute.* And with that, we entered the store and ended up by the puppies several minutes later. Dad was like, *They sure are cute, too, huh?* Mom was like, *Yeah, honey, they are.* I watched the puppies (which were quite cute, by the way) for a moment, rolling over each other and wagging their tails so fast that it looked as though they would knock themselves over.

I watched, but all I could see was Bear. How he used to romp up to me, big and fluffy with that doggy smile of his spread across his face. How he didn't mind when I laid my head down on his furry stomach to listen to his heartbeat. How he slept on my bed even though he wasn't supposed to. How he'd lain dead, a charred heap on our front lawn.

I didn't comment on the puppies' cuteness, and a second later walked over to the snakes. I saw my parent's sad expressions reflected by the store window. I didn't want them to be sad, but I couldn't have another puppy. Bear would always be my puppy. And I was scared what the Shadow Beast would do if I got a puppy.

I thought losing Bear was bad, especially how it happened. It was bad all right, but it was only the beginning of something much worse.

The next time the Shadow Beast visited me and did something really awful, I was eleven. But from the time it killed my dog until that day, it still paid its evil visits. I was the only one who ever saw it, though, because whenever I shouted that it was there, my parents would arrive a second after it fled or disappeared.

One time I was making a sandwich and it appeared next to me, big and wavy and black. Then it smiled down at me; I could see a more formed shape of it, and the next thing I knew, it had thrown down my mom's porcelain plate set, which shattered across the ground. And poof, right before my mom walked into the kitchen to see what had happened, it vanished. She entered and stopped once she saw the ground. I could only look at her with a piece of bread in one hand and the butter knife in the other with mayonnaise on it and say it wasn't me. I couldn't even reach the cabinet they were in without getting on the counter. It was the Shadow Beast. It came again.

She sighed and told me this needed to stop. (The Shadow Beast had written on my parents' bedroom walls, keyed their cars, shredded their credit cards, as well as scattering full bags of trash around the house; it also put a metal bowl in the microwave and peeled the wallpaper from the hallway.)

She said the Shadow Beast wasn't real.

Then she swept up her plates.

The next week I sat in the office of a man who had a bunch of framed papers hung on the wall. There were very nice couches and chairs in the room, and tons of books along the shelves, but they were thick and so must've been boring. He wore glasses that he peered over every time something he didn't believe came out of my mouth, which was pretty much whenever I spoke. It didn't work out; I quit seeing him after a few weeks. My parents worried about me a lot. Mom always asked how I was doing, if I needed to talk about anything. Dad tried to get me to throw the football with him all the time. I indulged them sometimes because it calmed them.

The Shadow Beast continued to occasionally make trouble at my house, but nothing too serious. I was almost always able to clean up after it before my parents could find out. But there were times when I couldn't.

The worst of those times happened when I was eleven. No one knew how to clean that one up. It was nighttime and I was walking through the hallway toward my bedroom when it began. My parents were in the kitchen, making dinner, chatting like songbirds.

I didn't fuss about The Shadow Beast so much anymore when it came. I didn't rush and try to follow it to whatever mess it wished to make, hoping to clean it up before my parents could find out. It had gotten to the point that I treated it like a bothersome bee. A bee that I sometimes swatted at but didn't get too worked up about because I never swatted fast enough…and I hadn't been stung in a long time.

That night was different, though. I could feel it in the air as the Shadow Beast passed me; a hot wind escaping a room once the door is opened. It hit me quick and burning, even nudged me a bit. I'd never been physically touched by it before.

I walked faster along the hallway, my bare feet slapping against the hardwood in rhythm with my accelerating heart. By the time I was at the end of the hall I was almost running. The air was hot; my lungs felt heavy and constricted; I didn't know which way to turn. To the left and I would head toward my room; to the right and I would head toward the kitchen. I looked left and right like a child waiting to cross the street. The difference of this encounter was obvious to me; my heart told me so. Panic started to seep its way into me and I was fighting the urge to just dash in one direction, yelling for the Shadow Beast to show itself. I was done crying wolf, though.

My fingers and legs were shaking, and my hairline was becoming damp. A feeling of weightlessness, yet of totally being grounded and unable to move, made a paradox in my chest. I felt about to burst with indecision, but then, off to the left in the periphery of my vision, I saw it, only a flicker.

In my room.

I dry swallowed and turned left. Walked slowly, breathing deeply, trying to calm the snakes coiling in my chest and the rats squirming over their tails in my stomach. I didn't run; there was no intelligence in rushing. Had to tread carefully because the situation—this visit— was too sinister to treat as though just another recurring nuisance. I wanted to call out to my mom and dad so badly.

The lights weren't on in the hallway, and I don't know why I didn't turn them on; they were only a few feet behind me, but I couldn't turn back.

The hallway felt unusually long to me. And for some reason, I was paying attention to the little details about the passage that I hadn't before. There was a stain on the floor to the side because of a tiny leak in the roof that my dad had been saying he'd fix for years. I never noticed until that moment that it looked like a shadowy face. There were several paintings hanging on the walls. In one the top of tall trees were depicted, backed by huge clouds that…

Of course, looked like shadows to me. Shadows with just discernable expressions of menace. The rain falling was saliva dripping over their sharp and bloody teeth.

I walked on, seeing shadows in everything. My room was dark at the end of the hall. I knew I was backlit by the light from the bathroom behind me. I didn't like that at all because anything could be crouching in the black pit of my room, marking my every twitch and jerk. And although I knew what was in there, and although I had never before been physically hurt by it, though first touched that night, my imagination gave me no pass. I became mad at myself; I felt crossed by my mind.

I continued on, almost to the end, to the complete darkness and the creature inside that awaited me. I didn't know what to expect and could never have guessed what would happen next. Not even my imagination could've.

The hallway lights popped on; my heart slammed into my ribcage and for a moment I couldn't breathe. Black spots dotted my vision. I was half bent with a hand on my chest, feeling as though vertigo were leading me in a dance. I steadied myself on the stand atop which a vase full of flowers stood. I looked to the right, confirming that neither of my parents had done it.

When I felt balanced, I tilted my head up and saw that my door was closed. That was the pop I'd associated with the light coming on. The Shadow Beast had shut my door.

The next thing I noticed was that I stood in front of a floor to ceiling window that looked onto our backyard. At first I thought it was the Shadow Beast because it was big and glossy and black. I stepped back, swallowing a breath.

Then I recognized it for what it was, and my fear grew. I was staring back at myself, surrounded by brightness as stark as blackness, as deep as madness. I stared back at myself, visible and bare, and my fear grew.

A tear slid over my cheek. I breathed deep and bit my lip. I don't know how long I stood there before moving, but when I did, I picked up the vase full of flowers and threw it at the window with a brutal grunt. A loud crash replaced the silence. Glass flew and my image became cracked and shattered, then fell like crystal rain to no longer be.

A thump to my right; the Shadow Beast was now at the other end of the hall. I don't know how it got passed me. That wolf-like appearance beckoned. It appeared to be howling, or laughing. Laughing at me. Then it was gone, wisped around the corner like the tail of a kite.

I followed.

Then the screaming started. I'll never forget that. Just as I'll never forget Bear. The sounds were worse than the actual sight of it.

And the actual sight was pretty bad because, you see, the kitchen is surrounded by windows, and no blinds were drawn.

GET THE BRICK

BY AMANDA LAWRENCE AUVERIGNE

The boys hoot and yell as soon as I step from the locker room.

I run out of the door and scamper across the wet tiles of the large swimming pool.

I skid as I turn a corner and before I know it, I'm sliding.

One of my friends reaches out and grabs me before I fall into the pool.

I thank her.

I hold my towel around my waist.

No way am I taking it off until I have to hit the water.

The boys in my class are standing in a large group across the pool. They are all looking at me and laughing.

They are such jerks.

Coach Medley is with them.

He's sitting at his desk in the middle of the testosterone-soaked group with his metal clipboard in his left hand.

The boys are whispering and pointing at us girls while we huddle in a shivering crab-like formation.

We all have on our towels and we're looking at the water in the pool.

The deep chasm of swarming filth that separates us from the idiot boys. Otherwise known as the Ridley Burnett High School gymnasium swimming pool.

We are all shivering.

We have just stepped from the showers. And we are half naked. A few of us probably are suffering from hypothermia right now.

We stare at the boys' loose fitting trunks.

The boys all smile at us and begin to strut around the pool.

Some of them stop walking and flex their pale non-existent muscles for us to see with ape-like grunts of pain.

Some of us yawn. A few of us laugh. One of us gags.

The coach gets up.

We can hear his arthritic bones crack as he stretches.

He looks at us with a grin and says some stuff we ignore.

I pull at the bottom of my suit. I stuff my hair into the tight rubber cap on my head.

The blasted thing is already giving me a headache. But no way was I going bareback in that pool. Not after what I had seen last week.

See, this senior, Tom Gerald, had gotten sick in the deep end of the pool after eating a six pack of Morten Fast Shack cheeseburgers, three boxes of onion rings and a vanilla shake in the locker room before class. Of course, Tom couldn't wait to blow spew until it was his turn to dive.

What happened was traumatic. I mean, I had to see the counselor for my PTSD you know?

If you really look you can see that there are *still* big chunks of green puke bubbling in the metal reservoirs on the sides of the swimming pool.

Enough said.

I'm trying not to stare at the yucky reservoirs and I jump when I hear a noise all around me.

It's the girls.

They're all squirming in their towels. Some of them are screaming. Two are crying. One is sneezing.

I look at Betty, my friend since Pre-K, and I ask her what's going on.

Betty looks away from one of the strutting boys she likes, Pete Miller, and she tells me that we have to take a swimming test.

So here it was, the ending to five weeks of hell.

To pass this class and not suffer the reek of this pool in summer school, we had to survive the ill-fated test of the waters.

We had to dive for the brick.

The boys were having a pre-war party.

They did a little dance of tribal warfare before they ran around the swimming pool.

The boys circled the large pool three times and they stuck out their chests in our directions each time they passed us.

We moved away from the laughing boys during each of their rotations and we gagged each time they tried to get close to us.

Coach Medley blew his whistle.

The boys ran around the pool one last time before they all lined up at the edge of the swimming pool in a straight line.

Just like kindergarten.

They all beat their chests while they struggled to breathe.

Coach Medley scratched his chest while he waddled over to the testing area.

If you can call a broken down diving board at the front of the pool that.

One of the boys stopped his alpha male chest thumping long enough to drag the Coach's desk and chair over to the testing area.

We girls all moved towards the boys. But we kept our distance. And our towels wrapped around our butts.

Coach Medley stops in front of the desk. He reaches inside the thing and he pulls out a big red brick.

I stare at the tiles beneath my toes.

A few of them are missing.

I look at Betty and say, "Coach Medley probably pulled that brick up from the floor."

Betty laughs and says, "You know there have been budget cuts."

I laugh so hard I almost drop my towel.

The Coach lets out a primal shriek before he turns around in a quick circle and throws the red brick into the water.

The brick hits the surface of the large scummy pond with a loud splat.

It sinks.All the way to the bottom.

Coach Medley rubs his hands and calls out the first name.

It was a girl.

We all look at Penelope Ardvan.

And we know by her last name that the Coach was going by ABC order.

Damn him.

That meant that I would be next.

Penelope throws off her towel. She runs across the tiles and jumps into the water.

Coach Medley sits down and he looks at his stopwatch.

Penelope leaps up out of the water like a mermaid. She's holding the brick in her left hand and she's swimming fast. She reaches the edge of the pool and places the brick on the tiles near the coach's feet.

Coach Medley shouts her time. He writes on the clipboard.

He bends down and picks up the brick. He leans back in his seat and he tosses the thing into the pool like a basketball.

The boys clap.

I watch Penelope climb out the pool.

The coach calls out another name.

It's a boy this time.

The boys let out loud hoots as Paul Bradley runs across the tiles. He yells before he jumps into the pool.

He hits the water in a clumsy belly flop.

The whole class howls in disbelief.

I hold my stomach.

I saw Paul grimace as he went under and I knew he was hurting.

Coach Medley stares at his watch.

I pull at my cap.

Paul jumps up from the water. He's holding the brick in his left hand and he's spitting out a lot of water.

Some of the girls make loud barfing noises.

Betty says she won't go in the pool because of Paul's nasty mouth germs.

Paul turns to us during his swim to the testing area. He raises his right hand and gives Betty the finger.

Betty lets loose with the cuss words and I flinch from her elegant ear scorching assault.

Paul turns from us and he swims to the coach and gives him the brick.

Coach Medley takes the rock and calls Paul's' time.

The boys shout.

Paul climbs from the pool. He rushes to his cheering friends and he lifts his arms in a sign of victory.

The boys jump, twist and yell around him.

Betty folds her arms across her bosom and says, "Boys are such idiots."

I pull at my cap and grind my teeth from the pain in my skull. I say, "Yeah, pretty much."

Coach Medley turns around and he makes a noise like a siren while he throws the brick over his left shoulder.

The red rock flies across the tiles and it misses Bill Hadley's slick head by a few inches before it hits the water.

The boys all laugh and cheer.

Coach Medley sits down with a slow nod.

I shake my head and say, "This test has lawsuit written all over it."

Coach Medley calls out a name.

All of the girls are looking at me. Betty is patting my shoulder.

I know the coach called my name. I was next.

Damn!

All the boys whistle and hoot.

I hear Paul yell, "Drop that towel!"

Betty says, "I'll drop kick you!"

The boys hoot.

Coach Medley says, "Settle down! Marnie Conrad. YOU'RE UP!"

I drop my towel and run across the tiles. I reach the broken down diving board and I take a deep breath before I leap off of pool's edge.

I'm floating for a brief second and before I know it, I'm in the water.

The first thing that hits me is the cold. I'm never prepared for the cold. It's like swimming in the arctic.

After a few minutes of swimming, I flip over and swim down.

As I get farther into the depths of the pool, I see nothing but murk.

The green light that had shined down on the pool from above fades as I go deeper.

I hold my breath and I exhale a few precious bubbles of air on my way down.

I look around and I see thousands of green snotty strands of slime floating around me.

I close my lips with a choke.

Can we say filtration system?

My eyes start to burn.

I open them and silently wish that I had taken Betty's goggles when she offered them in the locker room.

I blink a few times and I keep moving.

My left knee scrapes against something hard and I know I'm at the bottom.

Finally.

I flip up and land on my feet.

I exhale slightly.

The tiny bubbles of air pour from my mouth and disappear in the dark.

I walk slowly across the bottom and I wince from all of the unpleasant sensations that are cascading across my feet.

My left heel slides against something soft. The toes of my right foot touch something gritty.

I hear a low groaning noise and suddenly, the big toe on my right foot is caught on something.

I wriggle it and it comes free with a pop.

Oh yeah, I'm by the pump.

I move away from it and stop. I squint and look around.

I stare at the grimy floor and I see it.

The brick.

It's right in front of me.

I leap off of the bottom and swim towards it.

I exhale a little as I move closer to the rock. I reach out to the rock and I close my hand around the brick.

I lift it up.

It feels light.

I hear a loud swooshing noise behind me and I turn around.

I look around and I see a whole lot of bubbles.

They look black and shiny.

Weird.

I squint and look harder.

The bubbles fade and I see something big and white in front of me.

I move closer. Like an idiot.

My chest starts to ache a bit, and I let out more air. I blink several times and I gasp when the large white thing in front of me suddenly comes into focus.

It's a skull.

It's floating in the air right by me and the rest of its skeleton is sort hanging from the bottom of it.

The skulls' jaws are opening and closing. Black bubbles are pouring from its eyes.

The skull raises its arms and it moves them around in slow circles.

Long strands of slimy black slime are falling off of the thing's bones.

I look at the skeleton's middle and I almost breathe out my precious air when I see it.

The thing is wearing a pair of red Speedos.

The skeleton floats across the water and moves closer to me. It raises its left hand and it points at me.

It opens its jaws and the sound of muffled laughter fills my water-clogged ears.

At this point, I've decided that I've seen enough.

I push off of the bottom and I shoot up towards the surface.

I'm staring at the greenish light at the top of the water and I'm swimming for my life.

I move quickly to the surface.

I'm almost at the top and I look down.

The skeleton is right under me.

It's rising up fast and its twirling around in a fast circle. Black bubbles are coming from its eyes and mouth.

I scream and all of my air is gone. I look up towards the surface and I kick and flail wildly in an attempt to escape the bony horror that's floating under me.

After what seems like an eternity, I break the surface of the water.

I hear the shouts and whistles of my classmates and I don't' care.

I look at where I am and I choke with horror.

I'm in the middle of the damned pool and I still have to swim like lightning to get to the edge.

I take a few deep breaths and I spit and cough.

The water around me churns and I look around and see hundreds of black bubbles rise up on the water's surface.

The oily bubbles float for an unnaturally long time and as each one pops I hear a loud whiny voice.

"Ten."

"Points."

"If."

"You."

"Hit."

"His."

"Skull."

I scream and I swim to the edge.

I make it to the broken down diving board in no time. I can still hear that voice in my head as I grab at the edge of the pool. I'm still holding the brick in my left hand and I throw it before I grab at the edge of the pool. I pull myself out and I'm running.

I'm halfway to the safety of the locker room before I'm ambushed by my friends.

They put towels on me and I sob.

Betty rubs my face and asks me what's wrong. I cough up a lot of that nasty pool water and I'm rubbing my eyes, which makes them burn some more.

Betty is hugging me and the other girls are staring at me like I've lost my mind.

I take a deep breath to tell them what I'd seen and I stop when I hear this loud squeal that sounded like it came from a pig being slaughtered.

The pool becomes silent and everyone looks at Coach Medley.

The Coach is standing up and holding his left foot.

The brick is on the tiles near his feet.

It's broken in half.

The boys are standing around him and a few of them are laughing.

Pete moves quickly behind Coach Medley. He looks at me mouths the word, 'Awesome!'

The Coach stops his dance and he's looking at me. He raises his hand and he points at me while he continues to squeal like a wounded animal.

I don't understand half of what he was saying because I was still in shock, shivering from hypothermia and I was lightheaded. Oh, and a lot of the yucky pool water was gushing out of my ears but after I heard this loud pop I could hear everything.

By the time I got my hearing back to 100% and some of the shock of what I had just seen kinda' wore off, I was finally able to focus on the couch.

Coach Medley had stopped screaming but he was still screaming. In fact, he was starting to go a little hoarse.

Somehow, though. In between the Coach's curse words, loud sobs, womanly shrieks and rasping yells I finally understand what he's saying.

I have failed the swimming test. Because I broke his toe.

LISE

BY JAN VANDER LAENEN

"A near-death experience (NDE) refers to a broad range of personal experiences associated with impending death, encompassing multiple possible sensations including detachment from the body; feelings of levitation; extreme fear; total serenity, security, or warmth; the experience of absolute dissolution; and the presence of a light, which some people interpret as a deity."

(Wikipedia, *Near death experience*)

I am a simple man, on the brink of being uneducated. The story I want to relate to you here, the story of how I became the cold-blooded murderer of a beautiful, young, innocent girl and will perhaps be sentenced to life imprisonment for the crime, was not committed to paper by myself but, rather, by a female ghost writer and lawyer who listened attentively to my confessions over the course of six conversations with me, recorded these on a cassette tape and turned them into the story that is being presented to you now.

My name is Boris. I can be brief about the details of my family and country of origin: I must have been born just about thirty years ago in a mountainous region somewhere in Eastern Europe, but somehow ended up alone in Brussels, Belgium sometime during my teens, where I was cared for and brought up in a number of institutions. I had not had a criminal past – a police record as it is called - up to that time when I sent young Lise back to her maker: I was never involved in gangs of youths, and the so-called illegal substances or alcohol never appealed to me, nor did I ever have to force or pay for girls to provide me with their erotic services – as everyone knows, there are enough light-hearted, loose creatures running around in Brussels who find it hard to turn down the chance of a "roll in the hay" with a strong, healthy young man like me.

I am dark, tall, broadly built, with a beard and moustache, very dark eyes and short, black curly hair. My most distinctive physical feature is perhaps my *unibrow*, two thick eyebrows growing completely into each other above my nose and giving me a somewhat wicked look. There are many legends about people with a *unibrow*: they are said to be transformed into werewolves during nights with a full moon and are, according to the Italian professor Cesare Lombroso, disposed towards wicked behaviour or supposed to have brain disorders, such as the Cornelia de Lange syndrome.

But none of that applies to me; I have always been content with my own company in my little rented room on Place Fontainas and never got caught up in the futile problems of the rest of mankind.

I work as a cleaner at St. John's Hospital. People leave me in peace there. I take my lunch breaks alone in the canteen. And maybe they are simply pleased that I take on the more dangerous duties such as cleaning the rooms for patients with infectious diseases and radioactive areas without frowning with my meeting eyebrows. I, myself, have never fallen sick and it appears that, behind my back, I am called *le corbeau*, the raven, after the penniless souls that used to collect the corpses in the cities during plague epidemics and who had apparently developed immunity to the germs.

Once, somebody asked me at St. John's Hospital if they could take a photo of me. I had just taken a shower and changed out of my working clothes into my nondescript beige cardigan, trousers and shoes from the Salvation Army when a professional photographer approached me in the corridor. He asked me to stand against a uniform grey wall of the hospital, assume a normal, relaxed pose and then clicked his camera a few times. I have never been able to understand the purpose of this photo session. Until that day. Until the day that…

… my day's work was done. I had a wash at the hospital and put on my normal clothes. On the way home, I bought a loaf of dark bread at the baker's. There I was approached by a young, blond woman about twenty-five years old who introduced herself as Lise. She recognised me, having already seen a picture of me during an unusual moment in her life. I took her to my modest apartment. I made love to her in an ordinary way, her on her back and me like a growling animal on top. And she begged me never to leave her alone again.

Whether or not I slowly became attached to Lise is a question I cannot answer. Nor did I ever ask her if she took contraceptives or could have possibly saddled me with an offspring. But the fact remains that *she* gradually started demanding more *sadistic* performances from me.

It seems that sadistic and masochistic games are often aimed at reversing or, so to speak, upsetting the role patterns of everyday life. Lise was an attractive and well-educated girl and, judging by her clothes, jewellery and sophisticated make up, she apparently hailed from well-to-do circles and evidently had an equally healthy bank account, although she never disclosed anything about her background at the beginning. I myself am what can be described as a simple man with a humble profession who will never play an important role in society, will never exercise power or arbitrariness over his fellow-men, and who will have to live by his daily bread and a bit of love as it comes his way.

These were maybe the underlying reasons why our affair started to take on violent forms. At the beginning, Lise asked me to beat her around her face and body, a request that I responded to without any second thoughts. Then she came up with more sophisticated gear like little whips and handcuffs to shackle her to the end of my bed, cords to tie her up and a gag in her mouth so as not to be able to scream while I was physically abusing her and, in particular, targeting her anus for my penetrations.

Finally, on an autumn day, she fixed a date for a week or so later when I was supposed to kill her. She wanted to be strangled. With a chord. With a shawl. With a tie. With any object that would be effective. Prior to my murdering her, she would write a letter stating that the act had taken place with her full consent and that I was therefore to be exonerated from prosecution for premeditated murder.

"Would you like to know why I want to die?" she also asked me, whereupon I shrugged my shoulders indifferently.

Two evenings before I carried out her ultimate desire, she finally gave me an explanation for her death wish while she was sitting on my bed, continuously dangling her legs. Her words were as follows:

"I have already attempted to commit suicide. Some six months ago. Because of that, I was admitted to the psychiatric ward of St. John's Hospital, a ward which, as you told me, does not come under your cleaning responsibilities, so it is was unlikely that we would have ever met – I knew you unmistakably from a picture, though, but was only able to see you in the flesh for the first time in that bakery shop in Rue du Midi.

In the psychiatric ward, there was a lot of conjecture about the reasons for my desperate act. I come from a rich, strictly Catholic and well-to-do, middle-class family. I was the eldest daughter. Maybe I was harbouring feelings of guilt about my wealth and religious background. Perhaps I felt inferior about not being able to study at university. My love life was unravelled. My erotic life. Maybe I was abused by my father. Maybe I was seeking affection from the wrong kind of men, men with a *macho* image of exotic origin that wildly go on the rampage with my body as with the contents of my Chanel purse.

So I already have one suicide attempt behind me. Taking tablets. And a friend of mine found me just in time. I was taken to St. John's

Hospital by ambulance in great haste and landed on the operating table. And it was there that I experienced what is famously referred to as a personal near-death experience. Everything I have ever read in a women's magazine, matching my personal experience. I exited from my body. I could hear and see the doctors and nurses getting excited. Then I saw a dark tunnel above me, a tunnel with an indescribably beautiful light at the end. Never before did I feel so blissful as during those moments; no, I wanted to get away from this world, I wanted to go towards the light, to God, and the immense mercy and love radiated by Him. I felt my sprit, or soul, or whatever it was, floating upwards, towards the ceiling above the operating table. Then I just wanted to cast a glance at myself, at the body I was leaving, and I saw that there was a false ceiling about one metre lower fitted in parts of the theatre. On these false ceilings there were objects, including a basket of marble fruit and a crucifix. And a large coloured picture. A large colour photo of a full-length man, simply dressed and with a characteristic, almost fiendish dark head. His most striking physical feature was a *unibrow*, two thick eyebrows growing completely into each other above his nose and giving him a somewhat wicked look. The man in that picture was you, I recognised you in the bakery shop immediately. And that picture is the last thing I remember of my near-death experience before being reanimated and sucked back into my body.

"Along with all the related pain, physically as well as mentally."

"And what do you want from me?" I then asked.

"I did not want to mention one single word about my experience with anyone at the hospital. All I wanted was to simply go back to that light, that God, that mercy, that peace, in other words that paradise I was allowed to enjoy just a foretaste of. I am glad that I ran into you after searching for a number of months – I would not dare or want to ask anyone else to return me to that Paradise Lost with his own hands."

I nodded calmly and then killed Lise on the date agreed. I took her and during my traditional act of penetration I slowly but powerfully strangled her with one of my ties from the Salvation Army. And after that, I delivered her letter to the police station.

After the event, the details appeared to tally. In the operating theatre where she ended up following her suicide attempt, modifications had been introduced to provide scientific evidence concerning near-death experiences that are much talked-about yet disregarded as mythical.

False ceiling panels had been fitted on the side walls, with objects placed on them, i.e. a basket of fruit, a crucifix and a picture of me, the same one that the photographer had taken some time ago in one of the uniform grey corridors of the St. John's Hospital.

DAGGOTH THE DESTROYER
By John Pennington

<u>HALLOWEEN MORNING</u>

Andy Copeland sat down on the edge of his bed and started the painstaking process of stripping off all the heavy metal band patches that were scattered across his worn, filthy jean jacket. It was a difficult process, as Andy had always preferred to sew on patches to the iron-on type. He felt they looked better and were much more durable. Removing them seemed to be the best option to adequately clean all the dried mud and pig feces that caked every square inch of the jacket.

Andy slid the hobby knife beneath the first patch, the logo of the band Slayer, and carefully started to cut the stitching. He moved slow, not wanting to accidentally slice the patch, or worse, himself. As he cut, his only thoughts were of the ones who had done this to him. He envisioned them getting ready for their annual Halloween bash they had every year. They had no idea what was in store for them.

He finished with the first patch and immediately started on the next one. At this rate, he figured, it would only take him a couple hours to finish stripping them all from the jacket. It was tedious work, but Andy didn't mind. It made him feel like a warrior, preparing his armor for battle.

As he began removing the next patch, Andy smiled at the thought of the hell he was going to unleash.

THE PREVIOUS DAY

Andy opened his school locker and switched out his textbooks, preparing for his last class of the day—Agriculture. He hated the class, but it was a requirement to graduate and the only other alternative was shop class, which interested him even less than Agriculture. The only bright spot of taking the class was that he'd get to see Cindy one last time before the end of the day. They only shared two classes that year, so the last class was always the highlight of his day.

He had known Cindy Mills since the fourth grade, when her family moved into the house next to his. Over the next three years they became best friends, and often hung out and played together. But before their friendship could blossom into something else, Cindy's family moved away and they inevitably drifted apart.

Once they entered high school, she began to hang out with a new crowd. They were what the stoners called "preps", and their ranks consisted of mostly rich kids and jocks. The two of them remained friends, though not nearly as close as they once were. And when Cindy started dating one of the football players, Andy knew his window had closed. But he never gave up hope that someday Cindy would be his.

"Here you go dude," came a voice from behind him. He turned to see his cousin Ricky, whose outstretched hand contained a cassette tape. "Hot off the presses."

"That's awesome," said Andy, taking the tape. "I can't believe I got a copy of this. I can't wait to listen to it."

"Yeah, it is awesome. I listened to it last night. You won't be disappointed. But listen; don't go making a bunch of copies of it. It doesn't come out for another month and if it gets back to my brother that I gave anybody a copy, my ass is grass."

"Don't worry. The only person who's gonna hear this is me," Andy assured his cousin. It had been Ricky who first got Andy interested in heavy metal four years earlier, when he played him the new Iron Maiden album, *The Number of the Beast,* and from that moment Andy was hooked. He listened to nothing but metal from then on. And the heavier it was the better.

Andy turned back to his locker and grabbed a notebook and two cassettes.

"What are those?" asked Ricky.

"Oh, these are copies of the new Poison and Bon Jovi records that just came out," replied Andy.

"Poison? Bon Jovi?" mocked Ricky. "Don't tell me you listen to that faggy shit. You ain't turnin' queer on me, are you?"

"No," Andy shot back while closing his locker. "I made them for Cindy."

"Whoa, whoa, wait a second. You made her copies of those shitty records? The only way you could've done that is if you borrowed them from somebody else or went out and bought them. Please tell me you didn't buy those just to make her copies of 'em?"

Andy's silence let Ricky know he was on the right track.

"Jesus, dude. Can't you see she's just using you?"

"You don't even know her," Andy shot back.

"I know enough to know that she's using you."

"Whatever," said Andy, hoping to switch the subject. "Hey, you coming over tomorrow night?"

"No I can't," replied Ricky. "Parents are taking me with them to some lame-ass Halloween party. I can't get out of it."

"Man, that sucks," said Andy, before taking a look at the clock in the hallway. "I better get goin'. If I'm late to Ag one more time, Mr. Pearson said he was personally gonna call my dad. See ya on Monday."

"See ya," said Ricky, as Andy started to walk away. "Remember: no copies."

Andy gave him a thumbs up sign without turning around, acknowledging his friend's reminder. He made his way as quickly as he could to the Ag building, beating the bell by mere seconds, avoiding Mr. Pearson's wrath. The building itself was no more than a little shack where the class would meet before heading outside to begin the days assignment. Andy was not overjoyed when Mr. Pearson announced what they would be doing that day: working at the hog pen. Without a doubt it was the one thing he hated most about the class, and with the chance of rain at zero percent, there was no way to get out of it. The only thing that made the crappy news easier to take was the sight of Cindy, sitting two seats across from him.

She'd really blossomed since Andy first met her all those years ago. Gone was the gangly, rail-thin, boyish figure, having been replaced by many voluptuous curves. Her teeth, which seemed to have spent a lifetime hidden behind metal, were now perfectly white and straight. And her hair, that had spent its adolescence in an infinite ponytail, was now the gorgeous, silky mane that Andy feasted his eyes upon daily. The girl next door that got away from him was now a beautiful young woman.

Andy daydreamed about her frequently, and as with any other young man going through the growing pains of puberty, they were mostly of the sexual nature. Not all of them though, but even the ones that didn't always inevitably returned to where they began: with the two of them having passionate sex.

Andy was smack-dab in the middle of one of these daydreams when Mr. Pearson signaled it was time to head outside and begin the day's class.

"Mr. Copeland? Are you going to join us today?"

Upon hearing Mr. Pearson utter his name, Andy snapped back to reality to discover he was the only one still seated. This garnered a good chuckle from the rest of the class, especially the jocks.

"Uh… yeah. Sorry," said Andy, as he quickly gathered his things and followed the rest of the class outside.

The hog pen was located about a hundred yards away from the Ag building. It was an unseasonably hot day for early spring, and Andy found himself starting to sweat under his denim jacket. The heat also did nothing to help the smell emanating from the hog pen, and the closer the group got to it, the more overwhelming the smell became.

The group arrived at their destination and Mr. Pearson divided the students up into two smaller groups: one to handle and move the bags of feed and the other to distribute the feed to the hogs. The first group consisted of the stronger kids in the class, which included Kevin, Cindy's jock boyfriend. Andy was a part of the second group that was made up of the girls and the weaker kids in the class, which didn't bother him because it gave him more time to spend with Cindy.

"Hey Cindy," Andy said, walking over to one of the feed troughs where she was working.

"Oh, hi Andy," she replied, barely stopping her work to acknowledge him.

"So, I… um… I made those tapes you wanted," he said, taking the tapes from his jacket and handing them to Cindy.

"Oh wow, that was fast," she said, taking the tapes. "You didn't waste any time, did you?"

"Well, I didn't have much going on last night, so I went ahead and put 'em together. There was some room left on the tapes, so I put some other stuff you might like. L.A. Guns, a new band called Warrant, Def Leppard—"

"Def Leppard? Oh, I love them. That new song of theirs 'Hysterical' is great."

"Yeah, 'Hysteria'. That is a great song," said Andy, correcting Cindy, who was unaware that he had even corrected her at all. "So, what're you… what're you doing for Halloween?"

"I'm going to a party out at the Farm. The football team's putting it together. What are you up to?"

"Not much. I was supposed to hang out with my cousin, but he canceled on me. I'm probably just going to hang out at the house."

Cindy looked around and noticed a couple of her friends looking her way, whispering and giggling to each other. She turned back toward Andy. "Well, I better get back to work. Thanks again for the tapes."

"No problem. If… you know… need anything else just… uh… you know, give me a call. I'm usually home."

Cindy nodded at Andy, then turned and walked over to her friends. Andy watched her walk away and then headed toward the barn to get more feed.

"Hey Andy?"

Andy looked over his shoulder, toward the sound of Kevin's voice. He and the other jocks were standing near the pickup truck, its bed full of feed sacks.

"Come on over and give us a hand with this stuff," said Kevin.

Andy walked over to the group, unsure of their true intentions. "You sure this is okay?" asked Andy. "Mr. Pearson put me in the other group."

"Oh yeah, he'll be fine with it," assured Kevin. "Besides he went back to the classroom to get something and he left me in charge. And you look pretty strong. We could definitely use the help.

"Anyway," Kevin continued, as he gave Andy a couple playful jabs to the stomach, "you don't want to work with the girls and those wimps all day, do you?"

"No, not really," said Andy, smiling.

"All right then. Grab one of these bags here and follow me," said Kevin, grabbing a feedbag from the bed of the truck.

Andy walked to the truck and went to pick up one of the bags, but despite his best efforts, he could barely move its seventy-five pound bulk. Kevin, who was watching the scene play out, dropped his own bag and walked back to the truck.

"Here, let me help you with that," he said, lifting a bag from the truck bed and dropping it not so gently on Andy's shoulder. Andy winced a little at the impact and initial shock of the weight, but he hardly let it show.

"Let's go," said Kevin, lifting his own bag back up onto his shoulder in one quick motion. Following Kevin, the group started off toward the barn entrance, around fifty yards away.

Andy struggled to keep up with the rest of the group. The weight of the bag ground into his shoulder and made each step feel as though he had concrete pads on the soles of his shoes. But he was bound and determined not to fail. This was his chance to prove to them he wasn't the little wimpy kid they all thought he was.

A couple moments after the rest of the group had entered the barn, Andy lurched inside and dropped the bag of feed to the ground, much to the relief of his throbbing shoulder.

"Wasn't so bad, was it?" asked Kevin.

"No, it was all right," replied Andy, masking his pain.

"So, I got something to ask you Andy," said Kevin. "I saw you over there talking to my girlfriend a few minutes ago. So what… uh… were you two talking about? I mean, I ain't got anything to worry about, do I?"

The question surprised Andy. "What? No… no, it's not like that. We're just friends. I was just giving her some tapes I made for her, that's all."

Kevin moved in closer, appearing more menacing to Andy. "Really? You sure there wasn't something else going on?"

"Yeah… I mean, no. No, th-that was it," stammered Andy. "There's nothing else going on?"

Kevin smiled a big smile and backed away from Andy. "Yeah, I guess you're right. I mean, what would she see in a pussy like you anyway?"

The other boys in the barn started to laugh and Andy's heart sank, as he realized he'd been set up. Amidst all the laughter, one of Kevin's buddies spoke up.

"What's that?" he asked Andy. "Hey Kevin, I just heard this little twerp call you a homo."

"No I didn't! I didn't say anything," cried Andy, his pleads falling on deaf ears.

"Is that right?" Kevin replied to his buddy. "You know what I think fellas? I think Andrew here is a little too clean cut. Time to put some dirt on him, don't you think?"

A chorus of approvals came from the crowd of jocks. Andy tried to run, but his attempt to escape was a futile one. The mass of older stronger boys grabbed him, lifted him above their heads, and quickly made their way to the hog pens.

"Put me down, damn it!" Andy cried. "Put me down!"

Andy's shouting attracted the attention of the female group that was working nearby.

"You heard him boys," said Kevin. "Put him down."

The burly boys carrying Andy walked him over to the hog pen and tossed him over the fence. He landed on the ground with a wet thud, sinking a few inches into the soggy, muddy earth upon impact.

The jocks laughed and carried on as Andy wiped the filth from his face, in shock by what had just happened. It wasn't the first time he'd been humiliated at school, far from it, but this was easily the worst thing that had ever been done to him. He saw the girls group walking up behind the jocks. Several of them were pointing and laughing at him. Andy couldn't see Cindy, but he was sure she saw everything.

Then Andy saw one of the jocks picking something up from the ground—the cassette Ricky had given him.

"Look at this Kevin," said the kid who picked up the tape. "The dork must've dropped it when we threw him over."

Kevin took the tape from his buddy and looked at the label on the case.

"Metal?" Kevin scoffed. "You really need to stop listening to this crap. It's gonna rot your brain."

Kevin pulled the cassette from its case, and in a swift motion, snapped it in half. He tossed the broken pieces into the mud, directly in front of Andy. He looked at the broken, unspooled tape and then up at the crowd around him, which now included the group of girls.

They were laughing.

He finally caught a glimpse of Cindy. A faint smile grazed her lips, as Andy's eyes settled on her. Despite her best efforts, it was impossible to conceal the fact that she'd been laughing along with the others.

"What the hell is going on out here?" came Mr. Pearson's voice, somewhere behind the group. They all turned in unison to see the agitated teacher hurriedly making his way toward them. Kevin spoke up before anyone else.

"Andy here was goofing around on the fence, sir, and ended up falling in," he lied to the unknowing teacher. "I told him to knock it off and get back to work, but he wouldn't listen."

"Really?" asked the skeptical teacher. "Then why were you all standing around here laughing at him?"

"Well sir, he did fall into a big pile of pig crap," reasoned one of the other jocks. "It was kinda funny."

"Is that right? Let's see how funny you think a week's worth of detention is, Mr. Rokowski." Mr. Pearson looked around the group. "Anyone else think its funny?"

He received no takers.

Mr. Pearson climbed over the fence, helped Andy out of the muck, and the two of them headed toward the main building. The rest of Andy's day went by in a haze—taking a shower, getting dressed in an oversized gym uniform, and bagging up his muddy clothes in a black trash bag. He didn't bother telling Mr. Pearson what really happened. He knew nothing would happen to the jocks. The school's football team was undefeated and had a real shot at making it to the state finals. They weren't going to jeopardize that for some poor kid who nobody cared about.

But none of that even mattered to Andy. The only thing he could focus on was seeing Cindy's face and knowing that she was laughing right along with the rest of them. He'd never felt more crushed and humiliated. One of the few people he thought he could trust, who was the one he cared most for, had betrayed him.

After he had showered and dressed, Andy, toting the trash bag of dirty clothes, walked home. Mr. Pearson had offered him a ride, but Andy decided he'd rather walk.

Twenty minutes later, Andy arrived home to an empty house. A note tacked to the refrigerator, along with a twenty-dollar bill and the number to the local pizza place, let him know his father would be working late. His mother had passed when he was still a young boy and his father never remarried, or for that matter, even dated anyone else. It was just the two of them, and Andy had long ago gotten used to coming home with no one there to greet him.

He left the kitchen and retreated to his bedroom. Over the years, it had grown to become more of a sanctuary, a safe haven from the cruel world of high school he experienced every day.

Pictures of his favorite bands adorned nearly every inch of the room's walls, and were beginning to stretch their way to the ceiling. Alice Cooper lovingly caressed his pet boa constrictor, Megadeth's mascot, Vic Rattlehead, looked down from a nuked-out wasteland, while Judas Priest looked like they'd just stepped out of an s and m shop. They were the kings of the misfits, consolers of a generation of lonely, forgotten kids—kids that they themselves used to be. It was in these people and their music that Andy found something that he could understand, and in turn, something that could understand him and what he was going through. Something that would never leave him, never abandon him.

That would never betray his trust in them or his companionship.

Surrounded by the pictures of his idols, Andy dropped the garbage bag on the floor, sat down on his bed, and started to cry.

Astral Cross was one of Andy's favorite bands. They weren't his absolute favorite—that distinction belonged to either Kiss or Iron Maiden—but they were high up on the list. They were a black metal band from Denmark, whose roots traced back to the early '80's, alongside such black metal pioneers as Venom and Celtic Frost. Their first two records were pretty hard to come by; Andy had gotten copies from Ricky, whose brother lived in Europe and would send Ricky hard to find records. This included the band's yet unreleased third record, a record that Andy was overexcited to finally get to listen to, which now set in a broken pile of plastic and unspooled tape on the desk in his room.

Andy sat down at the desk and began the long process of putting the mangled tape back together. He started with untangling the tape itself, which, despite what it had been through, was relatively unscathed—a few crinkles and bends, but nothing major. After a long, meticulous hour of work, the tape was back where it belonged—on the two small plastic spools.

The tapes plastic casing however, had been destroyed beyond repair. Out of a stack of cassettes he had sitting on the desk, Andy chose the sacrificial lamb: a barely played copy of an album by the band Wingnut. His aunt had gotten it for him as a Christmas gift and he had only played it a couple of times. They had too much of that "pretty boy" sound for Andy's liking. He took the cassette from its case and began taking the screws from the corners.

Once he had it disassembled, he took the Wingnut tape from the housing and tossed it in the trashcan, replacing it with the newly re-spooled Astral Cross tape. He screwed the two pieces of plastic housing back together, then sat back in his chair and looked at the Frankenstein-esque creation.

Following a moment of silent, self-celebratory congratulations, Andy picked the tape up from the desk, put it in the stereo and pressed play.

"Andy?"

"Andy?"

"Wake up Andy."

"It's time."

Andy awoke still sitting at his desk, his head resting on the wood tabletop, a half-eaten pizza and a can of soda resting nearby. He lifted his head and wiped the sleep from his eyes, expecting to see his father. He looked around.

There was no one else in the room.

"Andy?"

Andy's head swiveled around looking for the body to go with the voice he just heard. Just as before, he saw no one. The voice was deep, and sinister in nature.

"Over here Andy."

He followed the sound of the voice to his stereo speakers.

"He-hello?" he asked, feeling a little silly that he was addressing his stereo.

"Hello Andy," said the disembodied voice, and the feeling of silliness was replaced by fear.

Andy looked closely at his stereo. The power was off, yet the tape player was still playing the Astral Cross cassette. Only Andy noticed something was off—the tape was running in reverse.

"I'm dreaming. This has got to be a dream," Andy said to himself. "I'm gonna wake up in a few minutes and everything's gonna be fi-"

"This is not a dream, Andy," assured the voice.

"If it's not a dream, then who the hell are you? What are you doing… talking through my stereo?"

"Who or what I am is of no concern to you. What I can give to you, however, is."

"What you can give to me?"

"Yes. I know what they've done to you Andy. I know what she did. I know everything. What would you say if I told you I could help you get even with them?"

Andy paused for a moment. "Why would you do that for me?"

"Simply, I need help to cross over to your world Andy. If you agree to help me, I will help you."

Andy remained silent, offering no answer.

"Think of all the things they've done to you Andy. We can make them pay for all of it. You and me. All you have to do is agree to help me.

"What do you say?"

HALLOWEEN NIGHT

By nightfall the annual Halloween bash at the Farm was in full swing. A large bonfire burned, giving an orange glow to the surroundings, as the high school kids partied, danced, and drank. The sounds of Bon Jovi blasted from the stereo that was set up about ten yards from the fire. The Farm was not so much a farm, more an old cornfield with a bunch of dilapidated barns scattered around it. How it came to be known as the Farm was anyone's guess.

It was pitch black outside when Andy arrived. His jacket was clean from all the muck and grime that caked it just hours before and the patches were all returned to their original places. He stayed in the shadows and surveyed the area. Almost everyone who'd been in Ag class the day before was there. He spotted Cindy and Kevin standing near the bonfire, laughing and drinking.

To Andy, Cindy was having a great time, hanging out and having fun with her friends. She looked as happy as he'd ever seen her look. She leaned in close to Kevin and kissed him.

Much happier than she could ever be with him.

Andy made his way around to the stereo, not directly out in the open, but not incognito either. He recognized the Bon Jovi tape in the first cassette deck—it was the one he'd given Cindy the day before. He opened the second tape deck and put his jury-rigged Astral Cross cassette in. He stopped the Bon Jovi tape and started his.

The stereo crackled back to life with the opening strains of the first song.

Daggoth the Destroyer.

The song started ominously, building on a droning organ that was accompanied by a choir of unearthly sounding voices. Andy stood with his back to the crowd of partygoers, who were, one by one, beginning to turn toward the sound of the unfamiliar music.

"Who turned off the music?" came a voice from the crowd. "What is this crap?" came another.

Kevin and Cindy turned toward the sound. Even though he had his back toward them, both Kevin and Cindy knew it was Andy.

"Hey wait a sec," said one of the guys standing near Kevin. "That's the kid from Ag class the other day. What the fuck is he doing here?"

The music started to pick up a little; a heavily detuned, distorted guitar came into the mix, playing a slow, bruising riff. Moments later, the song exploded into a full on assault. Andy remained silent, still facing away from the crowd.

"Hey dork?" yelled one of the guys in the group. "It's past your bedtime, isn't it?"

"Yeah, does your mommy know you're out this late?" asked another.

"No she doesn't 'cause she was at my house earlier sucking my dick for five bucks," replied a much drunker member of the crowd. Laughter erupted from the group, but Andy paid no notice. He stood perfectly still, back to the crowd.

"Leave him alone," pleaded Cindy.

"What? You got feelings for the little dweeb?" asked Kevin.

"No… I… he's an old friend of mine," replied Cindy. "Don't be so mean to him."

"Come on, babe. We're just gonna have a little fun with him," Kevin said. He turned to a few of his friends. "Let him finish though," he chuckled. "This is too good."

Everyone in attendance gathered around Andy to see what he would do. They were all giggling and snickering as the music died back down to an eerie crawl, reminiscent of something from an old horror movie. A single voice came in over the music, speaking in an unfamiliar dialect. In a call and response manner, Andy repeated everything the voice said, word for word.

Te illumno sa gren-na.

Drak-ni ent zarro ezzenal.

Andy finally turned to face the crowd. A few of them gasped at what they saw. His eyes, from pupil to the whites, were a deep red, like blood from a fresh wound. Dark lines ran under his eyes, making it look as if he hadn't slept in a few days. His face was gaunt and bony, like skin had been stretched over his naked skull. His lips were dry, cracked, and pale, and a white foamy substance poured from his mouth as he spoke.

"All right freak-o, you made your point—you're weird. We get it. Now knock this crap off or I'm gonna come over there and kick your ass," yelled one of the jocks. Andy did not respond.

Prini ent suca-ra bocca.

"I don't like this Kevin," whispered Cindy. "There's something wrong with him."

"Yeah, there is," Kevin agreed, although in a slightly different context from Cindy's assessment. He turned to look at one of his buddies. "Mark, go over there and turn that noise off. After that, I want you to kick the shit outta that geek and get him the hell outta here."

Cindy grabbed her boyfriend's arm and jerked him around to face her. "Kevin, goddamn it, listen to me. Something's wrong. I know Andy, he doesn't do things like this."

"I know there's something wrong with him. Your little friend there's a complete fucking spaz and he's starting to piss me off. Believe it or not, this may help the little dork. Maybe if we kick his ass enough he'll start acting like he's normal."

Hasa boccdini zree-ka te trepedis ot Haval.

Andy did not acknowledge Mark, as the jock and walked around him and toward the stereo. The older boy was a little frightened of what was going on around him, but tried not to let it show. The last thing he wanted was for the other guys to know he was scared.

Mark pressed the stop button on the cassette player. It did nothing. He hit the eject button. Still nothing.

Andy and the voice spoke in unison, growing louder and louder with each passage they spoke.

L'Chaka oc te zarro.

Pause, fast forward, rewind.

L'Chaka oc te tunda-ra.

All nothing. Thunder boomed from the night sky. Mark backed away from the stereo, fully freaked out by the scene.

L'Chaka oc te destricino.

"Andy, please stop," pleaded Cindy.

Daggoth resi-ra.

"Listen to her geek. Take your freak show and go home," threatened Kevin.

Daggoth resi-ra.

"Hey Kev? This is startin' to freak me out man," said Mark.

Daggoth resi-ra!

The thunder cracked loud, as a lightning bolt tore through the sky and struck Andy in the top of the head. His body crumpled to the ground in a lifeless heap, his hair smoldering from the impact. A wide array of exclamations poured from the crowd of onlookers, who were undoubtedly shocked by what they had just witnessed.

"Oh my God! Andy!" yelled Cindy, who was about to run to her friend's side, but was grabbed by Kevin.

"Jesus Christ. Somebody ch-check on him," said Kevin, unsure of what to do. Mark moved in to check on the injured boy. The smell of burning hair and charred flesh made his stomach turn to where he was sure he was going to throw up. He reached down and took hold of the Andy's limp arm, putting his fingers to the wrist.

"Oh shit man. He ain't got no pulse," yelled Mark.

"Are you sure?" Kevin nervously asked.

"Yeah, I'm sure. The fuckin' kid's de-"

Andy's arm twisted beneath Mark's grip and his hand clasped down on the older boy's forearm. Mark screamed and fell to the ground as Andy snapped his forearm like a twig, the bone splintering from beneath the skin.

Andy's metamorphosis was fast and violent. His clothes tore at their seams and ripped as he rose up from the ground, a good two feet taller than his usual five-foot-six. His hands stretched out and reformed, fingers turning into elongated claws. His knees snapped, buckling inward, like the hind legs of an animal and his skin smoldered and cracked as if it were on fire, turning a sickly, grayish-black color. Finally, his face split in two, erasing any trace that Andy had ever existed, revealing a horrifying death mask.

Ferocious red eyes stared out into the crowd, while two nasal cavities set where the nose used to be. A massive jaw jutted down from the cheekbones to the creature's large mouth, which was filled with rows of sharp, jagged teeth. The beast scanned its prey and let out an enormous roar.

Pandemonium quickly took over. The kids screamed and started to run in every direction, away from the monster. Fire exploded from the ground surrounding them, creating a circle of flame, negating their escape. The beast surged forward, killing and dismembering everyone in its path. Severed heads, arms, and legs littered the ground in the wake of the beast and some of the kids decided to brave the perils of the fire.

They fared no better.

Kevin dragged Cindy around by hand, looking for a way through the white-hot flames, but after only a brief moment of searching, he decided it was too risky to stay out in the open. They headed toward the only shelter held within the confines of the fire: an old, run down barn.

The couple hurriedly entered the building, the echoes of their friends being murdered behind them in the night. Moonlight peaked through the cracks in the roof, while light from the fire found its way through the rotted planks of the barn's walls. Even with all the light seeping through the cracks, the barn was anything but well lit, and Kevin and Cindy could hear the whimpering voices of a few others who had also taken refuge in the old barn. The two of them found a quiet, dark corner and hid in the shadows, listening to the death unfold outside, until, at last, there was silence. The calm was soon broken however, by the sound of hoarse, jagged breathing.

The beast smashed through the barn door, sending splinters and big chunks of wood flying everywhere. Screams broke out through the barn, pinpointing each of the screamers locations. Cindy almost screamed herself, and certainly would have if Kevin had not grabbed her and put his strong hand across her mouth. The frightened girl shuddered and cried at the sound of the beast doing its grisly business. Kevin held her tightly and whispered in her ear.

"It's going to be alright, okay? It's going to be all right. We'll wait here until it's gone. It can't see us; it doesn't know we're here, okay? We'll wait all night if we have to," Kevin said, as the last screaming voice was extinguished and all was silent again. They sat in the shadows and listened as the monster made its way out of the barn. Kevin let out a small sigh and relaxed his grip on Cindy's mouth, his hand wet with her tears. He turned her gently by the shoulder to face him.

"It's okay. We're just gonna wait here for a while, till it's clear. Then we'll-"

The beast's arms shot through the wall directly behind Kevin, its massive claws taking hold of the boy. Cindy screamed and fell backwards, in shock and helpless. Kevin shrieked in pain and fought to free himself from the creature's claws, which dug deep into his mid-section, gouging and tearing his flesh. The beast jerked backwards, pulling Kevin through the wall, to the outside of the building. It lifted the young man up from the ground by his arms and brought him up to match its eye level. The beast moved its demonic face in close to Kevin's and stared the boy down.

"Fuck you, you bastard," Kevin struggled to speak, blood trickling from his mouth, the result of the wounds to his chest. In a final act of defiance, he spit square in the monster's face.

The beast reared its head back and let out a gigantic roar. It opened its mouth wide and bit down on the top of Kevin's head, digging its sharp teeth into his flesh and cracking his skull. The young man tried to scream, but what came out was more of a whimper. The monster pulled back, severing the top of Kevin's head with its powerful jaws. His body went limp in death as the beast swallowed the crushed skull and brain matter.

Cindy exited the barn, unaware of the fate of Kevin, or the whereabouts of the monster. All around her were the dismembered bodies of her friends, scattered all over the blood stained ground. The fire that circled the area died down and vanished as quickly as it had begun, leaving the grounds in silence and darkness.

"Hello? Kevin?" Cindy whispered into the darkness. She received no answer, the only sound coming from the chirping crickets. She scanned the area for several seconds. There was no sign of Kevin, and, more importantly, no sign of the monster. She spotted the row of cars parked in a nearby field and wasted no time running toward them. Kevin sometimes left his keys in his truck, and as she ran, Cindy was hoping he'd done so this time.

She got to the truck and looked through the window and saw the keys dangling from the ignition just as she had hoped. Then, just as she was about to open the truck door, she heard the terrible sound of raspy breathing behind her. She turned slowly to see the hulking beast towering over her. She didn't bother to scream.

"Andy? Andy, please if you're in there, I'm sorry for everything they've done to you," she pleaded. The beast looked at her, but did not attack. Her pleads to the creature formerly known as Andy Copeland appeared to be working.

"Andy, I've always been your friend," said Cindy, tears starting to flow. "Please let me go. I-"

The monster grabbed her by the throat and violently slammed her up against the side of the truck.

"There... is... no... Andy... anymore," the monster said, in a slow, drawn out growl. Cindy screamed as the beast smiled and started to laugh.

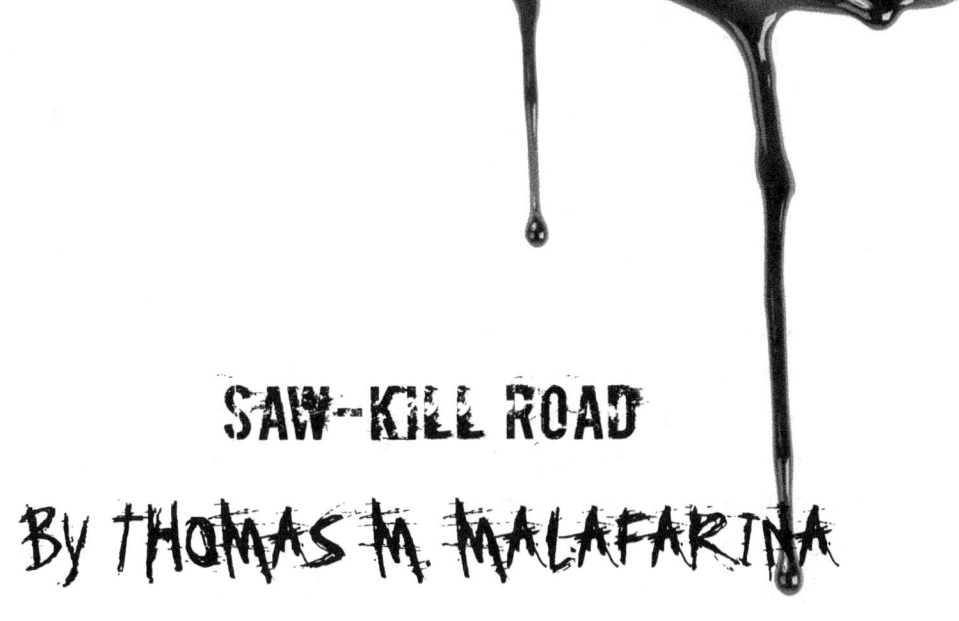

SAW-KILL ROAD

BY THOMAS M. MALAFARINA

The forlorn two-lane blacktop road snaked like a writhing serpent over its short half-mile length from end to end, connecting the busy Abington Lane with the mountainous Prescott Road. Its narrow winding countenance curved past the abandoned, once prosperous saw mill from which the road attained its name, "Sawmill Road". That is to say, "Sawmill" was its official name, as documented in the township archives. However, its unofficial moniker was much more menacing being known to locals, especially the children, as "Saw-Kill Road".

At the start of the twentieth century the sawmill had been a bustling enterprise, employing many local men; once a large two-story clapboard building, the wood sealed to allow its weather-resistance to fight off the elements.

Where the mill was level with the roadway two large barn-style doors opened to a dirt driveway allowing wagons to back up for loading and unloading of wood. As the land sloped downward a stone foundation reached five feet high to supported the building and provided a doorway access to a basement storage area, as well as windows for light. The ceiling of the basement area was comprised of thick wooden beams, serving also as the floor for the sawmill itself.

Its dark shutters in the sides of the upper floors could be open on nice days to allow the sun to shine inside and held closed during storms to prevent nature from damaging its many pains of hand-blown glass. At one time the mill had a gorgeous set of front stairs leading to a small front porch, constructed of wood from the mill, as was the beautiful oak entry door, with its four-pane window constructed of the same hand blown glass as was present throughout the rest of the mill.

Above the front door with its brass door knocker and crystal knob was a transom which held a custom made stain glass window bearing the name "Hanson's Mill" for the founder and owner of the mill, Jonas Jackson Hanson, known as "J.J." to his few friends and "the cheap limy bastard" to most of his employees.

Now, the mill stood in decay, its once beautiful wooden siding putrefying from years of exposure to the elements, fading to whitish gray, rotten and infested with insects. Rusted hinges hung loosely from disintegrating clapboards, some hanging by a single remaining corroded screw; a sad reminder of a time long ago when the mill's shutters hung proudly. Not only were the shutters now gone, but also most of the remaining glass pains had been either removed or shattered, leaving sharp jagged fragments in the frames, resembling hideous sharks teeth. A few may have been stolen by thieves hoping to get something for the custom blown panes, but most were simply broken by local vandals, for whatever enjoyment they might gain from such thoughtless actions. Behind the broken windows awaited nothing but the blackness of the abandoned structure and whatever else might lurk inside in the darkness.

The beautiful front door had likewise long since been stolen, allowing for a variety of woodland creatures to wander into the mill to take up residence. Perhaps the missing door was currently being used as someone's front door in a mansion in another state or another country, or maybe it had simply been burned for firewood. Its fate remained a mystery. Where the stain glass transom once proudly displayed the mill owner's name, nothing remained but an empty pitted wooden frame covered in spider webs; teaming with insects.

At one time a large double-sided fireplace was located in the middle of the mill providing heat for the workers in the winter. It led to an enormous chimney stretching high above the center of the roofline, making for breathtaking spectacle as it spewed its smoke into the icy sky during the coldest, most freezing months of winter. Now the chimney was all but gone above the roofline, its mortar disintegrated by years of exposure, its bricks having fallen to the ground below; many falling through the roof, making large gaping holes in the rotting shingles.

Through the center of the chimney large branches grew skyward from an oak tree that had taken root a few years after the mill had been shut down. Branches likewise protruded through the broken windows looking as if the tree and its mighty limbs might have been the only thing keeping the mill standing; which could very well have been true.

The locals called it "Saw-Kill" because of the mill's tragic history, or perhaps more accurately, the tragic history of the mill's owner, J. J. Hanson. The tale of Jonas J. Hanson had been a sad one when told with historic accuracy. However, through the years the tale had grown and evolved, each time being told with the addition of more fantastic and impossible elements, until it had become the stuff of legend. It was no longer simply a tragic tale but one of terror and mystery.

Hanson had been the only child of a British father and a German mother who had immigrated to the US toward the end of the nineteenth century. Shortly after his arrival, Jonas's father, William, built the mill and began growing his business. Jonas was born in 1880 and by the turn of the century the mill had become a prosperous business. Jonas took over ownership and operation of the mill in 1905 at the age of twenty-five when his father's died suddenly. The fact was, a heart attack had been the cause of his father's untimely death but through the years the story evolved to suggest young Jonas had actually murdered his father to get control of the mill.

The workers did not take well to Jonas running the operation, as they looked at him as having been privileged, being given everything as a result of the hard work of his father. Instead of trying to win the workers over, Jonas took a firm, autocratic approach, driving his workers with an iron fist, firing anyone who gave him even the slightest provocation. The economy was not prosperous in the poor rural Pennsylvania community, as was often the case in such areas, so the employees had little choice but to put up with Jonas's tyranny.

Jonas never married, and therefore never had any children. He took over the family homestead, a large farmhouse on the same parcel of land, but located several hundred yards in the woods behind the mill. His mother, Greta, lived in the house with him until she died of cancer, then known as "the waste of life", around 1920. Jonas soon found himself alone, in the big house and did not consider the isolation comforting.

Locals rumored his mental decline started after his mother's death. Many said the spirits of the dead parents haunted the homestead, tormenting Jonas relentlessly because of his poor treatment of the workforce. That particular rumor was probably started by a group of irate workers who hated Jonas and perhaps wished deep inside, such a phenomenon might actually have occurred.

Others, who dared to be so vulgar, hinted about an unnatural intimate relationship between Jonas and his mother after his father's death, which caused him to go mad with grief following her death. Whatever the reason, after a number of years alone in the "big house" as it was known, Jonas started to act irrationally and could often be seen carrying on conversations with people who were not present, some say his mother and father. This probably helped to fuel the ghost rumors as well.

Eventually, Jonas lost his mind completely and became stark raving mad. Unfortunately, no one realized the extent of his insanity until it was much too late. Until then, most of his employees simply thought is was a bit "off", and chose to ignore his steady mental decline in order to keep gainfully employed at the mill.

Then it happened. One day after the workday had ended and most of the workers had gone home, Jonas was hunched over his desk in his office, mumbling to himself as usual, working on the business books. A group of four obviously angry workers approached him demanding to speak to him about the working conditions. When he refused to speak with the men, they told Hanson they were forming a labor union and he would either have to give in to their demands or they would call a strike and shut the mill down.

Even though most of what they said was simply bluster, they're having just started talking among themselves about the possibility of forming a union, and were actually years away from making it a reality; Hanson did not know this, and in his decreasing mental state he could not distinguish between what was real and what might be fabricated.

He simply snapped. He reached into the top drawer of his desk, retrieved a Smith and Wesson 38 special revolver and proceeded to shoot each of them without forethought. One of the men died instantly when the bullet entered through his right eye, blowing out the back of his skull and spattering his blood and bits of skull and brain all over the back wall of the office.

One of the men took one through the neck and lay on the floor gasping for several long minutes as his severed artery pumped his lifeblood onto the floor where it pooled about him. The other two were not so lucky. Though one was shot once and the other twice, their wounds were crippling, but were not fatal. In reality, they would have been much better off had they died instantly. The two men screamed in agony and crawled toward the door trying desperately to get away from the homicidal mad man.

Unfortunately, they did not see him grab a souvenir baseball bat, which was presented to him by the company who purchased his lumber to make their sports equipment. But they most certainly felt it when Hanson tried to knock them both out of the park, so to speak. He shattered both of their legs so they could not escape the broke their arms and dislocated their shoulders so they could not fight back. Whether he originally planned on killing them with the bat or whether he changed his mind during the process, he only ended up knocking them both unconscious.

When the men regained consciousness they were in the sawmill, strapped to the saw table, legs spread as the belts above the table spun on their pulleys, powering the enormous saw blade, allowing it to spin above the table directly in front of them. Then the blade began its journey town toward them and within a few moments the screaming was over, as each half of both workers fell to the floor, the table slick with their blood, insides and stomach contents.

Apparently, Jonas had saved one bullet for himself and after his gruesome work was completed, he went back to his office, sat behind his desk and blew his brains out. The police investigating the crime scene were sickened by the manner in which he fell face-forward on top of his desk, his sodden brains oozing out onto a photo of his parents which had fallen down and lay beneath his ruined skull.

Paul Simmons was a twenty-first century transplant to the area, but knew about the history of the mill, having heard local children discussing it while they played in the streets of his nearby neighborhood. His subdivision was only about five years old when Paul and his wife, Laura, built their split-level home, completing it several months ago. Theirs was one of the last lots remaining in an already established and essentially settled development. They were both professionals, referred to as DINKS by their co-workers: double income – no kids. They both wanted to have children someday but so far they had not made any attempts to conceive.

During the workweek they both attended a nearby gym and fitness center, but on the weekends, weather permitting, they enjoyed walking along the country roads near their new neighborhood. They would leave the development and head east on Abington Lane until they reached Sawmill. Then they would walk the half-mile length of the road, past the sawmill; unconsciously keeping their distance from the ruins. Next they would turn right on Prescott Road and follow it until it intersected with the very steep Dairy Road, which eventually met back up with Abington Lane on the other side of their development, completing about a two mile circle.

Often, when he would walk by the mill, Paul would deliberately stare at the structure, wondering if the rumors surrounding the mill were true. He suspected they might be close to the truth although it probably was blown way out of proportion through the years. He often would feel a strange sensation in his stomach when passing the mill as if there was some force calling to him; urging him to come inside.

Most of the locals believed or wanted to believe the place was haunted, by the ghost of J. J. Hanson who was looking for another victim to saw in two. Paul, of course, did not believe in such local folklore, thinking it ridiculous. Even the nickname "Saw-Kill" sounded juvenile and corny to him. In fact, he was fairly sure once, several years ago, when he and Laura had lived in California, he had seen a sign in a seasonal Halloween store reading "Saw-Kill" road.

As he recalled it was one of those cheap foam or cardboard road signs, probably mass-produced in China or some other low-cost country, for a U.S. company eager for cheap labor. The sign had been designed with a green background and reflective white lettering, just like a typical road sign would be. It read "Saw Mill Rd". However the "mill" portion of the sign was obscured by the scribbled word "KILL" done in a way to appear to be written from dripping blood. Paul was fairly certain neither the workers in China, the businessmen in the United States or even the designers who created the idea for the sign had any prior knowledge of this particular Sawmill Road, in Pennsylvania, or its ominous history.

In fact, there were probably hundreds of Sawmill Roads around the country. He thought for a moment about a line he remembered from the promotion of the horror movie, "Nightmare on Elm St." which read, "There's an Elm Street in every town." Paul figured there must be a Sawmill Road in almost every rural community; hence the popularity of the novelty sign, he supposed.

Still he couldn't help but wonder about the strange feeling he had every time he walked by the mill. Although they had never discussed it, Paul and Laura would always walk by the mill in during the brightest part of the day. Once, about a month ago after a busy Saturday afternoon of shopping, they considered taking what they called their "Sawmill walk" but then thought better of it; both of them conveniently using the excuse they were too tired, when in fact the decision was based on an unspoken realization the sun was rapidly setting and it would be dusk as they passed the gloomy saw mill.

As Paul became more familiar with the area, he began to feel less apprehensive about the dilapidated mill and eventually had no trouble walking past it. In fact yesterday he had taken the walk alone; Laura was not feeling well; and he deliberately slowed down as he got to the mill, being bold enough to leave the road and walk up to the structure and stand within a few feet of its battered front stairs.

He now sat at the kitchen table having just finished his Sunday evening dinner and asked Laura if she was up for a walk; he suspected she might not be, as she hadn't seemed to eat very much.

"No." She replied, "I'm still not feeling so well in my stomach. I must have a bug or something. If I don't feel much better by tomorrow morning, I suspect I will be staying home from work."

Paul thought how odd it was to hear Laura consider staying home since she rarely missed work, no matter how sick she might be. "If you feel that bad, do you think we ought to take you to the emergency room?"

"No thanks." She said with a sarcastic laugh, "I would rather lie around here all night than spend five or six hours in a room full of sick and injured weekend people. You know how the poor people always use the hospital for their medical needs. The last time we were there many of the families seemed to know each other; like it is a party they all go to every weekend or something."

"Yes. I remember." Paul said, thinking about how about two months ago he had cut his finger doing yard work and Laura had to drive him into the hospital for stitches. It was a four-hour snore-fest before the physician's assistant even had an opportunity to look at his injury. "You are probably right."

"I think I will just go in and lie down on the couch for a while and watch TV." Laura said.

"Would you mind if I took our 'Sawmill walk' alone?" he asked. Laura looked out the window and noticed the sun was beginning to set. "Are you sure you want to do that?" she suggested, not wanting to express her apprehension too strongly, feeling somewhat foolish.

"Sure." He said, "In fact, I might even run part of the way to make sure I get back before dark. Don't worry, I'll be fine."

"I suppose, if you say so." Laura replied with discomfort. "Take your cell phone along with you incase you trip and fall or get hit by a car or something."

"I will." He said somewhat nervously, as he held up his phone to show her he would be just a phone call away. He walked her to the couch and made sure she was comfortable before kissing her goodbye and leaving.

Paul walked out the front door of their home and strode at a brisk pace through the development for about a mile, until the cement sidewalks ended abruptly at Abington Lane. Checking for oncoming traffic, he crossed Abington to the right side of the road walking steadily until he came to the intersection with Sawmill. "Saw-Kill" a quite raspy voice echoed in his head and he felt himself mouthing the words silently along with the thought. A cold chill ran down his spine.

As he turned right onto Sawmill Road he felt a strange sensation, as if he not only was not just turning onto another road but also was entering another world. He looked out along the curves of Sawmill, which seemed to take on a dreamlike, surrealistic appearance, knowing around the farthest turn in the road ahead, the ominous sawmill awaited like a hideous specter, hiding in anticipation of his arrival.

For a moment he thought perhaps he should simply turn around, head home and call it quits. He could always tell Laura he was too tired or he could say he got a cramp in his leg or some other excuse. But he knew if he did, she would know the real reason why he didn't want to walk by the mill. Although Paul was certain Laura would understand completely and not think less of him, he did not like the idea of her knowing he had backed out; she would always know he was unable to bring himself to walk by the mill alone at dusk.

Paul decided instead, he would walk at a deliberate pace up Sawmill Road with his head focused on the highway and do his best to not change the direction of his vision until he was well past the mill. He actually considered jogging past the mill to get it over with more quickly, but felt somehow, doing so might be akin to a cowardly act; the same as if he had turned around and gone home. So instead he walked with his eyes focused on the blacktop, purposefully moving up Sawmill Road. "Saw-Kill" he again heard a strange voice whisper in his mind. He tried desperately to ignore the strange voice, blaming it on an overactive imagination.

As he approached the area of the mill he heard the voice in his head grow stronger, taking on a tone, which sounded eerily insane. "Saw-Kill" the voice said repeatedly; first slowly, growing louder and more frantic with each utterance; "Saw-Kill, Saw-Kill, Saw-Kill" over and over. Paul stopped in his tracks in the middle of the road and slowly raised his head, turning it cautiously to the right; where the decaying sawmill stood. Instantly, the voice assaulting him in his mind stopped and was replaced by blessed silence as he looked at the opening where the front door of the mill once stood; a cavern of darkness resembling the gaping maw of some hideous demonic creature.

Paul realized the apprehension he had previously felt about the mill was now completely gone. In fact, he felt foolish forever having the feelings in the first place. It was as if he suddenly realized the mill was an abandoned building, a run down wreck, nothing more. He felt an incredible exhilaration flow through him as he stood in the waning sunlight of dusk in front of sight of the community's most feared legend and he did not feel anything but pity for the unfortunate, uneducated locals who allowed themselves to fall prey to such wild imaginings.

Before he realized he was doing so, Paul stepped off of the roadway, through the tall weeds and wild grass directly toward the front of the building. He stood for a moment looking up at the precarious structure as if defying it to collapse, which of course it did not.

He walked slowly around the left side of the building and saw the dirt driveway and large opening, where once two barn doors stood. He walked up the pathway to the opening and was surprised to see the floor of the mill appeared to still be fairly in tact and structurally sound; obviously constructed of thick wooden beams. He also noted there was still a fair amount of light in the mill entering through the broken western window panes coming from the bright setting sun.

Paul stepped cautiously out onto the floor, testing to assure himself the structure was as sturdy as it appeared. Before he realized it, he had taken several steps inside the mill and was turning to look down the length of the building. To his surprise, several hundred feet ahead, he saw a large worktable, above which hung the rusted pitted blade of the notorious saw. Looking up toward the ceiling he saw where once the huge canvas drive belts, used to power the saw had hung, now were dry-rotted strips hanging limply like giant pieces of pasta, useless for powering anything any longer.

He walked forward to the table and looking down noticed a dark brown stain soaked into the wooden slab. Looking up more closely at the rusted circular blade he saw a similar dark stain. "Blood" Paul thought, "A blood stain from the last night the saw was ever used." Once again the shiver returned and Paul started to feel a pang of apprehension and the resurgence of his earlier fears.

As Paul stared in amazement at the useless rusted blade he noticed it begin to change. Before his eyes, the rust began to flake off in thousands of bits of falling debris and orange dust, revealing a shiny metal blade below. The dark area encircling the teeth of the blade was now bright red and drips of blood began to fall from the teeth to the bench below. Above him, the rotted sagging canvas belts began to regain their luster and seemed to climb upward knitting themselves miraculously back together; repairing themselves, looking as good as new.

Paul tried to turn and run but was unable to move. Suddenly he felt someone grab him from behind. He turned to try to see who held him and saw the unthinkable: a translucent being stood behind him holding him securely, preventing him from escape. He could feel the impossible pressure of its icy death grip. He could not make out the thing's appearance but sensed it must be hideous. He felt his heart began to pound violently in his chest.

Then he heard the same familiar voice in his mind saying "Saw-Kill, Saw-Kill" over and over. He looked in the direction of the sound and saw a specter slowly walking from the darkness toward him. It appeared to be a man dressed in early twentieth century clothing, a business suit, which appeared to be stained with blood. As Paul looked closer he could see the right side of the man's skull was missing and his face was splattered with chunks of skin and blood.

Behind the specter, another creature came lumbering out of the darkness. It appeared to have once been a man, but now was something hideous. This poor creature stood naked, with no visible genitalia. From the place where its crotch should have been, a long line of awkwardly sewn stitching worked its way up along the stomach area, the chest, the neck and even the center of its face and skull. Paul understood what he was seeing was once, one of the unfortunate workers Hanson and cut in two on the very saw before him.

He assumed the creature holding him from behind must be the second of Hanson's victims. Paul tried to scream but found himself unable to utter a sound. The shambling creature next to Hanson came forward and grabbed Paul's legs, lifting them upward, placing them on the saw table. Unable to move, he was helpless to fight or escape.

Within a few moments the saw blade started to rotate, slowly at first then it began to spin madly, spraying droplets of blood down upon him. Soon the blade moved slowly down toward Paul's chest, as his mind screamed "Saw-Kill, Saw-Kill" just before everything went black.

Laura stood silently at the gravesite of her dead husband; dressed in widow's black, surrounded by friends and relatives. One by one the mourners approached her to offer their condolences until soon all were gone and she found herself alone. That was, except for one lone man standing next to the grave. She recognized him immediately as the local medical examiner. He had told Laura he would tell her of his final determination of cause of death as soon as he was ready.

The man approached Laura and said, "Once again, Mrs. Simmons, I am so very sorry for your loss."

"Thank you, Doctor Johnson. I appreciate it very much." She replied. Then wanting to get the unpleasantness over with she asked, "I was wondering… did you finalize your report… you know… on Paul's cause of death? Was it… was it a heart attack?"

"Yes, my dear. That was the cause. Again I am so sorry." The doctor replied.

Laura's face took on the appearance of resignation that often accompanies the feeling of closure in such situations. "Thank you for all you have done, Doctor." Laura replied, as the doctor turned to leave.

Walking slowly back to his car, the doctor saw his assistant waiting by his car to drive him back to the office.

"Did you tell her?" The assistant inquired.

"I told her what she needed to hear." The doctor replied, "Her husband had a heart attack and that is why he died. End of story."

"But what about…?" The young assistant asked curiously stopping short of completing his question.

The doctor stared at him sternly and insisted, "I told her nothing. As far as you and I are concerned, there is nothing else. And since you and I are the only ones that know any differently, I had better not hear anyone else in around this township repeating the story back to me, or I will know exactly where it came from. Do I make myself perfectly clear?"

"Clear as can be." The assistant replied. "I swear, I won't say a word."

With that, the doctor and his assistant got into their car and drove away in silence. The doctor was going over in his mind the incredibly impossible results of his examination. It was beyond his understanding, beyond his comprehension. When he autopsied Paul Simmons, he never expected to discover what he saw upon cracking open the man's chest cavity. No one ever would have expected to find the dead man's heart sawed cleanly in two.

ABOUT THE AUTHORS

A. J. French has appeared in Abandoned Towers, The Absent Willow Review, Short-Story.Me!, Black Lantern Publishing, This Mutant Life, theDF_underground, Fantastic Horror, Sex and Murder, Black Ink Horror, and Golden Visions Magazine. He also has stories in the following anthologies: Ruthless: An Extreme Horror Collection by Pill Hill Press, Deep Space Terror, By Mind or Metal, Novus Creatura, and Pellucid Lunacy.

Amanda Lawrence Auverigne writes dark fiction. "Get the Brick" is one of her tales. Please visit Amanda's website at http://auverigne.com

Anthony Bell lives in Washington state. He rides motorcycles, eats ice cream, and skydives.

Catherine Sisson is a 24 year old Aries pursuing a degree in Dietetics at the University of Arizona. This is her first publication, but not her last. She and her nonsexual life partner live comfortably tucked away in the desert, but not for long.

C.D. Reimer lives and works in Silicon Valley. His interests are ceramics, painting, tropical fish, and web programming. These keep him out of trouble when he's not fixing broken users and consoling hurt computers. Currently working on his first novel, a short story collection, and various short stories.

C.H. Potter was born and raised in the hills of Western New York. His work has also been published in The Copperfield Review and The

Monsters Next Door, as well as several anthologies from Living Dead Press, including Dead Worlds: Undead Stories Volume 1, The Book of the Dead Volumes 1 and 2, and The Night of the Wolf.

Washington state native author **Crystal Y. Connor**, now living in Seattle has been writing short stories specializing in Urban Fantasy/Science Fiction/Horror genres and poetry since before Jr. high School. Crystal's short story "The Ruins" earned a runner up placement in Crypticon Seattle's 2010 writing contest.

Daniel P. Coughlin is the author of two produced films "Lake Dead" and "Farmhouse" and a number of short stories published by such publications as Macabre Cadaver Magazine, Ghostlight, and Dark Gothgic Ressurected Magazine. He is a Marine Corps veteran and graduated with his bachelor of fine arts from California State University at Long Beach where he interned for his favorite director Wes Craven. Although born in a small town in Wisconsin, he lives in Orange County, CA with his wife Kelli-Rae.

Darren Gallagher lives in Ireland. He has been writing for two years. You can find his work in Static Movement, Pill Hill, and Wicked East Anthologies.

Eric Dimbleby has been contracted for stories that have been (or will be) in nine anthologies in 2010: "Zombie Zoology" by Severed Press, 5 separate anthologies by Pill Hill Press, "D.O.A." by Blood Bound Books, "Fearology 2" by Library of the Living Dead, "Fear of The Dark" by Horror Bound Magazine Publications, and "Inner Fears" by Static Movement. In addition, he has had several stories published in The Absent Willow Review and forthcoming in the e-zine Dark Valentine. For more samples and a history of his work, his website is available at www.ericdimbleby.com.

Ian Sandusky is an up and coming author, specializing in the dark and subversive, raised in Holland Landing, Ontario but currently residing in the Niagara Region. Ian currently attends Brock University, working on completing a Bachelor of Arts degree. His first book, GREY DOGS, will be released through the Severed Press (Australia) in Autumn, 2010.

Jan Vander Laenen (° 1960) lives in Brussels, Belgium, where he works as an art historian and translator (Dutch, French and Italian). He is also the author of eight collections of short stories, plays, and screenplays. A romantic comedy, Oscar Divo, and a thriller, The Card Game, are presently in the hands of a competent producer in Hollywood, while his short fiction collections The Butler and Poète maudit are eliciting the requisite accolades in Italy. His most recent publication are the tales "A Glass of Cognac" in "Bears: Gay Erotic Stories" (Cleis Press), *Epistle of the Sleeping Beauty* in "Unspeakable Horror" (Dark Scribe Press), "Fire at the Chelsea Hotel" in "Best Gay Love Stories 2009" (Alyson Press), and "The Stuffed Turkey" in "Best Gay Erotica 2010 (Cleis Press).

Jason Barney is 35 years old and lives in Vermont. He has had over 50 short stories published by various small presses.

Librarian by day, **Jason M. Bloom** haunts the stacks awaiting the cloak of night, when he can finally go home and start writing. His muse and beautiful wife Shannon helps keep the demons at bay, or draws them out, depending on the project. His work been published in the literary magazine Shoreline, the upcoming Pill Hill Press anthology *365 Daily Bites of Flesh 2011* and *Dead History II* from the Living Dead Press.

A native New Yorker who lives in the Finger Lakes area with his lovely wife Bonny, **Jeffrey Angus** has been writing for years. This is one of his first projects and is looking forward to adding many more to his portfolio. Screenplays and stage plays are his passion, but any tale that makes a reader want to know more is what he loves to do.

Jeremy Bush is a carpenter living in western New York with his wife. He has flash fiction forthcoming in Daily Flash 2011: 365 Days of Flash Fiction, The Journal of Microliterature, and Cup of Joe: Coffee House Flash Fiction.

Jessica A. Weiss spends her spare time picking through nightmares and horror films looking for new and interesting ways to put them back together. Owner of Wicked East Press, writer of short stories, and mother of four. Catch up with her blog The Writers Side Of The Looking Glass.

John Pennington was born and raised in Indianapolis, Indiana and he now currently resides in Bloomington. His most recent work appears in the Pill Hill Press anthologies Love Kills: My Bloody Valentine and Haunted. He is also contributing stories to two of PHP's upcoming flash fiction anthologies: Daily Flash 2011: 365 Days of Flash Fiction and Daily Bites of Flesh 2011: 365 Days of Flash Fiction.

Former English/Film Studies teacher **Ken Goldman**, an affiliate member of the Horror Writers Association, has homes on the Main Line in Pennsylvania and at the Jersey shore. His stories appear in over 550 independent press publications in the U.S., Canada, the UK, and Australia. His book of short stories, "You Had Me At ARRGH!!: Five Uneasy Pieces by Ken Goldman" (Sam's Dot Publishers) remains an all-time top ten best seller at The Genre Mall where (shameless plug alert) it can be purchased. Ken would be famous except for the fact nobody seems to know who he is.

Lee Clark Zumpe has been writing and publishing horror, dark fantasy and speculative fiction since the late 1990s. His short stories and poetry have appeared in a variety of publications such as *Weird Tales, Space and Time* and *Dark Wisdom;* and in anthologies such as *Horrors Beyond, Corpse Blossoms, Abominations, Withersin's Unkindness* and *Cthulhu Unbound, Vol. 1.* His work has earned several honorable mentions in *The Year's Best Fantasy and Horror* collections.

Lorraine Horrell resides in Ireland. She has had seventeen short stories published. She is currently studying for her diploma in creative writing.

Mark Wilson has been writing since the age of thirteen with the aspirations of becoming a published author. He lives in western MA with his partner and their kitten, Judas. He enjoys the company of the undead and things that go bump in the night.

Raised in Hawaii and educated in England, Las Vegas writer **Mason Ian Bundschuh** writes speculative fiction with a literary flair. Stop laughing, it's true. He's also a member of The Illiterati and the front man for the alternative rock band Atlas Takes Aim. www.MasonBundschuh.com

Matt Nord lives in Central New York with his wife, Karen, two sons, Jacob and Judah, and daughter, Jordan. He is an established horror writer with several credits under his proverbial belt, including short stories published by Living Dead Press, Library of the Living Dead Press , Pill Hill Press, Wicked East Press and Static Movement Imprint. His most ambitious project to date may be the collaborative novel he is currently spearheading with 18 other authors, and will hopefully see published before his baby girl graduates college.

Patrick D'Orazio resides in southwestern Ohio with his wife, Michele, two children, Alexandra and Zachary, and two spastic dogs. He has been writing since he was a teenager but only recently clued into the fact that unless he attempted to get published, no one else would really care. Approximately fifteen of his short stories appear or will be appearing in various anthologies from publishers such as Library of the Living Dead Press, Library of Horror Press, Library of Science Fiction & Fantasy Press, May December Publications, Pill Hill Press, and Dark Silo. Patrick's first novel, Comes the Dark, was recently released by The Library of the Living Dead Press.

Rebecca Besser is a wife and mother who lives in Ohio. She's a graduate of the Institute of Children's Literature, a member of Write-On Writers and the Ohio Poetry Association (OPA). Her work has appreared in the Coshocton Tribune, Irish Story Playhouse, Spaceports & Spidersilk, joyful!, Soft Whispers, Illuminata, Common Threads, Golden Visions Magazine, Stories That Lift, and The Undead That Saved Chirstmas charity anthology. As well as multiple anthologies by Living Dead Press (where she is currently and editor) and Wicked East Press, and one anthology by Pill Hill Press. For more information visit her website: www.rebeccabesser.com

Robert Freese has had nearly 100 short stories published in various genres. Christmas 2009 saw the release of his sci-fi/horror novella The Santa Thing. His first novel, Bijou of the Dead, will be released in October 2010 along with his paranormal book Paranormal Journeys. He currently lives in Alabama with his wife Frances.

Sarah Islam is a freelance writer and advertising consultant. Her work has appeared in local and in-flight magazines in India, Pakistan and Sri Lanka. She is currently working on her first full-length novel and lives in Calcutta with her husband and a house full of cats.

Thomas M. Malafarina is a horror author from Berks County, Pennsylvania. He has published two novels "Ninety-Nine Souls" and "Burn Phone" as well as a short story collection called "Thirteen Nasty Endings" through Sunbury Press of Camp Hill, PA. Thomas lives in South Heidelberg Township with his wife JoAnne; they have three grown children and three grandchildren.